CITY JUNGLES
A Tale of the Inner City

By

Anthony Spencer

This book is dedicated to both my sons:
Koy Anthony Nwadike-Spencer and Marquez Anton Nwadike-Spencer.
In memory of:
Veronica (Mum)
Andrew (brother)

CONTENTS

ACKNOWLEDGMENTS

Jeanette Johnson

Nadia Holmer

My Dad Andrew

INTRODUCTION

Three years and three months! What the fuck! How did this happen? How did I get so relaxed carrying weapons that I was picking up my kids from school with a loaded revolver down the front of my pants? How did things get so bad that I felt the need to be armed at all times?

The date was 7 February, the day was Friday and the year was 2002. I was back behind bars after eight years for pure progress, charged with serious firearms offences.

This wasn't supposed to happen. It really was for my protection. Protection from the violence that was now plaguing our streets today. Protection from those who wouldn't think twice about sending a bullet in my direction over the most trivial of reasons. Protection from becoming someone's statistic.

I was arrested on 7 February 2002 and on 6 August I was sentenced to three years and three months. But the story did not begin on that day.

It began on 14 October 1968. The day I was born in England. England, that's the story. The mean streets and jungles of the inner cities of England. The streets of London where I grew up. Tottenham, the original city jungle – A jungle with no monkeys on trees but nevertheless a jungle where only the fittest will survive, A jungle that I used to be a part of.

Thirty-nine months because the judges and authorities do not really understand the laws that operate in cities like mine across the world. To help the outside world make some sense of how things can turn out for a child born inside of one of these communities and anyone else who cares to understand our politics, I need to tell a story, a story about life in the city jungles of England. A story about the life of one of its members, growing up and rising from young punk to soldier and to general, all the time fighting to get and keep what was mine.

I say the city jungles of England because this is a book that any kid who grows up in any inner city in this country will relate to. I have read stories about the American ghettos and other ghettos, favelas and inner cities across the world and these stories are really no different to ours over here in Britain.

Although we did not grow up scared to walk down certain streets because we had the wrong colour clothes on, and although most of us here in the UK could not even imagine what life in a Brazilian favela would be like, when stripped bare the politics are the same. The needs, anxieties, worries, the injustices, poverty and violence are all too familiar. The lack of willingness by the powers-that-be to help runs right through. This is a story that will touch at least a billion people on this planet. A billion forgotten people who live in countries that can help if they really set their minds to it but choose not to, and instead choose the path of laws and restrictions, sanctions and labels that are meant to keep them where they are as long as they only kill and harm each other.

This is a story that will offend, disgust and even scare some people. It is a story that will shock some, but for those who have those mentioned reactions to this book, take a minute to understand the real purpose of the book.

My main intention is to lay bare the politics of our city jungles across Britain, with the hope that the next time someone like me faces a judge and jury for whatever it is they are charged with, just maybe they might see a reason for what drove them to where they have all congregated at that particular time, in a court room. And just maybe with that understanding will come help. Help not just for them but also their families. We have the capacity to do that.

The more of us understand and listen less to the press and their sensationalising and labelling of sectors of society, the more of us will press to even our countries out just that bit more so as to give more people the opportunity for hope and change.

It is also a book through which I hope to expose in some parts the hypocrisy of this Legal System we call fair, a legal system that can define my peer as a white, over-sixty citizen living in the countryside, while I'm black and live in an inner city. I would not class those people as my peers, but the system does. They could be my neighbours for years and still not understand me, nor I them. A system that reflects society will be a much fairer one. When the Asian police officers in Southall make up seventy percent of officers as Southall is seventy percent Asian, then we will be getting close to a fair society. When ethnic police officers in Tottenham make up the fifty percent of officers based there, we will be approaching a fairer world. Then the Mark Duggan type killing that sparked the 2011 riots in the UK will be cut, if not eradicated. I still have not come across a black person dying in police custody at the hands of black officers. If anyone knows of one please contact the writer.

The same goes for our courts, juries and the whole justice system. This is not to get ethnic people off, far from it. Indians in India with all Indian juries are still convicted if they break the law, so are Jamaicans in Jamaica. No, it is not about that. It is the fact that for a hundred years and before that, when black men got lynched because a willing white female sexual partner decided she would cry rape because she got pregnant, justice for ethnic citizens of western countries has been very poor to say the least. This is something that can be corrected but never will be.

Do I think writing this book will change that? Hell no! But this book may just affect one jury member in a case, who looks around them, sees ten white people and two non-white people, listening to a line-up of white officer after white office give evidence in a case involving a British youth of Pakistani origin from Southall and says to himself, "I need to really pay attention to what these officers are saying. I need to give this defendant the benefit of doubt." Rather than, "These are police officers, 'those' people are troublemakers anyway. He has to be guilty!"

If I reach just that one guy, I have achieved something.

We live in a system that favours the upper classes but hates to see the lower classes do well for themselves. We have loopholes in our laws for those who can afford to pay lawyers who know what they are. Loopholes in our tax systems that allow the rich to contribute less yet where they live have the best services.

Lastly, to any authorities that see this book as a book to comb through to see what crimes they may be able to solve, this book is not for you. Yes, there are some real events like the incident where I was shot outside my club. But that is as far as it goes. I have written this book, being careful not to aid or assist the police in solving any crimes. Therefore it is not a True Crime novel.

When you get to the end of the book you will see why. I do not want to spoil the genuine reader's journey through this book. Therefore the real truth is revealed at the very end of the book. I want this to be as real as can be to the reader.

The book does not start with my arrest, it starts at the beginning. The same beginning as most kids in these neighbourhoods. I hope the parents who read this understand that sometimes there is nothing you can do to change the path your child may head down, but you must not give up. And when the powers that be tell you it is all your fault as a parent, that is not entirely true. Yes there are some very useless parents out there, but even those were failed by the State somewhere along the line.

How do you explain it when a UK-born child has poorer spelling skills than a Romanian? I employed a Welsh guy and two Romanians later in life, in Spain. I was always astounded when I would read their notes to me written in English. My Welsh employee is a shameful reminder that we in Britain invest less in our own people than any developed nation.

So yes, they will try blaming and punishing you the parent and the newspapers who think just like them will point fingers and label. But do not pay attention to this, focus on helping our next generation of inner city dwellers to break the cycle. That is the most important job we have as parents. The more people from our backgrounds that break into the ruling classes, the more help the next generation will receive from the top.

Just as I end the book by declaring that I have no regrets, so do I begin the book by declaring the same.

I have no regrets.

CHAPTER ONE

Like I already said I was born on 14 October 1968 at the North Middlesex Hospital in Edmonton, North London. I was the third boy to born to Mr and Mrs Spencer.

They say you can choose your friends but not your family. And I would not change my family for any other. I had a very happy childhood as far as I can remember. I remember never being hungry or dirty and always getting what we wanted, and that's even though there were seven of us.

Two years after I was born, my mum got her wish. She had a baby girl. The only one out of seven, because the next three were all boys.

My father came to England for a better life in 1959, from Nigeria. He came with a bag full of qualifications to work for a bank he was already working for in Nigeria called The United Bank for Africa, or UBA. Mum always told us that on their way to England, they were full of hope and ideas for a better life. But they soon discovered that this country had no such plans for anyone of colour. It must have been a shock to their system!

You see, it's different for us born to this country but seeing how the system is still heavily weighted against anyone of colour, it's easy to picture how hard it must have been for our parents, who were immigrants.

My parents met the same year my mother arrived in England and fell in love. It wasn't long before my mother got pregnant and in 1964, they had my oldest brother, called Dillon.

After Dillon came Frankie in 1966 September. Now Frankie is the diplomat in the family. He was the United Nations of the family, peace maker. Today he lives with his family, well settled and very successful at his job. He never really got into any bad trouble. Like I said he was the diplomat, the one who picked up the pieces when Dillon or myself had fucked up.

Then came me. I am the one they call the hothead of the family. I inherited my dad's hot temper, which runs in the family. My parents always told me that they saw in me an impatience to grow up. A rush to become an adult.

Then came my sister Carol. We call her Cass for short. The only girl child. Now she's the calming influence in the family. God only knows what the family would have been like without my sister Cass. We all love her to death. She was born 1970, two years after me. My parents then had a four year break, and I have always wondered why. Therefore, 1974 February came the one we call joker in the pack. His name is Kevin. These days Kevin is my right hand man, just like I was Dillon's right hand in the past. After Kevin came Andrew. He came along in December of 1976, Sagittarian just like my father.

Andrew, rest his soul, has since died. He died in February of 1994 at the age of seventeen. He was killed in a car crash, in a car in which he was a passenger. The car had skidded on black ice on a cold February night. It skidded into the path of an oncoming car, which then hit the front passenger door side where my brother was sitting. But I'll get back to that later in this book. Andrew was the apple of my dad's eye. The shy man of the family. May he rest in peace. We all miss him very much. Last but not least loved, came Michael, or Mikey, as we all call him. The youngest of all of the family. He came along in 1980. He's now a young man in his own right. He was the one most affected by Andrew's death as they were very close.

Like I said, even though there were seven of us, we were relatively comfortable. My mother got a job at the Whipps Cross Hospital in East London. And with my dad's job at the bank we got on fine.

How they survived the racist policies of this country back then is a testament to the will of black people as a whole to do well at all costs. My parents would tell us of obstacles they had to overcome. Greedy White landlords and stuff like that.

My dad was a bit more fortunate as he worked for an African-owned bank. Anyway the family settled in North London, Tottenham to be exact. My parents found a four bedroom house on Lansdowne

Road N17 which is where I spent most of my childhood.

Growing up in Tottenham wasn't as bad as what my parents experienced when they first arrived. It was a pleasant part of London for anyone of colour being an area of at least fifty percent ethnicity. Today Tottenham has an Ethnic population of somewhere between fifty and sixty percent.

I don't remember a lot of the seventies politics apart from major events such as the Silver Jubilee in 1977. So I haven't got a lot to say about the seventies. I do remember the election in 1979, though, when I was going on eleven years of age, when Britain elected its first woman Prime Minister. I wonder when Britain will elect its first Black Prime Minister and then also when we'll have a first female Black Prime Minister. Maybe never!

Anyway her name was fucking Margaret Thatcher of the conservative party. The party of the rich, the judges and the snobs of society. The anti-working class party. The party that was in power for eighteen or nineteen years.

The party that was responsible for the break up so many marriages, the collapse of so many businesses, especially the small business man. A party full of thieves, homosexuals who pretended to be married, a party of sleaze. But at that time I knew none of this as I was only eleven when Thatcher was voted in. I was eleven years old and was already smoking. I'd had my first spliff or joint at that age thanks to my brother Dillon. I had also had my first sexual encounter and she was seventeen. I was nine years old.

So by the age of eleven I saw myself as a young adult. Looking back now that was a joke because I hadn't even begun understanding the politics of life and adulthood. When you're eleven, though, and having full on sex with a girl of seventeen, you sure feel like an adult.

Natasha, that was her name. Natasha Doting. Big breasts, big mouth, big bottom and big earrings Natasha!

Her bum was big, yes, but she was just right between her legs. So either I had a really large one for a kid my age, or her vagina wasn't as big as the rest of her. Knowing myself I'd say it was the former rather than the latter.

I was a tall kid, always have been. So I never did feel out of place in bed or out of it with her. Natasha gave me my first blow job, and boy that left a smile on my face for months. Her nipples were the first I ever sucked on sexually as well. And she loved that. I say sexually because I was breast fed by my mum.

I remember she would phone my house when my parents had left for work but before I left for school and she would say, "Come round after school yeah Anthony, 'Annie' needs you bad." 'Annie' was her vagina and 'Freddie' was her name for my penis.

And I'd say to her, "Annie needs Freddie, Natasha, not me. So if you want Freddie you have to talk to him not me." And then I'd say "Give the phone to Annie make her beg Freddie or he won't come over."

We would then put the phone down our anatomy, imitating a conversation between her vagina and my penis in which she would plead with my penis to come see her after school or something. She definitely knew how to make a young soldier feel seven feet tall. I remember always leaving her house down the bottom of my road with a spring in my step after our wicked sexual encounters.

I had other girlfriends at school who were my age, but none of them gave me sex. So big breast Natasha was my remedy when it came to sex.

Round about these times I'd started stealing and making a little bit of money. I started off shoplifting from local shops. I then went to school with whatever I'd stolen and sold the stuff. I was also baronning in school, baronning stuff I'd nicked from the shops. This, some might say, was a sign of things to come. A baron is a sort of illegal trader or loan shark, depending on what the commodity is.

For example, I would shoplift stuff like sweets, biscuits and bubble gum and go back to school and sell the stuff. Some kids had to leave the school at dinner time to buy these things, but if I had what they wanted, they could then purchase it directly off me, saving them the journey to shops. They could also get my goodies on credit if they didn't have my money on the day. The shops wouldn't let them have it so I did. At a profit of course. One, for two back. One packet of Smarties for two back and so on. Twenty pence for forty pence. At that age it was a profitable business, we called this sort of business double bubble. And I was beginning to be known as the baron.

Also at this time I started forming friendships, some of which exist to this day. One of the earliest friendships I formed during this period was with a kid called Danny Howard. We called him Toddler because he was shorter than the rest of us. Even though he was now grown and caught up with his peers the name has stayed with him to this day. Myself and Toddler have entered into a lot of ventures together over the years. We were friends for a long time but there is a sad twist to our story as friends, which I shall get to in the course of the book.

But at that time it was Toddler and the Baron.

There was also big-nose Kevin Brown. We didn't know it yet but this link up of like minds was to last a long, long time. They say birds of the same feather flock together and that's very true.

Anyway the three of us carried on terrorising the kids in school.

Not surprisingly, our activities came to the notice of our head teacher when I ripped a chain off one kid's neck because he couldn't pay me what he owed. The kid, Christopher, went to the teachers and grassed me up. I guess he couldn't go home without his chain and have to explain to his parents what had happened.

All hell broke loose when my dad found out and heard the whole story. I remember it was summer and nearly the end of the year. My dad had never before come to pick me up from school. A letter had been sent to my home but I thought that my mum, who was more lenient, would have responded to this letter. So I knew that I was in deep shit when I saw his car outside my school and saw him sitting in it. Fuck! I knew he would have had to take the day off and that wasn't a good thing especially as it was down to me.

The first thing he did was curse my friends Toddler and the Nose as we came through the school gates. He cursed and swore at them and told them to stay away from me. The next thing he did was slap me and then pulled me by my ears all the way to the passenger side of his car, opened the door, pushed me in and slammed the door shut.

You see, the thing with my old man was that he didn't mind what you did outside school as long as you did well and behaved yourself in school. The quickest and surest way to drive him loopy was to fuck about in school. He knew education was important and didn't like what I was getting up to in school one bit. He didn't want me to get expelled. To him that was a disaster of the highest order.

Anyway we sat in the car quiet while we waited for my older brothers Dillon and Frankie. Soon as they got in the car we were off home. I'm sure my brothers were just as shocked to see him as I was. He had to beep his horn to get their attention once they exited the school gates.

Do I really need to tell you what happened when I got home? My dad is African. He grew up with corporal punishment. I remember my back and backside were sore for at least a week if not longer. Today you can get arrested for beating your child like that, but not back then.

"The next time I have to come pick you up from school like that, you will either end up in hospital or a police station," my old man said to me when he was satisfied I'd had enough for one day.

But did that incident stop me in my tracks? It should have done, but didn't! And there were many more incidents like that where, as harsh as the discipline was by today's standards my dad was trying to do the best he could as he could see signs that weren't too promising.

Parents can be blamed sometimes for how their kids turn out but I can honestly say my parents were blameless. They honestly tried their best. I knew he wasn't hitting me because he enjoyed hurting his son, he was doing it because he saw a pattern then that was beginning. A pattern he was worried about. It was the only way he knew how to put a stop to it. He handled my brothers the same way and with the exception of Dillon and I, they all have turned out more or less the same - well-grounded and successful in their chosen fields.

Anyway I carried on along the same path, although it did not do my reputation any good the next day at school. Toddler and Kevin the Nose took the piss all day. Business was booming in school so how could I stop? I had found something that I was good at and put money in my pocket. I could afford to take a bus ride anywhere I wanted, pay for my cigarette habit and impress the girls and my peers. So I carried on, but this time as discretely as possible. My school work I made sure did not suffer as result of my black economy activities. Intelligence runs in my family anyhow so it wasn't hard to keep up. As long as I studied hard a couple of weeks before an exam I always managed to do more than scrape through. I was an intelligent pupil.

"If only you would apply yourself a bit more in school, the sky is your limit," Miss Sanderson, my maths teacher would say. But there was nothing wrong with my street maths. I could calculate sums owed to me in seconds, but school maths was something else.

So as long as I was making money, I did not care what anyone said. My pocket was always full of change and I did not need any teacher to tell me how much I was owed. Whatever business I had outside school, though, I made sure I left outside the school gates when I arrived in school in the mornings.

I have to say this, though, I am grateful for the way my dad was about school and studies because it made us realise how important education is and to take it seriously. I still believe that the best education is formal education in school, college and university mixed with the street education or street knowledge. You can never outwit an educated wise guy!

I went into the second year with flying colours and my street level education was going well at the same time too. I was building up a good reputation as a wise guy and a no-nonsense kind of kid. I was ready to fight the older kids if they upset my routine in any way while the kids my age just stayed well out my way.

Our criminal life was only just beginning. Toddler, the Nose and I were just another three kids in the inner city who wanted the same things that the rich kids in Chelsea or Cambridge had. But while their parents gave it to them, we had to get these things ourselves. Or so I told myself anyhow, because my parents were well able to buy me what I wanted and they did. Mostly. I just wanted more maybe because the kids I hung out with did really need to steal to get a spanking new pair of trainers or new coat and not a hand-me-down. We had Marks and Spencers underclothes, umbrellas and Chopper bicycles. Mine and Dillon's friends had to steal to have these. So when we stole it was more to do with being able to afford the things our parents would say no to. And the more I did the more I got hooked on making money and having the freedom money gave me as a kid.

I have remained addicted to making money ever since and also as much addicted to the freedom to buy what I want, go where I want, best clothes, shoes, clubs, women, cars, hotels or villas, holidays, the lot. I was hooked from a very early age.

CHAPTER TWO

I realised very early in life that making money was what it was all about. The road and the corners where we grew up were all about money. As long as you were making money and people knew it, you had and earned respect.

Respect! Anyone from our neck of the woods will tell you how important a word that is. Respect is what guarantees that you keep what you own. Respect guaranteed that no one took liberties with you. And people always try, trust me. But as long as you dealt with every situation you came up against in such a way as to retain your respect, then life was easier all round. Respect attracted the best people and the best girls to you in my young world, I was getting to understand.

It is very important to command the respect of not just your peers but also the older lot on the streets of any inner city. And at this early age it was becoming clear to me what you had to do to command the respect of others. The age was twelve.

With every punk I beat up, my respect grew. The more money I made, the more respect I earned. Even from my brother Luechie's age group. It was obvious that I had potential. But potential for what I didn't yet know.

But in the meantime I carried on the same path at school, baronning and earning. At this age I was full of ambition just like any other twelve-year-old. I didn't plan to go to prison at this or any other age. I didn't plan on becoming an armed robber or a gun slinger or anything like that. Things happen in an individual's life that turns him or her onto a different path from the one dreamt of as a child. In my case I still haven't sussed out what exactly turned me onto the path I took. And you will see exactly what I mean as you read on.

At about this time I joined a boxing gym. It was a boys club all the way over in West London, Harrow Road to be exact. My trainers name was I.K. or Isola Akay.

Boxing had a big influence in my life. It's an influence that I still carry with me to this day. I became fit and physical from a young age. And with that came the confidence and self-assurance I needed and still need to get through life, which can be a war zone at times. Especially if you grew up where I did and attended school where I did.

I was also interested in aeroplanes. I wanted to become a pilot. It didn't really matter to me what kind of pilot, commercial, private or cargo pilot as long as I was flying a plane. But I wish someone had told me back then that unless you had the right colour skin in this country not every dream was possible. They should have told me that certain professions are reserved and even now are still reserved for the faces that fit.

But regardless, I thought back then that I had what it took to become an aeroplane pilot. So I went ahead and studied everything about planes. I bought magazines, books and anything else I could get my hands on to do with the subject. And I can honestly say I still maintain this interest to this day. Funny isn't it. Back then I could tell you anything you wanted to know about aeroplanes. I knew where they were made, which country made which plane, how many engines each plane had and so on. At that time not a lot of black countries trained pilots, I knew I either had to train in America or Europe. If things had been different maybe my life would have taken a different turn to the one I took.

I was also very good at boxing. I had the right height, right reach and had natural strength to go with it.

"If you dedicate yourself to the work son, the world is yours for the taking," my trainer always said. Sounds familiar doesn't it? Yeah well that's the story of my life. But whatever I did dedicate myself to, I did do well at. But I was using the skills I learned in the gym to further my career on the streets of my concrete jungle. The more punks I knocked out, the more respect gained and the more people wanted to know me.

Let me just point out that when I use the word punk I don't mean punk rockers with Mohican haircuts. I mean my competitors on the streets. The other kids out on the streets looking to get ahead in whatever game they're in.

I remember my first one-punch knockout. It was around this time and outside my school. He was a Turkish kid two years my senior, called Val. He'd beaten up my friend Paul Greyer the day before. He had a sort of no-nonsense reputation, but for some reason never picked a fight with anyone his own size. Anyway the next day we saw him and called him over to where we were and then I told him to put down his school bag and have a go with me. I remember he didn't even get to throw a punch because the first punch I threw took him out. And it wasn't just his person that was knocked out, his reputation was knocked out on that day too.

Back in the outside world Margaret Thatcher was in power. She of the evil Tory party. I remember a lot of Black people foolishly thought things would be better. It was. But not for them. It was better for you if you were white, middle to upper class. For us lot in the inner cities of Britain it wasn't so. They closed down coal mines across England, which made whole families unemployed and on the dole. They crushed the trade unions, which were and still are the only means by which the working classes get their fair dues. And in the inner cities they put a lot more police on the beat. The police were given new stop and search powers, which they immediately put to use against the black and coloured peoples of Britain and any white people caught up in the inner cities. To them we were all undesirables. They didn't have to spell it out - it was all in their policies.

Immigration was tightened up against black and coloured countries. So if you were a white Australian or German your families back home had no problem visiting. But if you were a citizen of colour your families back home had problems visiting. We had trouble getting our families in Africa, Jamaica, India and so on to come over on visits. These policies left ethnic people in this country feeling let down and disappointed in a system they thought they could trust.

It all came to a head in April of 1981 after just two years of Thatcherism.

Brixton exploded! The result was the first of the riots in Brixton in the eighties.

I was going on thirteen and was just starting to understand the politics of the times but still didn't fully understand. I did feel a definite change in the attitudes of people at the time, even my parents and their friends complained a lot about these policies.

I remember walking down our streets and nearly always getting stopped and harassed by the police, whom we called 'the heat' back then. We called their vans the meat wagons because of the way they picked people off the streets, innocent or not, and carted them off to the police stations.

I also remember seeing television pictures of the Brixton riots of 1981. The way the news was reported left people in no doubt how the government saw the rioters. I'm not trying to make out that it was the right thing to do, far from it. But the Thatcher government left people frustrated and at their wits' end. And rather than look at the cause of the rioting they totally ignored these problems and instead concentrated on labelling these people as criminals and adopting even harsher measures. It was obvious to anyone in the inner cities that the riot of '81 wouldn't be the last the government was going to hear of the people in the inner cities. Back to '81, watching the news on the telly made me feel good. It was good to see the ordinary people putting up a fight, showing the powers that be that they weren't going to take things lying down. That they had had enough of the government sponsored bias towards the working classes.

There were upturned cars burned out on the streets, shops burned out and hundreds of police injured. A lot of shops were looted. But what pleased me the most was the police getting a taste of their own medicine.

But like I already said, instead of tackling the reasons for the riots, the Tory government went ahead and put more police on the streets and gave them more senseless powers, which they only abused and used against the same people. This only made things worse.

The eighties seemed to me the decade of unrest and riots. But Thatcher and her cronies didn't give a flying fuck.

In the mean time I juggled my street life with my boxing training. West London was quite a distance for a boy my age to go by himself so I rode up with my uncle George, who I can thank for getting me into boxing in the first place.

Also by now I was starting to get into bigger and better crime. I had by now discovered robbery and burglary. I saw these crimes as a way to earn even more money. Some of the people I was robbing were my dad's age. Once I got hooked on the buzz of having all this money it was hard to stop. To all those who think crime is easy money they don't know what they're talking about. It was far from easy money. I'd rather call it quick money. It was quick in the sense that you didn't have to work all day and all week to get paid. You could go out to 'work' and be back home in two hours with someone's monthly salary. So it was quick money but it sure was not easy money.

I was also now buying my own drugs. Weed to be exact. Weed was cheap then and always of good quality compared to what we get today. These days you pay good money for a lot of rubbish.

I was also starting to rave or party. Back then it was mostly house parties or Reggae dance hall blues. Because of my height and my brothers I was allowed into a lot of clubs and parties my friends weren't allowed in. But Toddler and the Nose, being my closest friends, were always let in as they were always with me and my brothers.

It became really tricky balancing my boxing ambitions with my need to make money on the streets. Something had to give because I was also at school and had my other aspirations like wanting to become a pilot. I had already started applying to Flying Schools in America and here in Britain. They all sent back forms and brochures, thanking me for my interest in their schools. That was alright until I saw the cost of the courses I'd applied for. In other words, it dawned on me that to be a pilot you really had to be a rich man's kid. Maybe if I was an only child my parents could've sent me to train as a pilot but I was one of seven and it was now becoming clear this was one profession I might not be able to get into. But I refused to give up. I bugged my parents all the time and didn't give up for years. All my mum would say was, "Tony when you finish school we'll see, OK?"

I know when it came to my dad he really wanted us to follow in his footsteps and work in a bank. He always involved us in talks about Banking and Economics and stuff like that.

When I turned fourteen in 1982 my brother Luechie was in jail at the age of eighteen. He had been remanded in custody for a string of robberies, some at knifepoint. Luechie was at this time earning good money on the streets, wearing nice clothes and had maximum respect for a kid his age. But his luck had run out. I remember going to visit him at the Ashford Remand Centre with my mum and my brother Frankie. I asked him what it was like in there and stuff like that. I remember the look I got from my mum when I asked these questions.

"Why, you plan on coming to join him?"

I really looked up to Luechie, and with him banged up in prison life for the rest of us was not the same.

On the way back from the prison visit, my mum gave us a long lecture about the whole situation and what it was doing to my dad and her. She was very sad about Dillon being in jail. We tried to cheer her up, telling her Leuchie was only on remand and could be coming home soon. And I also remember promising myself not to ever cause my mum the same grief and heartache. We knew my dad was blaming her for all of our wrongdoings, like she was sending us out to do stuff.

Luechie got six months in a young offender's institution and came out the next year. Meanwhile life went on for the rest of us. Frankie wasn't like Luechie. He was a speecher, a diplomat, while Luechie was all action, just like me. So with Luechie locked up, I knew my major backbone was gone even though Frankie was still there if I needed him. He wasn't a pushover. All it was is that Luechie had more respect on the streets than Frankie had. But life went on anyway. We visited Luechie in jail whenever he sent a visit order.

I was fourteen when Britain was at war with Argentina. But it was a war I didn't understand at the time, but do now. I remember wondering why Britain would go all the way to the Falkland Islands to fight for a land that wasn't really theirs. It was like Argentina coming to fight Britain for The Isle Of Wight or Jersey. Didn't make sense at fourteen but does now.

You see this was all down to greed and power. Just like my city jungle! Let me explain the comparison. It was greed and hunger that led Britain and the British to leave these shores in search of riches. And because they had the power they were able to grab and defend what they managed to grab. They grabbed the Falkland Islands years and years ago, and still had the power to defend it as theirs in 1982.

To be honest, yes I know the people of the island prefer British passports to Argentine passports, who wouldn't and yes I'm sure they would vote all day long to remain linked with the British than the Argentines, but that's only natural when generations have grown up only knowing English, Britain and the Queen as their Head Of State.

It does not make it right. The thing is for example, why was it that when China was strong enough to want back Hong Kong, Britain had to give it back. Failure to have done so, I believe, would have led to China invading Hong Kong. Now reader, ask yourselves this, do you think the UK would have sent ships to fight China in 1997 when Hong Kong was given back, or 1982 when they went to war with Argentina? Hell no!

They would have lost. And the US would not have got involved either. All Britain could do was give the citizens who wanted it a British passport. So we only bully who we can most of the time, do you get it? Same law often applies on the streets.

CHAPTER THREE

In 1983, I was going on fifteen and driving. I started driving even further out, like driving to my gym over in West London. My crew was still together at this time even though we were starting to get into more serious brushes with the law.

Round about this time, in the summer of '83, I saw my first murder. He was a drunk. It has stayed with me to this day. It is not something I would wish on anybody's child. Listen! We had stopped robbing people outside our local tube station. We were starting to go national. Our favourite haunting ground was the West End of London. The bright lights attracted everybody. The rich, the tourists, film fans and party goers. Homosexuals, straight couples, druggies and weirdoes. Anyway, it was an area for rich pickings to a kid from the inner city. Also at this time, a couple of the crew members had started driving as well, so we had about four cars between about fifteen of us. But we never drove to the West End. Instead we met outside TEE's Pool Café, which was one minute from the tube station. When everyone arrived, we'd set off on the tube to the West End and come back on the N90 night bus back to Tottenham fat with our loot. Watches, chains, rings and cash. On this particular night in the summer of '83 we'd been to the West End on one of those missions about nine of us. I'll leave out names because it's irrelevant to this story. Anyway it was a successful night as we were all nice and had enough things each to take to the jewellers in Tottenham the next day. It was jam packed up West. There was a big boxing match being shown on the big screen picture house at Leicester Square. I think it was Roberto Duran and Sugar Ray Leonard, but can't be sure exactly.

Anyway, when the clubs and pictures emptied out about 2 a.m., we all knew what we had to do. Without a signal or a word, the usual practice called every man for himself was on. When you got something, we'd run to Leicester Square Station or the nearest MacDonald's Restaurant and sit down like nothing happened to wait for the rest of the guys. These were the days before mobile phones, so we could only pre-arrange meeting points back then. Anyway, I personally grabbed an eighteen carat chain off a woman and robbed her husband of his gold watch and wallet. I was the third one to arrive at 'Mac Dee's' as we called it back then. Slowly but surely, the crew turned up one at a time, sometimes two together. When we were all together, the nine of us and a couple of Kentish town kids whom we knew but didn't show any respect, we moved on. I know this sounds bad, but please remember there are millions of people who have lived this way and changed, millions of people who still do and millions who will do in the future. Society will never get rid of this criminal behaviour until it understands that from the very beginning of time, when the rules we all now live by were written by the British, French, Spanish, Portuguese and much later the Americans, they were written in a way that has created all the problems we see today. The fact that alcohol and tobacco are legal and drugs isn't, is because they say it will be like that. It is not based on any scientific stats because if it were alcohol and tobacco would be far more illegal in terms of how many people they kill compared to how many people drugs kill combined per year.

Sometimes it is good to try as much as you can to imagine a different world. If so many things weren't illegal we would have less crime. Imagine a world where you got locked up for peddling tobacco of any kind. Two years in prison if you're caught with five packets of twenties. That's how easy this could have been reality if these people who came before us decided it would be that way.

Anyway, my lot headed for the night bus stop to catch the N90 back to Tottenham. We had to take a couple of back streets to avoid the heat (the police). We came across a drunk staggering along. We were just excited, talking about what we each just did. Anyway, one of us, can't remember who right now, decided to rob the drunk. He stepped over to the man with a brick in hand. Looking back now, that brick wasn't needed because he was drunk senseless. Anyway, bang! Right in the middle of his head. I saw him go dawn and start choking. The drunk man's pockets were searched with some success. Next his watch and whatever else he had was taken off him. He just kept on twitching and foaming from the mouth. He also had blood running from his head. How did we know he died? Because the next weekend there were police posters all over the place begging for anyone who knew anything to phone them and give information. I had witnessed my first murder. Things were just beginning to get serious, trust me. So we decided to give the West End a miss for a couple of months. We warned the rest of the crew not to go back up West for a while. This was as a precaution. No one wanted to get pulled in for shit like that. Especially when you didn't have anything to do with it. It happened so quick, we couldn't have stopped it even if we wanted.

Life went on anyway back in the jungle. We frequented the Broadwater Farm Estate in Tottenham, which was starting to take the shape of a frontline in Tottenham. For those who don't know what a frontline is, it's a street, an area or a housing estate where you could get any drugs, weapon and stuff. Similar to what a Red Light area is. Also round about these times, the Yardies started to feature in our local politics. But they weren't involved in any of our politics because we were the younger crew. We only purchased our drugs, mostly weed from these Jamaicans. Nevertheless we witnessed a few stabbings and heard about shootings involving Yardies.

My older brother Dillon's age group were more bothered about their presence than we were. I enjoyed listening to their stories of political warfare back in Jamaica. They either belonged to the PNP party or the Jamaican Labor party. Anyway at that age, it was all stories to me. They liked us English youths and we didn't mind them being on our turf. Not as yet anyway. I say not as yet because later on as we got older, they did get involved in my politics.

Life also carried on the same path in school. We were well known and respected. I drove to school, had new trainers on my feet all the time. Adidas Gazelles were the trainers of the day. Burberry clothes and drain pipe jeans and cords. Crime allowed me to keep up with the day's fashion with ease no matter what they cost. I have always been hungry for knowledge and this has never changed. I might never became a pilot, I still kept up with school work as much as I could. But this was more due to my dad's pressure than my eagerness to succeed in school work. At that time, I couldn't see how school work could help me when I was making a lot of money on the street.

But to keep my parents happy, I kept up as well as I could with school work. Being naturally intelligent, I put in just enough work to scrape through so everybody was happy, except the school authorities like my teachers and head teacher because they were well aware of our other activities and they didn't like it one bit. It was amazing in a way that I hadn't been thrown out because by this time Rodney and Nicky, my crew members, had been expelled - Nicky for stabbing another kid badly in the chest. He was at this time on bail for it and it looked bad. Rodney assaulted the PE teacher, Mr King. He punched Mr King in the face for leaving him out of a five-a-side football game. The head teacher was not impressed and Rodney was expelled. But we still linked them up during school hours and after school to make money. I only had one year left in school and I wanted to see it through, for what it was worth. Luechie, my brother Dillon, as we called him, didn't finish school, but Frankie did and I wanted to as well.

Boxing was also starting to take a back stage at this time. I'd had a couple of fights. Three to be exact. Won all three. The last one was the most pleasing because I didn't think I could knock out the guy. What was funny though, was that the boy, I think his name was Michael O'Leary or Leary, was from my home club in Tottenham. The Boxing club in Tottenham, called the Enterprise Boys Club, was the one I should have joined, being a Tottenham boy. So you could imagine how important it was to beat him. If only to prove I'd made the right decision to join the All Stars. Anyway, it was the South East schoolboys competition and I was in the preliminary stages when I came up against this kid. Three two-minute rounds. I was ready and rearing to go. I knew what I had to do. Take him out. – And take him out I did. I lost the first round because he was a fucking South Paw fighter. But once I'd marked him out, he was out in the third and the last round. My brother Leuchie and my uncle George, who got me into boxing to start with, were in the crowd and they were well pleased for me. My next bout was the next day and I knew I was ready, my aim was to at least reach the Semis. The next day I fucked up big time. I was fighting a boy from East London that evening. The fight started alright until I started to lose my temper. I couldn't stand losing, especially to an East End boy. I headbutted him blatantly twice in the second round and was disqualified and therefore lost. I was so upset that I wanted to finish the fight outside the hall.

You could imagine how mad my trainer was. He told my uncle to tell me not to come back to the gym for one whole month. He was really mad. But I only saw that month as a holiday, a time to get back to the streets and my crew. Looking back now, I wish I hadn't taken it that way. I wish I'd been a little more serious about the whole thing.

If only I'd put as much work into boxing and school as I did into being a little gangster, things might be different today. I sure would not be sitting in prison today doing thirty-nine fucking months. My second sentence in twelve short years. But anyway, as long as I was making money I thought my life was fine. I now turned fifteen in October of '83. I could probably pass for seventeen because I was very tall. I was still seeing Natasha. Remember? Big breast, big mouth and big earrings. I saw her only when my cock felt for her particular style of sex. Otherwise, I was out and about with other girls my age and prettier and more up to date with my thinking. Plus we were now at the age where they were now giving up sex.

Christmas came and went and a new year started as usual full of hope. I did my first smash and grab in 1984. I was fifteen. Smash and grab was more profitable and exciting than robbing people. And less chance of hurting anybody as well. Even more profitable than burglaries because you knew exactly what you were going for.

This was a gold shop located on Church Street Stoke Newington. Even though we had cars at our disposal and could steal cars if we needed to, this mission had to be done on bikes. BMX bikes were the bikes of the day. We'd graduated from Choppers to BMXs.

We'd seen this shop many times and knew this mission could be done. There's nothing worse than planning to do something only for some other crew to get there and do it before you did. It hurt when you heard about it. So we weren't about to waste time. It took two days for us to decide and plan what we had to do. Looking back now there is no way we could have pulled it off today. Anyway this was 1984 and we were still learning. Nicky by this time had been sentenced to five months in a young offenders' prison for stabbing the kid in the chest. We all felt for him. He was sent to Ashford. So Toddler, Brigadier whom we called Briggy for short, Gee Money at that time known as Gary and myself decided to smash up the gold shop.

The plan was to each have a carrier bag stapled to the inside of our jackets, get a hammer each and then ride up to the shop on our bikes. We would then smash the glass from the outside of the shop and then proceed to grab as much of the display trays as we could. It sounded simple and profitable so off we went. I borrowed my brother Andrew's BMX bike for the job. It all went according to plan with Briggy leading the way. I think the people in the shop must have thought we were vandals until they saw the shop display trays disappearing. By the time they ran out of the shop to grab who they could, we were already starting to ride off. Simple. We rode to Briggy's uncle's house round the corner from the shop. We wheeled the bikes in, still excited, adrenalin flowing from what we'd just done. Briggy's uncle's wife knew we'd done something because of the state we were in and also all the police sirens around the area. We went upstairs to his cousin's room to watch TV and relax and calm down. His auntie kept asking what we'd done and why the police was all over the place. She kept bugging us, in the end Briggy told her we'd been in a fight with some Stoke Newington boys. This explanation calmed her down and she got off our backs.

At this time all I wanted to do was see what I'd grabbed. When she left the room we couldn't wait any longer so we took our carrier bags out, comparing items and trays, weighing up the gold in our hands. I was happy with my lot. We all were in fact, so much so we didn't know Briggy's auntie had been outside the door listening. After a couple of hours when the sirens had died down we came back out and split up each with his own loot. We left the bikes in her back garden. We were sure every black kid on a BMX bike would be pulled by the police. I went home on the bus wearing one of my bracelets from the mission. A six ounce bracelet. Poor Briggy. His auntie told his uncle what had happened and what she'd heard us saying. The next time we linked Briggy he had two black eyes and a fat jaw. His dad and uncle had been responsible for his injuries. But he also had new clothes, about four thick chains round his neck, a bracelet and a bounce in his step. So we all took the piss out of him on our way to sell some of our gold. 1984 also saw my first serious arrest and first real threat of being locked up. It was silly really compared to some of the things I'd done and got away with.

It was April and for some reason, I was on the bus going to Blackhorse Road tube station to meet some girls with two punks I knew from the area. I call them punks because at the age of twenty-eight, which was the last time I saw them they turned out to be jokers, nobodies. Anyway, back then, they were alright just another two young soldiers on the block.

While on the bus, the tallest of the three of us, Chris, decided he wanted to rob this other kid on the bus minding his own business. It was obvious the kid was a broke pocket, meaning he had nothing to rob, apart from a skinny nine carat chain and a stupid watch. Anyway, Chris saw money in him. He walked up to the boy and popped his chain. He then searched up his pockets and even took his packet of Rizlas or cigarette papers. By this time the bus had got to our destination. Black horse Road. So we got off the bus. Because the kid was black and because I didn't have anything to do with the robbery, I didn't feel any urgency to get away. We didn't think he would flag down a police car and report the crime. But, that's exactly what he did. We met the girls outside the tube station and went to catch a tube to Oxford Street. I heard the police radios even before I saw them. When they appeared, they had this same kid with them. He proceeded to point us out as the three youths on the bus. Fucked! Fucking embarrassing, we got arrested in full view of all the other passengers waiting for the tube and in front of the girls we had come to meet. They put me in a car with a crazy police dog and the driver of the car. I was taken to Leyton police Station where I saw my two co-defendants. I wanted to strangle Chris. And I'm sure my stare said it all. We were there for two days and then taken to court. Chris was remanded to Ashford remand centre while me and Itchy, even though we were also charged with robbery, were given bail. At that time, robbery and especially street robbery was the number one public enemy crime. So I knew we were in big trouble. I didn't go and visit Chris in jail. I didn't think I could control myself on the visit. I was fifteen and a half and staring jail in the face.

The only thing that might have saved us was the fact he was a black kid. Black people did not trust or like the police at that time. It might have got better now and maybe will get better in the future. Luckily for Chris and thanks to Leuchie, I had a reliable solicitor and was able to get the boy's address. The solicitor was the same ones who had been handling Leuchie's troubles, so they took on my case as well. Every time we came to court I would not speak to Chris. Leuchie took the boy's address and went with his friend to apologise and use a bit of intimidation to make him see sense. Thank god he was black. A white family would have gone all the way, especially being that we were a group of black kids. Anyway, Leuchie's persuasive character brought the kid to his senses and eventually the case was dropped at committal when he didn't turn up. Chris was released from prison and I never ever went anywhere with him after that, even though we're still friends to this day. By this time it was July of 1984 and it was nice to not have a serious charge like that over your head. I enjoyed my summer. It didn't last very long though. Because I was soon on a robbery charge again.

This time in Watford, a town just on the outskirts of London. I didn't go out to do anything. I was with Toddler and the Nose. We had stolen some butterfly knives from a knife shop about two days before and were itching to put them to use. I was the first one to christen my knife, but unfortunately it happened to be my good friend and a staunch member of the crew Mark Greyer. It was an accident and it was also my first stabbing. The day we stole the knives, about twenty or more of them, we shared them out. I ended up with a gold-handled one with holes in the handle. Anyway, we went to play pool at TEE's cafe. I then started messing around with Mark. We were imitating a sword fight like you see in *Zorro*, the TV series. Before I knew it, I lunged at Mark mistakenly stabbing him deep into his shoulder. He was badly wounded and had to go to the hospital. I went with him and felt terrible. I then went to his mom's and told his sister as his mom was at work. Anyway, back to Watford. We'd gone to a park dance in a big park in Watford. That was all we'd gone there for. But sometimes, things don't go according to plan. Instead of partying, we saw so much easy pickings that we decided to rob some of these country folk. We could see a lot of the Londoners had the same intentions. But we left it till last when we were leaving to go home. Still all the time looking for the best thing to rob.

We found it! Two guys and a girl with them. We followed them at a distance out of the park. About ten minutes' walk from the park, we made our move. The butterfly knives came out and we stuck them up. We got some gold - quite a bit between the three of them - and some money. Wrong move! We were in the country in the outskirts of London and it was easy to spot blacks up there. Anyway, we thought we'd got away. We went to the tube stations but being in the countryside, the trains didn't run like in London. They run to a set time. We asked the ticket attendant how long we had to wait.

"Seven minutes mate," he said. "But there's another station on the other side of town though if you lot are in a rush." I think he meant an over ground train that also went into London from Watford but was in another location.

"Thanks mate," Toddler said.

But we chose to wait there anyhow. Wrong move number two. The train arrived and we got on it. But it had to wait because, as I said, they run to a set time, unlike London tubes, but also because it was the end of the train line.

While we were on the train, something made me go back out on the platform to keep an eye on things. So I left Toddler and Nose on the train and went out. What I saw was not nice. About one million police officers approaching the train. They had the three victims with them. But they walked right past me, stopping at every carriage as the doors were still open. I saw them pile on the train. I couldn't get out of the station as there were more officers at the exit. So I just sat on a bench on the platform like an innocent bystander. I managed to throw my butterfly knife and the gold behind me without being seen. I sat praying. After a couple of minutes I saw Toddler and Nose led off the train in handcuffs. The officers looked dark and evil when they walked past me. Then just as I thought my prayers would be answered, the girl walking past turned and that was it. She whispered something to the officer closest to her. He turned and looked at me and began walking towards me.

"Where have you been today son?" he asked me.

"I've come to the park with my sister and her boyfriend," I said.

"Where are they now?" he asked.

"In the park, officer," I said. "I have to get back to London cos I'm meeting my girl," was my explanation. He walked back again and conferred with the girl and the two guys. I sat still putting on as innocent a face as I could.

I saw him approaching me again and I knew it wasn't good.

"Have you got a pair of Sunglasses on you?" he asked. When I hesitated, he said, "I can search you if I want."

With that, I took out my sunglasses he took them and showed the victims. They nodded and then he turned to me and said, "You're under arrest on suspicion of robbery." And with that, I was on my way to jail proper for the first time in my life.

Again what happened in this next chapter of my life should have, on paper, fixed me, stopped me in my tracks, basically sorted me out. But it didn't. By the time I was released I was a lot more dangerous, more angry, more schooled in crime and more respected. All of these factors combined with my already wayward personality did not make for curing me. It only made me worse but better at it all.

So I began my journey as a prisoner.

CHAPTER FOUR

Yeah I was nicked and on my way to a proper jail for the first time in my life. These police officers were different from the ones down my way. They were proper cold and didn't take kindly to young thugs from out of town coming here and doing stuff.

"What's your name, son?" said the desk sergeant.

"Anthony Spencer," I replied.

"Address?" he asked.

When I gave a Tottenham address, he looked up, even more angry. "So those other two, did you say they're not friends of yours then?" he asked.

"No," I said. "I don't know them."

"But you three have given Tottenham addresses."

"So what?" I replied.

"Put him in cell four," he said to one of the officers.

It was a Saturday. Fucking long weekend it turned out to be. By this time I knew not to say anything until my solicitor got there.

My solicitor firm was called Joseph Jones Associates. When one of their representatives got to the station and came to see me, he said it looked bad. He didn't have to tell me, I knew it.

He sat in on my interview in which I made no comment. I was still denying knowing Toddler and Kevin, the Nose. I didn't have anything to say to the CID officers. Anyway on Sunday I was charged with three counts of robbery because there were three victims and they'd been robbed. I was finger printed, my photo was taken, and then back to the cell to be arraigned before a magistrate's court in

Watford on Monday morning. I'd never felt so far away from home. It wasn't a nice feeling. My mum and Frankie came up to the Police Station on Sunday evening to bring me my Sunday dinner and clothes and stuff. It was the best Sunday dinner I'd ever had, albeit in a police cell. The visit cheered me up a lot. It was nice seeing my family so far away from home. I held my mum's hands and told her it was my friends and not me who'd carried out the robbery. Frankie knew I was lying, but didn't say anything to her. They promised to be in Court the next day. I could see my mum was trying to hold back the tears. And when it was time for them to leave, it was my turn to fight to hold back tears. I kept reminding myself that I was now a soldier and soldiers do not cry. So I soldiered on.

Monday morning we were taken to court. By this time, though, it was obvious to the police that we knew each other because we'd been talking to each other, shouting from our cells. They knew they had the right people in custody. The country courts were intimidating compared to the London ones.

It seems as though you had to be over sixty and ugly to have a job in that court. No smiles, no warmth. Just cold. They read out the charges after we'd confirmed our names and addresses. I could see my mum flinch when the charges were read out. Or maybe it was the way the old bitch read them out. I forgot to mention the fact that Toddler and Nose were caught more or less bang to rights. They had their butterfly knives on them and some of the items from the victims. I'd managed to throw mine away. So I was just a bit better off than they were. Not much though. Anyway, back to the court proceedings. Toddler's solicitor was the first to have a go for bail. Then my solicitor and then Nose's. They were all sharp and said everything they had to say. I really thought we had hope. Nothing to do with it. We were all remanded in custody to Ashford Remand Centre in Middlesex. We were to be brought back up to court in seven days. And then I saw my mum burst out crying and I knew I'd done to her what I had promised not to do. It hurt to see her cry. I love my mum badly. Back down in the court cells we were refused visits from our families. I was just beginning to realize how serious this was.

On the van on the way to prison, I was not in a chatty mood. I just kept thinking back to all the good times I'd had and how different things would have been if only I'd stayed at home on Saturday instead of coming to Watford. That feeling is always the same on the way to prison. You can't help but reminisce about the fun times. It was the same feeling I had on the journey to prison all those years later in 2002 with thirty-nine months to serve. Anyway, it was the first time I was experiencing prison. Neither Toddler nor the Nose could enlighten me, nor I them, about what to expect in prison as it was the first for all three of us.

When we got to the prison, I remembered visiting Luechie my brother here when he was locked up. But it was different this time. This time, the prison van called a 'sweat box' drove us through the massive gates and into prison. It then drove to the reception area and we got out one at a time. There were other people on the bus who'd been picked up at various stops on the way to the prison. We were then locked in a room. All the new receptions in one room and the other rooms contained people who'd left the prison that morning to go to court and had come back. We were getting called one at a time by our surnames. It was hours before I was called up.

"Spencer!" one officer shouted.

"Yeah," I answered.

"Come this way," he said, more an order than anything else. He led the way through to a room where there were a couple of officers.

"Stand on that line," the Senior Officer said. "What's your full name?"

"Anthony Spencer."

"Date of birth?"

"Fourteenth of October 1968," I answered.

"Been in prison before?"

"No."

"What's your charge or charges?" he asked.

"Robbery," I answered.

"Another robber, eh? Any outstanding cases?" he asked me.

"No," I said.

"Next of kin?"

I gave my mum's name and address.

"Does anyone know you're here?"

"Yes."

"How tall are you? Actually, go and stand over there." He pointed to a handwritten measure on a wall. I stood up against it and another officer measured my height. "Five foot eleven," he said to the senior officer.

"Strip-search him," the Senior officer said.

I was then strip-searched and my bag of clean clothes searched properly. Being on remand, I was allowed to wear my own clothes, so they gave me back my clothes and then asked me to sign for my clothes and money my brother Frankie had given me through my solicitor in Court.

I was told I could have a shower. I badly needed one, so I was glad to hear it. After two days in the police cell, I was starting to smell.

After my shower I went in another room to join the queue waiting to see the doctor. This was the procedure for the new receptions. Toddler was next in the room. I was glad to have my crew members with me. The officers tried their best to scare you when they knew it was your first time. For some reason I didn't feel scared or intimidated. I was watching everything with a funny sort of interest. We got talking with some kids from Clapham Junction and Brixton. Each trying to impress the other. It helped that we were from out of Tottenham because Tottenham was well known for breeding tough soldiers. We weren't about to let down our town.

"Spencer."

"Yeah."

"Doctor to see you now." Another command.

When I walked into the room I was surprised to see an Indian doctor. He was the first non-white person in authority that I'd come across since my arrest on Saturday. It was now Monday evening. The policemen and women were white, the three magistrates in court were white, the Court staff were all white and all the prison officers I'd seen so far were white. So it was shocking but nice to see an

Indian doctor.

"Do you smoke?" he asked in a pronounced Indian accent and a smile on his face.

"Yes doctor," I said with a smile in return.

"Drugs?" he asked.

Leuchie already told me never to declare to them that I smoked weed, so I knew exactly what to say.

"No," I said. "I don't smoke drugs."

"Do you suffer from asthma?" he asked.

"No doctor."

"Are you suicidal?"

"No."

"Are you on any medication at this present time?" he asked.

"No," I said.

"Do you suffer from sickle cell or diabetes?"

"No."

"Have you ever suffered from any form of sexually transmitted diseases?"

"No," I said, laughing at the question.

The officer present in the room didn't find my casual attitude funny. He just stared at me. I ignored him and turned back to the doctor.

He closed my file indicating that the interview was over. I left the doctor's room to join the others back in the other room.

"Howard," the officer called Toddler.

"Yeah," Toddler answered.

"You're next for the doctor, come this way." So Toddler left the room with the officer. Back in the room with Nose and the other kids, I asked for a light off one of them and smoked a cigarette.

"What do they call you?" one junction boy asked me.

"Why?" I said with a little aggression in my voice.

"Nothing, just asking innit," he said with a South London accent.

"What do they call you?" I asked him.

"Square," he said.

"Boxer," I said.

"Do you box then?" Square asked me.

"Yeah I do. Do you want to try?"

"Cool man. What's up with you?" he replied.

"Nothing except I'm in jail."

"We're all in jail boxer, just calm down mate," he said.

Toddler came back in the room smiling.

"What's up?" I asked him.

"Did you see the Indian doctor?" he asked.

"Yeah," I said.

"Brown," the officer said, calling for Kevin the Nose.

When we'd all been seen, another officer came in the room with cell cards in his hands. He called out about six names including mine, Toddler's and Kevin's.

"Come with me," he said to all six of us. "Pick up a bag each," he said, pointing to kit bags that contained our kits such as bed spread, pillow case, PE shorts, blanket, vests and stuff. He also pointed to some plates, cups and plastic cutlery and told us to take one of each. One plastic plate, one plastic cup, one plastic eating bowl, one plastic knife, fork and spoon. After we'd all helped ourselves, he told us to follow him. We were on our way to our cell block and cells. By this time I was very tired and all I wanted to see was a bed.

I was allocated to a cell with the Nose. Toddler was next door to us with Square, the kid from Clapham Junction. It was late when we got in the cells and all the other cell doors were locked so we couldn't tell who was on our landing. The cell door shut and this was it. The real thing. I was in prison. I was fifteen years and ten months old.

I looked at the Nose and I could see he was very apprehensive, maybe even scared.

"You alright blood?" I asked him.

"Yeah boy. Prison you know. This is fucking prison," he said.

"Don't worry blood, we'll be alright. We're soldiers," I said to him to cheer him up. "I want the bottom bunk, yeah," I said.

"I don't mind which one I sleep in, I'm fucked," he said. I started making my bed and sorting out my stuff. I had a piece of paper showing my name and a number beside it. This was my prison number. I just stared at it. I was in prison. I just hoped I wouldn't be here for my birthday in October.

I got in bed and remember saying a prayer that I got bail from Court next week Monday. I was out like a light.

"Breakfast."

That was what I woke up to the next morning. A lot of commotion and keys and shouting. "Breakfast!"

For a split second I thought I was in my own bed at home and then it all came flooding back. I was in prison. The cell door was open by now as it was breakfast.

I looked out on the landing to see what was going on. Everybody was heading out of the landing with their plates and bowls in their hands. So I did the same and followed them with Toddler and Kevin the Nose.

When I got to the servery there was a big queue. I was very hungry. But when I saw the breakfast, I was not feeling so hungry any more. Shit! The state of the porridge. It still makes me sick today just looking at it. I took some tea off a fat screw as the officers were called. I also had some toast and a runny fried egg. I liked my egg fried brown. I had to force this egg down. I was in prison now and I had to eat. Everyone ate in a dining hall, so there was about seventy to eighty guys eating. I sat at a table with Toddler and the Nose. Nose took that sickly porridge and even seemed to enjoy it. But I think it was because he was hungry. I couldn't imagine anyone enjoying that shit. I just looked around at my new surroundings, hoping and praying I'd get bail next week.

I saw a few faces of people we knew from Hackney. I couldn't believe it when I saw my friends Reds and Curly. I called them over to join our table. They filled us in on how the place was run and how to get our weed in on a visit. They told us what we were allowed to have, who else was here and where they were. In short, they filled us in on the prison politics.

It was good to see our friends from the road even though they were from Hackney, which is up the road from Tottenham. Reds and Curly were good soldiers. I asked him about my crew member Nicky who was doing a sentence for stabbing the boy in the chest. Reds told us that he'd been moved to Chelmsford for allocation after he got sentenced.

Anyway he told us that there were more people we knew on other wings in the prison. We were on A-wing. But we were now five including our friends from Hackney and they knew the ropes in here so I didn't mind moving with them. After breakfast was the first round of visits. I was sure that Frankie and Leuchie would come up today with some food and weed. At that time you were allowed to have many things you're not allowed today. You could have cooked food, cakes and alcohol brought up on visits. It wasn't too bad then, it's a lot worse now.

Anyway, as I wasn't sure when I'd get a visit, I eagerly awaited, one knowing my brothers would not leave me to suffer in here. I was right. That afternoon, mum, Leuchie and Frankie came up. Boy was I glad to see them. Mum was sad, but was very worried about me. I told her I was fine and that I had some friends here, so I was OK. I wasn't about to show any weakness. When mum went to hand in my dinner, soft drinks and clothes, Leuchie passed me a little parcel of weed. Wicked! I was hoping he brought some but I wasn't going to ask him. Wicked! I was so pleased. When mum came back to the table she could see I was happy about something because I just couldn't stop smiling.

"What you smiling about?" she said to me and turned to Leuchie like she knew.

"Nothing, mum. Just glad to see you, mum."

"You sure?" she asked.

I was enjoying the visit so much. I was gutted when it was over. A screw walked up to my table.

"Finish off now."

It was hard, but I said my goodbyes. I couldn't wait to get back to

A-wing to show off and smoke a spliff with my crew and our friends from Hackney.

Getting drugs on my visit boosted up my reputation in a big way. Everyone wanted to know my crew. We were from Tottenham and were proud of it. I smoked my first prison spliff with the guys. It was wicked. Better than the porridge.

Before I knew it, it was Tuesday, then Wednesday. On Thursday, guess who came up with Leuchie to see me? Natasha. Big mouth, big breasts and big earrings. She looked good I can tell you. She made an extra effort today. Her earrings were even bigger today. It was so good to see her, I grabbed her and put a big kiss on her mouth. It was a surprise arranged by Leuchie. But deep down I wondered if Leuchie was fucking her now I was away. Oh well, I thought to myself. It doesn't matter, she wasn't my girl and he was my big brother.

I had two more visits on Saturday and Sunday. Monday was Court. In Court on Monday was the same as the week before. It was pure formalities. The ride in the Sweat Box to Court was horrible. We had to stop and drop people off at various courts in London before we went out of London to Watford Magistrates Court. By the time we got there, we'd been on that Sweat Box for over two hours. Horrible. I was cold and felt cramped up in the small space. I couldn't wait to get out and stretch my legs. The Court cells were even colder, but at least there was more space. This time in Court my Dad was there and wasn't happy. He'd had to give up work to come to court to put up surety for my bail. I could see he was fuming. He was a law abiding citizen and could not believe how his sons were turning out. My friend's parents were there as well. My solicitor went first this time, applying for bail on grounds that we were now offering the court a surety for my bail. But this didn't impress them. No bail, back to jail. I was sick to my stomach. The ride back was even worse. Depression set in when it started to dawn on me that I was stuck in jail and might not get to finish my final year in school. I knew this was probably why my dad had turned up today. My solicitor had come down to the cells and told me he was going to a Judge in Chambers for my bail application in two weeks at the most. And having then been remanded for fourteen days, I knew I had two weeks at least to spend in jail before anything could happen for me and even then bail was not guaranteed. Things looked bad right now and I wasn't happy. I really missed home.

When we got back to the prison we were passed through a bit quicker than the week before because now we weren't new receptions. This time I wasn't put in the same wing as my friends. Things were going from bad to worse.

"Where are you from?" I asked my new cellmate as I made up my bed.

"Tooting," he replied.

I knew Tooting boys were soft so he didn't impress me at all.

"I'm from Tottenham," I said.

"You just came in today?" he asked, making conversation.

"No, I've been here a week," I replied. Then I asked him what he was inside for.

"Robbery," was the reply.

"Me too," I said. "Three counts of robbery."

I could see he was impressed. He seemed alright to be banged up with. We went quiet for a while, each with his own thoughts. When I was ready to go to sleep, I took out a small piece of cannabis and proceeded to roll up a joint.

"What's that?" he said.

"What does it look like?" was my answer. "Do you smoke?" I asked him.

"Course," he replied.

"You want some?"

"Yeah man," came the answer. A bit too excited not to notice. I rolled up the spliff, had some and passed it to him.

I was tired from my journey to and from Court and after that spliff, my eyes couldn't stay open even if I wanted them to. I was sleeping in no time.

Morning. Another day in prison. I was getting used to jail now. I knew what to do and how to go about it. I linked up my crew in the Dining Hall and we had breakfast on the same table, discussing the events of the day before.

Thirteen more days before my barrister would go to a judge in chambers. It seemed very long. Anyway the next week, Toddler was the first one out on bail. He got bail with a two thousand pound surety. It was good news. He'd done sixteen days in prison. I reasoned that not having been caught with a knife or proceeds from the crime my chances of bail were good with Toddler being on bail. I missed him being there with us but I was pleased for him. I imagined him on the streets of Tottenham with the nice weather and back eating his mum's cooking. I couldn't wait for my time with the judge in Chambers. Kevin felt the same way. He wasn't getting as much visits as myself or Toddler, so I knew he was feeling it a bit more than I was.

My mum and older brothers made sure I was on a visit every weekend Saturday and Sunday and twice more in the week. I always had a fresh supply of clothes and also cigarettes and stuff.

The third week came and still there was no news. Then I got a letter from my solicitors telling me when they were going to apply for my bail. We were putting up five grand. I prayed and kept my fingers crossed. It worked. I was having dinner when a screw shouted, "Spencer 664."

"What Governor?" I replied.

"Pack your kit, you got bail."

I'd done exactly twenty-five days in prison. In all the excitement that I felt hearing that I'd got bail, I completely forgot about my friend Nose sitting on the table with me. I started running towards my cell, leaving my half-eaten food on the table before I remembered the Nose. So I stopped and called out to him.

"You've got five minutes to meet me at the wing office," the same screw said.

"Alright gov, I'll be there in two minutes," I replied, excited that I was at last going home.

I then ran to my cell with Kevin to get my clothes and stuff. In my cell I looked into Kevin's face and I didn't know what to say to cheer him up. I wished he was coming with me but it wasn't so. I left him all my food and drinks and stuff. I asked him if he had any messages for his people on the out. I tried to cheer him up telling him that he was bound to get bail now Toddler and I had made bail. I also told him I'd come up in the week to see him with Toddler. That seemed to cheer him up a bit.

"Spencer." That same screw's voice shouting for me.

I looked at the Nose and said my goodbyes. I was eager to get out but sad for him. Such is life like they say. I ran to the wing office with my kit bag and my stuff. I then went to the reception with the loud mouth officer.

He seemed upset that I'd got bail, but that didn't bother me I was going home. He could give me orders, but only in prison. Out on the street I'd been robbing big men like him since I was eleven.

Anyway, down reception, the officer told me my bail conditions.

"You must stay away from the witnesses. You must reside at your home address. You must sign on at Tottenham police station three days a week and also do not go within a ten mile radius of Watford. After every condition he read out I replied with an eager, "Yeah!"

I couldn't wait for him to finish reading the conditions. I wanted to get out before they changed their minds. At last I was taken to the prison gates. I asked the officer where the local station was and how far it was. When those massive gates opened, I ran and sprinted and then ran again till I was out of breath. Then I started to jog. I didn't walk in the ten minutes it took to get to the station. I was free at last. No more porridge, no more bang-up, no more orders from those punk screws. I sat on a bench waiting for my train to arrive. I couldn't wait to see my family.

I wrongly believed this was the end.

CHAPTER FIVE

For some reason I thought I'd get a hero's welcome when I got home. Wrong!

The only warm welcome came from my brothers and sister. They were truly glad to see me home. My mum was glad, I knew, but she couldn't show it because my dad was at home. He wasn't about to smile and welcome me home. He didn't say a word all night. But I knew he had plenty to say. When he would was anybody's guess. But I didn't let it dampen my joy of being home. I went straight to the bathroom for a bath after I'd said my hellos and greetings. I had a very long bath. First bath in weeks. It felt so nice. I relaxed in the bathtub, thinking about what the guys and especially Kevin was doing right then in prison. It was nice to be home.

"Are you sleeping in there?" my sister shouted through the door.

"No, just chilling sis," I shouted back.

"When you're ready, there's some rice and chicken in the oven for ya," she said.

"Wicked. I'll be out in a couple of minutes!"

I heard the front door open and heard Leuchie's voice as I started to dry myself.

"Leuch," I called through the now slightly open bathroom door. When he came up to the door, I put my hand out and he fist bumped me in the street style greeting.

"Welcome back man, how's things?" he said.

"Boy, sure I'm glad to be home bruv," I replied.

"You see the old man yet?" he asked.

"Yeah, but he ain't said a word, not a word," I said.

"Boy that's bad news, don't start relaxing yet seen."

"I know Leuch, right now I just want to get out of the way," I said.

"Anyway man, it's good to see you back on road." he said. "Where's your friend Kevin?"

"Going for bail next week." I continued. "But he's still there. I feel it for him."

"I saw Toddler yesterday, he said to big you up."

"Alright thanks. I'm gonna go look for them lot tomorrow."

"What have you got to smoke?" I asked my brother.

"Build a spliff when you're ready. I'm in the car outside with San. Come outside when you're dressed." With that he went outside to sit in his car. Leuchie and his crew were doing well. He was driving a Stag. The old school Dolomite Stag. A pretty purple one.

Anyway I went to my room to get dressed and there was a knock on the door. It was my mum. She came in and sat on my brother's bed.

"How are you son?" she said.

"Fine mum, how are you?" I asked.

"You boys will make me die young," she said. "I've got high blood pressure. All I get is grief from your father and heartache from you boys. Especially you and Dillon."

"Mum it was my friends Danny and Kevin who robbed the people, not me."

"Why did you stand up there with them? You could have walked away."

"Mum, they're my friends, we have to stick together."

"So if they jump off a bridge into a river would you still stick with them and jump in too?" she asked in a sarcastic tone.

"No mum."

"You missed your exams, you don't even care."

"Course I care, I'll take my O levels next year in College mum, don't worry."

"Your father's not happy at all, but we thank God that you're home."

I kissed her on the cheek and said thanks.

"Where's your friend - Mrs Brown's son?"

"You mean Kevin, mum. Yes, he's still there."

She shook her head again then said, "Are you hungry?"

"Yeah," I answered.

"Alright, I'll heat up the rice and chicken. Come in the kitchen when you finish."

"Thanks mum, soon come." I got dressed and went to the kitchen. The food smelt nice. Very nice. And I was ready for it.

Mom dished it out for me smiling because she could see how eager I was for my first dinner back at home. I helped myself to a big tall glass of orange juice with loads of ice. Then I settled down to eat. Mum went into her room, I suppose to talk to my dad. I waxed up the big plate of food and washed it down with the juice. When I'd finished and put the plate and cutlery away, I went outside to join my brother and his friend San in his car. The interior was nice.

"What's up, Boxer?" San said as a greeting when I got in the car.

"Yeah I'm safe," I replied.

The car stank of weed, but in a nice way. Leuchie passed me a packet of rizlas, the weed and cigarette. I put a spliff together in no time. They were playing a Pinchers tune on the car stereo. One of my favourite singers of the time. I finished rolling the spliff and lit it. The weed was wicked, Leuchie always had the best.

"So how was it in them places Boxer?" San asked.

Before I could answer Leuchie said, "Don't you know my brother's soldier?"

"Boy it was kinda rough you know but no big deal," I said.

"Rough like how bruv?" San asked further

"Rough like no-one should be there. Rough like the food's shit, rough like its dead. Should I go on, fam?"

"Nah fam, I feel you. Not good man. You guys need to take your time still," He commented.

By this time a Tiger tune I liked came on and the weed was starting to take effect. Leuchie turned up the stereo. We sat nodding to the music and smoking. I just wanted to be with people I knew tonight. I suggested we go to TEE's pool cafe down Seven Sisters to shoot some pool. The time was about nine o'clock and being summer it was only just starting to get dark.

Leuchie started up the car and we drove off. We stopped at a phone box to phone home. I phoned to let my mum know I was with Leuchie and hung up. We drove over to TEE's Cafe.

I just kept on staring out of the window; it was good to be back in the manor. When we got to TEE's cafe, some of my crew were there. Rodney, Gee money, BP, Vince and the only girl member of the crew at that time, Higgie. Her real name was Melanie. She was bad, a real tomboy. After the greetings and slaps on the back for being back out, I booked my game and waited for my turn. My brother and I were well respected in the manor. My respect seemed to shoot up since I got banged up. But I didn't want to get stripes in jail, I wanted to get my stripes on the streets.

After telling a few of my crew what had happened and how we'd ended up in jail, it was my turn to play. Leuchie dropped me back home at around eleven thirty that night and drove off with San.

My car was parked up down the road, so I walked up to it and jumped in. I tried to get it started, but it wouldn't start so I locked it back up and walked home. I made a mental note to change the fucking car. I needed to go make some money and fast. I let myself in the house and sat in the front room to play with my kid brothers Kevin, Mikey and Andrew. Kevin was now ten years old, Andrew was seven and my baby brother Mikey was four.

I sat in the front room for a while with them and then went to my room. I must have fallen asleep in no time because the next thing I knew was my dad shaking me awake.

"Wake up," he said coarsely. I knew this was coming but he could have let me stay asleep at least.

"Get up and come to my room," he said again and left. I looked round my room and the other beds were occupied with Andrew and Kevin fast asleep. I looked at the time and it was 3.30 a.m. I knew this was it. I had to go to face the old man. Oh well, I might as well get this out the way, I thought. So I got out of bed rubbing my eyes and walked reluctantly to their bedroom. I knocked on the door and entered. My mum and dad were sitting up on their bed quiet.

I stood up facing them. Not knowing what to expect. With my dad that could be anything.

"Anthony," he said.

"Yeah dad?"

"What are your plans now you have dropped out of school a failure?"

I didn't know what he meant so I stayed quiet. I didn't want to make the situation any worse. Though I was glad my mum was there.

"Are you deaf?" he asked.

"No dad."

"You want to be a robber, is that it?"

"No dad."

"Did I raise you to rob and stick people up like a high way robber?"

"No dad."

"Have you not got any ambition?"

"Yeah dad, I want to go to college and take my O levels."

"When?"

"In September dad."

"It's August now Anthony, and you could be going to prison soon," he said. "I thought Dillon was bad, but you are a walking disaster." He was referring to Leuchie. "At least Dillon waited till he was eighteen before going to prison. You are nearly sixteen and look at the trouble you are in."

I stayed quiet.

"I am really thinking of packing Dillon and you off to my mother."

My grandmother was back in Nigeria. That didn't sound attractive to me at all, so I stayed quiet still.

"You boys have had everything I can give you, but that's not enough. You want to get rich quick, is that the way I brought you up?"

"No dad."

"You boys bring shame to this family. I have worked hard, sometimes twelve hours a day, just to keep this family together and this is how you pay us back," he said. "You are a disgrace to all our people and you should be shot." By now he was talking quite loud.

"I'm sorry dad, it wasn't me, it was…"

"Shut up!" he shouted at me, cutting me off before I could finish what I was saying. "From now on your stealing friends are banned from my house, do you hear me?"

"Yes dad," I answered.

"And tomorrow, I want you to take your thieving self up to that college and register yourself for O levels." He was referring to Tottenham College of Technology as it was known at that time. "Let me come back and find out you haven't done it and see what happens," he added. "You'll be on the next plane to Nigeria. Is that clear or do I have to knock it into your head?"

"I'll register tomorrow dad, I promise. I'm putting in four O levels," I added. This seemed to calm him down a bit. But the lecture and abuse went on for another fifteen minutes non-stop. My mum was quiet the whole time. When he finished I left the room feeling relieved it was over. I went back to my bed and fell asleep.

I remember waking up and thinking I was still in prison; I was so relieved when I looked around and remembered I was now at home. A smile came to my face. I looked at the clock in my room, it was eight thirty in the morning. The bedroom was empty. My brothers were probably having breakfast. I stayed in bed another half hour before getting up ready to face my first day back on the streets. I had to go to the College first and then I had to go and make some money to sort out my car.

I was used to driving now so I wasn't about to go back to taking the buses. My mum was at this time doing temporary work at chase farm hospital in Enfield. So she didn't work every day.

"Morning mum," I said.

"Remember what your father said?" she asked, referring to my college registration.

"I know mum, I'll have breakfast and a bath and I'll be off."

"Alright, what do you want for breakfast?"

"Just cereal and coffee mum." Those were the days when sixteen-year-olds could drink coffee and we smoked with our kids in the car!

I helped myself to breakfast and then I went into the bathroom for a bath. When I was dressed and ready I picked up the necessary paper work for registration and told my mum I was off. What I didn't tell her was I had also picked up my screwdriver and gloves for what I had to do afterwards. Burglary.

I got Frankie my brother and our neighbour to give my Triumph a push start. It started up after a few tries. It was school holidays and a lot of families went away. So I knew if I looked hard enough I would find a couple of houses to drum.

It was eleven thirty by the time I hit the road. It felt good driving my own car. But I knew I had to change it soon because I'd had it a little while now and I had been stopped in it a few times so the police knew the car. Anyway, I managed to register for four O levels. English language, Government and Politics, Economics and Religious Knowledge. I was accepted for these subjects. I could see I would enjoy coming to this college, there were so many girls about, I was impressed. At this time, I didn't have a stable girlfriend, just girls I hung around with and sometimes had sex with. I was just about to turn sixteen.

When I left the College, I went to TEE's Cafe. It was empty, so I went to look for a house to burgle. I went to Southgate. Southgate was a middle to lower middle class area. I soon found one. I was committing a crime a day after being granted bail from the Courts.

I think I got about four hundred and fifty pounds from this particular move. I was happy with that. Four hundred and fifty pounds for a fifteen-year-old for a couple of hours work was a lot of money then. Things were a lot cheaper then too. I went and had my car washed and also bought a new pair of Adidas trainers. I went back home and showed my mum the paper work from college. I also put my burglary tools away, changed my clothes and went back out to TEE's Cafe with money in my pocket. I felt good. When I got there,

I saw Toddler for the first time since we had both been released. He'd been out about a week and a half by then. When I told him I'd just done a drum he was shocked. He said he'd held it down since coming out because he was scared of getting nicked. He thought I was crazy.

"A man's got to do what a man's got to do," I said with a smile on my face. I told him I was going to College in September to take O levels.

"When should we go to visit Kevin the Nose?" I asked him.

"I'm broke," Toddler answered.

"Don't worry," I said. "I've got some money."

It was decided we go on a Saturday. By this time it was nearly time to sign on at the police station, which was part of my bail conditions - and Toddler's, I might add.

Anyway, we went and signed on together. Back at home that evening, my mum asked if I'd signed on.

"Yeah mum, don't worry, I won't forget."

"Well, if you forget, you'll go back to jail," she said.

"Yeah, I know mum."

When my old man came home, I told him the progress I'd made with the college stuff and told him the subjects I'd entered for. If he was pleased, he didn't show it. He was good at not showing his emotions.

On Saturday, we went to visit Nose in prison. Boy it felt so good sitting on the visitor's side of the table.

"What you saying, Kev?" We greeted him touching fists.

"I'm fucking roasting here man. I ain't had nothing to smoke for three days," he said, meaning weed.

"Yeah we got some for ya," Toddler said.

"You know you'll get bail this week innit," I said trying to cheer him up.

"They're going up on Tuesday, I can't fucking wait," he said.

"Just cool Kev, you'll be out soon," Toddler said.

"Pass him the thing, no one's looking now."

As soon as he got it and put it away, I could see he was pleased.

"So what, we should see you on Tuesday when you come out then yeah?" I said.

"Course Box. I'm gonna pass by your mum's yeah," Kevin said.

"No, no fam. Forgot to tell you as well Toddler, my old man is not having it right now. He don't wanna see either of you two anywhere near my house." I carried on.

"Trust me, he's serious. I don't wanna fuck with him right now so call my house phone or something and if my dad answers just put the phone down. If not we can link up at TEE's café."

"Ok, I hear you," Kevin said.

"Anyway, how's things in here?" Toddler asked him.

"Same as when you left it," he answered and we all laughed. "Did you think it had changed?" Then he added, "Same food, same bullshit but a couple of new faces."

"Oh yeah, you know D Brown from Hornsey?" We nodded in response and he said, "He came in on Thursday for burglary. He's on my wing."

"Yeah big him up for us," I said.

Before we knew it, it was time to go. We touched hands again and said our goodbyes. He wasn't that depressed as we left him. He had something to smoke and his bail application on Tuesday to look forward to. But I was glad to be going home instead of back to my cell.

On the way home I suggested we drum a house near the prison with the hope it might be a prison officers house. Toddler wasn't too sure about it, but he agreed. So we went to a shop to get two screw drivers. We stole them. I didn't have my car because we'd come up on the train. So we knew if we did a burglary, we had to go for the little things such as money, gold, nice cameras and stuff that could easily fit into a bag. A bag we would take from the house.

About twenty minutes' walk from the jail we found an unoccupied house. I was first in. I went straight to the mantelpiece and looked at the photos.

I was disappointed not to see a man or even a woman in prison officer's uniform. But anyway we cleaned out what we could, got quite a bit of gold and got out as quickly as we came in. We were nice. I'd just done my first out of London burglary ever. This house seemed bigger than the ones I was used to seeing, and they had more top of the range electrical stuff and more gold. We also found about two hundred pounds in cash. I was happy with the loot. If I had my car the electrical goods would have come with me as well. It seemed profitable to go out of London. But I knew it was also more risky because there weren't that many black faces once you left London, so it was easy to get caught if you got spotted. Anyway we were happy with the day's work. We got back to town just in time to catch the gold shop to sell our stuff. Toddler was well pleased, it was his first earner since coming out. Then we had to go sign on at the police station. By this time, signing on was becoming a nuisance to my way of life. I had to stop whatever I was doing to go and sign. Oh well, I used to think. It's better than being banged up.

On Tuesday, the crew was back together in full. Kevin made bail. I was pleased for him. At TEE's Cafe, we linked up and went for a drive to meet some girls. We went back to Kevin mum's who worked nights. We played music, smoked and generally fucked about with the girls.

When Kevin knew I'd enrolled at College, he followed suit. He saw it as a way to avoid going to prison. It made sense, because even though we were out on the street, we still had serious charges hanging over us. Maybe that's how my dad saw it too. College started in September. Kevin was first to turn sixteen, then me in October and then Toddler.

College was enjoyable. I always used to go over to Kevin's and we'd ride to College together in my car. By this time, I was saving up for another car. I was also trying to sell the Triumph. There was nothing wrong with it, the body, engine and interior were in good condition. I was just fed up of it and wanted something new.

My parents were glad to see me at college taking my O levels. We were all still signing on at the police station and appearing at Court whenever we were required to do so.

We got committed to St Albans Crown Court to await trial. Meanwhile, life in College went on as usual. I put in quite a bit more work into it more than I did in school. A lot more. I also put in a lot of work and time into chasing the girls. Girls of all shapes and sizes were at College. And for some reason they seemed attracted to our bad boy reputation. So I milked it all the way. Could you blame me? Just before Christmas, I changed my car. At last! I got a six-year-old Capri mark one, metallic green, for nine hundred pounds. That was a lot of money at that time. He wanted a grand, but Leuchie and I got him down to nine hundred. Now I was really in business with the babes. I was still earning money on the side. By this time, I'd stopped robberies and concentrated on burglaries. They paid more and it was easier to get away with it as long as you didn't leave any prints and weren't spotted.

Plus, I was on bail for robberies, the last thing I wanted was to get arrested for more robberies as they carried more 'bird' or time than burglaries. I went to work about four times a week, so I always had plenty of money at College. It was good money for a sixteen-year-old. I'd go into College with a hundred pounds in my pocket. About this time Kevin also bought a car, a little mini Cooper, a black one. Toddler was the last to buy a car. He only learnt to drive in the mid-nineties, well into his twenties.

Christmas came. It was a nice Christmas for everyone concerned. I looked at it as possibly being our last Christmas before being sent down for the robberies in Watford. I'd heard about St Alban's Crown Court. I heard it was a hanging court. Meaning, no one got acquitted from that court. I'd especially heard about a judge called Hickman. He was nicknamed The Hitman. We heard he was a little old bastard who didn't like anyone not in his class. He especially had a hatred for blacks. I was praying he'd die before we came up to court the old bastard. Anyway I was expecting the worse from a court like that and a judge like him.

But meanwhile life went on as usual. 1985 started well. In College, new car, new girls around me. It wasn't too bad apart from the fucking case. Natasha, big breast, big mouth and big earrings had a son. It wasn't mine. I wondered if it was Leuchie's child. I'd stopped fucking her by now, but still stopped by her new flat every so often.

In January I witnessed my second murder. It wasn't pretty. All blood and more blood. There was a club called the Seven Ladies next to Finsbury Park tube station at that time. These were dangerous times as everyone carried knives. Nervous times. Everyone in my crew carried two knives each. Why? I don't really know. It was like the VISA advert, 'don't leave home without them' and we sure didn't. Flick knives were the knives of the day. Anyway, Seven Ladies was both a rave and a hide out for us. I'll explain. The raves were mostly on Sunday nights with one or more sound systems playing till the early hours. The tube station was so close that we used to rob people in the station and run into Seven Ladies and mingle with people and go on like nothing happened. On many occasions, police emptied out the club in search of my friends or others from Hackney, Stoke Newington or Finsbury Park. Tottenham, Stoke Newington, Finsbury Park, or Park as we called it, and the Hackney areas bred some dangerous soldiers and still is the same to this day.

Anyway on the night of this murder, Seven Ladies was on, so I know it was a Sunday. As usual, we arrived in three cars from Tottenham. There were about ten of us aged between sixteen and nineteen. It was about midnight when we got there. We paid our fee, a couple of pounds, and piled in. We went straight to the bar. I bought a Baby Sham as usual and proceeded to build a spliff. We met our friends from Hackney Eggy, Kenny, Curly and Reds from Ashford, who were now out of prison and a few others. A sound system called Fatman Sound was entertaining on this night.

After about an hour, a few of us went outside with dark intensions in mind. We stood up under the train bridge next to Finsbury Park Station. I can't remember seeing this man coming or which direction he came from. All I remember is seeing a man pinned up against a wall with a knife to his chest and another knife held by someone else to his throat. He was being robbed. I was gutted because as soon as a person had been robbed, we all had to go back inside. You stayed out and you got nicked simple, whether you had something to do with it or not. So you had to fly in the club.

Anyway back to this poor guy. He was tall and wore glasses. He looked well off. Why did he have to argue and struggle with them? He chose to. I remember seeing him go down clutching his chest but he still struggled. Wrong move again! He had all his stuff taken but yet he still struggled. Every time he took his hand off his chest, blood pumped out like he had a pump inside him pumping out blood. He then tried to grab hold of one of the youths and that's when he really made a mistake as now the kid had to get away at all costs. He was stabbed in the neck I think and went down. All this took about a minute and a half. In another thirty seconds everyone was in the club. The street outside the club was clear. Even the doormen were shaking their heads as they came in, scared to stand up in the street. I knew the guy had probably copped it.

The two responsible for that murder are still free and are now good guys in their own rights. The last I know of them they are now settled, reasonably good members of society. Good friends of mine from Finsbury Park. Anyway, back to that night. Sirens, sirens and more sirens. Sirens everywhere. For some reason the dance wasn't even disturbed even though the guy was lying about sixty meters from the club. No one poked their heads out to look. No one left the club. Not everybody in the club knew though, just the doormen and a few soldiers.

When the dance was over, we came out to about ten police vans and more police cars. The patch where the guy had lain was cordoned off. Police officers were asking everyone if they'd seen anything. They took down names, addresses and car numbers. They must have taken my number, but no one called on me. It had nothing to do with my crew anyway. Those were the good old days when everyone shut up and stuck together, not like today when sixty percent of the gangsters are part-time informers. Today they probably would have nabbed those two.

Anyway, February came and we were on the warning list for Court. The 'Warned List' meant your case could come up anytime in the next couple of weeks. You had to phone your solicitor firm every evening after six to find out if you were in court the next day. I was very nervous about this case. We were all first time offenders. We had no previous at this time and that was an advantage. But St Alban's was another story. It was a hanging court. I wasn't looking forward to doing time. Too many girls on the road to get stuck in jail. At this time I had what was probably my first stable relationship. She was tall, like I was, very fair skinned and went to my College. Her name was Diane and she was from out of Clapton in East London. I drove her home every day. It wasn't true love, but it was close. I was very fond of her and enjoyed spending time with her. So I didn't want to get banged up. I also had a couple of run around girls as my mum called them. My mum liked Diane especially for her mild mannered personality and her complexion. She didn't like me cheating on her. But I'm sixteen and entitled to a little fun at this age, I reasoned.

Anyway, Diane was worried for me as well. She knew about the case and didn't want to lose me. I think she was more in love with me than I was with her.

At the end of February, the case finally came to court. On the first day of the court case we had to pick the jury. Hah! That was like a joke. It was like picking between being shot by a handgun or a pump action shotgun! Whichever you chose, you were bound to be shot anyway. When we saw the line-up of jury members, we knew we had to go guilty or really leave ourselves open to be hanged. They were all white, from mid-forties and beyond, with some in their late sixties, and you could see 'hang them' written all over their faces. But we went ahead and picked the younger ones. When I say younger, I mean the ones not in their sixties. That took up the morning session of the day.

Over lunch break, our solicitors advised us to change our pleas to guilty. Seeing who we had for a judge. Fucking old hangman Hickman. Bad news. He looked evil. He was small and stared at you with a look that could hang you. I'd heard about this man even before I saw him and he came over a lot worse than people had told me.

Our families and the victims' families sat up in the court gallery. On the advice of our briefs after seeing the jury and the judge, we decided to change our pleas to guilty. It was the right move. We would have been found guilty anyway.

When court restarted, our briefs got up and told them we wanted to change our pleas to guilty.

So we got up and pleaded guilty to charges of robbery on three counts. That was it! Hickfuckingman wanted to sentence us there and then until our briefs asked for Social Reports to be done. Our bails were revoked and we were remanded back in custody for Social Reports or Probation Reports to be done. It was a four-week remand. Back down in the cells, it was beginning to dawn on me that I was going back to prison. Four-week remand, shit. My brief came down to see me and told me to expect at least two years youth custody. He said it didn't matter that we had no previous convictions or we pleaded guilty. He said the guilty plea was so we didn't get a much higher sentence.

"Where am I going from here then?" I asked.

"Chelmsford prison," he said. "Cheer up Anthony, I'll write to you in Chelmsford in a couple of weeks," he said.

"Tell my mum where I'm going so they can visit."

"Alright then. I'll see you soon." With that he went back to the outside world and left me there in the dungeons.

It was winter and freezing in the prison van or sweat box. I was deep in thought all the way to Chelmsford. Just like all the rides I'd had previously in these vans. We got to Chelmsford and the gates opened. 'Fuck!' I thought. This was one of those old British prisons you saw on TV programmes. Very cold and ugly. So were the first prison officers I saw through the small window in my box in the van. I wondered who was here from London that I knew.

"We're here, Box," Kevin shouted from his box.

"Yeah ugly innit," I shouted back.

"Sure is," Toddler shouted back.

Nicky, my crew member, was now on the street having finished his sentence for the stabbing, so I wasn't sure if I'd meet anyone here.

We got off the van one at a time as usual.

We were all in the reception room. We were new receptions again. Having gone guilty, we were now convicted prisoners. This meant that we didn't have the same rights as we had first time round. Then, we were only on remand and entitled to a lot more privileges. What privileges we had left I didn't know yet. We went through the same routine as in Ashford plus this time being convicted prisoners; we had our prints taken at reception and pictures taken. We were issued with prison clothes as we'd lost the right to wear our own clothes. The clothes were ill fitting. Especially for me because I was tall. The trousers were a bit on the short side and the shirt had a couple of buttons missing. I didn't feel like myself in them. We were allowed to keep our trainers on.

Then I was called into a room for the last time. This was to explain to me my visiting rights now as a convicted prisoner and other rights.

"Here's your reception letter," the ugly officer said to me in the room. "And there's a reception visiting order in it as well. It goes out first class," he added. "You are allowed one visit a fortnight from now on."

"When can I have a visit?" I interrupted him.

"As soon as you get your VO out," he replied and continued. "You can have three adults on your Visit Order or VO. The visits are half an hour long. The visit days are Tuesdays, Thursdays, Saturdays and Sundays. The other days as well as Saturday and Sunday mornings are for the adults on the other side of the prison. But that's not your business. You can have money sent in to you, but not tobacco or toiletries. These you have to buy out of your private cash to spend once a week."

When he finished telling me my rights and allowances and the do's and don'ts of his prison, he sent me into another room to wait. I was given my kit bag and piss pot to piss in at night as there weren't any toilets in the cells in those days. I finally got to my cell and the door was shut. I sat on the chair and looked around my new surroundings. The walls filled with writings by predecessors. There were two beds in the cell but I was by myself at that time. I wondered who they'd put in with me. I went ahead and made my bed up. The beds weren't bunked up, thank God. I'd just finished making my bed when the door opened again and a white guy came in. The door shut again.

"Alright mate," he said.

"Yeah," I said.

I'd seen him down in reception earlier, but hadn't spoken to him.

"Have you seen my mates?" I asked in his kind of lingo. We talked just that bit different from white guys unless the black guy moved among white circles, or the white guy moved in black circles. These days you couldn't tell a Turkish kid from a black kid, a white kid from a Somalian kid as long as they all came from some borough in London.

"Yeah, the shorter one's about three doors away," he said, referring to Toddler. "I left your other mate down at reception," he finished off saying.

"Ok bruv, cheers," I said.

"You from London?" he asked.

"Yeah, why?"

"I'm from Leyton, mate," he said. "You got long to do or you on judge's remand?" he asked.

"Judges remand, what about you? I said.

"Fifteen months for one poxy burglary."

"First time?" I asked.

"No mate, been here before," he said. "My name's Mark, what's yours?"

"Boxer," I said.

"It's my second sentence."

"What was the first one?" I asked.

"Six months for burglary."

"What's it like in here?"

"Not nice mate. Screws are bastards."

"Yeah I see it in their faces."

He laughed at what I said with his back to me, fixing up his bed. "What court remanded ya?" he asked still making his bed.

"St Albans Crown."

He let out a whistle and turned round. "What you up for?"

"Robberies," I replied.

"That's not a nice court to go for anything mate, they hang ya."

"Yeah I know. Thanks for making me feel better," I said.

"Sorry mate, I know how you must feel," he said. "How come you're up in St Albans?"

"Cos I got nicked in Watford."

"Anyway, good luck mate."

"How old are you?" I asked him.

"Eighteen mate. What about you?"

"Sixteen."

"They might let you off down to your age," he said.

"And it's my first offence."

"Oh well, you might be alright then."

"I hope so man, I hope so."

"I've got to write a letter to my mum so I can send this VO out," I said.

I wrote to my mom with a VO for her, Leuchie and Frankie. By the time I'd finished. I was ready to hit the deck.

"Turning the lights off Mark, alright?"

"Yeah."

"Breakfast!" the screw shouted as the door opened. I'd dreamed about Diane the night before. I was missing her already. Anyway, I had to soldier on, no matter what. I saw Kevin and Toddler at breakfast.

"Who you banged up with?" Kevin asked me.

"One white guy. But he seems alright," I said.

"Us two are banged up together," Toddler said.

"Is it? You lucky bastards," I said then. "Have you lot sent out VOs?"

"Yeah I have," Toddler said.

"Me too," I said. "To Leuchie and my mum and Frankie."

"I ain't," Kevin said.

"What are you waiting for? Christmas?" I said, taking the piss.

We had four weeks before going back and we would get visits from probation officers before then so as to get our reports done.

Probation came up the next week. It was a woman. She was OK as well. She gave me hope, telling me College would help and so on. The four weeks were up in no time and we were back in the dock facing that old fucker of a judge. After all the formalities and reports were read out he was ready to make his judgement or sentence. I can't remember the exact words, but it went something like this:

"Anthony Spencer, Kevin Brown, Daniel Howard, you have all pleaded guilty to offences of robbery. These are knifepoint robberies. This Court does not take kindly to offences such as these. I have taken into consideration your ages and the fact that none of you have ever been in trouble before this case. In the case of Spencer and Brown, I have taken into consideration your progress in College with studies. But this Court sees only one way fit to deal with matters such as these. Anthony Spencer, you will serve two years youth custody. Kevin Brown will serve the same two years youth custody, and Daniel Howard, you are sentenced also to two years in a young offenders institution."

And that was it. I was sixteen going on seventeen and starting a two year sentence.

CHAPTER SIX

Two years. But I knew I didn't have to do all of it. At that time you did two thirds of your sentence. I worked it out in the van on the way from Court. Taking away my first remand time and the second four week judge's remand, I had fourteen months to do. My parole date was six months away, but I'd been told not to expect that as it wasn't definite. So I worked at fourteen months. And being March 1985, I expected to get out in May 1986. Fuck! It seemed long at that time. Chelmsford prison was not like Ashford. Ashford was for remand prisoners and was strictly young offenders while Chelmsford was strictly convicted and also housed adults. That is people over twenty-one.

When we got back to Chelmsford Prison and told people what we'd got, they felt bad for us.

I went back to my old cell with Mark, my old cellmate from East London.

"What d'you get Boxer?" he asked as soon as I walked in the cell and put my stuff down.

"Two fucking years Mark."

"You'll have to do sixteen months out of that," he said.

"I've done two months so far, so we got fourteen left."

"That's not too bad then," he said trying not to make me feel too bad. "You'll be out soon."

"I'll miss everyone's birthday and mine, and I'll miss Christmas," I said.

"Don't worry Box, you'll be alright."

"Yeah, I know. I'm a soldier," I said, more to myself than to him really.

The next day I sent out another VO to my family. I was doing a longer sentence than Leuchie had done a couple of years before. By the weekend Leuchie, my sister Cass and my mum came up. The visit wasn't the best I'd had. Leuchie didn't bring me any smoke and it made me more depressed. They kept telling me to behave so I could be out on my first parole chance.

"How's dad taking it?" I asked Cass.

Mum jumped in and said, "How do you think? He's ashamed of you boys."

"I'm gonna see if I can take my exams in here mum. I think I can," I added. "I'll need my books sent in for me."

"Ok. But still behave yourself in there and get out. This isn't a life for young men," Mum said.

"Next time you lot come up can you bring Diane up with you?"

"Yeah, no problem. Mum has her number, when I get in I'll call her and fix something yeah," Leuchie replied.

In 1985, Leuchie was going on twenty-one years old. He knew if he ever got arrested again, it'd be adult prison for him. I was pleased he was staying out of trouble because I knew I'd be fine as long as my big brother was around to look out for me.

The visit came to an end as always. Good things never last as they say. I said my goodbyes, kissing my mum and sister on the cheek and turning and walking off before I said something stupid. I had fourteen months of this life and I'd only just started.

Back on the wing, it was dead quiet as usual. Chelmsford was always quiet compared to Ashford. They also had little petty rules such as no smoking on the landings and you always had to tuck your shirt in your trousers. They were annoying rules for anyone used to having their own way.

A couple of weeks into my sentence, I had my first fight with some punk from West London. Amos, I think his name was. It was over something so petty that I can't even remember what. It happened after lock up. So nothing could be done there and then. I waited till the morning to deal with the matter. We carried on arguing out the window till I got so wound up I shut my window. First thing in the morning, I came out with my piss pot full of piss and made my way to the recess where we all washed, brushed our teeth, used the toilet or emptied our piss pots. This time though, my intension was to empty my pot full of piss in his face. When I got in there, he was nowhere to be seen, so I put down the piss pot, still full, and started cleaning out my wash bowl to fill it up with water. I heard his voice approaching before I saw him. I picked up my piss pot and waited. He walked into the recess room with his cellmate, who was also from his manor. I turned, took the lid off the pot and whoosh! All over the two of them. And then I kicked off. The fight didn't last very long. Prison fights never do. The alarm bells go off, screws are there within minutes and it's all over. But I'd done what damage I could do to him in the limited time I had. About six screws were on me and the same amount on him also while the other screws banged up the rest of the inmates.

My arms and legs were twisted behind me. I'd been told by my brother never to scream because that gave the screws pleasure. So even though I was hurting in that position, I kept quiet. I was dragged down to what's known as a block. It's the punishment wing of the jail. Back to basics. No cell furniture. Just a bed. This was my first taste of the block. There were many more to follow over the years.

The screws who worked down the block were of a different breed. They tried their hardest to put on a mean face and spoke to you with no respect. But that was fine by me. I knew that on the streets, they were nothing. I'd take them out in seconds. I'd been taking out punks like them since I was twelve.

The next morning I saw the Governor as I'd been placed on report for fighting. This was, and still is, called adjudication. It's sort of like a Court within a prison. Kangaroo Court if you asked me. Anyway, I can't remember what my sentence was, but I remember him asking me if it was over now between me and the pussy from Kilburn.

I think I said yes because the same day we were back on the same wing again. But for me it wasn't over. I gave it about a week, in which time we'd walk past each other all the time and not say a word. I knew he was screwing about my piss being thrown on him. So after a week, I went in his cell and offered him out during the daily cell association time. This time I had Kevin and Toddler with me in case his cellmate jumped in. I wanted a one and one in his cell, no screws and no alarm bells. When he hesitated I punched him in the eye to instigate a response and therefore a fight and he went down on his bed. He still would not have a go, so after sealing my victory with a few choice words, we left his cell and that was that. I stayed in Chelmsford for about two months waiting to get sent to one of the young offender prisons around the country. Kevin was first to get allocated. He was allocated to Wellingborough Young Offenders prison, but wasn't yet given a date for his departure. Myself and Toddler were allocated to a young offenders jail called Warren Hill in Suffolk. But we remained in Chelmsford awaiting our transfer. After what I did to that pussy, nobody really bothered me or my co-defendants anymore. Apart from the screws that is, there were certain screws I would gladly have knocked out, but getting away with it was the problem.

Kevin was the first to leave. He was sent to Wellingborough. I didn't know where the fuck that was. All I knew is that we were all being sent further out from London than we already were. It was June 1985 by the time I shipped out to Warren Hill. Toddler didn't come in this batch with me. He came about three weeks later.

Warren Hill young offenders' institution was a breath of fresh air compared to Chelmsford. It was a more modern establishment compared to where I'd just come from. You had toilets in your cells, single cells and activities such as pool tables, table tennis, gym were available to us. It was a clean prison and with a much more relaxed regime. I was glad to be here. I met my friends from the manor there, Rodney Adams, Courtney Morgan and Lionel Walters, all from my town. Fiddles and Mikey Luke from Hackney to name but a few. There were a lot more country boys here than Londoners but the Londoners here were running things. They made their presence felt.

I got my first visit here soon after I arrived. Leuchie and Frankie came up with my mum. There was some bad news though this time. Leuchie had got himself in big trouble and it looked bad. He'd got arrested for a wages snatch. A wages snatch is a robbery really, only with this type of robbery you knew exactly what you were going for. A bag full of workers' wages. I can't remember the exact details of the incident, but he was in trouble because they had also beaten up the guy to get at the money. Anyway, he was looking at some time in prison himself now. And being twenty-one, now he would go to an adult institution. He wasn't happy at all and I didn't blame him. But he still brought up my smoke. His case wasn't coming up for a while yet so I knew he'd be coming to see me as long as he didn't get himself arrested while on bail. My mum now, she was another story. Angry and depressed at the same time. I think my dad blamed her for how we were turning out. But I don't think anybody was to blame. It was our environment and the need to own things our parents wouldn't get us because we were not behaving or because they didn't think we needed such expensive stuff as we wanted, or maybe because there were seven of us and if my parents tried to buy every one of us the high standards that Leuchie and I demanded, it would not be possible. But whichever one it was we were now addicted to having at all costs. Not that we were poor,because we actually had. But being boys we wanted more. And like a drug, once you're used to having money, you are hooked. I was hooked very early in life. Anyway, now I was convicted and was only entitled to two visits a month. I had to make my drugs last me. Because there was a few of us from town in the prison there was always something to smoke. I was put to work in the potato factory. It was a working jail and you had to work. The wages were slave wages. I say this because we produced potatoes, cleaned them up and then bagged them up for sale to other prisons and God knows where else. For this we earned about four and a half pounds a week. This was a proper operation with machines and an environment just like any outside factory. The only difference was that with the outside factory, I'd probably get paid round about two hundred and fifty pounds a week - fifty plus times more than we got paid in this factory.

On a Sunday, we'd go to church to meet our friends on the other wings. It was the only time I sat down and talked with Toddler as he didn't work in any factory. I should mention as well that that factory work was my first ever job and if that was meant to get me used to working so as to stop stealing, then it had the opposite effect. Getting four pound a week peeling, washing and packaging potatoes in a cold factory was no inspiration for anyone. If anything it totally put me off working a regular job.

Toddler was on Education. Education was better than what I was doing, so I put my name down on the waiting list for Maths and English and Cookery. Cookery because it was a chance to cook something different from what we ate in the prison. I'd heard good things about that class.

Then, I got in another fight. I remember this one especially because it was to do with defending my mum's name. See, from growing up as a kid with white guys I knew they had no respect for their parents, especially their mums, the way we did. Many a time, I heard my white friends call their mums slags, sluts or even worse. It was different for black kids, you didn't dare. I couldn't even raise my voice to my mum. She'd kill me. Also the quickest way to start a fight with any black guy is to say something about his parents, especially his mum. You could tell a white guy to fuck his mother and he wouldn't react. Try telling that to a black guy, see what happens. That's exactly what this fight was about.

There was a white guy from Essex right below me. His name was Gerard Langton. Gerry we called him. I got on with him alright. We'd chat out the window about the streets and all that. Even though he was from Essex, he was clued up to the max. Anyway, this night we fell out and he brought my mum into it, so I told him to suck his mother's pussy. I told him we'd sort it out in the showers next day. Everyone was excited the next day, looking forward to a good fight. How the screws didn't notice the number of people piling into the showers that evening is beyond me. Everyone had their soap dish and towels, pretending to be going in there for a shower. But it was the fight that really filled up the shower room. It was almost like a proper boxing match with my friend from Tottenham acting almost as a referee. He made sure when everyone who was anyone had got in that the door was guarded against interruption from the officers. They were on the landings minding their own business, not knowing what was going on. Like I already said, it reminded me of a boxing match.

"Round one," Rodney said.

Gerard didn't stand a chance for two reasons. One, he'd insulted my mum and two, I knew how to handle myself. He got beat up silly. Had him on the floor a few times. I let him get back up. As soon as he got back up, I started on him again. Banged his head on the shower room sink. There was blood everywhere. His blood. People even pulled me off him a few times so as to give him a chance to start again, but that didn't help him. He took a breather and tried to start again. That didn't help either. He was smashed up pretty bad. I made him apologise and beg, then I kicked him in the mouth and that was when I was satisfied. The fight lasted a good twenty minutes, which was a very long time by any standard. I'm sure Gerard has never insulted a black guy's mother after that beating he got from me. I came out with a few scratches, which I didn't mind at all. The next day Gerard went to see the doctor. His face was in a very bad way. I didn't feel sorry for him at all. I only hope he had learnt his lesson. We did start talking again after that though.

Diane! My sweetheart Diane. Prison had turned her into my sweetheart by now. Prison does that to you. You miss things when you're banged up that you take for granted when you're free. I knew I was getting a visit on this particular Saturday. So I put on my visit outfit, which at that time was a light green shirt and grey trousers. I knew Diane was coming up. She was always going over to my mum's house to visit. She also wrote to me at least once a week and sent me ten pounds every week. She was now working part-time so she could afford it. My mum also sent me money, so did my brothers Leuchie and Frankie, so my private cash balance was always healthy.

"Spencer," an officer called to me in the TV room. "Visit!"

"Ok, gov, coming."

I went to my cell smiling, fixed myself up and ran downstairs to wait for an officer to take me over. When I got there, I saw my mum and Diane. No Leuchie. I knew there'd be no smoke on this visit. But I was so glad to see my babes that I didn't mind. I kissed my mum first and then kissed Diane on the lips. She was a bit shy because of my mum but I didn't care, I was glad to see her.

"Alright mum, what happened to Dillon?" I asked.

"He ain't feeling too good, so we came up without him," Diane said.

"It ain't serious is it?" I asked, looking at my mum.

She shook her head to mean no and then asked, "How are you keeping?"

"I'm fine mum, I'm alright, especially now my two sweethearts are here."
That brought a smile to her face.

"And how are you D?"

"Missing you," Diane said.

"I'm missing you too, you know that. I ain't stopped telling you in my letters, have I?"

"Yeah I got one yesterday thanks," she said.

"Do you want coffee?" mum asked.

"Yeah mum, thanks."

With that she got up and walked over to the canteen in the visit room.

"I've got something for you from your brother Dillon."

"What? Did Leuchie give you something for me?" I asked shocked and excited at the same time.

"Yeah, a piece of hash."

"Oh my days, you're joking. I love Dillon, trust me. Where is it?" I asked her.

"You have to take it now because he said not to make your mum see it."

"Yeah I'll take it now," I said, looking around. God bless Leuchie, I thought to myself as she passed it under the table. Within seconds it was put safely away.

"Did you mind bringing it?" I said.

"No, why should I?"

I kissed her again, really glad to see her even more now. "Eh, I kinda love you, you know."

"You're only saying that because I brought your stuff," she said and gave me a questioning look.

"No D," I said, looking hurt. "I do check for you and you know it."

Mum came back with a tray full of goodies, Kit Kat, crisps, biscuits and drinks.

"What's that scratch on your face?" mum asked. It was one of the scratches I had picked up in the fight. Totally forgot about it and surprised too that she'd only just noticed it.

"Oh it's nothing mum," I said touching the spot.

"You've been fighting?" Diane said.

"No, far from it." Then, "I got it playing basketball down in the gym."

"How's Andrew, Kevin and Mikey?"

"Everyone's fine. Your dad got a promotion the other week."

"Yeah? That's good. What about Dillon's case?"

"I think he's up soon. So that's two of my sons in prison. I don't know what your dad and I have done to deserve this," she said sadly.

Diane touched her hand in a consoling way. I could see my girl and my mum were getting closer. As usual, the visit was soon over. Time flies when you're having fun. I kissed my mum on the cheek and she left the visit room, leaving Diane and I to say our goodbyes. I didn't want her to go. I wanted to have sex with her there and then. When I told her, she looked at me and laughed.

"Wait till you come home," she said.

"I can't wait D, believe me."

"You ain't got no choice!"

"Yeah, I know."

"When you coming again?" I asked her.

"I'll come on the next VO if you want me to."

"You know I do man."

"I love you," she said.

"Me too," I said.

And with that I let her go. I watched her tall self walking off. Then she turned and blew me a kiss and then she was gone.

Summer came and then autumn. Autumn of that year was an unforgettable period for a lot of people. September and October saw a lot of trouble on the streets of London. It was a time of unrest in the prison too. I'd since been banned from going to church because we kept talking all the time. It didn't make sense. If Jesus Christ and God himself could forgive our sins, why couldn't they forgive us? At least we made an effort to come to the house of God. The preachers weren't preachers, I reasoned, they were more like screws.

Anyway, we kept getting thrown out of Church for talking until about eleven of us were banned. How can you ban people from a Church?

These days many a vicar, pastor and even Bishops have been exposed as two-timing adulterers and child molesters. No one talks about banning them from church. They are accepted. Now even God himself didn't put up with that back in the day, he crushed Sodom and Gomorrah because of people like these but we're supposed to accept these sick people preaching to us on Sundays. But I'll come back to that in a later chapter. On the last occasion when we were thrown out of church, about nine of us were placed on report to see the stupid governor in the morning.

At the kangaroo court hearing down the block the next day. I was found guilty and told to stay down in the punishment block for I think it was three days. All the others got the same sentence or there about. Wrong move in my opinion. It was a wrong move because now you had nine friends on punishment at the same time. If that was meant to teach us a lesson, they were wrong.

We proceeded to smash up our cells and left the taps running in all our cells overnight. By the morning, there was a mini-flood and no sinks in the cells. My cell was fucked. I had about half a foot of water in my cell when I woke up. The officers were very upset to say the least. We were bundled into a yellow prison van, handcuffed two together and taken across the road to the other side of the prison and left on permanent bang up in single cells. The block was like a Bombsite. We got longer punishments for the damage we'd done to the Queen's property. Good. I enjoyed smashing it all up if I'm honest; I was quite an angry young man at this point.

It seemed as though the more they showed me no respect, the worse I got. Back in those days, it was nearly impossible to come across a black prison officer in the system. Also officers made a lot of racist comments and got away with it. I remember saying to an officer one time in a heated argument, "When I've gone home, you'll still be here doing time," meaning he'll still be working in jail.

And his response was, "Yeah and you'll always be black."

Poor bastard, didn't understand that I see being black as a strength as something I am very proud to be. But then it was a racist remark or at least it was intended to be a racist jibe. I hadn't said anything about his colour, but he thought that by saying what he said, he would hurt me. Poor guy. But that was typical of what all ethnic prisoners came across at the time and more than likely still do. It's much better now because at least you can complain about it officially and the more people complained about a particular screw, the lesser his or her chances of progress in the ranks or so they say it should be, but we still see this in the police today, where officers are not fired or reprimanded no matter what. Also there are a lot more black officers today than in 1985.

I was transferred back across the road to my original wing having served my punishment time for smashing the block cell up. A couple of my co-accused were moved to Rochester to do their time. It was good to be back on the wing with the guys.

I was finally accepted by the Education Staff and got my head down to do some studying. I soon discovered though that the standard was way below what I expected. It was like the prison authority thought we were all stupid. It was stuff I'd done in the third and fourth year in school. Much too easy and no good for what my intensions were. I'd had O levels in mind and these Maths and English classes were for beginners, but I stayed on because it was better than the potato factory. The cookery class was very enjoyable though. We cooked different meals. Meals we didn't get in prison and every so often, we'd make something West Indian. I enjoyed cookery. Plus we got about the same pay as I was getting in the potato shop.

Meanwhile, while we were smashing up the block, Brixton and my home town Tottenham were being smashed up and burned. For Brixton, it was a repeat performance of the 1981 riots. Only worse. The Brixton Riots of 1985 made me gutted that I was in jail and a lot of the London kids in Warren Hill would have joined in, no doubt about it. The police and the system needed reminding that they were stepping all over people's lives. Real people. I remember having a conversation out of our windows one night. Lionel, my friend, said he wished Tottenham police station would be petrol bombed and stuff like that. Well he sure got his wish. Because two weeks after the Brixton riots, Tottenham went up in smoke. The date was 5 October 1985. Nine days before my seventeenth birthday.

I couldn't believe it was happening and the scale of it. It wasn't a small time Riot. This was war zone stuff. Let me just say that I will not say too much about this incident for two reasons. One because I wasn't there and secondly because the police have recently re-opened the investigation of the murder of one of their members who was killed on that night. PC Blakelock was his name. It was the first time an officer had been killed during a riot in Britain and it hasn't happened since.

The riots had been sparked by the police and their heavy handedness when they went to raid Patrick Jarret's mum's house to arrest Patrick, one of our older lot from the manor. When they went into her home, they manhandled her so badly she was pushed down the stairs, broke her spine and was confined to a wheelchair the rest of her life. This came just behind the old black lady in Brixton as I mentioned, but on this occasion she died soon after due to their heavy handedness.

Brixton rioted at a huge cost to the taxpayer. Then Tottenham kicked off too. When Tottenham kicked off it was mayhem. We found out details on visits and through letters we received individually from our friends outside when they wrote to us lot from the manor. So when we pieced together all the different bits of information from what we each had, we then had a fuller picture of goings on.

We all were gutted we weren't out and in the whole mix of things. Then when all the dust had settled and the authorities and newspapers were going mad over the killing of a police officer during the riots, they arrested three people for the officers murder. Winston Silcott, or Stix as he was known, Mark Braithwaite and Ingib. Stix was my brother's friend and I knew him vaguely, Mark Braithwaite I knew from back in the days of Seven Ladies. But, the other kid I didn't know. Anyway back to the night of the fifth, the police brought it on themselves.

Many of my friends I'd left on the street were put on trial for affray and other matters relating to the riots. They all got heavy sentences. Three though, were charged with the officer's murder. The three got life sentences with Stix recommended to serve thirty years before release. All this was in 1986 though, when the cases came to court. All three were later released from prison and acquitted of the

PC's murder and the case re-opened.

Anyway, back to October '85. I received a visit from Dillon, Diane and my mum on the Saturday before my birthday. Dillon was full of stories about the riots a week before. My mum wasn't impressed. She saw it from a different perspective. She called them hooligans. When I said to Dillon that I wished I was there, the look she gave me could have killed me. He brought up my piece of hash as usual and they brought me birthday cards from my brothers and sister. It was a nice visit.

Leuchie's case was coming up soon as well. Actually, I think it was the last time I saw him before he went to Court. He was sentenced to four years. I was gutted for him. Four years at that time sounded like a life time. He was sent to Wormhood Scrubs. Scrubs was one of those prisons you used piss pots and stuff like that. I felt it for him, even though I was here doing my own time. He wrote to me regularly and I did too. I promised him I'd be there for every VO as soon as I was released. My release date was getting closer and closer.

My mum now had to divide herself between visiting Dillon and visiting me. I told her to slow down, that Frankie and Diane could come and see me. She would not have it.

Christmas came and went. It was now 1986. I'd spent my first ever Christmas in prison. It wasn't nice at all. I was to spend many more in jail, but didn't know it yet. I'd filled out my parole papers and was now waiting having seen the parole board. I wasn't expecting parole off these people, but I wondered in the back of my mind. Being on the Education classes had calmed me down a bit and I wasn't getting into as much trouble, not with the officers anyhow. One month went by, then another and I forgot all about the parole and carried on with life in prison. It was now February 1986. The Tottenham riots were still headline news nearly every day. The government opened an inquiry into how and why it happened. PC Blakelock and his widow were turned into national heroes. There was outrage from middle England, or Snobby England as I called them, about the inner cities and their unruly inhabitants. But where was their anger when innocent black old ladies were being killed and maimed in their own homes, minding their business or when black young men were being murdered in police custody and I bet if they had to live under the same pressure day after day for six years of this government as we've had to, they'd explode just like Tottenham and Brixton did. They couldn't understand or maybe didn't want to understand. Their lives were so far removed from the politics in the inner cities. The government of the day set out different rules to govern middle England and the flip side was what we in the inner cities experienced. The riots soon got them to sort out their ways, at least some of their ways. The papers were crying for the heads of those responsible for the police officers murder. The hanging debate was re-opened as is always the case when something like this happens in England. The racism hidden beneath the surface popped its head out as well. People calling for blacks to be sent home. They were ignoring the fact that the majority of us were British citizens just like them. They also ignored the fact that it wasn't just blacks involved in the riots. One of the three on the murder charge was Turkish. The riot itself involved kids, men and women from all races. They all had one thing in common that day. They'd had enough of the bullshit. But middle England chose to ignore the facts and saw it as a black thing.

"Send them home," was their cry. Send them home to where? Brixton, Clapham, Notting Hill, Leyton, Walthamstow? Because that's where it would have to be. I remember listening to a radio talk show at the time about the riots and race relations in Britain. I had to turn the radio off because I couldn't reach into it to grab those racist bastards by their skinny necks and strangle them.

They talked so much shit some of them had to be cut off by the presenter Robbie Vincent. He was a decent guy, he couldn't help the people who phoned into his show until they started to speak.

Anyway, March came and saw the start of the first batch of trials. I had done fourteen months by now and had two more months to do. Then I got a surprise. A nice surprise. I got parole. Two months of parole. On the day I got the news, I had gone to classes as usual. As I came back on the wing, the Senior Officer handed me a piece of paper. I read it over and over again. I had seventeen days left to do. Wicked, I thought. I thanked the officer and ran off to go talk to my friends.

I wrote home that night telling them I was coming home in seventeen days. I also wrote to my girl Diane. I saw Toddler the next day and told him. He was still waiting on his. Boy, was I glad to be going home. Then a second surprise, the week after, Toddler got his parole as well. While I had ten days left, he got his and had six days to do. I was very pleased for him. We wrote a joint letter to Kevin in Wellingborough telling him we were going home within four days of each other.

We hoped he'd reply soon before we went home. The day before Toddler left we met down the gym playing volleyball. He was so excited he couldn't concentrate on the game. We'd talk and say a few words in between serves and shots. When we came out of the showers, I said goodbye to him and told him to get some weed and champagne ready.

The next day he was gone. I had four days left now and counting down. These last days seemed to drag worse than the last year. But finally, the day came.

It was the tradition on my wing to get a good beating from your close friends the night before your release. I'd done it to others, but when it was my turn on the last night, I warned them that I'd fight back and made sure I watched my back at all times. I went and had a shower long before everyone else and I had a good size piece of stick next to me. I came out of the showers and went to my cell while everybody else was out and banged myself up. My friends came to my cell and tried to get the screws to open me up so as to give me the traditional beating. I'd outfoxed them. I had avoided the beating. I laughed at them from behind my door. It was all in good humour. That night I could not sleep. Early the next morning, I was passed through reception, taken through the gates and I was out.

Free again. I promised myself it would be the last time, boy was I wrong.

CHAPTER SEVEN

The yellow prison van dropped me off at the little county train station. I was given some money about thirty pounds I think and then they drove off. I wasn't alone. There were about six of us discharged on the same day. I remember going across the road to this sweet shop to buy cigarettes. It felt funny handling money. You always get that feeling when you handle money again after so long. I'd served fourteen months. I went to a pay phone and called my mum. My dad was at work, so I knew he wouldn't be home. Mum was excited hearing my voice. After I'd spoken to her, I called my girl Diane, told her to get her bed warm that I was coming home to give her some. I couldn't wait, boy. From the sound of her voice, I knew she couldn't wait either. I didn't know if she'd been seeing anyone, but I knew her well enough to know she was not one of those sex mad girls. I always had to speech and coax her into bed. And even then, it was still hard work. So going by that and the fact that she spent so much time round my mum's, I was pretty sure that I was the last one to get between her legs. And she sounded really pleased to hear I was out.

The train came and I got on it. I still had two or more hours before I would get to Seven Sisters Station. My local station. On the first train ride, I just stared out the window, daydreaming. I stared at the countryside speeding past my eyes. I hope it'd be the last time I came out so far for Queen and country. The train stopped at Ipswich. I got out to catch a train to Liverpool Street in London, from where I would catch a final train to Seven Sisters and Tottenham. On the train to Liverpool Street, I wondered if Tottenham still looked the way I saw it the last time I was around. I just wasn't sure what awaited me on the streets of my town. I wondered who was out and who was in prison. I promised to pay Leuchie a visit in jail the very next week. I also thought about things such as getting myself a car and some new clothes. The clothes I had on were old and ill-fitting. I knew I had to get a new wardrobe as soon as possible. I must have drifted off, because when I woke up we were a couple of stops from Liverpool Street. I was looking at London for the first time in thirteen months. Even though I wasn't on home soil yet, it felt like home now I was in London. I remember the weather was nice as well, which made me feel nice. I had big plans for this summer and the girls of London.

Sitting on a London tube made me very paranoid. I felt like everybody knew I'd just come from prison. Or maybe it was my clothes they were staring at. Anyway, I felt funny and couldn't wait to get home.

When I got to Seven Sisters, my local station, I smiled as I stepped out into the streets. I was now on my home soil. To all those racist bastards on the radio show crying for blacks to be sent home, I was glad I was home. I wasn't a stranger on these streets. I walked past TEE's Cafe on my way to the bus stop. TEE's was closed at this time of the day. I'd been at the bus stop about a minute when I changed my mind and walked back to the cab station next to the tube station. A cab would be quicker and I didn't want anyone seeing me in these clothes. During the cab ride, the driver tried to have a conversation with me, but I just responded in short answers. I was feeling too weird to talk to any strangers. The streets didn't show any signs of the riots. Mind you it was five months ago, so I wasn't surprised.

We went past my old college and that brought back memories. And then I was there. Home at last. I paid the cab driver and got out. I still had my door key so I let myself in. The screams frightened me for a minute until I registered that they were screams of joy from the three women in my life at that time. Mum, my sister Cass and Diane who had got a cab to my house after I'd phoned her that morning. Hugs and kisses. Boy, I was home.

Frankie, Andrew and Mikey were home as well, all pleased to see me. Kevin my other brother who was now eleven going on twelve was at school. Andrew was ten and Michael was six. Frankie who was two years older than me was nineteen and Cass was fifteen. Cass was very tall for a girl of fifteen. She had taken the day off school. Leuchie was the only one missing. He was just starting his four-year sentence.

It was a surprise to see Diane at my house. I didn't expect to see her there. I had planned to have a bath and a haircut then, put on better clothes and go to see her at home. But seeing as she was at my house, it was even better. It meant one didn't travel.

My mum disappeared into the kitchen to cook I suppose. I went into my shared room with Diane. Since Dillon went to prison, I now shared my room with just Frankie! The three youngest boys shared a room while my sister had the smallest room in the house to herself. Mom and dad had their room. At this time Frankie had a steady girl and was always out so I more or less had a room to myself. Anyway, I didn't have sex straight away out of respect for my mum. I waited till I came back from the barbers and had a bath. By that time, my mum had gone shopping at Tesco. I knew I plenty of time.

My first fuck was fucking special. It didn't last too long, but it was the best sex of my short life so far. Boy, did the earth move or what! Earthquake is the word that comes to my mind. I lay on my bed next to D. After a while, she asked if I was asleep.

"No, why?" I asked.

"Nothing, it's just that you gone quiet."

"Just thinking," I said.

"Was it wicked?"

"Earthquake," I said and looked at her. She was smiling.

"Who's been fucking you then?" I said.

"Fuck off Anthony," she answered, angry.

"Fourteen months is a long time," I said.

"Long time for you, not me."

"You're human D. A girl needs a man."

"Yeah and I've got my man and he's next to me," she said and kissed me.

"Yeah and who else?" I pressed on.

"No one else Anthony and you know it."

"Well it's you and no one else, right," I said in return. "Come here," I grabbed her and went again, this time taking time to enjoy what I'd dreamed about for so long. She got dressed and went and dished us out some dinner from the pot my mum had just prepared. It was ackee and salt fish. Jesus, these are all things I'd missed and dreamed about in jail. Mum came back with the shopping and had also picked up my brother Kevin from school. He was very happy to see me. Diane, mum and Cass put the shopping away while I watched TV with my brothers. I was waiting for my dad's return in a couple of hours. But in the meantime, it was nice being back with my family. And I was enjoying every minute of it. I wanted D to go home before my dad came home, so I told her I'd be over later and she left!

I went to my room to write Leuchie a letter. He was still in the scrubs I went out to post the letter and bumped into my friend Vince. Vince was shocked to see me out. We chatted for a long while and he told me he hadn't seen Toddler since he came out. He filled me in with the politics of the riots and who got what sentence and every other news and scandal that was going on.

He walked back with me to my house, we bumped fists, he said how good it was that I was home and left.

"You're home now?" My dad asked me when he came home.

"Yeah dad, good evening," I answered and greeted.

"Have you learnt your lesson or are you going to go back in there?" he asked.

"Dad believe me, I'm glad to be home and I will stay out."

"Your brother didn't learn. He's back there again isn't he? I hope you do better." He was referring to Leuchie obviously. "What are your plans?" he continued. He still had his briefcase in hand, I'd only just come home and already he was on my case.

"Back to college take my exams," I said. "I can now apply for a grant, so I should be alright," I replied.

"Good to see you home. I'll talk to you properly at the weekend alright! Think of your plans and we'll talk at the weekend. Your bad friends are still banned from my house. You think about the company you keep from now." He walked to his room.

I was back home and feeling free. Even though we were free, there were quite a few of my crew members locked up in prisons. This was a pattern that was now beginning. Some of us are out and some are in.

About these times, we started frequented a couple of pubs round Tottenham, the Bull on the Highroad and the Broads on Broad Lane. The Bull was a sort of raving pub while the Broads I can only describe as a drugs pub. It was a pub where you could get any drugs your heart desired. After my release from prison, my respect on the streets grew and a lot more of my brother's crew wanted to know me, especially because I reminded them of my brother. It was becoming obvious by now that I was more a leader than a follower. I was leading my crew and dictating what we did or didn't do.

It was spring by now so college wasn't starting just yet. I was back stealing within a month of my release. Doing burglaries and cleaning up the streets. By cleaning up the streets, I mean this, in the time I was away, some street soldiers had acquired stuff such as cars, gold and other things I wanted. Now we were out, we felt obliged to rob these guys whenever we saw our chance. Some of them were younger and some older than I was. Because of the reputation I had, it wasn't a problem robbing these punks. And also very few went to the police as they were known as criminals themselves, so it was a safe way to make money.

In no time, I had a couple of bracelets and other stuff from these kinds of robberies. 'Dog eat Dog' we called it. On the weekends we would go to the Bull pub and rave and spend money we'd made in the week.

I remember visiting Leuchie in the Scrubs with Frankie. I didn't like the atmosphere in the visiting room at all. They seemed to have something against my brother. It was the first time I'd seen him since my release. His hair was all bushy and he wasn't smiling that much. That was prison for you I suppose. I knew my brother was a good soldier anyhow and he'd take anything they threw at him regardless.

All the same, we tried to cheer him up as best we could. I passed him a half ounce of smoke, which was a lot at that time and hoped that would cheer him up even more. He had a long time to do still. But I promised him we wouldn't let him roast in prison. Back in the manor, the talk at that time was about our friends on trial for the affray charges relating to the riots in the Tottenham. The Blakelock murder trial had not yet started. Like I already said, I don't want to say too much about this topic. Very sensitive subject, the murder of a British police officer. . The only thing that saddens me is that the

Western countries have instilled in our minds - not me anyhow - that if you kill a normal citizen, it isn't as bad a crime as killing a police officer. Then they go further to sell to us that killing a white person is worse than killing a black person and in all black countries this has taken the shape of police and elite first, the average middle class person next and the poor and lower classes last. This principle is responsible for millions of unfair deaths every year around the world. I wish that when the police had crippled Mrs Jarrett on that October day in '85 that the newspapers had gone bananas, the country as a whole had been horrified and spoke with one voice to condemn these cowardly officers. But that isn't the world we live in. Why is Keith Blakelock's life worth more than the lady shot by police in Brixton. They are equally missed and mourned by their respective families and communities aren't they? So why when she died no one except her family and community made a fuss but when the officer dies all hell breaks loose. This blasé attitude towards some loss of life has to stop. A life is a life. I feel it for the family of police victims as much as I do for the fallen police officers or soldiers who serve Britain. One isn't more important than the other, just ask their families and you will see what I mean! Just think for one minute what the country would have said and newspapers would have done if a group of police men went into an old white lady's house in Buckinghamshire looking for her wayward teenager and end up killing her before they came out of her home. But even that wouldn't be as bad an uproar if an off duty police man was sitting at home and people came into his home looking for someone else they had an argument with and killed him before they left his home. This latter would be seen as an outrage and the hanging debate would start up again, the former example of the old lady will be a crisis of the highest order albeit they may not call for hanging to be brought back, meanwhile a lady in Brixton can be killed by white police officers and yet the papers see it as just that lower form of life so let's give it ten lines on page seven and move on.

Anyway, quite a few soldiers went down for these matters. It felt like nearly everyone I grew up with was away at this time.

In the summer of '86 I got in a serious fight outside the Broad Pub on Broad Lane. Some guy much older than me took my age and size as a licence to try to fuck with me. Wrong move.

It was over a pool game and he then threw his beer all over me. That was it. My knife was out in a flash, so quick he didn't know what hit him. I swung at his face, the left side as I'm right-handed. The cut even shocked me. It was a horrible cut. I could see his teeth through the outside of his face. The knife ripped open his face. The fool still tried to come at me, cursing and shouting, "He cut me, let me go, let me go."

I stood in front of him waiting for the people to let him go so I could put another cut in his face. The fucking punk.

My friends hussled me off down the side of the pub, over the road through the Tesco building and out on the high road. We disappeared in minutes. I could hear the police sirens heading towards the incident. My crew praised me for dealing with the older guy, who really was trying to push his weight about because we were young. I wasn't scared to go back there in a couple of days.

Cocaine. Then came cocaine. I had my first taste of cocaine in 86. I'd seen it before but never tasted it. Leuchie and his crew always had a bit of powder cocaine around them. And also, I'd seen people snort it in the Bull Pub during the weekend and raves.

Anyway, my brother's crew member, a guy by the name of Glady, was the first to give me a free snort. A couple of days later, I made some money and I told my friend Toddler I was going to buy some at the Broads. I purchased a thirty-pound wrap and went into the toilet with Toddler to snort some up. It was the first time we tried doing it ourselves, but sure wasn't the last time. I wish I'd known what I was getting involved in. But this was all big boy stuff to us and we were in a hurry to grow up. Back to the toilet and the coke. We laid out the lines on the back of our cigarette box, I went first snorting my lines in the best way I knew how, with Toddler watching the effect it had on me. Bang! A wicked rush straight through my body that made me smile.

"Your turn," I said laying out his lines for him. We'd found a new buzz, different from anything we'd ever taken.

When we came out of the toilets, I kept rubbing and cleaning my nose in such a way as to let the bigger boys know what we were now on. I booked my game on the pool table and no one argued. This became a regular thing. Buy our coke wraps, go in the toilet, snort some up our nose and put some in a spliff to smoke. It was the sweetest smelling drug you could ever smell. No other drug smelled as sweet. Anyway, it didn't take us long to get into a routine of always snorting and smoking cocaine. We still smoked weed of course, but there was no buzz like the coke buzz and this was just the powder form. I say this because later I got into the more purer form called crack or rock or base cocaine. But I'll get to that later.

With cocaine came the need to make more money. I was also getting fed up doing burglaries because it wasn't a guaranteed earner. Some days went well and some days were a waste of time and talent. I knew I had the talent to do bigger and better things. We soon turned our attention to selling weed. We sold weed at the Broad Pub in the day and still did burglaries when the time allowed us. We were having such a good run selling drugs at the Broad. The management of the pub were alright, they turned a blind eye to all the drug dealing going on. But the police was not about to be as alright about it as the pub landlord. I was pulling up in cab with my pocket full of weed bags to sell when I saw a number of police cars, vans and dog unit vans outside the pub one night. I told the cabbie to drive right on back to my house. Phew! If I'd been there ten minutes earlier I'd have been caught up in the raid. Yeah, they raided it good and proper and it wasn't the last time either. This time though, they missed me. I was lucky because I'd have had to throw the lot away from me. And I'd had quite a lot on me as my clientele was also growing steadily, but I was able to keep up financially with everything I had to do. I didn't have a car yet as my old car, the Capri, had been sold when I'd gone to jail.

But I still had good clothes and shoes and everything that an earner my age had to have. I was still visiting my brother in jail and even when I couldn't make it up, his girl friends came to see me whenever they had to go and see him. He had about three girls visiting him at that time.

My brother Frankie was working so he wasn't making as much money as I was. Round about this time, Frankie found out I was smoking cocaine and boy what a fight we had.

It was our first fight in years. The last being when I was fifteen when he stabbed me in the head with a fork. On that occasion, my dad had made him give me a piggy back all the way to a cab station to take me to the hospital.

This time though he was doing me a favour, but I didn't know it yet. He was fuming when he smelt the spliff I was smoking in our garden when my mum and dad had gone to work. He knocked the spliff out of my hand, which kicked off the fight. We fought and tumbled in the garden until I pulled back. He was my older brother after all, but if I'd wanted to really open up a hundred percent I would have won the fight. We stopped and then sat down to talk. He then gave me a long talk about the dangers of what I was smoking. I could have picked up something during the fight and harmed him, but I kept reminding myself that he was my brother. All that did was make me promise myself not to ever smoke it to his face again. And I didn't for many years.

Just before I started college in September of 1986 to take my O levels, I was determined to buy a car. I'd been saving for a few weeks putting a bit away under my bed every time I made some money.

My parents knew I was back with the bad company because I never asked for money. My mum I knew had been going through my room occasionally, so I never kept drugs in the house. Always in the dust bin out the back of my house.

In one of these searches, she found my bundle of cash and took it. When I came home that night and went to put down some more money, I found my savings gone. I went mad, turning my room upside down, making a lot of noise in the process.

"Is this what you're looking for?" my mum asked holding my money in her hand.

"It's my money mum, it's for my car."

"Where did you get this money?"

"Mum, that's my business," I replied, still vexed.

"You keep talking like that and I'll take it to your dad," she threatened.

"So what, it ain't his money."

"Anthony you're still stealing. You haven't learned your lesson. What's a young boy like you doing with seven hundred pounds? You don't work, how did you get it?"

"I'm holding it for my friend," I lied.

"So your friend can come and collect it from me then, yeah," my mum said.

"Mum, come on man, I'm starting college soon and I need a car. What's wrong with that?"

"Tony, you're seventeen, you just came out of prison and you're still robbing people and breaking into people's houses, haven't you learned that it does not pay?"

"Mum, you can't buy me a car, neither can dad, so I'm saving to buy one myself."

"Why do you need a car? You haven't even got a licence ." She shook her head and said, "Do you think I like visiting my children in jail? Or you must have enjoyed your time in them places so you want to go back is that it?"

"Mum, I promise you I ain't robbing no one or breaking into anybody's house."

"How did you get this money then?" she asked.

"I'm buying and selling things now."

"Buying and selling what, drugs?"

Shit, did she know, had she seen my stash of weed outside, I wondered, but I still played it cool.

"It's my car money. Please give it back."

She gave me a long look, threw down the money on my bed and left my room. Boy I had to find a hiding place or open an account, I thought to myself. I added the fifty pounds I came to add to the money, so I now had seven hundred and fifty pounds towards my car.

I was also still seeing Diane, my girlfriend, but since my release, we seemed to be drifting apart, but this was more down to my hectic and two-timing ways than of her making. Many a time she'd come round to see me only to find another girl at my house. She once scratched out this girl's face. It was the first time I'd seen her really lose her temper and it was a shocking sight - I didn't know she had it in her. She'd come round one morning and came round the back of my house as she always did. I was blasting out music in my room and didn't know Cass my sister had let her in. The door opened while I was kissing nympho Sandra's bare breasts. When I looked up, D was at the door. It seemed like forever before she finally shut the door. I got up and put on my shirt and ran out after her. She was at the bus stop round the corner when I caught up with her. Her eyes were red so I guessed she'd been crying.

"D, she's only a thing, she means nothing to me," I said, holding her by the shoulders. And then, "You know it's me and you."

She just kept looking away from me.

"D believe me, if you came back with me, I'll show you she ain't nothing to me!"

"She's something Anthony, that's why she's in your room!" Diane screamed so loud I jumped back.

"Listen, come back with me and I'll show you."

As we were standing sorting things out, who should come up to us but Sandra, the girl in my bedroom. Sandra was a street girl, unlike Diane who was a lady.

"Who's the red skin whore then?" Sandra asked.

Boy before I could tell her to shut up and fuck off, Diane was all over her like a rash. You see sometimes, it's good to let people let out their frustrations in their own way and I wasn't about to stop Diane from doing just that especially when I saw she was having the better of that bitch Sandra. In the end though, when it was getting too much people were starting to stare, I jumped in and pulled my girl off Sandra. I told Sandra to fuck off before I let Diane go again. I took Diane home, apologising all the way back. I had never seen this side of her. I didn't know she had it in her.

That same nympho Sandra worked for my local council. And she was sex hungry. Do you know that she turned out to be the first person to use a knife on me? Let me tell you what happened. About three months after that incident with Diane, I told her to come round to my brother Frankie's flat one night. I'd made sure Diane never bumped into her again after that time and Frankie had just got himself a housing association flat, a one bedroom. I was also on the list for a flat with the same people but was still waiting for my flat. But in the meantime when Frankie was round his girl's flat, I used his flat to entertain girls. Strictly girls cos he'd told me he didn't want any of my friends round there. Anyway on this night, I called Sandra round, ordered pizza and was having a night in. I started fucking her at about ten o'clock at night. I took a break, finished off the pizza we'd ordered and went back to the fucking business. By midnight I'd had enough and just wanted to sleep. Not with this bitch. You didn't sleep. She kept bugging me that she wanted more. She even started to make fun of me and calling me weak and stuff like that. I'd have carried on fucking the bitch if only to shut her up, but my cock was so sore it would need at least two days off to recover. I told her I was sore, but she would not have any of it. It got so bad I turned around and kicked her out of bed. I then picked up her clothes, went to the kitchen window, which looked out onto the street below, and threw them out on to the pavement outside. Knickers, tights, skirt, top, the lot. She couldn't believe it. I then threw her out of the flat and went back to bed, turning up the music so I could not hear her shouting and banging on the door. She got dressed outside because all she had on when I chucked her out was her jacket, which barely covered her big bum. Anyway I woke up the next morning laughing about the night before. I had a bath and went over to my mum's to change my clothes.

When I got home, there was a message from Sandra to phone her. I did and she cursed like a mad woman over the phone. In the end I thought I'd calmed her down and she said to come up to her sister's house on the Broadwater Farm Estate. I didn't know what she had planned for me. When I got there that night and buzzed their flat, she answered in a sweet voice and buzzed me up. I got in the lift and went up to the sixth floor. When the doors opened, there she was holding a big kitchen knife and swinging it after me with this horrible look on her face. I tried to fight her off with one hand and with the other hand I pushed the buttons in the lift for the doors to close. She caught me several times on my right hand, but luckily the lift doors shut. I pressed the ground button in the lift sending the lift back down to the ground floor. I looked at my hand and got really mad. My injuries needed stitching and I promised myself to take it all out on her brother Wayne who was a year older than I was. I didn't believe and still don't believe in beating up on girls, especially having had boxing training in the past. When I caught up with Wayne and told him what his sister had done, he was full of sympathy but I still took his chain and what money he had to compensate for my distress.

That bitch was the first person to cut me. But before all that happened, I'd started college and had bought my car. It was a bright orange Morris Coupe. It was bright and sporty and the girls liked it. My dad was not impressed. I remember I kept getting lectures about the police and driving documents. I had none. I didn't care though as long as I had my car, I was happy.

Round about these times and just before my birthday, the case of the Tottenham Three came to Court. It was major news with the newspapers screaming for their heads. All they knew was that a police man had been seriously hacked to death and someone had to pay. The press found them guilty long before they were brought to court. I remember reading these horrible lies about people I knew. We knew they were lies, but ninety-five percent of the country believed them. The jury had to be chosen from amongst this percentage of citizens. What chance did my friends have? None if you ask me.

But that's justice British style. I've got a lot to say at the end of this book relating to what they call British justice. But back to the trial, they called for hanging, they made up lies that the youths of Tottenham planned to cut off the officer's head and stick it on a pole and rubbish like that. It all made for a horrible reading. Painting a picture of savages in the inner cities. All this before and during the trials of the three for murder. Meanwhile on the streets, the police made their presence felt. They had new riot vans patrolling Tottenham. They had a lot more foot officers. It was like we were suffocating on the streets of Tottenham. This was the same kind of stuff that gave birth to the Brixton and Tottenham riots. It's like the police had not learned their lessons. Instead of dealing with the causes, they piled on more of the same.

The trial was a farce. We knew the outcome even before it started. They were found guilty all three of them. Winston Silcott was labelled as a gang leader and the leader on the night of the riots by the papers. So the judge duly sentenced him to life, recommending that he serve thirty years before consideration for parole. The other two, my friend Mark and the Turkish kid, got life sentences. I remember it rained and a cloud fell over Tottenham that day. We all felt sorry for the Tottenham three in my college common room. It was like one of us had died. I'm pleased though to say that today those convictions have been quashed! Two were freed immediately while Stix was still locked up for a separate murder. He has since been released.

CHAPTER EIGHT

Being in college was alright. While I studied for my exams, I was also building up a new clientele for my weed business. As usual, I was always flush with money compared to most of my college colleagues. I'd turned eighteen by now. Christmas and New Year's came and went. It was now 1987 and the streets of Tottenham, my city jungle, were starting to calm down after the trials of the year before. Police were also starting to let their guards down. Leuchie was still in the Scrubs and had been allocated to Camp Hill Prison on the Isle of Wight and was waiting to ship out. I always made sure that his girls had something for him whenever they visited.

1987 also saw my cocaine habit get worse. How I managed to keep up with college and cocaine is a testament to the natural intelligence that runs in my family. And it wasn't just cocaine, there were the girls as well. Loads of them and all wanted to know who the bad boys were. We had an entourage of girls always around us in the college common room. There was big Raymond from Wood Green, Wayne, nympho Sandra's brother and quite a few street guys in college at this time. You knew the bad boys from the rest and we were the ones who attracted the girls the most. We sent them to the shops to get us stuff, took them to flats available to us and generally had the run of the college. My bright orange Morris Coupe was doing the business when it came to the girls.

My parents, especially my dad, was off my back now I was in college. Round about this time, I stepped up my crimes. I was getting fed up of doing burglaries and it was getting harder and harder to sell the proceeds from these burglaries. My first clues as to what to get involved in came in the form of a house robbery we pulled off in Edmonton. It was a set up. This was a drug house where weed and hash was sold in large quantities. A dread was in charge of this operation in a terrace house off Fore Street. A good friend of the Dread had set him up. Myself, Briggy and Gee Money decided we'd go in on him.

Long before this mission, I'd come across a silver .22 calibre gun in a house I was burgling. I'd decided to keep the gun as things were getting serious on the streets. I only told a few close friends about the gun. Every so often I'd go back to where I hid it and pick it up just to get the feel of it. I'd never fired a gun at that time, so just holding it was exciting. On this mission, that said gun came in handy. The plan was to go armed with the .22 revolver and a couple of machetes. The night before the move we sat round Briggy's room discussing what we had to do. I wanted to hold the gun as it was mine. I had four bullets in the gun and made it known to my friends that I would not hesitate to let it off on anyone who got in the way. They agreed with my thinking about the bit of work the next day. I knew I was stepping into unknown territory. Like I said, I'd never fired a real gun before that day, but I knew in myself that if it came to it, I would take no prisoners. The thought of the mission both excited and scared me. I tossed and turned all night. The next day I was up bright and early and rearing to go. It wasn't happening till the night so I waited with Gary round Briggy's house. You see, we'd heard that this dread always had three or more other people in the house with him. We also knew he had a black Pit Bull dog in the house. What we didn't know for definite was how much drugs and money and gold we were likely to get, all we knew is they would have enough to feed all three of us and pay off the guy who set it up for us. The plan was for one of us - we chose Briggy being the shortest - to knock on his door and act like he wanted to buy nine ounces. When the door would be opened for him, Gee Money and myself would then rush in with me in the front because I had the loaded gun. When it got dark, I went to my hiding place to get my gun and got in Gee Money's car.

We drove to Edmonton and parked round the corner from the drug house. With our weapons well hidden from view, we walked to the drug house. Briggy stood at the door while Gee and I took up positions either side of the door and crouched low so as not to be seen when he came to the door. My heart was beating so fast by now that I just wanted to be in there and out. I took out the gun and made sure the bullets were first in the chamber and not the two empty chambers as I only had four bullets in a six chamber weapon.

Briggy asked if we were set and we both nodded back. He then pressed the bell and we waited. It seemed like ages and then, "Who goes?" the dread said in a Jamaican accent.

"I want something," Briggy said.

"You come here before?" the dread asked him in a suspicious way.

"No, but my uncle sent me," Brett answered. "Have you got?" Brett continued.

"It depend what you want seen?" the dread said. Still not opening the door yet but speaking through the letter box.

"Nine," Briggy said to him. Meaning nine ounces.

"Alright, hold on," the dread said.

We heard the door being unlocked and I looked up at Briggy just as the door opened. In the next second, we were rushing through the door and the passage into the house. We'd rushed in so hard that the door had been pushed on the dread, knocking him over. All hell broke loose. The dog was barking, the dread was fighting and a woman was shouting and screaming in the front room.

It took a second to control the woman and the dread. I was staring the dog in the face with my gun pointing straight at him. Gee had the dread in a head lock on the floor by the front door and Briggy had managed to calm the dread woman down. But the dog was still going mad. In the next second I squeezed the trigger and hit the dog in the side. Bang. It went down. My ears went deaf for a split second and everything was quiet. The dread had stopped struggling.

"Hold them, I'm going out to the front to see if anyone heard anything," I said to my friends. With that I went outside to shut the door and sat on the wall for a couple of minutes. Nothing. I think he was playing his stereo quite loud because I could hear it from where I sat. I walked back to the door and went in.

"Yeah, we're safe," I said putting the gun away. I looked at the dog, he'd stopped moaning.

"You fuck with us pussy and you get the same," Gee said, pointing to the dog. "We want everything and we mean everything."

"Alright man, alright man, just calm down seen," he pleaded. Gee still had him in a head lock in an awkward position on the floor.

"Where's the weed and money?" I asked.

"Come to the room," he said meaning an upstairs bedroom.

Gee and I led him into a room. As soon as you walked in, you could smell the pure smell of weed.

From under the bed he pulled out a fucking big bag full and I mean full of weed. I grabbed that off him.

"Hurry up, hurry up," I said.

He then reached in the wardrobe and took out a pouch. I unzipped it and it was full of cash. I punched him then and told him I knew there was more. I was right. He went into the bathroom cabinet and took out a bundle of cash wrapped in a red, gold and green towel.

"Where's the gold?" I said.

"Don't fuck you know," Gee said.

He took off all his gold and watch and gave it to us. With that we took him downstairs where Briggy had already taken his woman's gold.

We got sticky tape from the kitchen and tied them up. I kicked the dog into the kitchen and shut the door. Why I did this, I do not know to this day. Maybe I didn't want to look at it. With that we left the premises. We jogged to the car and sped off down the back streets. I was glad it was over. It was my first of its kind but there were many more to come.

On the way home we joked about how the dog went down when I shot it. We'd got over a kilo of weed and twenty-eight hundred pounds in cash. The gold was minor nothing spectacular. It was a decent move and we drank to the move at my brothers flat. I now had a key and I knew he wasn't there because the lights were out. We went there to share out the loot. We agreed to keep this move quiet due to the possibility of come backs. I had killed the dread's dog and we'd cleaned him out proper, there was a possibility that he'd want revenge. So in the meantime, I always made sure I watched my back and kept the .22 close at all times. This was a different crime. This wasn't a crime for the police. This was a jungle crime where you only had the victim to worry about.

Anyway, I turned over my share of the weed nicely because I already had a market for the weed. But this time I didn't have to buy the weed. I was smiling all the way to the Leeds.

I wanted more of these missions. But in the meantime, I did burglaries when I was idle to fill in the time. I never wanted to be broke. It was nice having money and I wanted more.

Round about these times and owing to the success of the drug house robbery, we got into robbing whore houses round my area. Stamford Hill to be exact. You had to know where they were situated though because these houses were not marked or anything. They were next door to normal houses and it was easy to hit on the wrong house. Stamford Hill was a predominately Jewish area and Jews mind their own business as long as you didn't trouble them.

I remember the first one of these whore house robberies we tried to do. It was a complete disaster. It was a house with about six girls in it. We didn't take firearms on these missions, just knives and machetes.

Anyway, we had this house tagged or watched for a couple of days. It was busy and looked promising. We knew that it was especially busy between eleven at night and two in the morning. Anytime after two would be a nice time to take it. If things went to plan we had all six girls' money from the night's work plus their jewellery plus whatever they had saved in the house. Before I go any further, I'd like to explain why we went in on them armed with knives and stuff, this was just in case their boyfriends or pimps or even their customers were on the premises. It wasn't to harm the girls in any way. On the night of this particular mission, we pulled up across the street from the house at about 10 p.m. The car was stolen so we didn't care where we parked.

We sat in the car smoking season spliffs. A season spliff is a joint with weed and cocaine mixed with a cigarette. We watched as car after car pulled up. Fat guys, slim guys, black men and white men, they all came and went. Every time a car would pull up, we would duck for cover so as not to be spotted. We sat outside the house for an hour and half and decided to drive about for a while. There were three of us in the car. We came back to the house at around one in the morning after getting some more drugs to smoke. At two o'clock or just gone two, one of the girls, an Indian looking girl, came out, looked up and down the street and went back in. When we looked back up, the passage light had gone out and we knew this was our time to move. We got out the car and walked up to the house. Briggy knocked on the window the way we'd seen the customers do, while Gee and I ducked under the ground floor windows. After a short while, I think it was the same Indian girl who came to the window. I hear her say "What?"

And Briggy said, "Business."

But I don't think she was convinced because he didn't look like the usual clientele. Anyway she shouted something through the window and disappeared back into the house. Fuck.

"Now what?" Gee said as we walked back to the car.

"I think she clocked," Briggy said.

I was fuming. It was obvious she would not open the door to him. Before we got to the car, I looked around for something to smash the window with.

"What are you searching for?" Gee asked me.

"I'm gonna smash the window and go in," I said. I found it. One of these metal dust bins with metal lid. It was next door to the whore house. "Come here," I said to my friends. I picked up the bin and walked to the window. In the next instance, the bin went through the window. At the same time the silent night was shattered by six girls screaming at the top of their lungs. But we were in the house. There were half-naked girls screaming and running out the back yard. At two in the morning any kind of noise was loud, much less six screaming girls. I ran out the back yard to try and bring them back in and keep them silent. It was obvious that wasn't going to work. They were fighting, kicking and screaming.

I heard Briggy shouting, "Let's get the fuck out!"

"Come on, let's go, let's go before the feds get here."

It made sense. I let go of the one I had and made for the front door with no success. I shouted for him to follow me to the window. Out on the street we could still hear them screaming. We got in the car and sped off empty handed. I was driving and told Gee and

Briggy to duck down just in case we were spotted by police. If that happened it was better they saw one person driving than three people in the car. We got back to town safely down back streets. It was obvious that we had to go back to the drawing board. If we ever had to do this sort of thing again.

"We should have grabbed her when she came out to look up and down the street," Gee kept saying. He was right, we'd fucked up. The way the girls were kicking and fighting, I knew they had stuff and money in that house that they didn't want to lose. We had to do better next time. We left the car on a back street and I left my friends and made my way to a cab station. My first stop was the Broadwater estate to the coke dealer's house. I bought two wraps, went to the all night pool house down Stanley Road to cool off. I didn't say a word to anyone when I got there that night. I remember seeing quite a lot of police on the road on my way there in a cab.

Back at college it was obvious I was falling behind in my work. My exams were coming up and I had to apply myself or fail. I was taking Economics, Government and Politics, English Language and Religious Knowledge. I promised myself to open a bank account with a cash point card as I had money everywhere in my mom's house. I had money in my clothes in the wardrobe, in my socks, my trainers and even in the cereal boxes in the kitchen. I did open an account and I was truly shocked when I counted all my money before I went to the bank. Seven thousand, four hundred plus. I was eighteen going on nineteen. That day I was so pleased I took one of my college girls to dinner up West. I had by this time drifted away from Diane, but still called on her occasionally to see how she was keeping. I still tried to get into her knickers, but she would have none of it. She said I had too many girls for her to hang around but when I was ready for her, she would still be there waiting.

After seeing how much I had, I was more able to concentrate on my studies and my upcoming exams. I still had my weed business, which was doing good, and still also had my cocaine habit. Around these times, I was getting pulled every other day by the police in my bright orange coupe. That car was getting too known for my liking so I decided to change it. I went to the car auctions at Seven Sisters with Gee to look for a car one Wednesday. I know it was Wednesday because that was the auction day. I had a thousand pounds on me, which in those days was enough to get me a decent ride. By the end of that day, I'd bought myself a decent Golf GTI. I had to go to my bank and get an extra six hundred pounds before driving out with the car. I especially liked the BBS. wheels on it, which suited the black colour of the car. I now had to sell the coupe so as to put some money back in my bank. Thankfully that didn't take too long as my brother Frankie was interested in the car. He paid me five hundred for the coupe. But him being the law abiding citizen he was, he sorted out the car and sorted out all the necessary paperwork for it.

After I bought my Golf, I settled down to my college work and cut down on the street missions concentrating more on my weed business. My friends would come round to look for me at home and I'd send my sister out to tell them I wasn't there even though they saw my car outside my mum's. I knew they'd call on me at college the next day. My exams came and I passed Economics, Government and Politics and RK with credits or 'C's and English Language I got a B in. I remember my dad being so happy he couldn't hide it this time. I woke up the next morning with two fifty pound notes and a note saying 'Well done' on my bed. At last I'd given him something he could smile about. That weekend I went for a drink with my dad for the first time ever. He bought me a Heineken, his favourite. I asked if I could smoke a cigarette and I couldn't believe it when he said yes. I was smoking a cigarette for the first time in front of my dad. He is a non-smoker to this day. He asked what my plans were now I had some qualifications to show. I told him I didn't know yet.

"You see how settled Frankie is now he's working. Got his own place, his steady girlfriend and never gets bothered by the police. Don't you want that kind of life instead of always watching your back and doing time like your brother Dillon?"

If only he knew that I had more money than Frankie had ever had he wouldn't say what he was saying. Still I was glad we were spending time together and wasn't about to spoil it.

"I've put my name down for a flat and I'll hear from them anytime now," I said.

"Yeah? So when did you decide to leave home?" he asked.

"When Frankie got his place, dad, and plus I've got girls now and need a place to entertain." I smiled when I said this.

"Girls?" he asked. "What's wrong with finding one nice girl instead of all these run around street things you call girls? What happened to that tall girl who used to come round the house?"

"You mean Diane? she's starting law school now."

That seemed to impress him. "Why not stick with her?" he suggested.

This was the first conversation of its kind I was having with my old man.

"Yeah I still see her now and again."

"You want another drink?" I couldn't believe he was buying me a second. By the end of that night he'd bought me one whole pint and two halves. Things were definitely getting better with the old man and it was a good feeling. I've never forgotten that night. We drove home joking about programs such as *Love Thy Neighbour*, which was one of his favourite TV shows. Just as we pulled up outside our house we'd drove past my golf and he turned round and said, "Nice car Anthony, how many people did you rob to buy that?"

"I saved up dad, ask mum."

"Saved up with what? I didn't know you had a job," he said.

And I didn't know he'd noticed. I had no answer for him, so I kept quiet while he parked up his Passat.

"Good cars Volkswagens," he said. "Look after it, OK?"

Wow things were really getting better, I couldn't believe that he didn't try and lecture me.

In the summer of '87 my flat came through. It was a flat above a shop in Seven Sisters on the Highroad. It was one of those flats you had to share with someone else. It had two bedrooms, a shared kitchen, front room and bathroom. I had to share with this dread called Mark Kemba. I'd met him a few times at the housing association meetings I'd had to attend in order to get the place. His parents were from Zimbabwe in Africa, but he was brought up in London. He was alright to live with. But first I had to decorate my half of the house and the way I wanted it done would cost money. We chipped in money together to get the stairs carpeted, fix up the front room and bathroom. But our bedrooms were down to us. I bought mirror tiles, which when put together made up pictures of ships on an ocean, for my ceiling. I bought a double bed and electrics to go with my expensive taste. The carpet was plush. When it was all done, it had cost over a grand. The DSS or Social Security had given me only three hundred and fifty pounds. I'd also got a couple of hundred from my parents. I was fucking proud of my new flat. Now I was really in business with the girls.

Summer of '87 also saw my return to serious crime especially after buying stuff for my flat and having bought my car. I still had my .22 piece and was ready to put it to work.

It was during this period that my friend Toddler badly stabbed a policeman who had tried to grab hold of me and would not let go no matter what I did to him. I can't say where or exactly when on the grounds I might incriminate my friend and myself. But this is what happened anyway. It was sort of like the drug house robbery we'd done before only this was a wealthy people's house out in the country and like I said I can't say exactly where.

It was my first aggravated burglary. It was a burglary in a way but instead of doing the house while the occupants were out, we made sure they were in so as to get more stuff. We'd been up this area before looking for a good sized house, almost a mansion. On this night in the Autumn of '87 we got into the grounds of a particular house and waited for the car with the man and his wife to pull up the drive way.

They came back at around eleven at night. The wife was first to get out the car, she opened the door and walked into the house while her husband got his briefcase out the boot of the car, she'd also left the door open for him. As he walked through the door, he turned around to close it behind him only to find me and Toddler standing there. I held a loaded gun to his head and put my forefinger to my lips indicating for him to keep quiet and not alert his wife. We had handkerchiefs over half of our half our faces so he couldn't see our faces. When he saw us, he dropped his briefcase and papers shocked at what he saw. We hussled him in and shut the door. His wife was upstairs and didn't have a clue what was going on downstairs, but we could hear her in the bedroom. I held his mouth from behind and led him up the stairs with Toddler close behind. I stopped just short of the bedroom and signalled to Toddler, he knew what I meant. He ran in the bedroom and grabbed the woman before she knew what hit her. When he had her under control, I came into the room still holding his mouth. I took out the role of masking tape we'd brought with us and proceeded to tie him up first starting with his mouth then his hands and lastly his legs. When I was satisfied he was properly tied up, I spoke for the first time.

"No one gets hurt as long as your wife gets everything we ask for OK."

He nodded and looked at her.

"What do you want?" she said.

"Where's the safe?" I said.

"We don't have one, but there's cash in the study."

I looked at him cold and he nodded. Toddler stayed with him while I went down with her to the study. She took out a key from the middle of a book on the shelf and opened a drawer, crying the whole time. I told her to calm down that we were after money and that we were very hungry kids from the ghetto.

The drawer she opened had a tin money box in it and a massive jewellery box also. I took the keys from her and told her to sit down.

I then opened the money box. Yes! I thought. It was full of cash. I played it calm. I opened the gold box next and boy I knew we had found it. Diamonds, twenty-two carat items and lots of one-off pieces. I put both boxes in a bin liner I'd brought along for that purpose. I took her back upstairs and winked at Toddler when I got into the bedroom. Everything was going as planned. When I got in the room Toddler showed me a man's Rolex Oyster he had taken off the wrist of the man. He then pointed at the woman's wrist. When I looked she had the matching women's wrist watch. They were both eighteen carat, his and hers Rolex. I stripped the watch off her as well as her other diamond rings and put everything into the bag.

"I know there's more, don't let me get wicked," I said. By now he was shitting himself and would have given me everything he had.

"You've got everything I promise," she sobbed.

I looked around the master bedroom and found a bar of gold, hallmarked eighteen carat and stamped nine ounces. Shit I thought

I'd never seen a bar so big in one block. I threw Toddler the tape to tie her up. As he did this, I kept searching the master bedroom. I found other little bits and pieces while Toddler relieved them of their wallets. This was a proper rinse out. All this took about twenty minutes. We cut the phone line as an afterthought on our way out. But then as we ran out on the street and started to take off our masks, we saw headlights approaching so we started to walk calmly, putting our heads down so as not to get recognised. When I looked up again, I noticed the shape on top of the car and knew it was a police car. The car was still approaching by now and still yet had not got to us. Shit.

"That's a police car," I said.

"What, should we run?" Toddler asked.

"No just walk."

It was going on twelve o'clock at night outside London and we were black men walking down an affluent road. It was obvious we would at least get stopped and name checked. We couldn't afford that, not after what we'd just done. As the car got to us, we noticed it had just one officer in the car.

"Alright boys," he said politely.

"Alright officer," we answered back, just as politely.

By now he'd stopped and was getting out. We'd also stopped.

"Where have you been then?"

"Oh we've just been visiting our girls."

"This time of night?" he said. I think he knew something wasn't right. Maybe it was the look on our faces or the bulge of the bag inside my jacket.

"What's that?" was the next thing he said, pointing to the bulge.

With that Toddler was off running and the officer jumped on me. We started fighting. I knew I was fighting for my freedom. I kicked, punched and did all I could. He held on to me like a Pit Bull. The next thing I knew Toddler came back and jumped on him and started helping me. He too was punching and doing all he could. I remember he had the guy in a headlock at one stage. Eventually I felt myself get free of his hold and then I broke free and started helping Toddler get free because by now this determined fucker had grabbed on to him. We got free but before I ran off, I picked up the bag that had dropped in the struggle. I didn't wait around. Straight to the car and on the motorway. I knew we hadn't got away as yet so I drove as sensibly as I could. Toddler was lying on the back seat. When we got on the motorway, he threw the knife out the window. The ride back was a very quiet one. And he lay on that back seat till we got within two miles of our turn off. Even then my palms were still sweating, my heartbeat so fast I was gasping for air. Toddler had saved my life and boy was I grateful. I can't say how much was involved, but the gold I buried in my mum's garden at the back of the house. It was a month before we decided it was safe to sell the stuff. We got nine thousand pounds for just the gold and another nine grand for the hot watches.

The officer was OK I'm sure and we got away with it. It didn't make the news, at least not the London news anyway. When he stopped us, he didn't even know what we'd done, he was just cruising down that street. I didn't feel like doing anything for a couple of months after that incident, not just because we had loads of cash from that one work, but also because I was paranoid after what had happened. We didn't tell anybody about it because we didn't know what injuries we caused and how big a deal they might make it and we trusted no one with that secret.

My birthday that year was wicked. I had a drink up at the Phoenix wine bar in Alexandra Palace. I invited a lot of people from college and those of my road friends who weren't in prison. That night I was given cocaine in the raw form for the first time in my life. What a fucking buzz that was. It was crack cocaine as it's known. I was given a white rock by my brother Leuchie's friend, a guy called Bad-Cock Charlie Williams. Bad Cock was a bad man. He came up to me and said, "Birthday boy build a spliff." And passed me this rock.

I put the spliff together and hit it. After a couple of pulls on it, he came back and said, "Yeah that's the original lick bruv."

I bumped fists with him and nodded my appreciation for the rush that was going to my head. It was very different from smoking powder that was not pure. Compared to this, smoking powder was like smoking cigarettes.

With every pull I took on the spliff, I smiled at anybody who cared to look in my direction. The house music seemed to go with the spliff. This was my party. My brother Frankie came up to me and shook his head.

"Happy birthday Anthony," he said. "I hope you're enjoying yourself. But you can enjoy yourself without that fuckery."

"Cool Frankie, it's my birthday man, don't start lecturing," I said, still beaming.

"Alright bruv, just enjoy yeah,"

Girls came up to kiss me and wish me happy birthday. I searched out Toddler and passed him some of the spliff.

"Taste this," I said, smiling mischievously.

"What is it?" he asked.

"Washed up shit," I said. "Believe me, the living rush."

He walked off with the spliff and went to the bar. While I went looking for Charlie Bad-Cock to get some more. I wanted more of this fucking buzz. Diane caught up with me and pulled me to one side.

"What have you been smoking Anthony?" she asked me.

It was obvious Frankie had sent her over.

"Who me? Nothing to worry about D," I answered.

"I see you've invited all your girls. When are we going to have time to dance then?"

"In a minute," I said. "I'm looking for someone."

"Someone or something?" she asked with a questioning look on her face.

I think she knew I was smoking shit, but I didn't care. I wanted some more of that buzz.

I found Charlie and called him over. I then took out a crisp fifty pound note and gave it to him.

"Give me some more," I said.

"Alright, come in the toilet."

When we get to the toilet, he took out a big piece of rock and a knife and then cut me up a nice piece.

"Here, this is more than fifty pound worth. True it's your birthday, you get the birthday boy treatment."

"Wicked Charlie, hear what when you get out there get Toddler and tell him to come to the toilet," I said as he was leaving the toilet.

I was just starting to break of pieces of the rock into my spliff when Toddler came in.

"Buil'a spliff," I said.

"How much do you want?" he asked.

"Listen, just build up and stop asking stupid questions," was my answer.

Charlie had given me at least a gram for my fifty pounds. This buzz was just so nice it was to lead to my downfall, and the longest sentence of my short life.

But at this time I didn't know it yet. I had girls, money in the bank, a nice car, jewellery like dirt and I was still only nineteen. I was enjoying myself. It was nice knowing that over a hundred people had turned up for me and I was feeling high as a kite and happy. But worse was to come.

CHAPTER NINE

I woke up with the living headache in my own bed in my own flat. Diane had come home with me and we'd had a wicked sex session. It was our first sexual encounter in about a year and boy it was worth the wait. There is only one word to describe sex on a coke buzz and that's "OMG!" She was seeing some boy from her college at this time but I knew that all I had to do was to promise to dedicate myself to her and she'd be mine. The problem though, was I wasn't ready to make any such promises to any girl. But I would not have minded a visit from her every now and then but I knew Diane wasn't a two-timing sort of girl. Hell, I was even lucky to have got her into bed. I also knew that this college boy of hers was nothing serious. He was only there because I wasn't. On the way back from my party the night before she went into a long lecture about us settling down and rediscovering what we once had. While all that was going through my head was to take her home and fuck the living day lights out of her.

Cocaine makes you horny and crack cocaine makes you twice as horny. When we got in I put another joint together, but this time I put weed in with the crack to calm me down a bit as I was hyper. I really wanted some dirty sex but I knew I was with the wrong girl for that so I was prepared to settle for calmer sex as long as I was with her that night. Kissing was Diane's thing. She loved it when I kissed her and caressed her nipples. We could kiss for a whole hour, I swear, and it'd still be very nice. Her pink nipples would stand up as soon as I started feeling them up and kissing her. She soon melted to my touch and I knew I was getting her that night. I took her clothes off in a flash before she could change her mind. But there was no need to rush because I could see she was just as eager now I'd got her in the mood. Her height was just right for me. I was six-three and she was five-eleven. She knew what made me tick and that was her hand caressing and feeling up my balls. She put her hand on my balls and with the other she held my cock. At this time I was so charged and excited I could have laid her out and fucked her there and then. But the night was still young so why rush? I put my hand between her legs and played with her clit. Her legs parted, allowing me more room to explore and caress, all the time still kissing her. She kept groaning and kept her hands on my cock and seed bag. I was ready to go; Diane always had this effect on me. So with my legs, I parted her legs even wider and positioned myself ready to penetrate her now wet vagina.

"Not yet babes," she whispered. "Not yet."

"Nice?" I asked her, whispering back.

"Yeah boy," came the answer.

I tickled her pussy with my cock, getting her even more wet and excited. Her legs were even wider apart by now so I let my cock go in just enough to make her feel it but not going in all the way.

"Yes babes, I want it now," she cried.

But still I teased putting just the tip of my cock in her wet pussy and then pulling out.

"Now Anthony, now."

When I finally pushed in all the way, it was like coming home after a long period away from home.

She let out a small groan and gripped me with her long legs. I knew she liked it nice and slow, so I gave it to her, just the way she liked it. To my surprise she said, "I want it harder babes, harder," and that's exactly what she got, trust me. I didn't realise how bad I'd missed her and her pussy. I rode it like a true jockey.

"Can I touch your balls now?" she whispered.

"Yeah babes," I said. I was ready to explode, I'd held back long enough. As soon as her soft hands touched my balls I felt my spunk rising to the top. Blam. It was like the world stopped and shook at the same time. We held each other tightly while our love juices flowed. And then it was over. Diane. No one had the same effect on me in the bedroom as she did. We just lay there quiet and still holding on tight. I didn't want to let go or withdraw and I could tell she felt the same way. We laid there for about ten minutes with the only sound in the room being our breathing. When I finally withdrew, I leaned over to the bedside cabinet and passed her some tissues to clean herself up and I did the same.

I lit the rest of the spliff and enjoyed the sweet taste of a season spliff after good sex.

"Did you miss me Anthony?"

"Boy, couldn't you tell D?"

"I've missed you. But it doesn't have to be like this though. I'm getting my own place soon as well."

"I'm too busy right now and you're at law school as well, do you think we could see each other all the while like you want?" I asked her.

"You can start by cutting me a key to this place. That way I can come straight from college most nights."

"Are you sure it's what you want after what happened with that stupid bitch Sandra?"

"Well it's up to you then, if you cut me a key then you can't have your slags coming here. You think about it."

I promised I'd give it a thought and with that we must have fallen asleep. The headache the next day wasn't too bad after Diane made me breakfast and brought it to the bedroom. As soon as the breakfast was done I put the tray down and pulled her into bed! All she had on was my t-shirt, so it was back on the racetrack for round two. It was gone noon by the time she was dressed and ready to go home. We'd had a bath together, which was nice as well. All in all it had been a night to remember my nineteenth birthday. I drove her home to Clapton and made my way back to town.

I stopped at Toddler's to see how he was feeling after the party and drugs the night before. His mum answered and said he was still sleeping so I left a message and went home.

About these times we used to go to a night club called Maxim's Club on Friday nights in Stoke Newington. This was a reggae night spot with a lot of Yardies both men and women as regular revellers. Yardies were now starting to feature in my everyday life. They seemed to be the main pushers of crack and Maxim's was one of the main outlets. I remember back when we went to Seven Ladies to rave and all you'd smell was weed. In Maxim's all you seemed to smell was crack. But it was a regular Friday night rave spot for us.

Anyway, one Friday night we went out to Maxim's with the intention of raving but I also had a few weed bags to sell if anyone asked. We'd been there a few hours when I spotted this punk from Holloway in North London called Paul Simpson. Now Paul Simpson was not a gangster although he liked mixing with us. He was a nine-to-five worker and worked for a firm that repaired gold, so we thought at the time that he was a good man to keep in touch with. About a month before the night I saw him in Maxim's, he'd asked me to sell him an ounce of weed on credit and that he'd pay me at the end of that month. I agreed even though I didn't know where his mum's house was but I trusted him, especially being a punk and a worker. The end of that month came and went and there was no sign of Paul even though he knew where my flat was and knew he could push the money through the letter box. Another week went by, still no sign of the punk. I was at this stage beginning to think he intended to take the piss. I am paranoid like that. It's the same kind of politics that nearly got me six years back then.

Anyway, back to the night at Maxim's night club, I saw Paul for the first time since he took the ounce of weed off me on tick. I couldn't believe he was there especially because I knew he also worked Saturdays. When I was sure it was him, I told Toddler to entice him somehow and bring him in the toilets. I then went in there to wait, hiding behind the door so he wouldn't see me as soon as the door opened. It worked. Toddler got him clean into the toilet before he noticed I was there.

"What's up Paul?" I said to him.

"B-b-boxer, I was gonna come check you tomorrow," he stuttered.

"Yeah?" I said. "Well we're here now so you can pay me my money."

"Boxer, I only came out with forty pounds, I didn't think I'd see you here."

I pulled out my knife and held it so he could see I wasn't fucking with him. He had two thick chains, one with a pound sign pendant and the other a dollar sign pendant hanging from it. He also had two bracelets, small ones. Nothing compared to what I had on.

"Boxer, I swear to God, if you wait till tomorrow, I'll bring round your money." All this time there's people in the toilets and people coming and going all the time, but I didn't even care or notice them.

"Paul, you know you took the piss when all I was trying to do was do you a favour."

"I know Boxer, that's why I will definitely bring the money round tomorrow."

"Take off your chains and bracelets," I said to him, still holding the knife.

"Please, Boxer. Talk to him for me, Toddler. I won't let you down," he pleaded.

"You disrespected the man already," Toddler said to him, making it obvious he was on my side. Paul was on his own.

"Take them off," I repeated.

"Boxer I swear, please," he pleaded again but this time he'd started to take off his chains.

"When you pay me my hundred and twenty pounds tomorrow you'll get your things back."

That seemed to cheer him up a bit but he was still taking his time giving me the stuff. I don't know why I did it, but then with one swing of my knife, I cut him across his forehead. He screamed and tried to run out of the toilets but Toddler held him back. He had to face the music.

"Take them off now, I ain't playing unless you want another cut." With that he hurriedly took off all his gold and handed them over. By now he was bleeding all over himself and the floor. I took out my flannel and passed it to him to clean himself up.

"It ain't a bad cut. Couple of stitches and you'll be safe, right. Next time when man do you a favour, don't take the fucking piss," I lectured him.

"Can I get back my things when I pay you?" he asked holding the flannel to his head and tears in his eyes.

"I'll think about it Paul."

"Get a cab to the hospital Paul and get yourself stitched up," Toddler told him as we left the toilets and went back to raving. I didn't even see him leave, that's how quick I'd put it out of my mind. I didn't class this as a crime. I was collecting my debt.

So you can imagine how shocked I was when police came crashing through my door at seven thirty the next morning telling me I was wanted for robbery. I woke to about six CID officers standing around my bedroom.

"What fucking robbery?" I said angrily.

"Get dressed, you're under arrest for a robbery that took place at Maxim's nightclub last night."

It was then it dawned on me that Paul had gone to the police. They then picked up all the gold on my bedside cabinet for evidence.

"Listen you fools, that's my fucking gold," I protested. Paul's gold was in my jacket pocket in the passage but they didn't know it.

I got dressed while they watched carefully.

"Can I make a phone call?" I asked.

"Yeah, down at the station," a CID officer said.

"What station?"

"Stoke Newington," they said. "We also have to search your room." And so they searched, but the only thing they found was the knife I cut the boy with and an empty cocaine bag, which the officer sniffed and passed to another officer.

"We'll sort out the gold at the station."

I prayed that they would not search the jackets in the passage. Because the flat was shared, they only searched my bedroom. When we got to the passage, I picked up a different jacket and walked down the stairs with them behind me and a couple in front. When I saw the damage they'd done to my door, I cursed their wives, mums, kids and anyone else I could curse. I was still cursing their families when I got to the station.

In the station when I was getting booked in I looked up at the names and saw Toddler's name up the board. He'd also been arrested, probably by a different squad. I couldn't believe that punk had gone to the police. I had to somehow get to a phone and get somebody to move the jacket with the gold in it. I knew that once they found out that Paul's gold was not among the gold they had, they might go back to my flat and search it up properly.

I got a phone call at around nine that morning. I called my flatmate Mark and talked to him in Patois and a mix of coded talk telling him to move my eight-ball suede jacket. I then crossed my fingers and hoped for the best. I also called my solicitors and told them to get there to the station. I was right about the search. They must have taken the gold found in my room to Paul to identity and obviously they weren't his so around midday I was taken back to my flat. The eight-ball jacket was gone. The search was a waste of time. I didn't keep nothing incriminating in the house anyway and the jacket with the gold had been moved. I made a no comment interview but was still charged and kept at the station to appear in court on Monday. On the Monday morning my mum came to court to put up our family house as surety for bail. Both myself and Toddler were granted bail on two thousand pounds and a curfew of 8 p.m. to 8 a.m. Because my people were in court, my surety was signed there and then and I was let out while Toddler had to go to Feltham Young Offender's Prison to wait for his bail to be signed.

I was free. I remember it was December and really close to Christmas, which is what made it even sweeter being free and also I knew that being out the chances of this case going anywhere would be next to nothing.

I went back to the police station to collect my gold from the bastards. The look on the CID's face said it all. He was gutted I was on bail. I just smiled as I checked my property.

"Don't get too comfortable, we've got you on this one son. Six years this time," he said.

"Yeah, yeah. Anything you say punk," I said as I left with all my gold. While on bail, I made a couple of trips to Feltham Prison until Toddler's people signed him out. I felt guilty for him because he hadn't really done anything to be locked up for, I'd done everything, but still that punk Paul went and involved him.

As the months went by, it was obvious that the boy was

determined to lock us up. And also he hadn't paid me my money so I kept his gold and waited for the trial. My bail restricted my movements badly. A lot of the police officers in Tottenham knew me by sight so every time I moved at night I had to get a girl or a friend to drive my car. Or else I got cabs up and down to do what I had to do. It was a tricky situation. I knew that all they had to do was catch me between my curfew hours and I was straight back in custody. Also I could not contact Paul directly. I sent girls to his workplace to make him see sense, but that didn't work either. The police had worked on him properly as they were determined to have us locked up for this petty thing. They knew we were becoming very dangerous, but didn't know how dangerous we really were. If only they knew.

The trial came up in April of '88 at Snaresbrook Crown Court. Our families were all in court. Paul's word was the only evidence against us. The jury this time was a lot friendlier than the one at St Albans, a mixture of young and old, black, coloured and white. I knew we had a better chance than we had a few years back.

I was in the dock with Toddler. The case opened with the prosecution calling us names and all that kind of stuff and making Paul out to be some good boy. Our barristers let it be known that Paul was at the same night club as us, so if we were bad for being at such a club, well so was he. The case started normally. The next day my barrister came down to see me and told me something that gave me hope. I should point out that on the first day of trial, they had withdrawn our bail so we were now in custody and going to court from jail. Anyway, my barrister had read Paul's statement in which he kept referring to me as Boxer all through and referred to Toddler as Toddler. He had not once used our real names. But because the police knew who we were, we were arrested anyway. So my barrister was excited because he was sure that he'd seen a case or heard of an old case in which the defendants had been acquitted on the grounds their nicknames weren't their real names. He was positive that given time he could find this law in a book. He had to find it so as to prove it to the judge. When we went back up, he asked for the jury not to be brought up as yet as he had a law point to put to the judge. The judge listened to his argument and was not impressed. But he granted him an hour to search out this old case. After an hour searching through the library in the court house, he could not find it anywhere.

When the court reconvened, he pressed the judge to grant him more time so he could go to a law library somewhere in London to look for this book. Reluctantly he was granted two more hours with judge telling him that if he didn't find it this time, the case had to run its course. My barrister thanked the judge for his patience and the court was adjourned till after lunch.

We were taken back down, all the time keeping our fingers crossed and hoping the barrister would find this law book. And boy did he or did he. After lunch we were brought back up into the court. The judge, the court staff and our barristers were already there but the jurors were still not called back yet.

The case re-opened with my barrister repeating what he had told the judge earlier in the day. Then he was asked if he'd found the law case to back up what he'd said. He then read from this big old law book, which in effect stated that we could not be tried on the basis of our nick names. When he'd finished reading from the book, the court was quiet while my barrister handed the book to an usher to hand to the judge so he could read it for himself. While the judge read it to himself, my barrister turned around and gave me a smile. I was still not too sure so I just nodded back. In the end, the judge called for the jury to be called back up. When the jurors were all seated in their right order, the judge went into a long speech, quoting from the law book several times. He seemed very upset when at the end of his speech he directed the foreman of the jury to find the two accused not guilty and thereby acquitting us. But all this still had to be done formally, so he turned to the jury and said, "How do you find the defendant Daniel Howard?"

"Not guilty," came the answer from the jury foreman.

Then next he turned back to the foreman again and said, "In the case of defendant Anthony Spencer, how do you find the defendant?"

"Not guilty, your honour," he said again.

The judge then turned to us and said, "Anthony Spencer and Daniel Howard you are both free to go."

All this before Paul Simpson had even given his evidence. I was still a bit shocked at what had happened as we walked out of the court room. Outside the court room we were congratulated by our people with hugs and kisses. I searched out my barrister and shook his hand enthusiastically. I could have kissed him the way I felt. He was fucking brilliant.

And then I turned round just in time to Paul Simpson and two CIDs on the case walking past, I shouted, "Six years officer? Hardly!"

But they just kept on walking. Two years later in 1990, I was in a designer clothes shop when who walked in but the same Paul Simpson. I hadn't laid eyes on him since that case. As soon as he saw me, he turned and walked straight back out. I didn't go after him though. I'd learned my lesson with guys like him. We call them one-day-bad-boys. They mixed with bad boys one day and police the next. He was an original one-day-bad-boy.

It was now summer of '88 and a new kind of music and rave was coming on the circuit. Acid music. We were pioneers. Also Leuchie who had by now done over two years was coming up to his release date. I looked forward to having him back on the road. I visited him during this period and boy was he massive or what. I went to the Isle of Wight and a prison called Camp Hill to visit him with my mum. The fucking size of him. I knew that Leuchie was coming out to take no prisoners. Back on the streets cocaine was taking all the money I was making and a lot of my savings, but it was a while before I realised. I just kept on going to the cash point and withdrawing, never putting nothing back. I was also making money all the time but most of that went on cocaine as well and the rest on high living. It got to a head in the summer of '88 when I got itchy for big money. I knew I had to hit the pavement or empty out my account, so I started looking for the right move. It came by the way of an African girl who worked in a factory in an industrial estate in Tottenham Hale. She was a cocaine user like me and had a flat on the Broadwater Farm Estate. One day I got talking to her and she told me where she lived. About a week or so later, I went up to her house with a half-ounce of powder cocaine. I knew she knew how to wash up powder into the crack form, which was all I smoked by then. She'd told me to come over anytime I had powder and she would wash it up for me. I went over that night anyway with Toddler and she was in. She was pleased when I handed over the half ounce of powder. While it cooked in a pot on the fire, she took out a plastic Coke bottle with a broken pen sticking out the side held in place with chewing gum. On top of this

Coke bottle she had put a piece of tin foil held in place with rubber band.

"You ever piped cocaine?" she asked us in her African accent, showing us the Coca Cola bottle.

"What do you mean by pipe cocaine?" I said.

"I mean put cocaine on a pipe and smoke."

"No, why?" I asked her. Her name was Tina.

"No?" she asked. "Well, hold on, I'll show you when the first piece of rock comes out the pot."

"All we do is smoke it in spliffs Tina and right now I'm not interested in nothing else," I said.

"That's waste man, you have to try this. Just wait."

When the first pieces were ready, she put a little rock on top of some ash she had placed on the foil at the top of the bottle. She took a lighter and burned the rock and at the same time drew the smoke out through the half pen in the side of the bottle. I watched as the Coke bottle filled with smoke and then emptied as she drew out all the smoke. I was fascinated and watched her reaction closely. When she'd exhaled all the smoke, she smiled and said, "Try some, trust me."

"Go on then Tina, I'll try it." I looked at Toddler and said, "Are you gonna try it blood?"

"Yeah man, it looks safe," was his answer.

She changed the ash on the foil and put on a fresh lot. She then put a little rock on the ash and passed me the bottle, which was really a crack pipe.

"Hold it carefully Boxer. When I start burning the thing, just inhale all you can and take your mouth off the pipe OK?"

"Yeah, let's go," was my reply.

The rush I felt when I'd inhaled the smoke in the bottle was out of this world. 'Shit!' I thought to myself.

"You like it Boxer innit," she said, smiling. I couldn't speak for a while so I just nodded. She then repeated the same process with Toddler and I could see he felt that fucking rush. I took my jacket off and told her to give me another one. And another. And another. This was wicked we kept on saying. What was meant to be a short visit turned into a crack party between the three of us. We didn't leave her flat till around 5 a.m. that morning.

The following night we were back there again, doing the same thing. It was during one of these visits to Tina's that she mentioned her factory to us.

"We all get paid in cash on a Friday. It's very easy to take the place. All there is, is one Indian man and us workers."

"How much money do you reckon we'll get then?" Toddler asked as we all smoked the pipe. By now Tina had made two extra pipes so we didn't have to wait in turn.

"Toddler on any Friday at least fifteen thousand easy," she answered.

"That sounds alright," I said.

That money was needed boy because smoking cocaine was expensive and piping it was a lot more expensive.

"When can we move to this factory of yours?" I said.

"Whenever you boys want. You do know I have to get a cut?"

"Of course," I said. "That goes without saying."

"What about next week?" Toddler asked.

"Yeah, that's possible. It's up to you boys."

"Next week Friday," I said to Toddler.

With that we carried on smoking our crack pipes till the early hours. In the days leading up to the Friday we paid the industrial estate a couple of visits to work out how we would do the move and get away. We had all the information we needed with regards inside the factory, but we still had to work out the surroundings and a getaway route. We settled on taking the factory as he arrived from the bank in his blue Suzuki van following information we had. We knew what time about he would arrive with the money. It was easier that way than going into the factory and taking him there. On the day, we borrowed a garage car from a man we knew and changed up the number plates. We went outside the factory and parked up, smoking crack spliffs while we waited. Then we saw him arrive in the blue van.

"Ready blood?" I asked my good friend Toddler.

"Ready from I was born," came his answer.

We jumped out of our car as he parked his van and walked calmly towards him. I was armed with a.38 revolver with six shots and Toddler had a .22 with two shots. And we were masked up. As it turned out we didn't need the weapons, it was like taking candy from a baby, believe me.

The first thing I said to the Indian factory owner was, "Get back in your van," showing him my gun pointing at his stomach.

"Ok, OK, please don't shoot. All of it is in the bag on the backseat."

Fuck, it was so easy. It's like he was expecting us. Maybe the gun and the masks was what frightened him most.

"Yeah OK, just get in the van," I repeated. I got in front of him while Toddler ran round to the door and opened the backdoor.

"Got it blood, come," he said to me.

"Stay in your van right. Don't fucking move until we're gone."

"Ok boss," he said nervously.

I jumped out of his van and ran over to our car, which was still running. We were gone in seconds. All this had taken less than two minutes, if that.

Back at the garage we parked up the car and gave the guy one hundred pounds from my pocket and got into my golf and drove off to my mum's house. I went to my old room with Toddler to count our loot. It came to just over twelve thousand. So we both had five and a half between us. And the rest we set aside for Tina. Her cut came to just under fifteen hundred. We also decided there and then that we were going into the cocaine trade with some of our cash. We settled on three grand, which at the time would get us about three ounces of cocaine in the powder form. The weed business was nowhere near as profitable as the cocaine business. We put aside fifteen hundred each toward our new business.

We split up then, deciding to stay away from Tina's for a couple of days. By this time we could make up our own crack pipe so we didn't need her for that anymore. I went to my flat to put down my money, then make some calls about getting hold of some coke. That night I called Tina from a pay phone to tell her we had some cash for her. I didn't want her thinking we had pulled a fast one on her. She got her money. And boy what a crack party we had round my flat that night. While we waited for our parcel of three ounces to be dropped off, we went over the Broadwater estate to purchase about a half ounce of already washed up coke and came back to my flat. We smoked till the early hours of the night. Smoked till we were sick. I remember going to the window gasping for air every time I took a hit. We took it in turns at the window, me and Toddler, but always came back to the pipe for more.

I had put two and a half thousand away through the cash point so I didn't mind blowing some on a crack party, plus we'd already put aside fifteen hundred a piece for our crack business. I was happy to spend some on smoking that night. We crashed out in my bedroom still dressed up in the clothes from the night before.

Remember when I said in an earlier chapter that the yardies were not yet involved in my everyday politics? Well they were soon to be.

By buying and selling cocaine, which is what I was about to embark on. I was getting into their business but didn't know it yet. I knew though that selling coke while being a user was not too smart, but I didn't care.

The next day after our binge we got hold of a Yardie called Greedy. He got us the coke we wanted. Three ounces. He also washed it up for us and promised us he could get it for us anytime we wanted. He gave us a telephone number. This was before the mobile phone came into being for us, so it was a BT line number we had to make do with.

Just after all this but just before my birthday, my brother Dillon was released from jail. He had served over two and a half years. We were all so pleased to have him back. He was now twenty-four years old and going on twenty-five. I could see he was ready for some serious stuff. My old man took him out for a drink first and then he came out with Frankie, myself and his friend San and a couple of girls the next night. We pumped him full of drugs, mostly weed and drinks. While we were out, I filled him in on the latest news. I told him, I was in the cocaine trade and he seemed very impressed. He wanted to come in with us as well, which made sense to me. So I told him we would sort out the nitty-gritty details later. He was just out after so long, I wanted him to chill out for a bit and enjoy his freedom. That same night we all went to our regular haunts in town.

Yeah it was nice having Dillon back on road.

CHAPTER TEN

I wish mobile phones were invented earlier. Selling cocaine, especially when you smoked it as well, was a nervous and paranoid lifestyle. The best policy as they say is not to get high on your own supply. But having started smoking the stuff before we were selling it, that was easier said than done.

With Leuchie out of jail and coming in with us we were going to make a go of it. You see Leuchie hadn't tasted crack as yet. He'd been banged up when crack came on the scene while Toddler and myself were slowly but surely working our way to becoming crack addicts. Anyway, I gave my brother a grand to sort himself out and get on his feet. With the rest of my money, I traded in my Golf GTI for a three-year-old, much newer model of the same Golf GTI, but this one was a lot faster.

We started off selling our drugs on the Broadwater estate, which is called the Farm for short. It was and still is the closest thing to a frontline in Tottenham. We had no trouble fitting in as we were known to people there since we were kids. Except the Yardies who hated competition. They saw us as kids and thought they could move us off our own plot. A plot we fucking grew up on. Wrong move!

It started in a subtle way. They'd make stupid remarks every time we would make a sale. Or they'd try to take a customer away while myself or Toddler was serving up the punter. We always stood our ground. It was obvious we were heading for a clash. Because we were already known in Tottenham a lot of the punters who came by, came straight to us. We weren't the only English youths on that line. There was an equal amount of us English youths and Yardies. The battle lines were drawn. It was only a matter of time before someone got hurt and I was determined it would not be me.

Life went on anyway in the meantime. We would phone greedy to get more stuff wash it up, put a piece away for ourselves to smoke at night and the rest we would cut up into little rocks. We would then divide it up between me and my partner Toddler and then head for the farm where we would be all day till we sold out. On a good day we'd net eleven hundred each and still have a piece put down from earlier to smoke after work. Of that eleven hundred, about five hundred each would go back on the next parcel and we would do the same thing all over again. It was good money but the tension was building up on the farm.

And then it happened one afternoon. A punter jumped out of a cab and made his way straight to Toddler. He was Toddler's regular man. But before he could get to Toddler, he was intercepted by this Yardie called Prang. Prang was tall and in his thirties. We would not have done that with his fucking customer so we weren't about to have this.

"Oi, you coming here or what?" Toddler called out to his punter. But Prang was by now holding on to the guy and would not let go. We knew this was a test we couldn't fail. So we walked over to where they were and told Prang in the best way we knew how to, that what he was doing was a liberty.

"Fuck off. Ah my yoot this seen," he said, meaning this was his punter and to fuck off and then turned back to the punter and said, "Wey you ah look Star."

We both looked at each other me and Toddler and I knew we had to do something. Everybody was watching for our reaction. Meanwhile the punter was confused and didn't know which way to turn.

"Prang, you're taking liberties, let the guy go. We wouldn't do that with your customer," Toddler said.

"So wha'? Me done tell you already, fuck off," came the answer.

With that I grabbed the punters shirt and yanked him away so now it was just me and Toddler facing the fucking guy Prang. But still we didn't really want to start anything with him. As soon as I'd done that he walked over to a dust bin and pulled out this fucking great big chopper. I didn't stand around and neither did Toddler. We had to make a quick get away because all we had on us was lock knives, which was no match for what he had. We knew the estate back to front so we were able to get away. I cursed blue murder when I linked up Toddler about half an hour later.

"Blood we have to go back over there, what you saying?" Toddler said.

"Listen, you see that pussy hole, he's as good as dead. Did you see the size of that chopper?" I said.

"Should we draw for the .22 and go back?" he asked.

"Come then. Let's get a cab."

My car was still on the estate as I'd had to escape on foot. I was fuming. We went and put down our drugs and picked up the .22. It still only had two shots in it.

We jumped in a cab and stopped the cab just outside the farm and walked into estate. I saw the look on their faces when we came back. Only about an hour had passed since the last incident. Prang was nowhere to be seen.

"Where's that pussy hole Prang?" I shouted to no one in particular.

"In that food shop," our friend Briggy, who'd only just turned up, shouted back. He'd obviously heard what had happened when he'd turned up. It was obvious they'd all been talking about what had happened.

Anyway the food shop was further up from where we always stood up to sell our drugs. So we walked on past the group of bystanders. Everyone kept their distance. The food shop was called Miss P's. It was owned by an elderly black woman whom everybody respected. The last thing I wanted to do was shoot up her place and kill that pussy in her shop. As we approached miss P's I said to Toddler.

"Give me the bucky." Meaning the .22.

"No this is my thing, he dissed me not you."

"Give it to me blood, let me pop him."

"I'm safe, I'll do it," he said.

When we got outside the shop, we stopped at the door. I could see him through the window paying Miss P.

"Prang you pussy hole come out here now," I shouted. By this time all the drug dealers and the people on the line were standing around watching. I didn't see Toddler take out the gun, but Prang did. The guy's amazing. The next thing I knew he was over Miss P's food counter and throwing himself out her back window. By then he'd disappeared from view but all we heard was crashing glass. So we and the crowd ran round the back of the food shop chasing him. He was about a hundred feet away from us by the time he came into view. I couldn't believe how fucking quick this idiot was.

"Shoot man, fucking shoot him," I said as we chased him.

Pop! Pop! Twice Toddler pulled the trigger and twice he missed. The fucking man kept on running. When we stopped chasing him, I turned to Toddler and nearly took his head off.

"Why didn't you wait for him to come out before taking out the bucky?" I said angrily.

Yeah it's true, I should have. Fucking lucky dick head. Shit, I fucked up," he said stamping his foot on the ground.

"Big time man. You should have waited for him to come out then popped him one in the stomach or something," I said.

"Anyway come let's head out before feds get here," he said.

The crowd was by now starting to disperse. And everyone knew the police would be here soon. Someone must have heard those shots. It was broad daylight as well so we ran over to my car with Toddler still holding the gun and left the estate.

"Blood don't say a word, I know I fucked up," he said as we drove out the farm.

"You just wasted two bullets blood. Now he'll be looking for us. Toddler you should have done better than that," I said, still fuming. While we drove down Lordship Lane, about three police cars went driving past with their sirens heading towards the farm. It was obvious this was to do with the shots fired. We just drove on to our hiding place for our drugs and guns. We took the rest of that day off. I phoned Leuchie to come over from his girl's. This was some serious shit now. That prang was no push over. This wasn't something we could just forget. It had to be sorted out somehow. We waited at the Phoenix wine bar for Leuchie to come over. He came in with San and Bad Cock Charlie.

"It was you two shooting up the farm today innit," Bad Cock said. They had heard about the incident even before we said a word.

"Leuchie man this idiot tried to chop after us with this rusty chopper so we went to the lock up and came back for the fucking guy," I said to my brother.

"Was it Prang?" San asked.

"How you know?" I said.

"Some girl was showing us," San said.

"Yeah man, he took the piss. About he's taking my punter and telling me to fuck off," Toddler said.

"So why you never smoke him?" Leuchie asked Toddler.

"Go on, tell him," I said.

"Boy Leuch, I missed him twice."

"You can't miss man like that. Then you really got trouble," Bad Cock said.

"We already done fall out with that lot years back, remember Bad Cock?" Leuchie said to Charlie.

"Course I remember. How can I forget? Them man don't change. Always trying to chuck it."

Apparently the same guy Prang and another Yardie called Dues had had a falling out with my brother and his friends years ago. I was only just finding out about it. They had kidnapped Bad cock, put him in a car and drove over to Brixton. They had then phoned Bad Cock's people and wanted a grand that they claimed Charlie Bad Cock owed them. They kept him from one evening until early hours of the next morning. They stripped him and left him over in South London. He got a Cab back in his boxer shorts nearly freezing to death. But on that occasion I think he truly owed them that money. But he wasn't saying. This was different. Prang had taken liberties. And we had reacted.

"Leuch, I need shots for the .22, who's got?" I said to my brother.

"How many do you need B?" Leuchie asked me.

"Boy it's empty, so six cos I ain't playing with them Yardies."

"Just cool right, don't get yourself banged up for idiots like dat. We'll work out something seen," Leuchie said to me.

"Hear what, we're gonna go take a drive through the farm and see what's going on. I want them man to know it's my little brother they're fucking with. You two stay here, we soon come." With that the three left the Phoenix wine bar.

While they were gone, I played pool with Toddler but our hearts were not in it because every game we played took twice as long as usual.

It seemed like ages before San came in and called to us. We followed him out to his car with my brother and Bad Cock in it.

"Jump in your car and follow us," My brother said.

When I'd turned my car round, they started up and we followed. They drove back into Tottenham, past the farm to a gambling house called Cee Jays. We parked up and they motioned for use to come in. It was a place frequented by Yardies and we knew it.

"Why we coming here Leuch?"

"Don't worry, just come," he said as someone peeped through the spy hole and opened the door.

"Wey ya sey Leuchie," This guy greeted my brother. We walked in and it felt like walking into the enemy's camp. Even though I trusted the company I was with, I kept my hand on my already open knife, which was in my jacket pocket. And also kept my eyes open.

"Where is he?" Leuchie asked this Yardie called PJ that I knew. He was in his thirties and this gambling house was his dad's place.

"He soon come. Sit down and wait," PJ replied.

"Who we waiting for?" I asked my brother.

"Prang," came the answer.

"What, you mad or what Leuch?"

"Just shut up and sit down," he said.

"You got something Leuch?" I meant a weapon.

"Just cool," he said.

Prang came out the back into the room and to my surprise he was fucking smiling and walking over to where the five of us sat.

"You cool now yoot?" he asked me, but I didn't answer him. Didn't say a word. He probably thought I pulled the trigger.

"Me love see the yoot dem stand up fe them rights. Ah nuh nottin seen. Wey ya say blood?" he said to Leuchie.

"Boy Prang, you can't go bullying the yoot dem, you know. Ah my likkle breder dis. I want this ting done right here so. You never get hurt and you never hurt dem. Call it ah misunderstanding."

"Ah true man. Ah misunderstanding," he said, and then, "You cool though Leuchie."

"Yeah me cool Prang. All this have to stop right here blood. You ah big man fe dem. Yoot dem have fe mek money too. You fe 'llow dem Prang." Meaning he should just leave it and let things go with us.

"Leuchie hear me blood, me sey it done. Me love how your likkle breder handle himself. It done seen," he said, trying to reassure us that the beef was now over and no one needed to take it further.

"Alright then Prang, we gone seen. Later."

We got up and walked out of Cee Jay's.

"Leuchie you sure it's over with that punk?" Toddler said.

"You lot still watch your backs, can't trust them fucking Yardies an inch," he replied.

"I need the shots for the .22," I said.

"Bad Cock can sort it out in the week," Leuchie said to me.

"Yeah Boxer, check me weekend and we go see a man," Charlie assured me.

"I'm going to mum's to sleep Leuch, I'll phone you tomorrow." It was about 1 a.m. by now and I didn't feel safe sleeping at my house that night I remember. Nowhere safer than mum's house.

This happened between my twentieth birthday and Christmas of '88. But it wasn't going to be my last encounter with the Yardies. The next one nearly cost me my life. But at the moment life went back to normal and Prang truly had written it off and kept himself to himself. So did the rest of the Yardies on the farm. We had our regulars and no one tried to deal with them. Neither did myself or Toddler try to take anyone else's customer. No matter who they were. But after that incident we kept the .22 close by. And people knew it. It was just a dash away from where we stood up to deal. And I wasn't going to miss like Toddler did, I promised myself. We weren't on the line everyday though because our cocaine habit was growing by the day.

Christmas '88 was Leuchie's first Christmas in over two years and he made sure he enjoyed it to the maximum. We had a drink up round my flat on Boxing Day '88. Even my flat mate Mark Kemba had a few friends round. Our guest list was like a roll call of a mixture of thieves, gangsters, fraudsters, armed robbers, burglars and even murderers and girls galore. It was a night to remember, just like my birthday the year before.

But I look back now and it's sad to say that of all the people who were there, only a few have survived the drug epidemic that at the time was just starting. Only a few of those there that night are still on the right track, majority took to drugs and are now fucked up or locked up doing long stretches trying to feed their drug habits. Or dead.

I'm pleased to say that even though I'm in prison in this point in time, I can be counted as one of those still on track. So are my brothers Dillon and Frankie. But back then it was nice having the who's who of North London in my flat drinking Champagne and smoking shit and having a wicked time. The next day there were still people crashed out in the flat at noon, that's the sort of drink up it was.

About these times also saw the beginnings of Acid House music, which evolved into another type of music known as Jungle Music, then evolved again into what is now House and Garage. Like I said in an earlier chapter we were the pioneers of Jungle Music.

Acid music as it was known then brought a new earning opportunity to the wise guy. It brought us in contact with workers, idiots, country bumpkins and rich kids. Hell, when I got into acid music, I even stopped stealing for long periods at a time. That's how much money there was to be made. With Acid music came ecstasy pills, speed and trips. All drugs that didn't exist at all in our everyday lives. I can't remember how or exactly when I got into acid music, but I do remember my first acid rave proper. I mean proper because before that rave, we had been hearing the music now and again at clubs such as Heaven's in the West End and Phoenix wine bar and such places. It didn't impress me until the rave on New Year's Day at Kings Lynn in Cambridge. It was a rave called the Rain Dance. It was being advertised on radio stations and clubs, so about fifteen of us, men and women decided to go up. We had about eight cars between us and hit the motorway. From the directions we had we were supposed to stop at a petrol station. Meet up with people who were organising the event, and move on to the real venue once we were given the correct venue location. When we get there, there were other revellers there. It was like a meeting point. Eight cars turned into twenty cars with the rest of them complete strangers we'd met at the petrol station in Kings Lynn. People from all over the country. Anyway Rain Dance was the rave that got me hooked on acid raves. They had funfair rides and tents where the DJs played. Being a street guy, these raves meant money to me and my friends. It was like people had money to burn. They just wanted drugs, drugs and more drugs. Soon after we got well into these raves it became obvious to us that a lot of these people didn't care what they took, a lot of them didn't even know what the drugs tasted like or looked like. So what we began doing was making up our own drugs and called them whatever we liked, I'll explain. There were different kinds of ecstasy pills. Red and Blacks, Love Doves, Brown Biscuits, Yellow Biscuits, New Yorkers, Brown Burgers, the list went on and on. Now there were a lot of real pills such as vitamin pills that were sold in chemists, which looked exactly like a lot of these ecstasy pills, or E's for short. All we had to do was walk into a chemist and buy say a bottle of vitamin B6 tablets, which looked exactly like New Yorkers.

For £2.99, you could get a bottle of B6 with a hundred pills. Each pill we then sold for £15. You work it out and you'll see we made fifteen hundred pounds for a £2.99 layout. And this was just one scam. We also made up Trips. I saw Trips for the first time when I started raving acid raves. But I sold fake trips to so-called trip heads. It was a fucking joke. These guys would even search you out and ask for more, then bring their friends back to buy some more. Because they honestly believed that what you'd sold them was the 'good stuff', what a joke. I loved the early days of acid. It kept me from hitting the pavement. Even though it was a purely weekend thing, Thursday through till Sunday, the money kept me in the lifestyle I was now long accustomed to.

We even got better at faking these E's and Trips. We found stuff that was bitter enough to dip the normal tablets in so they tasted like E's. The doves were the hardest to crack because they had the logo of a dove on them. But we soon found a way round that too. We had a man in Leyton, East London who spent all day every week carving doves on normal vitamin pills, obviously for a price. £2 a tablet. We then sold each for £15. That wasn't bad considering a real pill cost about six to eight pound to be resold for the same £15 we were selling ours for.

All we did in the week was travel from chemist to chemist searching for pills that looked closest to real E's. It was a very profitable scam. I couldn't see the point in buying real E's when most of the people you sold them to didn't know what the damn thing looked like or tasted like. Why spend seven hundred pounds to make fifteen hundred when you could spend three pounds and make the same fifteen hundred. On Thursdays we would go to Rage at the Heaven's night club, on a Friday was Ealing Boulevard, on Saturday was the big tent raves day, the day when we would go outside London to the massive field raves like World Party, Fantasia, Biology or Ram Dance and then Sunday was the day we enjoyed some of the money we'd made. We didn't sell fake stuff at the Sunday raves such as Turnmills and Linford Studios. These were raves for us wise guys. Every man and woman was sensible. Turnmills started at 4 a.m. on Sunday and finished at 10 a.m. And then it was home to rest before leaving at around 10 p.m. that same night to Linford Studios in Battersea.

I remember we would be coming out of Linford Studios on Monday morning with our dark sunglasses on, while people were going to work. The stares we got at traffic lights on the way home said it all. We must have looked evil with our shades on because people didn't stare for too long. But fuck them, they were going to work while we had just finished work, which started since Thursday night. On Tuesday it was back to making up 'drugs' and Thursday we started the cycle all over again. It was better than standing on the farm selling crack and arguing with Yardies. We enjoyed the music and the clueless punters enjoyed our make-up drugs. As usual in Britain, the powers that be and the police hate to see us normal people enjoy ourselves. By mid-'89 they started trying to clamp down on these raves. Especially the field ones, which were the most profitable.

We would turn up only to find police cars driving up the roads leading to the rave and turning people back. That's always the case with everything the majority of the country enjoy in this fucking country and beyond. They never last. As I said earlier the world would be so much better if we had the opportunity to rewrite the rules they laid down for us all a very, very long time ago. Once the government and the higher classes haven't got an interest in it, it's only a matter of time before it's stopped. Glastonbury still goes on today even though more drugs are consumed there than is consumed in the whole of the UK in a two month period, you know why, because the organiser is a Toff, a land owner, one of the upper classes. Let you or I common man have tried doing a Glastonbury type thing and it wouldn't be long before the police and your local council tried their best to shut you down, quoting how many casualties they have had, how much drug taking took place and blah, blah, blah.

The Notting Hill Carnival is not the same event I used to attend back in the day. Every year they change it and change it until today it is unrecognisable to those of us who grew up in the eighties and before. All this because they have tried to stop it but couldn't because it has grown to a cultural event and brings lots of tourists to London otherwise they would have stopped that too.

No one has tried to stop all that blood sport the upper class enjoy. They call it a sport sitting on their horses and having their dogs chase and rip apart some poor animal. And yet the same people condemn bull fighting. This country, and especially the upper classes, is full of hypocrisy.

Anyway about these times, acid music started hitting the headlines as something to be condemned. We didn't care, we went to every rave we could find and the money kept on rolling in. But the more money I made, the more crack I smoked. In 1989, just before my twenty-first I met a girl that remained a big part of my life for a long time and became the mother of my first son. Her name is Sandra. The night I first saw her and our eyes met, I knew this was someone I could roll with. All six foot of her. We were at a private party in Clapton. I'd gone there with a couple of friends and she'd come with her sister. She was taller than my ex girl Diane and dark-skinned and was pretty but not as pretty as Diane was. I only found out when we'd started seeing each other that she'd seen me first and had said to herself, "I want that guy."

When I laid eyes on her, I thought the same thing. She was the tallest girl there that night. I asked her to dance and she agreed. The chemistry was there but I didn't know at that time she'd end up being the mother of my sons. We had a few more dances and I couldn't pull myself away from her. She was the tallest girl I'd had the privilege to dance with. She made that party a night to remember. She left early though because she had to drop her sister home. The night ended with us exchanging telephone numbers. Soon as she left, the party was over for me, even though there were other girls there I could have checked.

The next day was a Sunday and as soon as I got up and got dressed, I phoned her. We spoke for a while getting to know each other. I knew at that time that I needed a girl that could hold my interest and take and put up with my lifestyle. I didn't get to visit her at her flat for another couple of weeks. I remember my first visit to her house. It was a Sunday. She had cooked some chicken and rice, which reminded me of my mum's cooking. That's always a good sign because I've always liked a girl who can cook. I took some weed round and after dinner we watched a film, I think it was *Babylon*, and smoked weed. I was glad to know that was all she smoked. She also worked, which was good in my books. I asked if I could stay the night, but she refused. I didn't mind, it was the answer I wanted, even though I would not have said no if she'd agreed. She had a nineteen-month-old son, Romaine, who was a cute little boy. She was the first girl I'd dated who was already a mum. But like many young black girls, she chose a deadbeat for the father of her son. It was a new experience for me at the time but one that didn't put me off her. Instead it made me want to help her out. I wasn't sure what type of father or step-father I was going to be, but I was prepared to learn something new. It was like having a readymade family of my own.

It was a few days later before she let me stay the night and what a night that was. The sex was great. I knew I'd found a good thing. She lived in Tottenham, but came from Edmonton originally. She was born in March, which made her six months older than I was. She was not a street girl and wasn't known to people. From what I'd heard about her from a few people who knew her in her children's home, she was tough and fiercely independent. Her mum had died of diabetes when she was fourteen and herself and her sister and brother had been taken into care. I had a few friends who grew up with her and they spoke of her with maximum respect. They nick-named her 'Aluminium Draws' because no one could get into her knickers. I liked what I heard and no strange guys came knocking on her flat. I knew this was a good girl. We spent Christmas '89 together. In February 1990, she became pregnant. Boy, I couldn't believe I was going to become a dad. I had virtually moved in with her by now. Seeing as my place was a shared place, we had more privacy at hers. It was my first time living with a woman and it was nice. I attended every hospital appointment with her and looked forward to the birth of my child. I wanted a son. It was becoming obvious that if anyone was going to settle me down, it would be Sandra.

I still had my crack habit but this I kept from her for as long as I could. To be honest I didn't even know I had a habit at this point. I don't think any of us knew or called it a habit. We just smoked what we smoked and got high on what we got high on. I smoked crack round my flat with Toddler and the crew and sometimes by myself. The fucking drug was starting to clean me out by then, even though I was making plenty of money. Sandra tried to get me to save but every time I'd put some away, I'd soon ask for it to buy more smoke. I was still going to acid, which at this time was changing slightly into hardcore. Crack was also now coming into the raves. And with crack came violence. The scene was changing. Sandra was still working and looking after the home now we'd settled into an almost husband and wife routine. She still kept a slim figure, which I loved very much. . I like them slim and tall. Even though I wouldn't have minded had she lost her figure because it'd be down to her pregnancy. I knew she wasn't happy with the life I was leading though. I stayed out till the early hours and came in buzzing on crack. I'd be sleeping when she was going to work and wasn't at home when she came in from work. It didn't take her long to work out what I was on, but she still put up with me. We didn't argue at all or fight because our personalities complemented each other. I tried to be normal for her but that was difficult when you have a drug habit. I was finding myself nearly broke all the time even though I made good money and I knew it was the crack but couldn't stop it. My car was now five years old and needed changing, but I was more interested in smoking than changing it. I still showered Sandra with gold and bought her nice clothes and presents. There was always shopping in the house. These things I made sure I kept up, but cash I didn't seem to have anymore.

Remember when I talked about my next encounter with the Yardies, which nearly cost me my life well that happened in this period when I was always finding myself broke. It was in the summer of '90, Sandra was about four or five months pregnant. My habit was so bad I was getting in the habit of doing switches. I'll explain. You see back then crack was mostly sold in twenty pound pieces wrapped tight in tin foil. So a switch as we called it is when you made up your own wraps, putting peanuts the size of a twenty pound rock in a piece of tin foil and making it look like a legit piece of crack. You then took these pieces to a dealer, pretended you wanted to buy his or her rock and then replaced or switched your peanut wraps for his or her legit crack wrap. Depending on who you did it with, it worked most times.

But on this particular night in the summer of '90 I was caught out and would have lost my life if it wasn't for my quick thinking. This quick thinking was to save my life again in 2000, ten years later when I was shot. I'd gone over to Stoke Newington's Sandringham Road, which was North London's prime frontline back then and walked down the line. I walked up to this girl whom I didn't know. You couldn't do it with people who knew you. Anyway she looked like it would work with her.

"I want three rocks," I said to her.

"You have your sixty pounds?" she asked me.

"Yeah, but I have to see the size is right first yeah."

"See dem here," she said in her Jamaican accent, passing me three rocks.

I inspected them for size and agreed to take them. "Yeah alright they're safe," I said. I then put them in my month, where the other three fake rocks I'd prepared already were. Of course I knew which were which. Anyway I put my hand in my pocket like to take out my wallet, which was all part of the act. I searched all my pockets still acting and said, "Shit babes I left my wallet in my car."

"Gimme back me things and go fe your wallet," she said.

With that I took out my three switch wraps from my month pretending they were her ones and gave them back to her.

"Listen, wait here right, I'm just going to my car to get my wallet. I want them same ones, they're alright," I said. With that I started walking off like to walk back to my car with the legit wraps in my mouth. The bitch was smart. I had taken about ten steps when someone grabbed my shirt, nearly ripping it off. I turned round to find the now angry bitch behind me.

"Ah weh dis you gimme back," she said.

"What you talking about?" I said pretending not to know what she was talking about.

"Ah no my bloodclaart ting this," she screamed. "Gimme me back my fuckin rock dem."

"Listen, let go of my shirt now, I just gave you back your fucking rocks."

I didn't know she wasn't working by herself. Within seconds of the commotion, I was surrounded by about nine or more Yardies. Fuck. I knew this was trouble. She still was holding on to me. What had happened was that as soon as I'd turned round and walked off, she'd unwrapped one of the rocks I gave back to her and discovered what I was up to. But I wasn't about to admit trying to switch her especially not now that I was surrounded. I had to see it through and maybe make her think someone else had done it to her before me. That was the plan. So I kept on protesting my innocence but they weren't having any of it. The next thing I knew, about six knives were showing and then bang! Someone hit me with a stick in my knee. Bang! In my head next and boy I knew I had to leg it. It was going to be the knives next, these guys hated switchers. I was outnumbered, unarmed and in danger. I turned and ran as fast as my legs could take me. I could hear dozens of feet chasing and they were shouting and telling me to come back. No chance. I ran out onto the high road and nearly got knocked over crossing the road. Still they chased. I ran along the high road knowing that if I flew over a wall with the same momentum I could kick in somebody's front door. I did that, I jumped over one of those short walls you get in Stoke Newington and made for someone's front door, all the time hearing them not too far behind me, the door gave way on the first attempt. I think that's when they stopped. But I didn't know because I didn't look back, I just kept on going through these white people's house to their front room where a man was sitting and watching telly. I didn't even look at him, I ran past him and kicked in his backdoor and out into his garden and over his back wall into the next house. The poor guy must have thought he was seeing things sitting there minding his own business in his own house, only for his front door to come crashing in and a black man come running through his house and out the back door. Anyway I flew a few more walls till I knew I was safe. I sat down then in someone's garden breathing heavily from the chase. I couldn't believe I was still in one piece and not full of holes. It was then I noticed blood pouring from my head where someone had hit me.

Damn! I thought. That was close. I picked myself up and came back out on the street. Looking up and down to make sure those Yardies weren't about. I sat there in my car for a while just staring at the rocks in my hand. I took some tissue out the glove compartment and held it to my head wound. I knew I'd come too close for comfort. And you know what? Instead of going to a hospital to get the wound taken care of, I went to my flat to smoke the damned rocks. That's what crack does to you. When they were smoked, I went home to my pregnant girl, she took one look at the wound and ordered a cab to take me to the hospital. She stayed there with me while I was seen to and stitched up. Bless her! I still haven't told her to this day how I got that scar in my head.

After that incident I knew something had to give before I killed someone or got killed myself. One thing was for sure, I had to hit the pavement real soon and make some big money, I couldn't go on like this. The next real big money I went for, I fucked up big time and was banged up. Being on crack seemed to bring nothing but bad luck. We were still selling drugs and all that, but anyone will tell you, no amount of money can support a raging habit. You had to be importing it yourself. I was spending about six hundred pounds a day on crack. That was serious money. I knew people with worse habits. I needed big money. I needed a big move as my baby was on the way. It came in November just about five weeks before my son was due. I had gotten inside information from one prostitute I knew in town about a factory where they collected cash sometimes for their industrial laundry services. I was told that it had to be a two or three man job and we all had to be armed and fully loaded. They took the money out the safe and went to a bank on Thursdays to deposit. I was told I could net as much as fifty grand. It looked too attractive to turn down. But with the money problems I had I thought I'd do this one by myself. Wrong move. Anyway this factory had a shop floor and an office upstairs. There was an outside stairway leading to the office in which just the manager sat but there was also a stairway inside the factory leading from his office down to the factory floor.

I looked at this factory for two nights on the trot and decided that I definitely could take it alone. If I went up the outside steps and kicked in the door I could be in the office robbing him while the factory staff downstairs were working away. They wouldn't know what was going on upstairs in the office. At least that's what I thought.

On the day of the work I went and picked up my.38 and a green rucksack. I drove up in my car, which was fucking stupid anyhow because I could have been spotted driving off even though I parked a good five-minute run away from the place. Drugs make you do stupid things like that.

Anyway, I walked calmly to the factory after I'd parked up in an alley. I got to the stairs, walked up and kicked in the door like I'd planed. I was now in the office face to face with the guy. To my surprise I met him actually counting out a heap of money on his desk.

"You make a sound and you can kiss your life goodbye," I said calmly.

I threw the rucksack over to him.

"Put all the cash in that," I said. "Don't even try being a hero, I hate heroes, I chew them up for breakfast and spit them out," I said to him. I was so fucking eager. "How much have you counted so far?"

"Twenty-four thousand," he answered while he stuffed the money in my rucksack.

"And how much is there?" I carried on.

"I don't know mate, about forty."

If only I'd known that every word we said was going out to the shop floor over the Tannoy system in his office and to the whole factory. The whole fucking factory could hear every word we said. But I still was there thinking it was just him and me.

"Hurry up man," I said again. When he'd put all the money into the bag, I took the phone off the hook and put it in the rucksack and turned to walk back out down the outside stairs. What I saw made me blink several times.

It was like the United Nations outside at the bottom of the outside stairs that I'd just climbed up a few minutes before. There were Indians, Chinese men, white men, black men and women. The whole fucking factory having heard what was going on over the Tannoy had come out to wait for me. I was fucked. I had a gun with six shots in it and was facing fifty or so people.

"The police is on their way so you best stay where you are," one man said as I started walking down the stairs slowly.

"Yeah? Do you think this is a toy gun? Who wants to try?" I said as menacingly as I could even though I was very worried. There was no point in shooting at them so I pointed the gun upwards and squeezed the trigger letting off a round in the air.

"You lot still want some?" I said still coming down the stairs.

"You can't kill all of us," the same guy said. "If you drop the bag, we'll let you go."

"Fucking get out of my way now," I said pointing the gun at this guy now.

All they did was dress back as I walked towards them. I took a step forward and they took a step back, two steps forward and they took two steps back as I was now getting desperate. Still no sign of them giving up their ground. So I dropped the rucksack on the ground as I could now hear sirens getting closer and closer real fast. When I did that I saw a gap open up between them. I saw my chance and still pointing the gun at them I dashed through the space they'd made. But it was too late. I didn't even make it to my fucking car. Armed police were arriving just as I turned the corner. I kept on running until they drove up beside me, nearly knocking me over with their open doors.

I dropped my gun and put my hands up. I knew it was over. Looking back now the sentence I received for that crime helped wake me up to kick my cocaine habit. I didn't kick it as soon as I came out but the suffering I went through for the next years played a huge part in me kicking my habit forever, but that was still five years away and I am proud to say I've never touched crack or cocaine ever since. The year was 1990 and the month was November. My first son was born just over a month later. I missed the birth. I was gutted and still am gutted about that till this day, even though he is now twenty-three years old.

CHAPTER ELEVEN

Yep! I was caught bang to rights on this one. And I knew I was in serious shit. It had been raining on that day as well but it didn't mean a thing lying on the wet ground with my arms stretched out sideways. I was told by the armed unit to put my face down, so even my face was right in the wet and cold surface of the road.

"Just keep still and you'll be alright," one officer said. I couldn't see because I was face down.

"Get the weapon out the way," another one said.

"Is it loaded?" one asked.

"Yeah," came the answer after about fifteen seconds.

I lay on that fucking road for about ten minutes until about another six squad cars arrived. But I knew that at least two weapons were being pointed at me all the time. As I lay there that day, many things went through my mind all at once. I wanted to fire at them or just try a kamikaze move and rush the officers. But it's like they could read my mind because they just kept telling me not to do anything stupid. Finally, I was cuffed and told to get up. When I looked up I was shocked to see the number of people around watching the drama. By now I was wet and dirty from lying on the ground. I was put in a van with armed police officers and taken with sirens blazing to Stoke Newington police station. I remember staring at the streets wondering how long it would be before I was back out on my corners. One thing I was sure about though at that early stage was that there was no getting out of this one. So I looked at the streets with the look of someone who knew he was going away for quite some time. With the sirens blazing, it didn't take long to get to the station. On the ride to the station, the officers did not say a word to me. They just stared with this cold look in their eyes watching for any movement I might make. But I could also detect some fear in their stares. Fear of the unexpected I suppose. They didn't know what I was thinking and what to expect.

When we got to the station, a welcoming party was awaiting me. About one million officers just standing around. Some in uniform, but most in plain clothes. I'd been to this station before. Years back on the robbery charge at maxims.

"What's your name son?" the sergeant asked.

"Anthony Spencer."

"Address?"

I told him my flat address, not Sandra's.

"Date of birth?" I told him that too.

"Can you take these fucking cuffs off? They're breaking into my skin," I said.

"You know why you're here?"

"Listen, answer the questions first and then the cuffs come off when you get in the cell," the sergeant said. I was by this time surrounded by the tallest and biggest officers they could find in that station.

"I ain't saying jack shit till these cuffs come off," I said.

"Ok, put him away."

These burly officers walked me to a cell and banged me up, taking the cuffs off at the door before they slammed it shut

The gun with bullets had my prints. They'd also got back the money. So I was definitely going down but with no money on the outside and Sandra was expecting our first child next month. I knew that drugs were to blame for this, nothing else. I kept thinking that I should have taken the advice I was given and went on this work with another two people at least. It probably would have turned out differently with another couple of pairs of eyes watching for anything out of the ordinary. We definitely would have spotted the crowd gathering outside if I had someone else with me. Damn. I sat in the cell holding my head in my hands, deep in thought. Then an officer came to the door and asked who my solicitors were. I told him and he fucked off leaving me to my thought. I thought of Sandra and the baby to come and how long it would be before I was with her again. Things I remember didn't look good. I just wanted to go sleep and wake up to find it was all a dream.

And I did go to sleep funny enough. When you're on crack, you don't get much sleep so it wasn't long before I fell asleep. But when I woke up, I was still there in the same cell and an officer was telling me that my brief was here. I got up to go to talk to the solicitor in the private room. He shook my hand and the first thing he asked me was, "Why so many witnesses Anthony?"

At that time I didn't yet know about the Tannoy system that had alerted the staff. I was thinking more along the lines that I'd been spotted by a worker who then got the other workers involved. So when he asked me that question, I didn't have an answer for him. I just shrugged.

"They've got so many witnesses who saw you and they're taking their statements right now. How are you anyway?" he asked.

"I'm fine. I need to call my girl and my mum. Can you sort that out for me?"

"Yeah, no problem. First though I need to know a few things. Did you have a gun and was it loaded?" he said.

"Yeah."

"Did you discharge any rounds?"

"Yep."

"At anyone in particular?"

"No, in the air."

"How many times did you fire?"

"Twice I think."

"What happened to the money?"

"I dropped it. I fired into the air to get them to move out of my way. It was either that or fire at them fucking bastards. In the end I dropped the money when I heard the sirens close by just so I don't shoot anyone. There were too many of them."

"Ok. Did you hurt anybody at all?"

"No."

"Did you point your weapon at the officers when they arrived?"

"I wish I did. But no."

"That's good Anthony. Now I need to know if you want to make a statement or not," he said.

"I'm making no comment to their questions."

"Are you going to fight it, then?"

"I don't know yet, what time is it?"

"Oh just gone nine p.m.," he said.

"Shit I need to phone to let my people know. I'll probably be here for a couple of days. I need to change these clothes."

I wasn't allowed a phone call that night. I was placed on a rule called' incommunicado'. This means that the police think it best that you don't contact anyone apart from your brief. I'd been in the cells since about 4 p.m. At around 6 p.m., I was driven to my flat to carry out a search. When we arrived, Mark, my flat mate, wasn't there thank God. My bedroom and the shared areas were taken apart piece by piece. All they found was a little bit of weed I always kept as reserve for when I was at mine. Then it was back to the station. They must have contacted my local station because no sooner was I put back in the cell before they came back and put the cuffs back on me and said we were going to my other address, which was Sandra's flat, which we had now been sharing for nearly a year. I only had weed at her flat so even though I was upset that her place would be turned upside down, I wasn't too worried. I did make them know that she was pregnant so to go easy when we got there. I saw her surprised look when we got there and she opened the door to about nine CID officers with me handcuffed to one of them.

"Babes I'm sorry you know, I don't know how they found out about this place," I said to her when I had the chance to speak close enough. "How are you feeling?" I asked.

"I'm alright. What have you done now?" she said with a very worried look.

"I can't even talk right now. But don't worry it ain't as bad as it looks trust me," I lied. It was a terrible situation really. I was thinking anywhere from ten years in prison for what I had just been arrested for. But I didn't want to alarm her at this point.

"Do you need anything?"

"Yeah my clothes and some food. Bring them up to Stokey police station in the day tomorrow please. Phone Leuchie and tell him what's happened and tell him to phone my solicitors and find out the score. He'll understand."

"Is that where you are?"

"Yeah, at Stokey. Listen babes, don't worry about all this just look after yourself right now, OK?"

The officers carried on searching while my girl and I carried on talking. I was still cuffed to one of them while Sandra was told to stand in the kitchen doorway so she was about ten feet away from me. She really looked pissed off and worried. But I kept trying to reassure her. I don't think it worked though. They found the weed, but that's all they found again and left the flat after about an hour. I got back to the station and went to sleep cursing the day I picked up a crack pipe. I still hadn't even been interviewed by the end of that first night so I knew I was in for a long stay at the station. I slept blissfully due to lack of sleep for so long. The next day I was allowed to talk to my girl and my mum. She, my mum, broke down over the phone and hung up. I wasn't allowed a visit, but I did get a change of clothes that day and some food. The clothes were needed as I'd been put in the white boiler suits and my clothes taken for forensics. My interview isn't worth talking about as it was all one-sided. They talked and I kept quiet. I was charged with Armed Robbery and discharging a firearm in a public place. It was only after the interview that I found out the reason why the shop workers had been outside waiting for me. The officers in the interview had mentioned the fact that the Tannoy system had been on. When they said this, they looked for a sign or a response from me, but there was none. But deep down inside I cursed myself and wanted to cry when they told me they had counted the money and it had come to thirty-nine thousand pounds. If only I could get a second chance at this I thought, but it was now too late. I'd had my chance and blown it. After being charged and remanded to court the next day, I was taken back to my cell. I think it was that night there and then that I swore never to touch that evil drug cocaine again. But first I knew I had to get my sentence and finish it before the true test would begin, how long away that was,

was anyone's guess at that moment. Court the next day was buzzing with police activity. Sandra, Frankie and Leuchie were there. I'd told them not to bring my mum because I didn't want her hearing what I was charged with.

Obviously I was remanded in custody to await trial. When I got to Pentonville prison in November of '90 I was like a celebrity, but didn't feel like one. There were so much Tottenham and North London people that I knew in that prison at the time. The police had a lot of success that year - it was unbelievable. That was the same year that Operation Bumble Bee, which was an operation to net burglars, started up. This was the same period the police had set up a fake sting jewellers in Tottenham to net robbers and they were all in Pentonville prison. So much known faces it was upsetting to be one of their successes. But I knew it was the crack epidemic that was the cause of so many of my friends and associates finding themselves behind bars. I knew this because every one of us without exception had been on crack on the outside. It was in our stories, our conversations and it was finding its way into the prison as well. I was determined though to use whatever sentence I received to kick my habit. A lot of my friends respected the fact that I had gone for big money but the way I see it, what's the point going for it but getting caught? You're better off free than banged up no matter what you tried to go for. They only saw it that way because they were in for burglaries, robberies and the likes. I would not have minded too much though if I'd got the money and then got nabbed later, at least then I knew my girl and child would be alright financially. I went in jail with just my Golf GTI and my gold collection to my name. No cash. That depressed me because I knew how much money I'd thrown down the crack pipe. My car and most of my gold didn't keep for too long after I'd got banged up. What was the point?

Anyway, back in prison I settled down to a routine going to court every other week until I was committed to await trial. When I saw how many witnesses the police had and what their statements said I agreed with my solicitor to change my plea from not guilty to guilty. The witnesses all said the same thing and I had no chance if I'd elected for a jury trial. So I settled down and waited for my sentence day to come up. Meanwhile being on remand meant I was entitled to a daily visit. Sandra, bless her, was there every morning even though she was expecting our little one.

. Without fail, my girl was there every day helping to keep my spirits up. And then she came up one Wednesday in December and told me to get ready for the news that she'd had the baby on that day.

"It's coming today Anthony, I know it," she said on the visit.

"But how are you so sure?"

"Listen, tell your brothers to start coming up for the next week or so because I just know it's today."

"Babes, I don't know how you can tell, but if you say it's coming today, then I won't argue. Phone Leuchie and tell him to come up on the visits and phone my mum so she can be there with you."

"I already phoned her this morning," she said. And boy was she right or was she right.

That very night she had my first son. I already had a name for him in my head. Koy Anthony.

On the next day, Leuchie came up on a visit. As soon as I saw him I knew Sandra had had our baby.

"Congratulations, rude boy. You had a boy at one thirty a.m. this morning. You've got one strong girl there, make sure you take good care of her bruv," he said as he sat down.

"A boy Leuch, wicked." All I kept saying on the visit was, "I've got a boy, I've got a boy." I was happy and depressed at the same time. Sort of like a bittersweet feeling.

"How are they? Who was at the hospital with her?"

"Mum was there. And I was outside the ward as well as Frankie. That boy is a true Spencer, trust me. Long legs and light just like us."

"How's Sandra?"

"She said to tell you, you got your wish. You got the boy you wished for! She says she'll be up as soon as she's on her feet. Have you got a name for him."

"Yeah. I'm calling him Koy with a K."

"Ok! That's a wicked name B," he said with a smile, I remember. Then he carried on to say, "That's an original name blood. What does she think about that?"

"He's my son, Dillon. But she does like the name though."

143

Leuchie also brought me up a fat parcel to celebrate the birth of my son. I remember walking off that visit and one fucked up prison officer by the name of Mr Ward, saying, "What you so happy about?" he said it like he was upset to see me happy.

So I told him, "Why, because I'm a father. My woman's had a baby boy ." I couldn't be bothered to argue and curse. When I got back on the wing, the boys were slapping me on the back, bumping my fists and generally happy for me. But when I banged up that night, I felt so sad I couldn't go to sleep I remember. That same night, the night officer on duty after lock up was an African man. At this point there were now a few black and Asian officers I'd noticed since I came back to prison. Or maybe it was because I was in a London jail. But either way it was a bit better. I called him to my cell and told him my woman was in the North Middlesex hospital because she just had our baby. I begged him to phone the hospital and pass a message on for me, just to let them know I was thinking of them. I couldn't believe it when he said he'd try. I didn't count on it though, I thought he might be fobbing me off, so as not to dampen my happiness. But to my surprise, he came back and told me he'd got hold of her ward and had passed my message on to the nurse on duty. And when I did eventually see Sandra, to my surprise he had made that call that night and she had got my message, which she said cheered her up very much. I'll never forget that screw and wherever he is today, I hope good things happen to him. I don't want to sound cynical or pessimistic but I do not think a white officer would have done this for me. This is why it is so important in a multicultural society to have a reflection of society all the way from the road sweepers to the police, to the Courts, to our judges, House of Parliament, local authorities and all areas of society. Ok I committed a crime yes, punish me yes, but having empathy sometimes comes from sharing the same life experiences and understanding people.

Anyway Sandra spent three days in the hospital. A day after she came out, I got called for a visit and I knew I was about to lay eyes on my boy for the first time. When I came out I didn't know who to hug first, Sandra or Koy. But she solved that problem for me. She passed him over and I took him and just stared at him. I looked at his hands, his feet, his face. I just stared with a smile on my face. She was smiling as well.

"What do you think babes? Your mum said he's a true Spencer," she said, smiling. I leaned over and put the biggest kiss I could manage on her lips. He was a true Spencer.

"Sandra, what can I say? We did it boy. Shit man. I really wish I was out there with you guys, babes."

"He's got your eyes and look at his feet just like yours." And then she told me how she'd got the message from the night screw.

"Did he give you trouble coming out?" I asked her.

"Yeah a bit. Just like his dad."

"I apologise on his behalf seeing as he can't speak," I joked.

"You can hold him better than that you know he won't break!" she was referring to the way I held him gingerly, letting me know I could hold him better and showing me how to.

"He eats all the time and he's got a loud month another trait he's got from you." I didn't want that visit to finish. I just stared at Koy and I even got to feed him on that first visit when he woke up. He was a hyper baby then and still is an active boy today. Love him to death. Anyway back in the real world, I couldn't stop boasting how handsome my boy was to my friends back on the wing. My heart was outside with them all the time, hoping they'd be alright. I knew I had a faithful woman and I was right. But I just prayed that nothing would happen to them. When I look back now I can see how funny or weird life can be. I say this because I was a month into my time in jail when my son was born and then nine months from my release years later when my brother was killed in a car crash. It's like a new life came at the start, but then a life was taken at the end. But I didn't know it at the time. I do remember going to church after I got sentenced and praying for all my family members. Praying that everybody should be there when I came out of jail. The worst thing that can happen to you while you're banged up is to lose a family member. And it happened right at the end to me. But all that was yet to come.

Christmas of '90 was very depressing for me. I didn't know how many more I would face in jail. I was still awaiting sentence so it was anyone's guess. Eventually my day for pleas and direction came up in February of '91. This is when you tell the court if you're pleading guilty or not guilty. I pleaded guilty, knowing there was no going back. I was now at the mercy of the judge on the day of sentencing. I was to be visited by the probation service after which I'd be brought back up for sentencing. So the horrible waiting went on. I just wanted to get it over and done with, so I could work out exactly when I was back on the road.

My son was now going on three months and was looking more and more like me as the weeks went by. Sandra always complained about his restlessness. He was wearing her out and keeping her up at nights. I felt bad that I wasn't there to give her a hand. Thanks to my mum, she got a break now and again. Remember Sandra did not have a mother, having lost her mum at fourteen, and any help my mother gave was very much appreciated. She still kept up the visits so much so that I wasn't getting visits from anyone else, not even my brothers. At the end of March '91 my day in Court came. They read out the circumstances of the robbery and all that and boy it did sound bad. The only thing that sounded good in my favour was that I didn't aim my gun at anyone or hurt anyone physically. Also the fact that I pleaded guilty went in my favour and probably the probation report stating that I had a young child and all that helped a bit.

By the end of that day I'd been sentenced to six years in prison. The judge said he had nine years in mind, but had run the other three years for the firearm concurrent to my six years because of the mitigating circumstances. And the fact that I hadn't fired at no one.

Was I chuffed with the six years? Yes I was. I was expecting seven to nine and even as much as ten. I knew people doing ten at that time for the same thing. So yes I was pleased it wasn't worse.

Sandra wasn't though. I got a visit in the court from her and my brothers and sister. I worked it out that I'd be out in November of '94. She didn't like the sound of that at all considering it was March '91. But then at that time your parole on a six year sentence was after two years although this wasn't guaranteed. And then you had another chance at parole after another year. So in principle in November of '92, I had a first go at parole and then again in November of '93 and only after that if I ended up doing the whole two thirds of the sentence would I then look to be out in November of '94. I broke it down this way to ease her into it gently but this also helped me in my first couple of years to deal with the thought of spending the next four years locked up. That cheered her up a bit. They all told me to behave myself so as to come out on time. I promised Sandra I was through with hard drugs as it was the reason for my downfall. But anyway I went back to prison with six years to finish or four years to be exact, before I could really be tested on the promises I'd made to my people. Now I had truly started my sentence. Six years sounded long that first night. But I wasn't gonna buckle or get weak. I'd done the crime, so I was prepared to do the time.

But I had a serious problem. How to look after my family as I'd always done on the outside, but to do it while locked up. I had my family but that wasn't going to be the answer, not for four years. It was too long to not imagine Sandra and the kids being in hardship at some point. Sandra still worked but she also now had a second child and if you count her looking after me with what little she had and visiting God knows where I would end up, it was like having a third child. The answer came in the Ville, as we called Pentonville. Heroin. Heroin wasn't a drug I was familiar with. I came to jail and realised what heroin could do for you, if you could get it in. It seemed as if everybody smoked that shit except me. Pentonville at the time seemed like a junkie convention. I didn't know too much about it until I got to that prison. I soon found out how profitable dealing heroin inside was. Fucking profitable. As I hadn't saved or left any money outside for my girl, I knew I had to make some inside. For a ninety-pound parcel you were guaranteed at least four to five hundred pounds back and that was after getting yourself sorted with everything that makes a man's sentence bearable inside. Things such as food, drinks, tobacco and later, phone cards. But in Pentonville at that time they didn't have the pay phones yet. So for every ninety pounds I spent outside, I handed back over four hundred pounds and always had munchies and tobacco and my smoke, hash or weed, which I swapped with the junkies, giving them a small amount of brown for a big piece of hashish. My people didn't even have to bring up hash for me when I discovered brown. With the brown trade, I knew my sentence would go a lot easier for me and my girl. So with the expertise I'd gained outside dealing drugs, it didn't take long before I was raking it in again. It felt good earning money inside. I found it a buzz that I could be locked up and still earn. I am a natural born earner. The pressure started to ease off my girl as she now had some money to take care of things and even some to save. I didn't feel bad dealing to these junkies. They were junkies. I saw it as a favour I was doing them because if I didn't have it, they'd be sick and ill. Some of them even gave me their wedding rings and some went out on visits and took their wives or girls jewellery to purchase that poison. I could not believe how profitable this drug was and still is, in prison.

But with the profits comes trouble from both inmates and officers. Nothing remains a secret in prison for long. Brown junkies are worse than crack junkies I soon discovered. They suffer serious pains when they haven't got and at that stage they'd even sell their wives for a smoke, whereas the crack buzz is a psychological one. No withdrawal or pains. Brown junkies in my books are the lowest of the cons. I'd only been doing business inside prison a couple of months before my first lesson of how these junkies are occurred. You see, when a junkie wants it he can talk and swear on everything he holds dear knowing full well it's all bullshit talk. Talk just to get his drugs. But being new to this trade I was a sucker for these sorts of speeches. I was losing money all the time when people would approach me for gear on tick or credit and end up moving to another jail. On this occasion this punk had twenty pounds for me when I found out he was going to be moved to a prison called Highpoint the next day. A friend of his told me just so he could get in my good books. When I found out, I called him in my cell and asked him if he was moving, when he said yes, I'd had enough of these junkies by now, so I lost it. I took out my prison tool, which was a piece of razor stuck into a toothbrush and melted together so the toothbrush had the razor stuck at one end. I swung the blade around the back of his neck, bringing it back around the front of his neck below his windpipe and close to his collar bone. It cut him in a semi-circle way from the back of his neck to the front. He went down holding his neck and begging for mercy. I told him that was for his other mate who had also pulled the same stroke a few weeks earlier and the rest of the junkies that thought they were smart. Then I told him to keep the twenty pounds and take the scar with him to his new prison. I also told him to clean up his blood from my cell floor. All the time I had my good friend Eggy from Stoke Newington keeping watch outside my cell.

The cuts weren't bad because the razor was thin and didn't inflict too much damage. The sort of cuts you didn't even have to stitch up. But it was noticed by the screws. The next day the boy left for Highpoint. About a week later around 6 a.m., seven officers came into my cell to turn it over. They were searching for drugs and weapons. I knew not to get caught with brown in prison as this led to extra charges in a proper court and more time on top of whatever time you were already serving. So I always slept with my parcel plugged up my bottom. Pretty uncomfortable I can tell ya, but these are the things we do for money and survival. This is the sort of thing that middle England would never understand. So when they came in on me, they found nothing. My weapon I kept in a friend's cell. But all the same I was told to pack my stuff, that I was moving to Brixton prison.

No notice, nothing. This was the first of six or seven moves in this fashion that I had to go through. My wars with the junkies and authorities had just begun. I suppose after that incident I could have stopped selling the nasty drug, but I had to support my family outside. It was risky because I was risking getting more time added on and it was unsettling because once you're marked as a dealer inside, a lot of prisons watch you when you get there and the first sign that you're dealing and you're off again. Six or more times I changed prisons but it had to be done. It kept me in things I needed and kept my family relatively comfortable. So off I went to Brixton to be allocated to a serving prison outside London.

I arrived at Brixton prison in the summer of '91. I arrived with brown left over from Pentonville prison so I didn't have to call up for more. I carried on dealing even though I knew I was marked and being watched. My first day in Brixton was depressing. It rained all day and I just stared out my window thinking about Sandra and Koy and Romaine of course. Brixton has that effect on you. It was a depressing prison. You got no favours from the screws. All they wanted to do was lock you up, feed you then lock you up again.

I went on my first visit in that jail and couldn't even hand out the money I had on me. The visit room is so small and compact it was impossible to hand it out. On top of that I was being watched so I told Sandra to hold on until I left that jail. She had some money put away by now anyway so I knew she was alright.

I went back on the wing determined to bug the screws for a quick move. About two weeks after I arrived there the screw in charge of allocating came to see me. I was allocated to Highpoint. I couldn't believe it. It was the same prison where that junkie I'd cut up in the Ville had gone to. I asked when I'd be moving and was told in another couple of weeks. I went without a visit because seeing as it wasn't possible to do anything on the visits and I only had to wait two weeks, it wasn't worth calling up for a visit. I eagerly awaited my move from depressing Brixton prison. I spent exactly five weeks in Brixton when my day came. I'd only seen my girl once in that time so I was looking forward to my move. I got to Highpoint prison in August of '91. It was my first adult prison outside of London and what a revelation it was.

We had freedom I'd never experienced in a prison before. Compared to Brixton it was like being outside. You were open from 8 a.m. to 9 p.m. You could walk about all day and the best thing of all was the card phones on the wings. Now this was where being a brown dealer really started to pay off. One ten pound bag, which was equivalent to about two pounds worth on the outside, got you five two pound phone cards. The same ten pound bag got you a gallon full of prison brewed alcoholic drink. This drink called hooch could get you drunk and merry if you got the right brew. The jail was full of brewers. That same ten pound bag you could also get cash for and the jail was full of cash. This is where having heroin and not smoking it really was a money earner. But like I said, I was already tagged as a dealer. So with this in mind I went about my business as quiet as possible. I didn't want to be moved and end up back in one of those lockdown jails in London. My girl was up within a week with a fresh parcel from Leuchie. And at last, I handed out my money, which I'd had now for about seven weeks or so. I think it was well over five hundred pounds at this point. There wasn't a lot of cash in Brixton as the visits were tight so what I sold I mostly sold for food, tobacco and hash to smoke as I couldn't get my own in. I'm sure Sandra was shocked to see me making so much money inside. But she was also grateful for this because I know it made life easier. She had given up work to look after Koy at this point too, so anything I could make inside came in handy. And also I paid for her fares to come up even though I was banged up. I knew the money was in safe hands as well and she wasn't going out blowing it and doing stupid stuff. With the arrival of my visit came the arrival of a fresh parcel. One of the first things I did on arrival at Highpoint was to ask if anyone knew where that punk I cut up in the Ville was. You see Highpoint has two sides to it. North and South side. I was on the South side, which housed the more dangerous or serious inmates while the North side housed the others. I found out he was on the other side. As free as we were on the South side, I heard the North side was a lot freer. It didn't surprise me. Anyway my business went on as usual and as low key as ever. But sadly it didn't take long for them to catch on. Like I already said, nothing stays quiet long enough in prison. Two months was all I lasted in that prison. One morning, just like in Pentonville, the screws unlocked my door to tell me I was going back to Brixton prison. I was gutted. I knew it was down to informers who owed me bits and pieces. Someone had probably put my name in the box saying I was bullying him. Which is the only way some of these dirty people know to get rid of their debts. So instead of grassing up blatantly, they sneakily wrote a note and put it in the letter box that would get to the officers. As we all put letters in the box to post out, you would never suspect anything if you saw someone walk up to the box and stick an envelope in it. The only thing is, when the officers emptied out the box the next day, they would be able to see any sneaky messages meant for them as we weren't allowed to seal our post anyway. So I was on the move for a third time back to that hell hole. The ride to London was depressing. I wondered where I'd end up from Brixton prison. I was doing too long to be kept there, I had to be re-allocated to another serving jail. It was the same routine again back in Brixton. Lock up, feed, lock up, feed. I'd only been there a couple of days when I flipped during one of these feed times. The thing is a lot of prisons prefer using assistant screws as servery workers. We call them assistant screws because they're inmates with screws' attitude. They smile, drink tea, make tea and have it with screws. These guys would inform on you with no remorse even though they're supposed to be one of us. It was over chips and sausages. I approached the screw boy serving the chips and quietly asked him to give me a bit more chips as I was starving. Now a sensible inmate would do it no problem but when it came to this screw boy, he spoke loud so the screw could hear him say he could not do it.

"Come on mate, just a bit more," I said, still speaking quietly.

"Can't do it mate," he said back aloud.

So I put my hand in the chips tray and picked up a big handful. But before I could get it in my plate, the fuckin inmate screw boy grabbed my hand with the chips like he'd personally paid for the chips. I wasn't taking that. Screw boy or not. I jumped over the counter, before he knew what hit him I was all over him like a rash. Bust lip, bust nose. The screws grabbed me and had me on the floor in their so called hold. I was dragged down the punishment block and stripped of my clothing. This was the first of many occasions where I was stripped. Anyway they took all my clothing and left me in a bare cell called a strip cell. I was still fuming but felt very vulnerable with no clothes on. It was my first visit to Brixton block and I didn't know what to expect but I'd heard about how the screws went on down the block. I geared myself up ready for what was to come. But no one came and nothing happened. A couple of hours later about ten screws and a deputy governor came to my cell and told me I'd be left down there on GOAD. Stands for Good Order And Discipline. This means they think you're too risky to inmates or staff to be on a normal wing in other words. I was also put on report for the fight. I was glad I'd plugged my parcel of brown that was left because they would have found it during the fight or when I got stripped. I was down the block for four weeks before they found a jail for me. Wayland was my fourth move. I was glad to get out of Brixton prison believe me.

Now Wayland was another story. It was like Highpoint, only more violent and too many people on the same thing. There were dealers everywhere you looked. Brown was everywhere. Knives everywhere. It was a jail you had to step cautiously or you might be stepping on someone else and they wouldn't be happy about it at all. I met a few of my friends from London in Wayland. And it wasn't long before we had a firm. Patrick Campbell, Blinky, Simon Chucky, Mark Lambie and myself. We had a solid team and weren't taking prisoners. We were armed and dangerous.

In no time we had a piece of the jail cornered. House block four to be exact. We even took over the pool room on house four. Other people came in there but they knew whose pool room it was. By this time I'd got well into working out down the gym. I was getting larger and larger. Wayland was alright for a while until the screw guessed what we were up to. I didn't live on house four but I was always there. The thing about Wayland though was that I didn't stand out like a sore thumb. There were too many other wise guys, so moving me would have been pointless.

I had my first birthday in prison on this sentence in Wayland. I remember getting a wicked visit from Sandra, Koy, my mum and Leuchie. I'd been in jail now for just under a year and still had three years to go. Time seemed to be flying I remember. I couldn't wait for the New Year and I was happy in this prison. Then the prison authorities decided to have a clean-up of the prison and surprise, surprise, I got caught up in it.

I remember being woken up one morning and told to pack up, as usual, and hustled off to reception. When I got there, I was checked through, handcuffed, and my bags were sealed. There were two hired coaches ready and waiting. When I got on one of these coaches, it was already half filled with other inmates I knew. It wasn't too bad, I thought. At least I wasn't alone. The coach I was on was headed for Wandsworth jail in London I found out when I got on. When they had everybody they wanted on it, it left Norfolk and hit the motorway for London. I was on the move again and I'd only done over a year. I wondered where I'd end up from Wandsworth jail this time, because Wandsworth was an allocation prison. When we got there, it reminded me of Brixton. Same old style building and probably would be the same sort of regime. I was coming to Wandsworth for the first time and didn't know what awaited me, but I was ready for whatever it was. I also had my firm from Wayland with me intact. The ride on the coach was lively as you can imagine. We were all undesirebles travelling together and it was fun.

Wandsworth prison was my fifth move in thirteen months. This I knew was a terrible record. The way I was going I soon would run out of places. I still had just under three years to go. Anyway I plodded on like a true soldier. Wandsworth was a true no nonsense jail. You could even see it in the screws. Being outcasts from one of the worst category C prisons in the land didn't help. And it showed in their attitudes towards us. Some of my co-passengers were taken straight to the block. I was among the lucky ones who went on to a proper wing. A-wing was supposed to be the longest or largest prison wing in Europe. I can't remember which. Anyway it seemed to take all day to feed this wing. It was back to the feed, lock up, feed, lock up routine once again. Remember back when I done my first sentence and I had that falling out with the guy from West London called Amos. The one I emptied my piss pot on. Well, I met him again in Wandsworth. But this time he was doing twice my sentence. Twelve years. Soon as I saw him on my wing, I knew it'd be only a matter of time before we would catch up again. I'd won that last argument, so I knew he'd probably want a 'part two' to it. So I geared myself up for the worse. I was right. About ten days after I arrived, we were down the gym. Now the gym had the nastiest showers I'd ever come across in my life. After the gym session, everyone stripped and waited his turn for the shower. There were about six showers to be shared between twenty or more inmates per session. So you had to wait for one to be free. Anyway there I was stripped, soap and flannel in hand waiting for a shower. I notice Amos still had on his PE kit. I ignored this fact and jumped in to have a shower when I found a free one. I kept my eyes on him all the time and just as well I did. Soon as I was soaping up, I noticed somebody pass him a piece of stick and saw him walking towards me. All I had for defence were my fists. If only he had a bigger heart, he could have hurt me pretty badly. I had the bigger heart on the day. There were no screws about, so I had to fight. And like my boxing trainer said a long time ago, 'the best defence is always attack.'

The fact that I attacked instead of standing there saved me from serious injury. He walked in the shower room, stick in hand, swinging aimlessly. I think he managed to hit me twice only with the stick before I wrestled him holding him close to me so he didn't have room to hit me. I wrestled him naked to the wet floor in the shower room. I was on top of him still moving my head this way and that way to avoid his swings with the stick. While avoiding his swings with the stick, I was head butting him, punching when I had the chance and generally going crazy on him. I knew I couldn't get off him and give him the room to swing at me. The screws noticed the commotion because someone shouted, "Screws."

I still didn't let go of him until I saw someone grab the stick off his hand. I punched and kicked him a few more times before we separated as the screws were now nearly on us. None of us wanted to get nicked for the fight. When the screws came in, I was back under the showers and he was just standing there making out like he was waiting on a shower. The stick had disappeared the way it appeared. That's prison for you. But I hadn't lost any stripes. He had blood coming from his face and he hadn't been able to use his weapon properly. I was lucky though that it wasn't a knife he had.

Nothing stays quiet in prison though, like I said. He was moved to another wing the same day. I think the blood on his face gave him away. Or maybe he was worried about comebacks after what he tried to do. I say try because he didn't actually hurt me.

I had a horrible Christmas in Wandsworth, my second one now in prison. It was now 1992 and I wasn't due out until '94. I was allocated to Parkhurst prison. Parhurst prison was the big sister prison to where Dillon had been sent a few years back, Camp Hill. I had been re-categorised to a B category. So where Parkhurst was a CAT B, Camp Hill was a CAT C. I suppose after my record so far, no category C prison wanted me. By this time I'd stopped dealing brown. Sandra had saved enough money by now so I could take a break while I was in Wandsworth. I just got my smoke when I went on visits. I looked forward to my move to Parkhurst prison as I knew it would be better than where I was. Parkhurst I'd heard was a prisoners' prison. Run by prisoners for prisoners. I was wrong. It really was an extension of Wansdworth. The officers were in charge and those inmates that had clout were white bad boys who colluded with officers when it favoured them but would murder you in jail at the drop of a hat. The jail was the most blatantly racist jail I'd ever come across. Both from inmates and screws.

In February after three and a half months of fucking Wandsworth I was finally on the move to Parkhurst. The trip wasn't just long, it was horrible. We had to cross the channel or sea or whatever it was, locked in the Sweatbox. Now I understood what Dillon meant when he told me about this trip years ago. While the driver and his companions went upstairs to the ferry lounge, we were down with the cars and lorries. And being winter I remember the sea was rough and it felt like the ferry was ready to go over at any time. No one came to check on us or make sure we were safe. If anything had happened, we'd have been first to sink with the cars and lorries while the other people were rescued. The thought was horrible; I couldn't wait till the ferry made its crossing.

When we got across the fucking water, I was relieved not to have drowned in my box in the van. We first had to stop and drop people off at Camp Hill, which I remembered when I saw it. The last time I saw it I was a visitor, free as a bird, this time I was a caged animal staring out from my little box window. Then the next stop was yet another prison, Albany, before we arrived at Parkhurst. The Isle of

Wight was more or less a prison colony. Three huge prisons. Those who lived on the island were either farmers or they worked in one capacity or another for the prison.

Parkhurst is a formidable jail just to look at. Recently they had a jailbreak from Parkhurst. I don't know how it could have been done without help from people or a person with keys or something. When that van pulled in that day in February of '92, I knew I was in a proper jail. Parkhurst prison housed some of the most dangerous prisoners in the land. And here I was at the age of twenty-three arriving there. I was determined not to let myself down in anyway. I had a sentence to serve just like anyone else. I was going to hold my own here, regardless of what happened.

With those thoughts going through my head, I watched as these massive gates closed behind the van. I was now the furthest I'd been from home, in the toughest prison I'd ever been, categorised the highest I'd ever been categorised and feeling the loneliest I'd ever been.

The prison van drove through the next set of gates and what I saw was an old hanging jail. I was sure that just like Pentonville and Wandsworth this jail was also once a venue for hanging prisoners back when Britain still hanged its people.

I was filled with deep sadness. Sadness I wasn't going to show to anyone at all. Just that type of sadness that you kept in and soldiered on.

Parkhurst here I come.

CHAPTER TWELVE

Back To The Future

So there I was all those years later and still had not learned my lesson. Sitting in another police cell with another firearms charge. It was now 2002. Labour had been in power now since 1997, and was to remain in power for another eight years until 2010.

Five months before this, 11 September 2001, or 9/11 had happened. The world was changing in a way none of us could have ever imagined.

My arrest and charge this time was not about me committing a live crime. I was being watched by the Trident Squad. This was a squad that was set up due to a lot of black on black shootings in our inner cities. This squad would later be assigned to deal with all gun crimes in London. Shootings and gun crimes in general became an issue that crossed racial barriers. The Indian and Pakistani youth were now getting heavily involved in drugs and guns, the Kurds were heavily into guns and heroin supply, the white older guys as well as the up and coming lot were shooting each other and even the recently arrived Somalians were starting to make their own noises.

So Trident was now charged with dealing with all gun crimes across London.

At the end of 1997 I finally split up from my son Koy's mum after eight years. I was now in a new and exciting relationship. Along with that came new ventures. Less street, more business with a dash of the streets.

By 1998, I had got into promoting garage raves and events. I started out of a small wine bar that only held about 150 people. The wine bar was owned initially by the first cousin of my fiancé at the time, Marcia. I decided to buy a percentage of the place. With that I started the only garage event in the hood.

It was an instant success. Within a very short time we were too big for the venue. It was at this time that I started my first ever business venture, Many Many Promotions. I have since operated many more both in the UK and in Spain, where I lived from 2004 to 2014.

I was so proud of setting up a business that for the first time since leaving college I thought I could impress my dad. I thought my dad would finally be happy that I was now doing something tangible. But I was wrong. My dad has a way of seeing through things. And boy, was he right or what!

I decided to recruit doormen to work for my company in 1998, firstly as a way to save on paying overheads to door staff agencies. At first I only had the one weekly event so, as there wasn't enough work, I allowed them to freelance all week and work for me on my Sunday event. Then I moved the company into other sectors to try to maximise potential. We went into four categories. Event promoting, event managing, door staff agency and debt collection.

During the week I used my door staff as debt collection agents. We collected for good guys and bad guys alike. We collected for baby mums ripped off by guys who sweet talked them, for printing companies who hadn't been paid for their work, for DJs owed money by promoters. The more our reputation grew the more work we got. And to be honest I don't recall a single debtor that got away. You did pay a high price for coming to us however, because we kept half the debt we collected. So we always told people to try every other means before approaching us. Basically, when they were sure the debt was practically written off we then stepped in. At least they recovered half what was owed rather than lose it all.

My events were also getting known. We had the heavy weight champion of the world at the time Lennox Lewis attend my event once, we had Bruce Scott the boxer who was a regular, we had the hundred-metre British sprinter Dwain Chambers attend a few times. I had people from Manchester, Birmingham and all over the UK attend my events every week. I had two main events by now. A Saturday night event at the Leisure Lounge in the City and a Sunday night event I'd started at the wine bar. That was the most popular one.

I later started a Sunday night/early hours Monday event at Trends in Hackney to replace Fulvia's Grays Inn Road event, which had been dying off for a while due to shootings and violence.

By now I had made my home base the Trends nightclub in Hackney. Trends had never hosted such events. It was known for its reggae events and Yardie gun shoot outs.

People thought I was crazy taking such events that are normally in the city or in central London to the inner city and to a club like trends with its reputation.

But I made it work. We became a full blown Sunday night to Monday morning weekly event.

I also had by now, a full team of doormen. I was also now able to hire them out to other events and make more money that way. All in all these were good times.

From 1998 all the way to 2000, the millennium and beyond. Then the raving scene really started to get dark. Shootings of people, of clubs and lots and lots of guns turning up at the club doors.

Remember when I said my dad was right? When I had boasted about my new venture two years previously? Well I would see what he saw in a few months' time, when I was shot outside my own club and event!

But by the beginning of 2000 I could only see things going my way.

At this time I was in talks with two other very well-known promoters. They were the two guys behind Freedom and Telepathy, a huge drum and base music event that had huge following among ravers. They were looking at the possibility of taking on a night club formerly called Shenolas or Bellair or numerous other names, located in Stratford.

The intention was to get involved with them and then I would have a much more up-market home base for my Sunday night event, which was now the talk of the town. We were regularly getting 500 to 600 people a night. If I could move to a bigger and better looking venue I was positive I could move attendance into the 700 to 800 range and more.

But in the mean time I kept doing what I was doing.

When I said I was now into business with a dash of street, I meant that I was still involved albeit not to the same degree as before '98.

I was always up for a quick move on a drug dealer. Or anyone I thought wouldn't go to the police. I had a good team of real soldiers who didn't give a fuck. Guys who will do what it takes to get what we came to get.

I was also selling bullet proof vests and bullets too. I had made a contact before 9/11 happened where we got bullet proof vests and bullets of all types from Turkey. But this stopped after security was stepped up after 9/11.

But I managed to find a way to carry on as I had built up the demand for my goods by telling all the different gangs that the other sides were buying up vests like crazy.

I would say to a friend from say a Brixton based crew that their enemies in New Cross had just bought fifty vests and 2000 bullets.

"How come you and your guys are only buying bullets bruv?" I would ask.

"What do you mean, Troubles?"

"Bruv do you know how much people have died with a gun in their hands?" I would reply.

"You and your people have got to start thinking about protection too, it ain't all about having guns and bullets, fam."

"I have as much vests as you guys need."

"For how much then, fam?" would be the usual question asked.

"Five hundred pound a pop, fam," came my reply. I was making 1000% as I was paying 50 pounds for each.

I would then repeat the same thing to the other side and so on. I single-handedly created a market for vests in the early 2000s all the way up until my arrest for the firearm in February 2002.

So on with Trends nightclub and my events.

We were by this time the premier place to be if you wanted to really party on a Sunday night into Monday morning in the underground Garage circuit.

We would be leaving my event with shades on at 7 a.m. as ever, while 'Joe and Jane regular' were off to work! Funny, but we had now been doing this since the eighties when acid came in as I mentioned in previous chapters.

Summer 2000 was great. I had one off events in the West end by now that were always packed.

On 30 September 2000, a Sunday night, myself and my head doorman/body guard Bigsy, a Jamaican with a big heart, were outside smoking cigarettes.

We had just finished with the crazy rush my Sunday night event always had at round about 2 a.m. to 3.30 a.m. This was when we took in the revellers from all the other clubs but whereas they all closed at 2 a.m. and 3 a.m. we went on till 6 a.m.

Anyway this night was exceptionally busy. Turned lots of people back as they were armed. My rules were: no weapons in my club, leave them in your cars. Quite simple really but not as simple as it sounded in reality, trust me.

I managed to run the only event where enemies could come to and be sure that at the least they were safe within the confines of the club. What happened outside was always out of my control.

There were sworn enemies dancing only feet from each other. Although there was always the possibility of violence, between myself and my door staff we always kept a lid on any potential explosion of violence. Until 30 September 2000.

As I was saying, myself and Bigsy had just found the time to breath and have fags outside after the crazy rush of the night, when we heard on our walkie talkies, "Code red, code red."

This was our code for all hands on deck or all muscle needed right now!

We ran back inside only to see about ten guys beating up this one little guy. They were hitting him over the head with champagne bottles, fists and feet.

The guys doing the attacking were my very good friends while the guy they were attacking was a stranger to me. I remember when this guy and his mate came in. They weren't our regular Garage music heads, this is why they sort of stood out to me and I had never seen them in the two years I had now been promoting.

To my shock there was Happy, a friend of mine out of Brixton, standing at the top of the stairs with a pistol in his hand taking aim at the guy getting the beat down. It looked to me as if he was just waiting for an opening or a clear path to this guy then he was going to shoot. He didn't have a clean shot because not just his guys but also my doormen were all now involved in the fracas. My doormen were trying to break things up, his guys trying to get the last hits in.

I was the only one who noticed Happy at the top of a flight of about eight steps taking aim.

I shouted, "Happy, No!"

I ran up those steps three a time and got to him in time to jolt him out of his mission. I grabbed him and his gun hand.

"What the fuck you doing?" I shouted at him. "Put that shit away now. How the fuck did that get in here?"

"Relax Troubles, relax," he says.

I decided to leave this for now as the imminent danger of Happy shooting this guy in my rave had passed.

I then turned my attention to the fracas still going on. My doormen had managed to pull the 'victim' away from the mob. I put victim in inverted commas for a reason. You will understand why, later on.

By the time he was pulled away he was a mess. His head was busted open, his eyes were swollen, his lips were fucked. Basically he was fucked up.

Myself and Bigsy took him outside, staggering from the beating. I leaned him up against a parked car and helped him stay up until he started to get his senses back fully.

"Where's your friend that came with you?" I asked him. "Where's your brethren?" I asked again.

"Inside," came his reply, still on the dizzy side. Just as he said this, out came his mate.

"Listen bruv, your mate just got rushed, don't know what he did, but he's wounded. Take him hospital now."

Bigsy chipped in and said, "Yeah man, take him hospital."

So off they went after a minute. As far as myself and Bigsy were concerned that was the end of it. But I still had to find out what happened to make them rush this one guy.

Not to mention the pistol in my rave!

So I went back inside to find out. After talking to the main players I found out that he had done the unthinkable.

I recalled that when Happy and his crew arrived, they came with their girlfriends. There was about nine or ten of them and they all had their girlfriends with them. Two of the girls were arguing loudly when they got to my door. The other girls were trying their very best to quell the arguing.

We had to kind of rush them through security at my door just to get them in. This explains why at least one weapon got in.

Anyway, the arguing between these girls carried on inside. From what I was told happened next, one of the girls started crying. And while the guys were trying their very best to stay out of it all, this guy, the one who got the beat down, someone unknown to all the players in this story, decides to get involved. Un-fucking-believable!

He apparently, shouted at the crying girl something along the lines of, "Stop your fucking crying," "Where's your fucking man?" "Stop your foolishness and go to your man."

With that all hell broke loose.

"Who is this guy?"

"What the fuck are you getting involved in girl's argument for?"

With this they started attacking him. Even the chicks jumped on him.

After hearing this I thought well he kind of deserved a lesson but he did not deserve to be shot.

I then turned my attention to Happy and that strap in my rave. It is much easier to stop an armed raver at the doors than it is to get him out when he already got through. And when they are your friends, it is even harder.

So I spoke to Happy and told him to go put the gun in his car. I decided it was better to get the rave back on track and not follow him up and down until he did as I said.

Once things settled down, I went back outside with Bigsy. Bigsy's car was parked right outside the club doors but a bit to the left, if you stand with your back to the doors.

At around 3.30 a.m., about forty-five minutes after the incident with the gun inside, I was standing on the pavement leaning with my back against the wall while Bigsy was sitting in his car, with the car door open and his feet on the pavement. We were just talking.

Next thing I see is, to my left, a figure approaching us. At first I couldn't see the face as he was still about twenty metres away.

As he got closer, we were finally able to make out that it was Mr Victim himself!

The same guy that was so wounded a short while ago that he could barely walk.

Shocked, I said, "What the fuck are you doing back here?"

He replied, "Them guys still in there?"

"What guys?" I said. Knowing full well he meant the guys that had beaten him up.

"You know, them, man," he replied.

"Bruv listen after you left, I threw them out too." I said. "Call it a day and go home because you ain't getting back in here."

Even though the guys were still in there, I lied to save any kind of plans he had. But I sure as hell weren't gonna let him back in.

He decided to walk off back the way he came, to my left.

Bigsy said to me, and I'll never forget this, "Why you let him walk off with his gun?"

"What do you mean, how you know he's carrying?"

"Are you mad? Look at him, he's a little guy just got rushed by nine or ten man. And then come back on his own to try go confront them," said Bigsy. "And you don't think he's strapped, fam?" He carried on.

"You know what bruv, he already got smashed up tonight, let him go. He definitely wasn't gonna get in," was my response.

And with that we carried on with our normal banter and forgot about the guy.

But, about ten minutes later I looked to my right this time, and could not believe my eyes when I saw a figure that looked exactly like this same guy.

That other corner he was approaching from was further away.

"Bigs, you won't believe who's coming back, fam."

"Who? The same boy?"

"Yep, look!" I decided I was going to take this guy much more seriously this time, So I said to Bigsy, "Listen, I'm gonna let him get closer and then I'm gonna show him my strap so he knows what he's really dealing with."

"Yeah I'm getting mine ready too," Bigsy replied.

What most of my ravers and friends knew, that maybe this guy didn't know, was that my event was probably the only event where all doormen were armed and most wore Vests. And I too was armed.

So I let him approach, kept my eyes on him, and as soon as he was close enough to hear me and see my weapon, I said, "What bruv, you came back again?"

But before I finished my next sentence with the action of showing him my pistol, all hell broke loose.

I was just about to say, "Listen this is what you have to deal with mate, you ain't coming back in. As I already told you." At the same time showing my gun.

I think I only got as far as, "Listen, this is wh-"

The next thing I see and hear is a flash and a bang. And then more flashes and more bangs. I truly believe what I did next saved my life. In a split second I realized that this little fucker had opened fire on me. A guy that I'd saved from my own friends only an hour or so before.

Now there are three steps from pavement level to the club door. Two steps and then the third step is the ground floor level of the club. I carried on pulling out my weapon but crucially, I started to climb the two or three steps backwards into the club. As I was on the pavement before the shooting started, the fact that I climbed those stairs proved to be my saviour.

By the time I'd got to the top step and level with the club, the whole time facing the shooter, I felt a burning sensation go through one leg. At the same time, I was now through the door and had my weapon pulled out. Next I heard the shatter of glass. I was now behind the huge club doors and out of the line of fire. I had my gun in hand by now so the next thing I did was what came natural. Retaliation! I leaned back out, using the door as cover, and pointed my gun into the darkness and squeezed. Nothing! Damn! My gun was still on safety mode!

So I pulled back in, took it off safety and squeezed again. Squeezing off two rounds. By the time I'd let the second round go, I knew it was a waste of time. At the same time, I noticed that Bigsy, who was sat in his car, had also been shot at. His windscreen shattering was the breaking noise I'd heard earlier during the incident. He was just also pulling himself together as I was.

All of what I have just described took about ten seconds. From when I went to give him a warning and show him my weapon, to when he started shooting all the way to when I fired back and noticed Bigsy was also shot at, all of that was in ten seconds or even less.

Then, I remembered the burning sensation I'd felt in my right leg. I said to Bigsy, "I think that fucker got me fam. Think he got my thigh."

As we made our way upstairs through the club, people were running out. They'd heard the shouting and screams from people on the ground level of the club who had heard or even seen what happened. I made it upstairs where my crew was. They took off my three quarter length leather coat I had on. They spun me around to see where I may have been shot.

A group of about ten or fifteen people ran outside, to look for this guy. They jumped in cars, scanning the area. Finally found out I had picked up two shots. In both my legs. Surprisingly, I was still able to walk. We shut down the rave, wrapped up our weapons as we knew the police would be there soon. At least six shots had just been fired. I fired two of those and he had fired at least two maybe three at me and two at Bigsy. Bigsy came out of it with no injuries but his windscreen was shot up. I was the only casualty.

Within minutes the pain kicked in. I got Danny the owner of Trends nightclub to drive me to Homerton Hospital. Just as we were leaving, the police arrived. The club had emptied by now. This was still just about 4 maybe 6 minutes from the first shot being fired. I made a quick getaway to get to the hospital. I had promised myself years before that if anybody that I cared for was ever stabbed or especially shot, I would not waste precious time calling an ambulance. Same rule applied if I was the casualty. The ambulance gets there but do not approach especially if it is a shooting incident. The police then take their time waiting for an armed response unit. By the time they give the OK for the medics to come to your aid a crucial thirty to forty-five minutes could have passed.

I was a witness to this strategy or procedure a year earlier at one of my events when an ex-soldier called Jamie was shot and killed. My first serious incident. I was to have two more after that, one being mine. But out of respect to the dead I will only fully discuss mine.

So we sped the ten or so minutes to Homerton. We got there and Danny and Bigsy disappeared. I limped into casualty and announced loudly, "Can I see a doctor, I've been shot!"

I'll never forget the look on the faces of waiting patients and hospital staff alike. A big black nurse on duty ran over to me. "Where have you been shot?"

"In both my legs as far as I know." It still was all just about twenty minutes since all hell broke loose. So to be honest its best to assume you do not know everything yet. I was rushed through to the emergency room, put on a gurney and then they tried to cut my clothes away like you see in movies and reality TV. I had also had this happen to me before and was another one of those promises I'd made to myself, that I would never again let them cut my clothes away if I was alert enough to stop them.

So I refused and offered to take them off. I still have those jeans today in 2014! Still with the four holes. Two entry holes and two exits.

So I'm whisked off to X-ray to see where the bullets were and what other injuries I may have. While in X-ray, the two members of staff appeared confused. I was in there far longer than I should have been. They kept whispering to each other and going back to the X-ray results.

Eventually they came over to me and the main nurse carrying out the X-ray said, "You are a very lucky man. We can see you have been shot in both legs. We can't find the bullet, so we think it has come out. And we also think the one bullet went through both your legs," she continued.

"Ok," I said, still listening.

"So you have been shot in both legs by the one bullet and remarkably both times it missed your thigh bones." She then added, "The chances of being hit in one thigh and missing the bones completely are slim never mind two. Very lucky, Mr Spencer."

So now I was getting that feeling that I was gonna be OK. I had actually come through this OK.

Now my thoughts went back to the events of the last hour and a half or so.

I was pissed off to know that someone I had stopped from being shot had come back and opened up on me. I was now thinking, I should have let Happy and his boys finish him off outside.

Then as I went over it all it hit me that had I stayed on the pavement level as I had been, this shot would have struck me in the abdomen for sure. The fact that I had climbed the 3 steps backwards had elevated me enough that when he fired his second, maybe third shot at me I was high enough off the pavement that they struck me where they did.

I called my fiancé to tell her what had happened, only to find out that the word had already spread far and wide that I had got shot.

Next the police came. I had already been told by the hospital staff that I was being segregated from other patients as was routine in these types of shootings. So when about eight armed officers came into the room I was being held in, I wasn't surprised.

It was now about 5.30 going on 6 when my girl arrived. Bigsy bless him had sorted himself out and had also returned. My brother Dillon was also outside the room.

The police insisted on not letting anybody in to see me. This is where I truly lost it. I hadn't been angry the whole time. Before I lost it, I was just more offended and pissed off than angry. Pissed off that someone I saved had tried to kill me. But now the emotion was pure anger. The officers' boss tried to calm me down explaining that they couldn't allow anyone in until officers from Trident had spoken with me. When that didn't work, they then agreed to allow Marcia to come in and see me.

At around 8 a.m., three plus hours after the incident, the doctors were finally satisfied that I was all clear of any imminent danger. They said they wanted to keep me in for at least twenty-four hours.

I had one question for this doctor. "Can I discharge myself?" I asked.

"We would not advise it, but seeing as they are flesh wounds and no bones have been touched, I suppose you can come in for at least a week for us to dress the wounds and make sure they do not get infected."

"You cannot discharge yourself yet Anthony," said the top police officer.

"Why not?" I asked him. "If the doctor says it's OK and I say I'm OK to go, then who are you to tell me I can't?"

"You need to stay here until the officers get here to speak with you." He added, "It is much better you wait here at the hospital."

"Well I'm going home," I replied.

"Ok I will get the necessary paperwork done and you will have to sign a document stating that you have discharged yourself," said the doctor and walked off.

"Anthony you will leave us no choice but to arrest you if you leave this hospital," said the top officer.

"What? Arrest me? For what? For discharging myself? Are you fucking joking?"

"No, for discharging a weapon," came his calm reply.

As I stared at him, my brain asking questions about what he meant, he answered my main question.

"We know you fired back. We know you had a weapon." He continued. "You can either wait and be interviewed when the Trident officers come on duty in an hour or so or we can arrest you and take you to the station, where they will speak to you."

With this I thought, 'You know what, seeing as I was already having a terrible day, fuck this, let them go ahead and arrest me.'

And so it ended with me discharging myself and promptly being led out of the hospital with all these armed police officers and placed in a van.

Pissed! At least they had more sense than to handcuff me. By now it's just gone 9 a.m.

We head to a police station in the square mile, in the City of London. There I'm kept in a cell. Can't believe I've been shot but still I am the one in a police cell. So I kick into custody mode and ask to call my lawyers. I don't even know what I've done wrong at this time. I know they're saying they know I fired back, how they know? Not sure. They haven't said I was under arrest for that, they got no gun. I'm under arrest at this time for obstructing the police. So you can see I'm all confused right now.

At around 11 a.m. now Monday morning, Trident officers arrive. Told them I wasn't prepared to speak to them until they tell my solicitor what I was there for. Eventually sat down with my solicitor and was glad with what she said.

"They are happy to let you go home Anthony, they just want to ask you a few questions about what happened last night." Then she dropped the bombshell. "Apparently your rave has been under observation for some time. And they saw what happened. All of it."

Whow! When? How? Who? Was what went through my mind. But I kept my exterior calm and did not flinch.

"Ok," was all I could say. "But I want you in there with me."

"Ok then, are you ready?"

"Yep let's get it done, I need to go home."

So I went through the usual routine of, "Who shot you?" "Did you see them?" "What was it about?" "Was it about drugs?" "Did you have a firearm?" "Did you discharge a weapon?" etc, etc.

Then, "You do know if you don't co-operate with us you cannot claim funds from the crime victims funds?"

I honestly looked at these officers and thought, are these guys serious? But I just didn't answer. What made them think I wanted any money from their poxy fund. Fuck their fund.

So that was that. I was released and on my way home. The end of a very mad day that will eventually lead to the reason I was now sat in a prison cell on a firearm charge.

Because from that day, 30 September 2000, I never again went anywhere - and I mean anywhere - without my trusted strap on me, under my car seat or very, very close by!

Even a trip to the newsagents on a Sunday morning, I would be strapped.

Now from what I later heard, the idiot that caused this whole episode with his lack of tact in speaking to people and getting involved in an argument that had nothing to do with him was later shot himself. Apparently five days after he shot at me. Do not know what became of him to this day.

I had daily appointments with the hospital for a week to keep my flesh wounds clean. On my first appointment later on in the evening of my release from hospital, I get there and tell them my name and why I was there, the lady I was speaking to turned round and said, "Oh, so you're Anthony Spencer?"

"Yes Why?"

"We have had lots of calls inquiring about you. We could not find you in any wards so we didn't know who they were talking about."

"Oh really?" I said. "I was shot last night but I discharged myself at around nine a.m. this morning."

"Well lots of people have called in asking if you were here and what had happened with you and wanted to know if you were OK," she said.

I left the hospital and drove over to Trends, the scene of my shooting. It was still all cordoned off. A couple of uniformed officers stood outside. I couldn't see me having my rave the coming Sunday as usual. I know some of you may think I was mad to be considering my next event at the same spot, less than twenty-four hours after being shot, but as we know attack is the best form of defence. Showing my face and keeping my show on the road was important in letting people know that I wasn't affected by what happened.

By this time the finishing touches were being put to the new club that we called EQ's nightclub in Stratford, East London. We expected to open to the public in about two weeks. This meant that I only had one more Sunday at Trends. We had already had flyers printed weeks before and had been handing them out to ravers and also announcing we were moving during the events. So people already knew. My birthday was in two weeks as well so I had a big show/opening night planned.

But I still had to deal with coming back to work on the following Sunday, 7 October.

On around the Wednesday I got calls from a few people asking if I had gone past Trends lately. I said no not since the Monday the same day I saw the two cops outside.

When I asked why, they laughed and just said, "Drive by there, fam, you're not gonna like it, though."

So I think it was Thursday that I drove by and boy was it annoying. The police had put up these large metal boards that they generally put up at the scene of any serious incident where they need 'information' from the public. One of these was right by the fucking club doors. Unbelievable!

I was thinking, 'How the hell am I supposed to have my rave in three days, when everyone knows I'm the shooting victim, and they have to walk past these notices asking for any information.'

Friends and family advised that I should just close the event for that week seeing as we were moving anyway the following week. But

I thought it was best to soldier on and keep the show going. I even had to talk Danny into opening as he also had doubts.

So we did just that. Come Sunday the seventh, a week after the shooting, the metal boards were still there, the ravers came, we made sure we were on high alert, but I warned everyone that I had found out that the police had some observation post opposite the club but I didn't know where. So to warn them of any illegal activities they might be involved in outside. The night passed off well, it was our last night in Trends.

The next Sunday, 14 October 2000, was Club EQ's opening night as well as my birthday night. I had stars like Romeo of So Solid and a host of A List DJs entertaining. It was a great feeling to have a new home for my events and a handsome home it was. This did not last long however. Within two months of opening, a good friend of mine was dead outside the club.

I did promise earlier that I would not discuss the dead or go into their stories out of respect to them and their families. But I need to write this so the reader can see how situations around you can influence your life drastically.

I had my biggest event to date planned for Christmas Eve 2000. It was going to be a fantastic event and I was hoping to get upwards of a thousand people. It had all started off as I envisaged. Got busy real early. It promised to be a great night.

It always seems to kick off at about the same time. This was two months after I had been shot. At around 3 a.m. I and my ever loyal bodyguard Bigsy spotted some commotion in a corner of the club. A group of about eight, maybe more guys were scuffling. We ran over along with my other door staff, who were on duty in the main room. Before I even got to them I knew this was a problem because the faces I saw standing in that corner earlier were really sworn enemies. They only tolerated each other at my events. But you knew that it was a time bomb waiting to go off if, the wrong thing was said, the wrong action was taken or just anything in general that could spark the fuse. The saddest thing of all was all sides were my friends. Some I grew up with, some I'd rolled with on many different levels and many only came out because it was my event and they felt safe.

When we got to the problem, it was really a flare up caused by my friend from Hackney, Jay's people being told by one of their girls that someone from the other side, my real crew, Mark and the rest had tried to approach her in some way or another. This then led to verbal insults and then a bottle of champagne being thrown at my lot. So it kicked off. We jumped right in and broke them up. In the fracas, one of Jay's guys discovers that his Rolex watch had fallen off his wrist. So now his whole crew want to block the exits as they think Marks people or people around them have seen the watch and didn't want anyone leaving. So I instruct my guys to turn on all lights so we can all search for this fucking watch. The party goes on but lights are on in full and not much partying is going on.

I recognized at once that this situation was potentially more dangerous than most people realized as both sides were capable of wiping each other out and I was prepared to bet my bottom dollar that between them they had enough weapons outside to take on a small army. So as Jay's people and some of my doormen carried on looking for this watch, I called Bigsy and my most trusted doorman Robin over and told them it was imperative that we split these guys up. We had to get one side out of the club and hold the other back at least 20 minutes or so before getting them out. We could not run the risk of a shootout outside and someone being smoked. So I gave instructions on how to go about this. Meanwhile I went back to trying to find this guy's watch and to see if we could tell who may have picked it up in the confusion. Lights are still on.

When after about ten minutes of searching we could not find the watch, he decides he wants three thousand pounds from myself and my partners. Compensation for his watch! Jokes, I thought. In the end he helped me decide which side I was going to put out first. Remember these are all people I've known for a very long time. Way before I was doing raves. So I told Jay to calm his crew and that I need them out as I didn't want them to run into Philly, Mark, Shots, Malkie and the rest of my crew outside. I think he agreed with me as they really did not pursue the Rolex matter much more and took their time leaving. I went with them along with Bigsy and other doormen and we watched them leave and walk towards their cars. Phew! One mission accomplished, or so I thought. Next mission was now to keep my guys in the club for at least twenty or so minutes before letting any of them go outside. So I went about this mission with military precision. And succeeded. We kept them in for as long as I thought was enough time for Jay and his crew to have been well away from the borough not just the area.

Then I went outside with Mark and the rest and said my good bye. It was now maybe 3.45 a.m. on Christmas morning.

We all went back to partying and working and forgot all about it. The rest of the night passed off with no further situations. This had been our first real serious issue since EQ's opened. At around 5 a.m. when revellers started leaving, I started to get calls from people I'd seen leave like a half hour before saying there was a road block on the road and no cars had been able to leave since leaving the club. I didn't understand what was going on so I went outside to have a look. And to my surprise the road was packed with cars that were stood still. This was not good as only about fifteen percent of people had left the club. Majority were still inside. If the road was this bad now, it was going to be terrible when people really started to pour out.

So I took a walk up towards the top of the road where the traffic started. When I rounded the bend I saw lots of police cars and officers. It didn't make sense what I was seeing so I carried on walking until the road straightened out and I could see there were even more officers, some in forensic white suits and I also saw there was a forensic tent in the road, slightly to the left but in the road itself and not the pavement. As there were about three clubs including ours on this road I just assumed it was some incident related to the other premises. But it all looked very, very serious.

I found the closest police officer and asked him what was going on. He said he could not say and asked who I was. I introduced myself and told him I was the organizer of the event in the EQ's and that at 6 a.m. I would have about 700 to 800 people leaving all at once, so wanted to know what was going to happen.

Can't recall exactly what he said. Anyway I walk back to the club and tell my DJ and MC to tell the people that there had been an incident about 200 metres from the club and the roads were blocked. I told them it had nothing to do with us so they shouldn't worry. This was what I thought at this time.

When we start turning the revellers out, the traffic was still bad but we noticed that the police were going to every car individually to get the details of everybody within the car and then letting the vehicle through the check point they had set up. So traffic was moving but really slowly.

It took me the best part of an hour to get through and then I drove past this tent I had seen earlier when I'd walked up. I could not see into it but experience told me there was a body lying in the road inside the tent. You couldn't tell if this person was run over, was shot, beaten or collapsed from being drunk.

I sort of put it out of my mind and carried on home to get some sleep before Christmas day festivities kicked off at home. I must have just started to drop off sleeping when the first calls hit my phone. It was one of my guys, the second lot that I had let out of the club after the scuffles.

"Yeah hello fam," I answered the phone.

"Bruv have you heard?" came the voice on the other end.

"Heard what fam?" I said, still in sleep mode.

"Don't you know what happened after you let us out last night?"

"No fam, what happened? What's going on?"

"Booooy, after we left man, them idiots were still there innit. Someone blocked their car in so they couldn't get out. We walked past them as they're trying to get their car out."

By now I sat straight up, thinking oh my God, don't tell me that body on the street had something to do with us and our night!

"Yeah and what happened?" I asked.

"Well we walked past them and no one said nothing. But Philly and Jay caught up in some name calling shit and next thing I know Philly ran over to their ride and grabbed the steering wheel." He carried on. "Us lot was shouting to Philly to leave it man cos them man didn't look like they were trying to beef really. Then as me and shots are going over to the ride they must of thought we was coming over to do something."

"Yeah and then what happened?" I asked, trying to get to the bottom.

"Next thing I know fam, I hear the car start crashing into other rides blocking them in as they're trying to get away, Philly, all now was still holding on to their ride and throwing punches or something. Before we reach the ride, they broke free from the rides blocking them in, start driving off, then I heard boom!"

"Who shot who?" was my next question.

"Philly dropped off the car as they sped off and landed on the road fam."

"Oh no, no, no, no," was all I could say. "Don't tell me that was Philly lying in the tent on the road, fam. Did you lot go over to see if he coulda made it?" was my next question.

"We went over to where he fell off the car and fam he wasn't good man. They got him in the head innit cos that's all they had to shoot at. His whole head was in their car tussling with them."

"Oh fuck. Fam he's gone. When we left this morning there was bare traffic on the road. Down the road they had them forensic tents with bare forensic officers. The fucking last thing I thought was that this had anything to do with us."

"Where's everybody?" I then asked.

"Boy, the ride is burnt out, man's gone home," he replied.

With this I knew my Christmas was not going to be a very good one. I had just lost a very close friend. Even though I tried my damnedest to avoid something I could see was possible. Who would have thought that some fool would choose their car to block in and therefore ruining my plans to keep these guys apart. And as far as I know they shot my friend because they were scared of being trapped in a car and shot at. This was the beginning of what made the police determined to stop my events. I tried to go back to sleep. But couldn't as more and more calls came in asking me if I'd heard what happened and who it was. In the end I gave up on sleep.

I also knew the club was in big, big trouble. I had a New Year's Eve event planned a week later. That was in doubt. This was my main income and I knew it was now on shaky grounds.

The club was shut for the next two weeks. All events were cancelled. Forensics were camped in the club for about a week.

As if this wasn't enough, when we re-opened in late January 2001, the council started to come down on us. So much so that as a promoter, I was told to submit my DJ line up to my nearest police station two weeks in advance. This was unheard of. They basically wanted to vet my DJs. When I asked why, I was told there was intelligence on DJs and their following fans. That some DJs had more gangsters or rowdy people who follow them than others. So basically if they didn't like my line-up they would refuse me permission to have a rave. About May 2001, I moved my event to club Aquarium. The only club I know with an in-house swimming pool. I did this in an attempt to move further west and get away from the confines of the police and council. I changed the name of the rave to Strawberry Sundays.

Things settled down a bit more. We had an uneventful next six months or so. Christmas 2001 came and went and we welcomed 2002. Although war was on the horizon with 9/11 having just happened and Tony Blair and George Bush junior on the march to get the Taliban, it was a peaceful Christmas as far as we were concerned.

I was still packing my weapon every single day. Until one day in February, the seventh to be exact. The day started off like any other day. It was a Friday and I had my usual appointment to pick up my son Koy from school along with his older brother Romaine, my step-son for eight years while I was with their mum, but still maintained a steady relationship with him even after five years now of not being with his mum.

As normal a day as it was, it did start up with some bad news. I got a call from friends to say someone we knew, who had just got released from prison in Manchester and had come down to London as a lot of different Manchester crews were now in London, had been shot and killed in an ambush on a BMW in South London. I was told to buy the evening standard of that day.

On that same day, remember my bullet-proof vest and bullets business? Well that day I had about three people to meet. So I went about meeting all the people I had to meet and dropped off what I had to drop off.

What I didn't know was that my whole movements on this day were being watched by the police and SO19 firearms officers!

After finishing my bullet and bullet proof runs, I headed towards my sons' school in Northolt, west London. On the way I stopped in

Wood Green and bought some Kentucky fried chicken and a drink for the drive but I also remembered to buy the Evening Standard like my guys had told me to do.

When I looked at the front page, I saw a shot out BMW and my friend lying dead on the front passenger seat. I didn't have time to read it all so I kept it on the passenger seat next to me so I could snatch moments to read the story from the newspapers perspective. We already knew who, why and details of what happened. But it was always good in a way to see what the rest of the world made of it all.

So I started my journey west on the A406 north circular road. As I drove I ate my Kentucky meal. I got to the usual traffic jam approaching the Hanger Lane round about after about twenty minutes of driving on the north circular. This traffic was always notoriously slow. Always! So now I had the perfect opportunity to catch up with the newspaper story.

So I started reading and inching forward as traffic moved, being careful not to kiss another car in my attempt to read and drive at the same time.

I suppose the fact that I believed I wasn't committing a crime at that time, the fact that carrying a gun was now second nature to me, the fact that I had carried one now daily for nearly a year and a half, even been stopped by police with my gun and got away with it, led me to not even monitor what was going on around me. But I think even if I had tried to be alert, knowing what I know now, I still would not have seen it coming. They were that good. The vehicles they used were totally blended with where I was now living near Stamford Hill in Hackney/Tottenham, a Jewish area where old Volvos and old estate cars were a regular sight.

So, I carried on reading and driving my car as slowly as the traffic allowed.

Next thing I notice is about twelve or fifteen armed men with unconventional weapons surround my car shouting stuff I couldn't hear. Honestly, I was so relaxed and not expecting anything at all that it must have taken me about five real time seconds for it to sink in that this was the police and they were talking to me!

Then their words started to come through my ears.

"SHOW US YOUR HANDS!"

"DON'T MOVE!"

"GET OUT OF THE CAR!"

"DON'T MOVE!"

"ARMED POLICE!"

"KEEP YOUR HANDS WHERE I CAN SEE THEM!"

All these different commands were coming from all different officers. My brain was scrambling to work out just what the fuck was going on.

In all that chaos I noticed they were also filming with a camcorder! There was a cop slightly behind my driver's door with a camera.

Then my eyes fell on one particular officer. I can't tell you why I noticed him. I have gone over it so many times and told this story so many times and the only thing I can think of was he just seemed to twitch, he looked unsettled and he, barked the next command at me amongst all the other commands they were all barking at me.

He said, "UNDO YOUR FUCKING SEATBELT AND GET ON THE GROUND!"

Then they all started shouting the same thing. "Undo your fucking belt and get on the ground!"

In a split second I realized I couldn't. My gun was right by where the belt clip was to undo the seatbelt. On my left side, in my waist band. There was no way I was going to reach for that side at all.

So quick thinking, I shouted back, "No! You fucking come in and undo my belt!"

"I SAID UNDO YOUR FUCKING SEATBELT AND EXIT THE CAR WITH YOUR HANDS UP!"

"Fuck you! You come in and undo it!" I shouted back. "My hands are on the steering wheel," I then said, keeping my hands firmly on the steering wheel.

This stand-off went on for about a minute from the time I noticed that one officer changed the instruction to when they could see I wasn't going to budge. But all in all it had now been about three minutes since they surrounded my car.

Eventually that same guy, the one who was twitching relented, lowered his Heckler & Koch machine gun and opened my car door. They leaned in, undid my belt and yanked me out of the car and onto the road face down.

I couldn't believe it! Not again! Armed police, on the road face down just like back in 1990.

They picked me up after handcuffing me, put me in one of their cars and began clearing the motorway. As I sat in the car I really then started processing what just happened. Firstly, I still had my gun in my waistband because they hadn't searched me yet, then there was the twitching officer, then the change of commands to undo my belt and the filming cop. It dawned on me that they probably set out to kill me on that day. Just like they shot Mark Duggan in 2011. Years later.

Why do I think this? Two weeks before this, a good friend of mine from East London, Crackers, had a narrow escape from the same police crew. They actually shot at him after he had stopped. Luckily for him the bullet hit the metal that divides the front door from the back door on the driver's side. When the bullet hit, it split into fragments. One piece carried on and struck him I think in the face, while the other fragments lodged in the side door panel and went elsewhere. He floored his car and so did not give them a second chance to take another shot. He managed to get away and go into hiding. He contacted his mother who called Scotland Yard direct and accused the police of trying to kill her son. She told them that if he was wanted she would bring him in personally to Scotland Yard but not to the same officers who had just tried to kill him. So I was in no doubt that today was supposed to be my death day! You know, like your birthday?

I think I threw them into confusion by refusing to undo my belt. I believe if I had reached for my belt, they would have shot to kill me and claimed that I was reaching for my weapon, which was in exactly the same place as the seatbelt buckle. I will return to my opinion about the killing of black and ethnic men by the police later in this book. I have seen too much to not believe that a very long time ago the police probably set a quota on how many of us they kill in any given year.

So, back to my own situation.

My Mercedes 500SL which was what I was driving at that time was moved off the motorway. Then an officer came and explained to me why I had been arrested. They still hadn't let on that they had been following me for days. So I still did not know this.

I was then transported to Stoke Newington police station. Again!

On the ride back to North London my mind refocused on Koy and Romaine. Koy had now turned eleven and Romaine was fourteen. Although they could get home on their own I felt the need to ask to contact them to tell them I wasn't going to make it for our in-the-week date. So I asked the officer to allow me to call my kids. They agreed, so I was able to tell them not to wait for me at the school and go on home.

Now the next issue was the gun I still at this point had in my waistband. So as the officers were trying to talk to me I began my attempt to at least dump it somehow, even though my hands were cuffed. I began trying to loosen it, dislodge it and generally try to get it free enough to let it drop.

Anything was better than having the gun on me! At least I had a chance if it wasn't found on me. I could claim a stitch up and all sorts.

By the time we got back to North London the gun was so loose but not completely free that when they pulled me out of the car, as soon as I stood up straight it fell out. Fuck! Fuck! Fuck!

And so began my last day of freedom for nearly two years. And just like in 1994 when I lost my brother Andrew before I got released from my other serious sentence, I would lose another family member by the time I was released this time too.

CHAPTER THIRTEEN

Return To The Past

So back to the early 90s and my first firearm sentence!

Now I was in Parkhurst having a real miserable time of it. The distances to travel for visits for Londoners like us were diabolical. There was a bus ride that picked people up at different spots in London and brought them up to the jail. But it was such a journey that it wasn't something you wanted to put your family through very often. My visits went from two a month to mostly once a month and sometimes twice.

It was also much tougher to get the drugs in at Parkhurst. The screws were more alert and generally a lot tighter, security wise. As miserable as things were for me, there was a blessing in disguise coming my way, but I didn't know it yet.

The dreariness of Parkhurst got me back in the gym doing my boxing training once again. First time in years. I focused on getting fit and somewhere in the back of my mind was the question, 'what do I do when I get out.' So I started to see myself getting back into boxing, this time though I knew I'd be more committed to it as I was older and wiser. So I put my all into trying to do as much on the inside to help me minimise the catching up I definitely would need if I went back to boxing.

It didn't take long for me to get into another mix-up though. This time with officers. Over a pillow! Can you believe it?

Basically my cell was searched one afternoon and the officers were probably upset they did not find anything that they took two extra pillows I had on my bed, leaving me one. Anyone who's ever been in prison will tell you how flat these prison pillows are. I always get additional pillows by hook or by crook and it is always a battle to keep them especially when you have petty officers who just want to make your life a misery.

It started by me refusing to lock up unless I got my pillows back. I was told I didn't have a doctor's certificate and therefore couldn't have one. I was given a 'direct order' as they call it, to return to my cell. I just felt at this point that I had nothing to lose so I refused. This led to the officers blowing their whistles, which was a sort of alarm to call for back up.

So it kicked off. Me against about ten officers. They won, of course. And I was carted off to the block. I wasn't to know it but this was a blessing.

I had my next visit while in segregation. It was impossible to have a decent visit while in segregation. I'd had lots of them before now but the Parkhurst one was the worst I had ever encountered.

One morning at around 7 a.m., while still in segregation, my door opened and I was told to pack my stuff and be ready to ship out in an hour.

"Why, where am I going?" I asked.

"Just pack your kit son, you will be told at reception," came the officer's reply.

I thought, 'You know what, it can't be no worse than this shit hole.' So I went and got showered, packed my belongings and waited for them to come back.

When I got to reception about an hour later, I was told I was being moved to Maidstone Prison. Didn't know where that was, what the jail was like or anything. When I asked another inmate at reception if they knew where Maidstone prison was, I was shocked to hear what he told me.

"Mate," he said. "That is in Kent. I hear they got a swimming pool there, you can wear your own clothes and you're out of your cells all day."

"Seriously?" I asked, not sure whether to believe him or not. "What, a swimming pool for inmates?" I asked. "Are you sure bruv?"

"Yeah mate, I've got mates there right now. And it's easy to get to from London and all."

He went on. "Nah mate you're laughing bruv. You just got a touch leaving this shithole to go there."

"Where are you going?" I asked.

"I'm going Wayland," he answered.

"Yeah I've been there mate. Got chucked out. It was OK really. Screws are not too bad. And you can get a shag on the visit if you get the right tables in the back corners. They dim the visit room lights once visits start," I told him.

"Sounds alright," he said, then asked, "what's bang up like there then?"

"Not bad. Out from about eight-ish until lunch and then from two-ish until tea time. Then you're out until eight and bang up," I added. "Plus you're allowed to roam from wing to wing and go see your mates on other wings."

I started looking forward to my next prison with excitement. A prison with a pool? Wow. If this was true, I was going to make sure I didn't get in any bother so I could stay there for as long as possible if all I was hearing was true.

Well I set off on my journey with another couple of inmates who were also being moved to Maidstone. I found out that they had requested a move to this prison and had to be good to get this move. So I couldn't work out why I was being moved to such a good prison. But during the journey, I got to find out more about this place. It just sounded like the place to be. The swimming pool was confirmed, even by the officers overhearing our banter, wearing your own clothes as a convicted prisoner was unheard of at that time. It is much more common now, but not back in 1992. Huge sports facilities, relaxed atmosphere. But what got my ears twitching was what one of my fellow inmates on the bus said. He said it was a good place for Home Leaves.

Home Leave is when you are allowed out of prison to go home, usually for a weekend, and are trusted to return. Generally, if you do return, it opens doors for you to keep getting more leaves and eventually parole or an open prison.

"My mate's doing a nine, and he's just had a Home Leave even though he's still got three years left of his sentence," he claimed.

"No way!" I said, not believing that this was even possible.

The people I saw get home leaves in all the other jails I was sent to were inmates that had months left. Like three, maybe six months left. So hearing that people were getting home leaves after serving just a third of their sentences and with more time than I had left to do was very, very promising indeed.

But then I thought, nah, those things only happen to those who haven't fought the system, kept their heads down and basically towed the line. I was hardly that. So I didn't let it fill me with false hope. But it was good to know that these things were possible.

By the time we arrived at Maidstone I couldn't wait to go in and get to my cell. It was the first time that my spirit and soul were at peace about arriving at a prison.

After getting processed through reception, I was sent to my wing. When I got to the wing, I put my stuff down in my cell and took a walk about. What I saw astounded me.

There was a kitchen for inmates to cook! What? Everybody was easy going, the staff were joking and laughing with inmates, phones everywhere to call home up until 8pm. I asked about the swimming pool and I was directed where to go. It was an area of the prison called The Sports Field.

I made my way there. When I got there I was truly impressed. It had a running track the same as any sports centre on the outside, which ran around a huge football pitch. Not your regular prison indoor gym astro turf that some prison gyms had. This was huge and outside. To the right, there was an enclosed part with a door. When I went through the doors I saw it.

A fucking swimming pool. This was too much. I felt like I had died and gone to prison heaven!

Then I went into the gym proper, where weights are kept. Great I thought. And for the first time I was in a prison where you just walked out of your wing and went gym as you pleased. Just like you were outside. I went downstairs in the gym and saw what made me even happier. A fucking punch bag. And skipping ropes. This was too much.

It was now summer of '92 and the sun was out on this day in July. I was getting close to my second full year in custody. In November I would be half way to completing my sentence and be up for my first parole too. I had to do two thirds or four years to get out without parole, but was eligible after a third or two years. I knew with four months to that first parole date I had no chance of getting it as I hadn't been the best prisoner out there. But you had another one after a year from that first one normally. So the way I saw it, I was aiming to maybe get my head down now and look towards November '93 for a possible successful parole bid.

This place had the potential to keep me at peace and get on with my sentence in the best possible way as to give myself a chance at parole on the second attempt. A year off my time was a huge amount of time to get back.

While all this was going on in my mind, I went and made a call. Called Sandra to let her know the good news. That I can cook my own food. The canteen sold everyday groceries like a supermarket. I had never seen this before. That I could wear my own clothes, that they had a swimming pool and more importantly they had a punch bag. I could now start training here and get myself to a fitness level that would allow me to give boxing another go. It really was ironic that my mind had only recently started thinking about getting back into boxing and here I was in the first fucking jail I'd ever come across with a fucking punch bag and three or so skipping ropes. Wow. I was twenty-three going on twenty-four so there was still time. I also told her that getting to Maidstone was easy and not an all day trip like Parkhurst. Just a matter of the tube to an over ground station and a twenty minute or so train ride to Maidstone station. From there the prison laid on busses at regular intervals for the short ride to ferry visitors to the prison.

I also told her about the home leave potential and my parole plans now I was here. All in all it was the best day we'd had in two years. We could finally see light at the end of the tunnel.

When the workers in the prison started to go back to their wings I ran into a few people I knew. One was Suttie from West London. Rest his soul. He died in an ambush just over a year after he got out in '95.

Suttie and I served our time side by side. He was serving a seven-year sentence. I got a job in the same factory as him. We worked in the tailors along with my homie from Tottenham, Peter A.

I settled in real quick, I started running and boxing training as often as work allowed me to. It was easy to get a firm schedule going with the regime as it was. I also kept up my weight training and strength work. I had one thing in mind at this point; I would take up boxing again when I get out.

I took advantage of the pool to polish up my swimming. At school I never completely learned to swim. I can honestly say that thanks to Maidstone prison I came out a good swimmer. Who would have thought that!

I also have to credit Maidstone for teaching me how to cook properly. And I'm serious.

Before I was locked up, I could cook the normal - Spag Bol, breakfast fry up, boiled rice and what I may have called a sauce to go with it by frying meat and dumping shit loads of tinned tomato on the meat and stewing it down. At that time in Maidstone there were so many accomplished chefs that my cooking skills, which I have to this day some twenty-two years later, came from being around those guys. The right seasoning for the desired flavour, the right way to really create a sauce from scratch, how to make it as thick or as thin as you want it. Cooking Indian, Caribbean, English, and lots of Anthony specials. The thing with cooking is once you get a hold of it, it makes you experiment with styles and flavours and cook stuff no-one's taught you to cook. You sort of branch out into your own flavours and style.

So I got my head down and just enjoyed the freedom I now had. For the first time I came across officers I could have a laugh with. I was actually starting to like some officers. A situation that I never thought was possible before I got to Maidstone.

Maidstone also had a large amount of high level, white old-school gangsters. The ones from the Kray Twins days and the Great Train Robbery days. The days before our time.

There was Bobby Knapp, old boy, well old boy to me at the time. He was probably only a couple of years older than I am now at forty-five years old. Bobby's crew of blaggers or armed robbers were the guys who probably are responsible for the type of security vans we now have. Back then they specialised in stopping a money van at gun point, jumping on to the top of the van and then proceeding to open the van up like a tin of sardines by cutting parts open and then literally peeling the top back just like you would a tin of sardines. They then jumped down into the van and emptied it.

Then there was Freddie Forman, the old-school mate of the Krays. His son was in *Eastenders* for a while, Jamie Foreman. Don't want to go into all those there but there were also black notorious gangsters from Liverpool to London. I managed to get on with the older and the younger lot. Then there was Terry the Tart!

Terry the Tart was a black, old school armed robber who was a Rastafarian but also gay! Pardon? I hear you ask. Yes and there's more. He sold heroin in prison. For those who don't know what that combination means let me explain.

Firstly, even though he was a Rastafarian, he was as bald as they come. He really didn't even qualify to be called a Rastafarian anymore. His dreadlocks only went around the sides of his head and at the back. The whole front of his head all down to half his sides were gone. If he was white he would be the comb over guy on TV. Anyway, this guy seemed to only live in a bathrobe. A bathrobe and the noisiest flip flops you ever heard. You could hear Terry the Tart coming down the landing a mile away. No one else sounded that way.

As I was dealing H myself, I got to know what this guy did and the true politics of the scagheads, or junkies to most of you. As I said earlier in the book, these guys will do anything, say anything and promise anything as long as it got them a fix. Maidstone was definitely the wealthiest prison I had ever been to up to this point and maybe even since, with regards to inmates. Well at that time anyway. I am not sure what has become of it since the early nineties, but back then a very large amount of inmates had money personally, had many wealthy family members, had access to lots of money or had wealthy friends who made sure they were OK on the inside. The amount of money to be had was ridiculous. I made more money regularly than I'd ever made anywhere else. Let me explain what I mean by regular. I was sending out money on every visit. A lot of money! 1.2k, 1k, 1.6k, 600 and so on. I was handing out jewellery of all sorts. Wedding rings was a big favourite, chains, rings and the occasional item from the outside, taken off a loved one to use as currency on the inside. Then I was also selling to people on the inside and collecting funds on the outside so the money never came through the jail at all.

So back to Terry the Tart, I got to discover that he wasn't always selling his H for money and commodities but was selling his stuff for blow jobs!

Most people don't know that UK jails are very, very different to US jails in regards to homosexuality. You can be gay in a UK jail but you best not let anyone know about it. You may like men but when in the gym you best not let your eyes linger in a funny way on another guy's body or genitals. It could be very bad for you. I don't have anything against gays but whereas in the US the 'baddest' guys have a 'bitch' or even a few 'bitches' and are proud of this and then when they were released from prison, go home and back to a heterosexual life, here in the UK it is completely not like that.

So Terry getting blow jobs from some of his customers was a whole new thing for me when I found this out. This was why he always was in his bathrobe the whole day long except for when he had visits.

When I asked about him and where he was from and what he was in for. I found out that he was doing time for a string of armed robberies. I knew he was serving a nine-year sentence but not what it was for. I was also warned about him, to not confuse his blatant homosexuality for weakness. He was a very dangerous character. Apparently he was notorious in West London.

Anyway as summer '92 rolled on, I really had settled into the most peaceful personal regime possible. I was nearly at the two-year point and my parole papers would soon be issued to me to start the parole process, which was due that November. I had heard of lots more people by now who had gone on home leaves with huge amounts of time left to serve compared to myself. Guys serving a ten-year stretch still had four whole years to serve were going home for weekends. I was shocked at this but excited too that if they could get it with so much time left maybe I could get it once I had done two years in November and had my parole answer back, whether it was a yes or a no. I started day dreaming about the possibility of seeing the outside again in a few months, being with my son for the first time at home and being with his mum. Being free albeit for a few days. Remember up until Maidstone my release date to see the outside world again was November '94, now I was trying to taste freedom in less than five months.

I asked for advice from a couple of friendly officers and senior officers regarding my chances at getting a home leave that year. Every answer I got from them was positive. The biggest test was the first one. The first time you were trusted to go out. If you repaid their trust by returning firstly and secondly returning on time and in a fit state, as in not drunk or high, then you had a free run at going home every three months and more in-between if you used family crisis as a cover story. So with this I started counting down the clocks to November or December when I could apply for a home leave.

My parole papers came in August I think. Filled in what I had to fill in. Got my MP, the late Bernie Grant of Haringey, to write a pleading letter for me through my Sandra. Got the probation report done after a visit by them to the jail. All was in and it was now about waiting for an answer. I know I wasn't expecting it to be fair, but I suppose it's like gambling, even though I don't gamble. A gambler always thinks he's in with a chance. So there were always those moments when your mind drifts and you imagine a screw coming to your cell and saying, "Spencer? You got your parole son, you're going home in two weeks."

That vision flashed past my mind more than a few times. But I always brought my mind back to reality.

My son Koy's second birthday was on 11 December, so I started planning my home leave for that period. Luckily his birthday that year fell on a Friday. So in late October '92, I put in an application for a home leave from Friday the eleventh until Monday the fourteenth. I put it in with plenty of time so they couldn't tell me it was back logged or wasn't sufficient time or any other excuses. Plus it would have been for after my first parole answer, which the officers advised me to do. I had my mind set on being there for my son's second.

So I awaited this parole answer not so much for the result but for the home leave. When I finally got my answer it was just what I expected. A refusal! The grounds were mainly my disciplinary record since being locked up. I accepted this and looked forward to the prisons answer to my home leave application.

It came in early December! Oh… My… God! I was going home!

May have just been for the weekend, but I was going home. I was going to be with my family. I was going to spend my son's second birthday with him. I was going to have sex again. I was going to eat home-cooked food! I was over the fucking moon.

Who would have thought so only nine months before when I was stuck in Parkhurst down the block? I ran to the phone and called home. Gave Sandra the news. She was in disbelief too. First thing she says to me was, "Anthony just make sure you go back!"

I was going home in about eight days from when I got my answer. I started to make arrangements to pick up my stock of weed and heroin to bring back. By now I had saved up more money than I'd ever saved when I was out. So where as I heard of a lot of people who went out and had to commit crimes to have a good home leave, I was sorted. A large majority of convicts have no savings outside when they are incarcerated. I was one of those. But thanks to the trade inside I was flush-ish. When the new fifty pound notes came in, the current red ones, I saw it first before Sandra ever did. One day she came up on a visit and I had a bundle of cash to hand out, I think around five or six hundred pounds.

I said to her, "Have you seen those new fifties yet?"

"No," she replied. "Why?"

"Well when you get home have a look in the bundle, the new fifty's in there," I said, well proud of myself.

"That is mad, so I'm outside and ain't seen the new money and you're inside seeing it before me!" she said shaking her head.

"Well what can I say?" was all I could come back with.

So I was OK financially to have a great home leave, get my son a great birthday present and treat Sandra to something to say thank you for hanging in there this whole last two years. I just knew and felt the worst was now behind us.

When the day finally came, the only butterflies I had was the type you get when your sentence is over and you're going home for good, as anyone who's ever been banged up will tell you. The only thing was, I was going to be back here behind bars on Monday.

But I will never forget when the huge prison doors opened and I was on the other side. The freedom side, first taste of freedom in two years, one month and four days! Sandra had come to get me with my friend Skip and his chick, our friend too, Maxine, as well as Koy.

It was the start of a great weekend. It was particularly sweet because the policy that existed in Maidstone at the time that allowed me to get out for a weekend was not common in the penal system. With two years to my release date, ninety-nine percent of jails would never have let me out. Most will do with six months or less remaining. Some will only do three months or less. So this was so much sweeter to think that my bad behaviour had actually led me to that moment in time.

I had a blast. I drank proper alcohol and not prison hooch for a change. I smoked lots of weed that first night, celebrating my temporary freedom and my son's birthday. Although I smoke every day in prison, I mostly smoked hash and on the odd occasion skunk weed. Usually when I brought mine in. Lately I had just focused on getting heroin in as I swapped small quantities for large pieces of hash from the junkies whose friends and families only brought them up hash but they wanted more. So being out I was smoking the real stuff. High grade weed or sensimilla.

Then came the night and the kids had gone to sleep. And it was me and Sandra. And all them nights I hadn't given myself a hand job, all them wet dreams, and all the sexual scenarios I'd played out in my mind since the day I got arrested two years before were now about to be fulfilled. What can I say, it was like an explosion of a volcano. It was like being in a real sex movie. This was the longest I'd gone without sex in my life since I lost my virginity at nine years old.

We did it sideways, frontways, backways, longways, shortways and every which way! Then we did it upside down, inside out, outside in and downside up!

"Oh my gosh, do I really want to go back?" I said, out of breath after the last one for the night.

"Hmm hmm, hmm hmm Anthony, don't even start going there," she said to me, also out of breath. She carried on. "They let you out before we ever thought you would see road, don't fuck it up man. You even said if you go back you can come out every three months, ain't that what you said?"

"Yeah I know Sandra."

"So ain't it better you go back, come home again in March and in June and then September and before you know it your second parole is ready to go through? Then you don't go back, go on the run, can't stay here and be with your son and then when - not if - you get caught that's you done with home leaves."

"I know what you're saying Sandra, but it's hard. You don't understand," I said, lighting a cigarette.

"I know it's hard Anthony, but it will be a nightmare for all of us if they had to come looking for you every five minutes here. Kicking the door down and upsetting the boys. And then when they get you, you could end up in some far place that's not easy to get to," she said. "Right now you're settled there, it's easy for me and the kids to come to see you. You can get three visits a month instead of two like all them other places. Please Anthony, just let's enjoy this weekend and go back on Monday."

Still thinking, I said, "Yeah you're right. Let's enjoy the weekend."

It's funny what happens to your mind when you do get out on a temporary release. Before you get out, most people have the best of intensions and do intend on returning. But the minute your first night is nearly over and you start thinking about Monday and returning, the chemistry in your brain starts doing funny things. You start remembering all those nights you wanted a cuddle from your girl and only had the pillow for company, all the lock downs, all the hardship and all the pain deep in your soul from being inside and you start to think the one thought that never crossed your mind before. You start exploring the possibility of going on the run and taking your chances.

The thing is though, this is a very risky policy. Many inmates have come back with further court cases picked up from being on the run. Guys who were finishing off their original sentences, went out for a weekend, didn't return because they figured, "Fuck it, I only have six months left, I can do that later when they catch up with me." But then get caught doing an armed robbery or something even more serious that their original crime and come back to finish that six months and another ten years.

So this was torture for my whole being. But I put it to the side and carried on enjoying my brief time outside knowing I was going to come back to deal with it on Sunday night and all day Monday.

Still I went about doing stuff in preparation for going back to prison. Preparing to go on the run I could do on Monday. It was a great weekend all in all. Didn't party or gallivant, just spent precious time with those I missed the hell out of, my family. I went to see my mum and dad and saw my brothers and that really was it; mostly it was Sandra, the kids and I.

By the time Monday came I think I pretty much was resigned to going back. The more I thought about it the more I knew it would be a bad move. I had way too much time left. I thought it was best that I use my brain and gift of the gab to squeeze out more time out from prison and make the next twelve months to my next parole as easy as possible. Now they had trusted me it was vital that I use it to my advantage.

And so came the hour to drive back to hand myself into the prison's custody. We all got in the car, myself and Sandra, Skip and Maxine. It was the shortest, long drive of my life. I'll tell you this for nothing, even on the drive back, I was still contemplating telling Skip to turn around.

I was filled with great sadness as I looked out the window at all the sights like someone who knew they weren't really sure when they would have these views again. Because let's face it I could get turned down for my next applications for a home leave. Nothing was guaranteed except my release date two years away. Christmas was around the corner, like ten or so days away. All these factors played on my mind big time as we drove through Kent heading towards the prison.

When we arrived, I felt like a beaten man. This is the only way to describe it. Like a man who was resigned to his fate. A man who knew he was walking to his own death. OK not as bad but the feeling was the same. I kissed Sandra and hugged her and then waved good bye to them for the last time. I then had to walk to those huge doors but this time I was going in and not coming out again for God knows how long. I walked up, knocked on the huge doors and was let in. My brief taste of freedom was over. Once the doors shut behind me, I went into a different mode. I started to look forward to telling my guys what the outside was like. I was also fully loaded with all types of drugs. Heroin, weed, hash and ecstasy pills. I was also starting to think of my next reason to go out again even before I had been processed back through the prison gates. When I got back to the wing the guys welcomed me back heartily. Those in my crew knew that they were going to be sorted. Whenever someone goes on a home leave they share stuff with those closest to them in the prison. Everybody around me smoked well for at least two weeks after my return. Christmas was a really good one. You could buy chicken and turkey and lamb or beef. Because this was a prison where you could cook, they had to sell all this stuff. I think we had to order our whole chickens or turkey a week or two in advance.

New Year's came and we welcomed 1993 gladly. I might sound crazy to some but I had been waiting for 1993 since 1990. Why? Because I could finally say, "I'm out next year," even though it was only 1 January. I knew with or without parole I was going home next year.

I carried on with my boxing training regime. This then gave me a fantastic idea. I was going to apply for a leave to go to see my old trainer at the All Stars gym to see if I could sign back up with him. I knew the officers knew I was training hard. They knew I used to box so it would make sense if I told them I wanted to go re-establish my contact with the gym. At first, if I'm honest, it was all about being out again before March. I could either apply for a compassionate leave, which needs a somewhat serious family crisis to qualify or a work leave, which is where you are going out to set up job or work opportunities for when you get released. So I went for the latter.

I got in touch with my old gym and got Mr Akay to write me a letter of invitation to the gym so he could assess my fitness, my skill level and all of that to determine if I had a future with his gym. I got the letter by the end of January and put my application in. My plan was that if I got the gym home leave in February, I would then put in for a normal leave in April and then another in June and before I knew it half the year would be gone.

My plan worked. I got a work release type leave for four days! As long as a normal home leave but with no weekends. I t was from a Tuesday to a Friday. I was over the moon. 'This thing really worked, wow!' I thought.

Sandra was ecstatic. I was coming home again just two months after my first one and with my normal one due another two months from then. Now some people would go out and not even bother with the gym. But the truth was, I genuinely believed in myself and honestly wanted to give boxing a go again.

So I went out and spent Tuesday with my family. I had Wednesday and Thursday to do the gym thing and had to be back at 4 p.m. on the Friday. I went on over to the gym on Wednesday. It was good to be back in a real blood and sweat boxing gym again after so many years. Mr Akay put me through my paces, shadow boxing for a long time while he watched me closely. At the end of that day's session we had a chat.

"OK son, come over here," he called over to me. "So how long did you say you have left?" he asked.

"Well I have nine months to parole and I think I can get it, but if not next year November," I replied.

I could see him doing his sums and then he said, "Twenty-one months? Nearly two years isn't it?" he said really rhetorically.

"Yep," came my reply.

"Long time man. What did you do son?" he asked.

"You really want to know boss?" I asked not sure whether to tell him the truth or not.

"You don't need to tell me, but I'm just curious."

"Armed Robbery," I said. "Got six years."

"So are you serious about the game or do you think you might get distracted again once you're out?" was his next question.

I gave it a thought for a second, looked him dead in the eye and said, "I believe I'm ready this time. I want to come off the streets. I've been through a lot, good and bad. But now I need to do this before I'm too old to take it up." I continued. "Do you think I can do well from what you saw today?"

"You do have something son. You always had something." And then, "If I remember correctly you had a great right hand and a lot of power in both hands. Power is always the last thing to go. If you get your head down, dedicate yourself to the sport, follow instructions and live well, who knows? You could have something."

Wow! That was all I needed to hear from this great man who had trained countless champs.

With that we called it a day. Went in the showers and got dressed. I had one quick favour I needed to ask him. I felt rotten considering the chat we just had. He knew I was supposed to come back in the next day, but I had other ideas. I wanted to beg off from coming in that following day. Fancied spending it home as I only had that Thursday left and had to go back in on Friday.

So as rotten as I felt asking I went ahead and asked anyway. "Boss listen can I ask you a favour? I only have tomorrow to spend with my missus and kids, would you mind terribly if I took tomorrow off and I will promise that I will keep up the training regime. I can ask for another release in six months' time so you can see if I'm still on course?"

I would have given a penny for his thoughts as he stayed silent for a bit then said, "It's OK son. Enjoy your family and stay in touch. Yes let me take a look at you again in six months."

So then I returned home to enjoy my last remaining hours at home with the family. As much as we were able to cook in Maidstone, it still was different eating at home. There were different types of meat you couldn't get on the inside like oxtail, neck of lamb, goat and so on. So when I came home on home leave I tried to get Sandra to cook all those things I couldn't cook inside. So dinner at home was always special.

As 1993 rolled on, I got more and more home leaves. I also got the work leave to go back to the gym in August of that year. This time I made sure I attended both days of training and assessment by Mr Akay. He was pleased with my progress and was genuinely giving me hope that I was doing the right thing and heading the right way. We planned another visit for early 1994. I went out in the summer once or twice, went out again in the October near or around my birthday but was close enough to my birthday to count as being out for my birthday. By now, I'd been given a job on my wing as a cleaner. Now this was a milestone for someone like me. Guys like me do not get given cleaning jobs. When you are anti-authority, stubborn and a general pain in the backside, they do not make you a cleaner or give you work in the kitchens or on the servery serving food to inmates. These jobs are seen as jobs for inmates who have got their heads down and sometimes inmates who will grass to officers about anything. This was the first ever job of this nature that I ever had, even in young offenders institutions. Mind you it's funny how people desire these jobs in jail but would never do it on the outside. I know I would never be a cleaner on the outside cleaning people's shit!

Getting given this job was like some degree of confirmation that I was on a smooth path to parole for sure. I had been out about four times by the time summer of '93 came around. By the time my parole papers started being processed the second time in September or thereabout, I had been granted another leave for October. So all the signs that I may be out that year were there.

November came and went but no answer to my parole. From experience most inmates and officers will tell you that the later your answer is to come back the more chance that it will be granted as they might not be happy letting me off a whole year but will be OK letting me off eight or nine months. So Christmas came and went. Finally my last fucking year in prison arrived. The year 1994. Wow!

No one really knew how long I had waited to see 1 January 1994. To think we are now twenty years down the line in 2014 is truly amazing because looking back at how long it took from January 1991 when I was on remand to January 1994 it feels like those three years took longer to pass than the last twenty years since '94!

I celebrated hard. I could finally say, "I'm out this year!" But little did I know the year was not going to be a good one for myself and my family. January came and went and still no news on my parole. Every time Sandra and I discussed it on visits or over the phone I maintained my view that they didn't want to let me off a year but I believed I would get something off. In private I had this vision that the officers would call me into their office one day and say, "Spencer, you got your parole son. You're going home in two days!"

But then at the beginning of February my hopes came crashing down with a bang. I got my parole review answer. The parole board turned me down. That was now it. There were no more paroles. I was staying in until November '94. This wasn't so bad. Because time had flown by while I was waiting for their answer. It was now February. There were only nine months left. Compared to the time I had put behind me, what was left ahead was nothing. So I mustered my strength and made a call to my missus. She was the one that would feel the disappointment the most as she really had her heart set on my being released early.

So I called her. At this time we did not know that this was going to be the first of our two very difficult phone calls in the month of February 1994. I told her, explained to her that this was it but to look on the bright side, there were only nine months remaining of this very long journey. Plus I was lucky that we had had some release from this from time to time now, for over a year with the home leaves. I told her I would apply immediately for another leave as soon as possible. I had gone out just before Koy's birthday in December and it was now early February. Did my best to cheer her up and make her look on the bright side.

I knew it was my bad behaviour before Maidstone and probably my drug dealing in Maidstone and other prisons that was my downfall. Although the officers were OK with me and me with them, I knew that they probably knew I was dealing. There were quite a few dealers there and we really never got hassled the way you would have done in many other jails. But if they knew, then there were obviously reports, if there were reports then parole boards and authority personnel can see them. I had accumulated quite a decent amount of money on the outside so I had no regrets. I set about applying for another home leave to go out that month, February. By now because I had gone out quite a few times now, the processing time for approval of my request was a lot shorter than it was a year before.

On 24 February 1994, I was cleaning my wing as I did every morning, when I got called to the office at around 10.45 a.m. There was a weird mood with the officers that I couldn't put my finger on. Some didn't want to look me in the eye, others had their heads down. The senior officer says, "Spence, call home son. I'm afraid it's not good news. Your missus just called in."

"Really? Why, what's wrong?" I asked him, concerned, maybe to get some clue of what was waiting at the end of the phone line.

"Call home son," he said, kind of in a consoling way.

Now I was concerned, confused, worried with a hundred other

emotions running through my mind as I went to my cell to get a call card to call.

Called home. The phone was picked up by Sandra, crying badly. WTF!

"Sandra what's wrong, what's wrong?"

"I'm so, so sorry Anthony, your brother just called."

"OK stop crying so I can hear you. What's wrong, who called and what's wrong?"

"Leuchie called. Andrew died this morning," she said, sobbing badly.

"What? Which Andrew? My little brother Andrew?"

She couldn't answer I think, because I still wasn't sure what she was saying. So I asked again.

"Sandra did you just say my little brother Andrew died this morning?"

"Yes. I'm so sorry Anthony. Leuchie was in a state. He died in a car crash. There were three of them in the car. Leuchie said he was the only one who died. They're all at your mum's now. I'm just getting ready to go down there with the boys."

I remember letting the phone drop from my hands in disbelief after hearing what she just said. The phone stayed hanging, while I just leaned on the phone box itself with my arms and my head resting on my arms. I probably stayed in this position for a few minutes. I could hear her calling me faintly from the hand set hanging down.

I finally picked back up the phone and put it to my ears. Still in deep shock.

"Are they sure it's him?" was all I could ask. "Who was he driving in the car with, do they know yet?"

"I don't know yet Anthony, your brother called about ten minutes before you called. I called the prison as soon as I got off the phone to him and waited for you to call. I ain't spoken to anyone else."

"Alright, listen get yourselves ready and go to my mum's. I'm gonna call my mum see if Leuchie's there. And then I'll call you back," I said starting to pull myself together.

My next call was one of the most difficult calls I have ever had to make. Called my mum.

"Hello?" I said when the phone connected. "It's me Anthony."

I could hear really loud wailing and crying from many different voices. I couldn't tell which was my mum, which my sister and who exactly was at the house crying. It was just a loud jumble of crying and wailing voices. I wasn't even sure who had answered the phone.

"Hello? It's me Anthony, who's this?" I repeated.

"Aaanthooonyyyyyyyy. It's aunty Felicia..." she cried out, still sobbing. It was my aunt Felicia. I knew this was really happening. It wasn't a dream.

"Aunty what happened? Sandra just told me."

"My dear you need to come and be with your mother. She needs all of her children with her," she said, still crying. What she said made me feel so bad, I couldn't even begin to tell you.

"Aunty, I know, I know. I have asked them to let me out this month. I should be out next week for a weekend. But I'm gonna ask them for a compassionate leave and see if I can come home tomorrow Friday or Monday," was all I could say.

"Can I talk to mum?"

"My dear, she can't talk. It's too painful. She hasn't said anything all morning, only tears." Then, "Anthony when are you coming home? Your mother needs you all here."

"Aunty, can you tell her I'm calling. I need to talk to her," I said, ignoring her question. I didn't want to make any promises until I spoke to the officers.

"Wait let me tell her, I don't think she will even hear me." And then I heard her say, "Veronica your son is on the phone, and he wants to talk to you. Can you please come and talk to him. It's Anthony!" Then after a little pause, with crying and sobbing still in the background, she carried on. "Veronica, it's Anthony on the phone, please be strong. Be strong for the family. Please. We will get through this in Jesus name. Please be strong. Andrew would want you to come through this..."

I listened to all this and my heart and my every being wanted to cry with my family but I just couldn't get the tears up. Oh my God, I had forgotten how to cry! I couldn't cry to save my life. I couldn't cry for my own brother. I couldn't cry with my mum in her hour of need. As I held on to the phone listening to the goings-on at home, I was completely oblivious to the fact that I was at the entrance to the wing where the phone were. There was a whole other world going on behind me. I was totally not aware of anything other than what was going on at home. I might as well have been there, I was there in spirit. Suddenly, I heard Luchie's voice say to my Aunty, "Aunty give me the phone, let me talk to Anthony."

"Here son, here talk to your brother. Tell him to come home. Your mum needs all of you now!" My aunty just didn't understand I was somewhere at her Majesty's pleasure. You didn't just walk out and say, "I'll be back soon, my brother just passed away!"

"Troub?"

"Yeah Leuchie man, what the fuck happened man?"

"Mum said last night he must have gone out at about ten with Strekker and BJ. She must have asked him what time he was coming back and he said about 1 a.m."

"Yeah?"

"She went sleep and the next thing she knew was when she woke up this morning. She went to get ready for work and never even remembered that he went out." I waited, so he could continue. "She says about nine thirty this morning the door started to knock in a funny way. She said her heart went like she knew the knock wasn't right. When she opened the door, there were three police people at the door. They asked her if this was Andrew's house and who she was. Then they came in and said Andrew was in a ride with two other people. The car skidded and a next car came and hit them on the side where Andrew was sitting. He didn't stand a chance Troubs, man. They said he passed on the spot," he finished off saying.

"So where's Strekker and BJ? What happened to them?"

"BJ's in a bad way cos he was at the back and on the same side as Andrew. But Andrew's side got the full hit from the other ride. I hear BJ's brain's all swollen and shit. Strekker's in hospital but he ain't as bad. He's cool. He's gonna come home. Fucking nightmare, fam. Do you think them pussy holes will let you out?" he asked, meaning the prison bosses.

"Soon as I come off the phone to you lot I'm gonna go change the dates I did ask for before. I was getting a home leave this month or early next. Aunty has been killing me so as soon as I get off I'm gonna go ask for Monday coming. Compassionate leave."

"So where's Andrew now?"

"You don't wanna know," he replied. "Go talk to them pussies and see if you can come home. Mum would be glad if all of us was here still. Even if they can give you a couple days out."

"Yeah, fam, I will. Do you think I can chat to mummy?"

"You know what Troubs, even if I did pass her the phone, she won't make sense. Call back after a few hours. Call back when you lot come out after lunch bang up. I think she needs to sleep and wake up."

"Is everyone OK yeah?"

"Yeah fam, everyone's feeling this right now but you know we have to be tough for mum and Cass. And aunty and that." he said. Then carried on to say, "Go talk to them and call back. Don't stress, right now there's nothing you can do fam. So just try speech them to come home ASAP."

"Alright Leuch. Gonna call back around two. You still gonna be there?"

"Yeah man, I'm here all day today, tomorrow and until we don't need to be here no more."

"Ok, Sandra and the kids are coming down as well. Gonna call her now to let her know to hurry up and come. Then I'm gonna go ask for compassionate leave. Leuch, I can't fucking believe this."

With that we hung up. I had been on the phone for about an hour. I was sweating, my legs were weak, I was shaking too but I just couldn't cry. The officers noticed I had got off the phone and signalled me to come over.

"You alright son?" The senior officer asked me. "If there's anything we can do, let us know. We are sorry for your loss." So they already knew.

I said, "Can I see a governor today boss?" And, "I need to apply for a compassionate leave to go home."

"Here fill in one of these, and put down what you want to see the governor about and I will try my best to get you to see one today. At the worst you will see one first thing tomorrow," he said, handing me the usual form to request an audience with the governor.

"Cheers gov."

As I walked off, I began to hate myself and blame myself for not behaving for so long on this sentence. Because if I had, I would definitely have been out by now and would have been there for my family.

Little was I to know that this was not the last time I would lose a very close family member at the end of my firearm sentence!

Andrew was only seventeen years old. I had just spoken with him over the prison phone less than a week before. Now he was gone forever.

CHAPTER FOURTEEN

Ok so I was in custody when my brother dies. Anyone who's ever been incarcerated will tell you that the main nightmare scenario is that you lose a child, your spouse or partner, one of your parents, brothers/sisters and then the list goes down to other relatives and down to close friends. But losing someone while in prison is something I wouldn't wish on an enemy.

For the following few days, which included a weekend, I was allowed some space by my crew and even the screws to mourn. I got my Audience with the Governor on the Saturday, believe it or not. I was grateful for her speedy response to my request for an audience with her.

I think by the time she came to see me, she had heard from the screws about my loss and had already had it approved for me. The good thing was I was already in their good books as someone who could be trusted to go out and come back so the vetting process was not a strict one.

She said I could go home on the Monday. I had spoken to my mum at this point, but it wasn't the best call at all. She was in so much pain that talking to her was torturous to me being inside and not being able to comfort her. I felt that telling her I was coming home on Monday for four days may give her something to ease the pain for even a minute.

On Monday when I got home, my mum's house was like a funeral parlour. It was still tears, tears and more tears. But still I could not cry.

It was good to be able to help in any way I could. My dad was being very moody and solemn, my mum was inconsolable, my sister who was very close to Andrew, may be the closest in the family to him besides Mikey was traumatized. My youngest brother Mikey who was the one immediately after him was confused and needed shoring up. I felt like I couldn't leave for now, like it was down to myself and my older brother Leuchie to see this family through the worst crisis my family had ever experienced. My dad was obsolete. He was just plain angry. But we knew he was angry because he didn't know how to show hurt. So he also needed help really. So as soon as we could, myself and Leuchie sat down and spoke.

"Have you cried Leuch?" I asked him.

"Boy, I tried but couldn't. May be it's cos I'm still vexed that of the three of them in the car, he's the only one that never made it out."

"I don't even think I remember how to, fam. Been wondering why I ain't cried for our little brother."

"Don't let that get to you man, it's better both of us stay strong for the rest of them and then when it's all done we can cry all day long," he said.

"You're right, fam, you're right," I said, deep in thought as I spoke.

"Has anyone been to see him at the mortuary?" I carried on.

"Yep, me and dad went on Friday night." Then, "They had his head in a bandage. His eyes were closed. Looked like he was sleeping, Troubles. I even spoke to him as we were leaving. I told him to get up now. Told him it was his last chance to prove he wasn't gone for good. I said, 'Andy if you don't stand up now and come with us you know we're gonna leave you here innit?' But bruv, he didn't move, he didn't say nothing. I think that was when I let him go. It's deep."

"Booooy!" was all that came out of my mouth. It was both a sigh and a response all at once as I processed what Leuchie had just said. "How was dad?" I asked.

"What, you mean at the Mortuary?"

"Yeah. How did he react when he saw Andy?"

"Troubles, to be honest he was just calm. He looked sad, angry and speechless all at the same time. He touched Andrew's hands, his forehead, felt his ribs on both sides and then he just said, 'Children are not supposed to go before their parents.' After that he didn't say much more. We were there in the room with him for about ten minutes, fam."

Andrew was named after my dad. He was also Andrew. His namesake was gone.

We carried on talking for a while longer until we got to the topic of who was to blame for our brother's death.

"So do you know what they were on? Were they on a move or raving or what? Where the fuck were they going?" I asked.

"Strekker I hear went home yesterday Sunday. His big brother Lincoln called me yesterday to tell me. BJ's too bad to even try find out. So if you want we can go over to chat to Strekker to ask what really happened."

"Yeah come we go chat to Strekker after. Kinda wannna know really what went down. How our little bro got to come off worse in all of this madness, do you know what I mean?"

"Sure do. Let mum go to bed first. Right now every time I've left the house she wanna ask a million questions even though I don't live here. Let her go to bed yeah, otherwise she'll worry."

"Ok bruv, I hear you."

That night we went over to Strekker's mother's house to visit with him. Although it might have come across like we were there to offer our get well soon wishes, we really were there, I think, to find someone to blame.

What Strekker said to us during this visit would determine what we did next, Leuchie and I. You see Leuchie's crew was the older lot to mine. So we rolled in different crews. Andrew was born in 1976, which made him eight years younger than I was, so his crew were much younger than Leuchie and I. But we knew some of his people and also knew their older brothers or sisters if they had any.

His mother apologised to us and expressed her deep sympathy to my family. She asked for my mum's number to call and offer her sympathies, which we gave to her. I think she was a bit worried seeing Andrew's two notorious older brothers at her house. One was still in prison and only out temporarily - me! We finally sat down with Strekker in his older brother Lincoln's bedroom.

"Trust me Leuchie, if I could have swapped places with Andy right now I would. Please believe me," was the first thing he said looking us both dead in the eye. "I tried my best man, I tried to hold the ride straight when we started skidding and spinning but I couldn't stop the fucking ride from spinning and spinning and then when I thought it stopped spinning, that's when I heard the crash from the other car. I didn't even see it until it hit us. And then I woke up and Andy and BJ weren't moving." At this point he started crying. But as I looked at Leuchie and he looked at me, I knew he was thinking what I was thinking. We will not be fooled by tears!

So I asked, "Where exactly was you lot going?"

"Just over to Leyton to link two sisters, then we were gonna go drop BJ off at home and then drop Andy and that was it."

"How fast was you driving to where you started spinning and couldn't control the ride. You must have been flying Strekker man," I commented, looking for an answer.

"No Troubles, the road had ice or something cos I wasn't speeding, fam. I was starting to slow down to turn onto Blackhorse Road and as I went to turn we just started skidding into the next lane with oncoming cars and that's when the other ride must have hit us." He continued, "Trust me, we weren't speeding like that."

"So what's the police said to you?" Leuchie asked him. "Did they say whose fault it was?"

"They ain't said nothing to me. They asked what happened and all that but they haven't said anything else to me."

"Leuchie, Troubles, believe me, Michael's wounded about it all. He can't believe how a little drive about to go check chicks can end up like this," his brother Lincoln said, referring to him by his first name. Lincoln had been sat there the whole time not saying a word.

"You lot wanna build a spliff?" Lincoln asked.

"No, no we're OK," Leuchie replied before I could.

"Troubles, when do you have to go back?" Strekker asked me.

"Friday."

"Will they let you out for the funeral?" Strekker asked again.

"They should still. Been coming out now about a year and a half,"

I replied.

"Can I ask you lot something? Would you lot let me carry his coffin with you lot's family please. You know he was my key and right hand and I was his for years. Me and you lot's brother have been tight from junior school. We grew together. Please let me do this with you lot. It would mean a lot to me. And I know he would do the same for me if it was the other way round."

"Ain't up to us, fam. And we still wanna hear what police are saying about the whole thing. Can't sell it to my dad if the police end up saying it was something you did that caused our little brother to die in your ride, do you know what I mean?" I said to him.

"Yeah I hear ya, but trust me I wasn't doing nothing wrong. We was just cruising like normal."

"We'll see what dad and them lot say and let you know, yeah?"

With that we left the house, passing his mum again on our way out. She was again giving us words of kindness and told us she would always remember our brother and our family in her prayers. We thanked her and left.

Went back home to a very down and depressed home. A home in mourning. In all this I had forgotten about the joys of being out of prison on leave. It was a bitter sweet leave. One I couldn't really enjoy the joys of being out and when I found myself doing something that would normally be a reminder that I was out, I felt like stopping it. The four days I was out flew by. All sadness. By the time I went back to prison my parents, well really my dad had not confirmed my brother's funeral date. So I obviously had to ask permission to go out again at some point when my dad figures out when Andrew was going to be laid to rest.

Being back in prison was even more depressing than being in my depressed home. Gym was tedious, work was laborious and even calls home were not as upbeat as they used to be. They were down and depressing. This phase lasted until the funeral.

Now I did not realize that my dad, being Nigerian, would mean his culture took over the formalities of my brother's death and funeral arrangements. In the Nigerian culture parents do not bury their children. This meant that when a child dies before the parents, relatives take charge of funeral arrangements - aunties, uncles and the like.

It wasn't until towards the end of March that my brother's body was released. The police conclusion somewhat backed up what Strekker had said. It basically said the car lost control on making a right turn and skidded on black ice before being hit by another car, which also couldn't stop on time due to black ice. They did not charge either of the drivers with any offences in relation to my brother's death. So there you go, he'd gone and that was it. Couldn't say we were happy with that. When these things happen, a part of you wants someone to blame.

I got leave for three days to attend the funeral in early April. I had been to funerals of young people in the past. But I had never been to a family member's funeral before never mind an immediate family member.

I will not go into this in depth as it serves no purpose. My dad attended but my poor mum was made to stay home, partly her wish and partly tradition from my dad's culture.

The funeral passed off OK, but anyone of us kids will tell you that from that day in 1994, my mother never ever recovered from the loss of her child.

I tried to put all that sadness behind me and focus on training and plans for getting out. I was being released in about five months when summer came round. I was being offered CAT D status by officers. They were telling me to apply for an open prison place and were basically saying they would back my application if I did. This was a coded way of saying, "Apply for it and we will see that you get it."

I thought about it, spoke to people who'd been to one of these places and thought about it a little more. I heard good things like going home every weekend, having your own cell keys therefore can come out as and when you wish, working outside the prison, which means being out every day and getting much better pay than in a prison, but not quite the pay levels of a normal worker doing the same job. So in prison you may get £5 a week, in a CAT D working outside, you'll get £25 for the same job while on the outside you get £200 to £250 or something. But on the downside, it was very restricted, you couldn't fuck up at all, there were no second chances, there were lots of grasses, which for me still making money on the inside meant I could be stitched-up, raided, found in possession and then more time and not in a pleasant jail.

I had to weigh up all of these against being in a jail where I was OK, making lots of money, was relaxed and I could go home every six to eight weeks. In the end I decided to stay at Maidstone.

The months rolled on and again as anybody who's ever done time will tell you, at this point everyday counted. Every day was a historical day because you had never had ninety days left, seventy-two days left, forty-one days left and so on. I was in touch with All Stars Gym regularly, and at this point I felt fit and even fighting fit. As my release date drew closer, I stepped up my training regime. The closer I was to being released though the more I was nervous about being back out again. What worried me the most was my resistance to crack cocaine. I hoped I had beaten it by now, but was not a hundred percent sure. This was my main concern.

The whole time I had been away I had heard stories of what guys' girlfriends, partners and baby mums were getting up to outside while they'd been away and it wasn't pretty. Those guys who didn't know what the future held for crack users at that time had partied with their girls using crack cocaine and now they were away, their girls were partying with whosoever had crack for them. Guys who were lucky enough to have been on the outside all these years I'd been away were now totally fucked in a way we had never seen before in our neighbourhoods. Stories we were hearing from all corners of the UK were scary to say the least. This was what scared me the most.

But, I put all that to one side of my mind and soldiered on to my release date, glad I didn't smoke crack cocaine with my missus.

I remember getting to ten days, then seven and then three days. Wow! It was finally here? I finally finished four whole years in prison? How the fuck did I do that?

Then it finally came, my last night in prison. I had given away so much stuff. I had a TV I'd smuggled in on two separate visits. One was to get the TV in and the second visit was to get the charger in. The TV's screen was as big as an iPhone screen today but a lot more cumbersome and the charger was even bigger. It was bloody expensive to run by batteries so to run it I hooked it up to the florescent light in my cell. I gave this and other homely comforts I had accumulated on the inside away to my tight friends. I was a bit sad on that last day to say goodbye to my guys. But that last night I could not sleep. I was filled with anticipation of what awaited me on the outside now I was free. When morning came, I was glad I had slept a bit. I was up sharp and ran to go shower. The time had finally come.

After breakfast I was called to the office and asked if I had all my gear and if I was ready to proceed to reception for release. Are you kidding me bruv? I was ready like Freddie mate!

After being processed, returned my stuff and all that, I was waved good bye by the screws and let out the first gate as usual. Then the second opened and I walked through to the other side. I heard the door start closing and this time I knew it was the last time it would close behind me. I wasn't coming back in a few days, this was it, I was free for good.

My brother Leuchie was outside with Sandra and the kids. Koy was a little man now - he was nearly four years old. Sandra said he'd been kicking the huge wooden doors with his little legs shouting, "Daaad, daaad!"

We walked to my brother's car and left. When we got home I put my stuff down and began the task of easing back into the life of freedom. Pretty soon after my release, I started looking about putting my life in order. Earning money was top of the list, going to the gym was next and then getting a car was third. There were more goals but these were the top three. Within a week I had been to the gym twice, which I was proud about because it was one of my major doubts before my release as to whether or not I would keep the regime going and if I would be disciplined enough this time to keep up the training and dedication it takes. So week one I was pleased with. Then about making money, I had spent a good deal in the months since my brother's death. All the goings and comings, getting myself Sandra and the kids new summer stuff. Being in Maidstone was expensive too. We wore our own clothes so if you were a top boy then you had to look the part. You had to eat well, that costs money too. So I needed cash fast before money ran out and I needed a car. I left Sandra two cars when I went in. One she sold and one she kept. But that was now nearly dead and was no good really. I set about building up a drug business. I had sold brown in prison because that was the number one drug. Now I was back in the manor, there wasn't a lot of junkies around that we knew about. But there was now a thousand times more crack addicts out here. And they were now starting to look just like the American addicts we used to see in documentaries about crack cocaine in those days. Men and women. It was shocking to me. What was a recreational thing when my generation and slightly older first picked it up had now turned into something like a plague! I had been taken off the streets just in time before my addiction got worse, but I do believe I never would have ended up like these zombies out here - rather I may have ended up dead from having it all the time or in prison for much longer because of the level of crime I would have gone to in order to fund my habit. I still would have looked sharp clothes-wise and had a nice car and an orderly home. But it would have fucked me up just the same. So crack cocaine would be the obvious choice for me to peddle to get back on my feet, right? Wrong! I figured I didn't want it around me. I figured having my own supply might lead to me getting high on said supply. It was a safer bet selling brown as I didn't indulge in it at all. I actually can't stand the drug and its smell. So the next problem was where and to whom was I gonna sell this. I had to be very ingenious about how I went about it. Just like I did later on with bullet-proof vests, that was how I created a market out of nothing.

I first secured a start-up quantity of merchandise, a couple of ounces, then I took about four sheets of A4 paper and scribbled my nickname and my mobile phone number on these pieces of paper in straight lines going horizontally and down vertically. I then cut them to individual pieces. I had hundreds of them when I was finished. I put them in match boxes and went round to all the social security offices within the radius of where I felt comfortable to travel for now, to deliver the products. I went to Tottenham obviously, went to Hackney, went to Walthamstow and went to Edmonton all over about a week. I went back to the same places many times. I gave anyone who looked like a junkie my number and many I gave free samples to.

Even before the week was out, I started getting calls for sales. It was instant. It was a brilliant move thought up just in my little big head. I was in business. Within a month of coming out I bought a little decent runner of a car. It was the old Ford Fiesta XR2. Never forget it. It was white with two red stripes going down its sides, and fast. It was just before Christmas 1994 and I was getting regular business enough to be OK for now. But it needed me being available at all times if I wanted to keep a fledgling business going and keep my clients and get more. I found gym starting to suffer. My first Christmas and New Year in four years was fast approaching and I wanted to make it special. Koy had his first proper birthday party for his fourth that December. We had a McDonald's party as they used to have them then. This was a big thing really as he had never had a birthday party until then. So things were settling in nicely. Christmas came and went. It was great waking up on Christmas morning at home smelling food cooking. Watching cable TV as it was then. Watching all the Christmas favourites, *Only Fools And Horses* and the likes. Remember, these days prisons have TVs now but back in the early '90s there were still a lot of prisons where you sloped out because we had no toilets in the cells. So although I had a mini TV smuggled in, I didn't have it the Christmas before. It was just a joy being home at Christmas and really remembering what it was all about again. We went out later on Christmas day to my mums and then later to Sandra's dad's house. He had also cooked. We took lots of doggie bags home with us. Plus we still had our own food at home as we'd also cooked. Then came New Year and that was a blast too.

In the time I had been away, the Acid Music we used to rave to had turned into Jungle Music and was now evolving slowly again into what became known as UK Garage. I went out on New Year's Eve and came across my first true test with crack cocaine since my release about seven weeks before. I went out with the crew. More and more of us were now out after the blitz of '90 and '91 by the law. We went to a new place that had been around since I'd been away. A place called Roller Express. As we walked in the sweet smell of burning cocaine hit us. Bought my standard bottle of champagne and settled down to rave. I had my pills and weed, that was it. I was doing well not indulging in the cocaine thing. I was buzzing from the music, buzzing from being free, from seeing a new year in on the outside and just plain buzzing on life. Toddler rolled a coke spliff right next to me but it wasn't just him, the rest of the crew were smoking and passing coke spliffs around. This is where the devil is truly evil. I wasn't the only one not smoking crack in a joint. There were a few guys who were also trying to do the right thing. As the night went on and the rave got sweeter and sweeter, I finally succumbed. I asked Nicky 'Skitz' to give me a rock. I then went ahead and did what I saw as a compromise. I rolled what we call a Season Spliff. Remember? This is when you put a mixture of tobacco, weed and crack in rolling paper and smoked it. It has a balancing effect. The tobacco allows it to burn in an even way, the weed tames the effect of the crack and its aftereffect of wanting more but at the same time gives you the desired buzz from smoking coke. The quantity of weed to crack determines how much coke hit you got. So more weed means less crack hit and more crack and less weed gave you more of the crack hit. I rolled one of these, confident that this was just to enjoy the moment. I convinced myself that I had suffered a great deal and I deserved to let myself go for the night. This is what the devil does to your mind. It convinces you to do stuff you know you shouldn't be doing, but… Oh my God! The spliff was just so nice and suited to the mood I was in that my night just got better. We partied on and soon I felt I could do with another.

So this time I asked who in the crew was selling. I didn't want a handout. First time, cool, but seeing as I wanted more I decided to buy. My old friend Rabbit was at hand to supply. I purchased what I thought would be sufficient for that rave and went ahead and rolled another one. As I rolled this second one, I started hating the fact I had to pay for it. I could be selling this stuff if I wanted, why was I buying from my people? Although I don't mind supporting my guys, I was better off buying a chunk just to go out and sell on the nights out and have some for myself to smoke too. I had a lot of my junkie clients asking me for crack all the time. I always referred them to my old friend Fiddles from East London to sell it to them. So we worked as a team. He sold the white stuff and I sold the brown stuff. I had no intension of selling this stuff until tonight when I paid for some for personal use. So I made a few more seasoned spliffs, we raved the night out and went home.

When I awoke on the afternoon of 1 January 1995 after my night out, I found a good sized piece of rock that I still had left from the night. I did not want to go home with any left as I was worried I may then put it on a pipe and freebase it. That was a no-no at all costs. That was the most destructive way of smoking the stuff. The whole night out got me thinking seriously about going into the crack business. If only on weekends for raves. There was just so much money to make on that scene. Everybody and their aunties seemed to smoke it now. When I was out, before I got locked up, it was just us earners and bad boys and girls who smoked. Now it seemed everyone did it. Some you could see were really just weekend coke spliff smokers while others were addicts who were only smoking it in spliffs at that time because they were out and could not smoke a crack pipe. I think by the end of that night when I wasn't tempted to freebase or even smoke some of the rock I had in a spliff, I thought I knew I had beaten the habit. So I decided I would buy a good quantity and go into business.

Wrong Move!

The year started well. All was OK at home. My mum was getting back to an acceptable level of normality. It was now nearly a year since Andrew died. We always still talked about him and still missed him terribly. I decided to take Sandra and the kids on holiday. We booked a flight to Amsterdam for ten days that would include a drive to Belgium for two days visiting Antwerp and the chocolate regions. The kids had never been away and neither had Sandra. It was her first ever plane ride. We went off and had a blast. This was what it was all about. These were the things I'd sat in my cell missing and promising myself I'd do when I came home. A lot of the time we say these things to ourselves when our freedom is snatched away from us but yet when we get the opportunity again to do it, we don't because we're consumed with the life.

So it was great to smoke weed in Amsterdam and taste chocolate in Belgium. My crew didn't travel much. Those who did at that time went Jamaica with their parents or Africa or India, wherever it was their parents came from. It wasn't like it is now where we go anywhere we wish to go holiday. So I took some photos with me holding a huge weed spliff and standing next to, shaking the hands of or putting my arm on the shoulder of policemen. I knew this would shock my guys. We'd all heard you could buy weed in coffee shops but I wanted to show them I could smoke with a policeman with a gun on his waist next to me and it was all good. Wow, what would it be like if we could have that here in England? All in all it was a memorable first family holiday for me. It was the first time I will take my own family away on a holiday and it felt nice. I did this as frequently as possible over the next years and even up to last summer 2013. This time to The Seychelles.

But back to '95 as they say. I got into dealing crack cocaine alongside my regular brown stuff. As the days went by without me breaking my discipline to not smoke it, I grew more and more confident that I was cured. So the weekend after that New Year's Eve, we all went out again. Again I smoke my seasoned spliffs, my E's and drank my champagne. Great night. The money I made from the rave was a huge bonus to what I was already making. I don't recall exactly when I decided to start smoking seasoned spliffs at home but it wasn't long after that second night out. I remember convincing myself I was over the craving you get from it in withdrawal, so I went ahead and rolled my seasoned mixture of tobacco, weed and crack cocaine. At this point I would say I put about forty percent tobacco, thirty percent weed and thirty percent coke. It wasn't long before I was putting thirty percent tobacco, thirty percent weed and forty percent crack. Then then fifty percent crack. Then soon it was thirty percent tobacco as it needed that to burn right, five percent weed and sixty-five percent coke. All the time convincing myself I wasn't freebasing so I was OK, but at the same time putting up the quantity I put in a joint so I could taste the crack more and more. But still putting some weed in it as I knew the weed did calm the buzz and craving to some extent.

By the time my brother's first year memorial came round in February I was already fully back in the mix. But I still was not freebasing. Until one night, for the sake of sex. I ran into one chick I used to see back in the day behind Sandra's back. This chick had been at college with me so we go further back than Sandra and I. Her name was Monique. Anyway, I hadn't seen her for years. We spoke on the roadside and arranged to meet up. I knew I was in for some. It was now March; I had been faithful to Sandra for the first time ever for about four months. But the itch had started. That night I made my excuses at home and off I went. I took weed, crack and a drink with me. I didn't think she smoked, I only took them with me because this was what I smoked to relax. Anyway I get there and we start chilling and catching up about old times. I pull out my drugs and start rolling a joint. When I take out the crack to add to the already prepared mix of weed and cigarette, I asked her if she was OK with me doing a spliff at hers. She asked what I was smoking and I told her what it was. Her next question threw me off.

"Don't you lick the pipe?" she asked, which means 'do I freebase.'

"Nah, used to babes but since I got out I'm staying away from that," I replied.

"I do. When I have it," she said.

"You do what? Smoke pipe?" I asked, stopping what I was doing and looking at her.

"Yeah, but like I said not like them cats out there just dabble really when people round me have it or when I got some spare money."

"Why, do you wanna smoke some now? I got some for you still if you wanna."

"Can I?" she asked.

"Go on then, have you got a pipe?"

"Nah but I can make one quick time though." She said, getting up to go to the kitchen.

As she left, I started remembering how nice sex was when you are freebasing. There was nothing sweeter than taking a long pull on the pipe while a chick gave you a blow job. I don't want this to come across as sexist because any woman who has smoked can tell you what their favourite turn on is when getting high. What they ask a man to do to them when taking a pull. So it isn't anything other than my story and what my turn ons may or may not be.

"Ant, light me a cig and just let it burn in the ash tray please," Monique shouted from the kitchen.

"No probs," I replied, coming out of my reminiscing mode. But the more I thought about it the more I knew I wanted this again tonight.

When she came out of the kitchen she had a plastic Coca Cola bottle converted to suit the activity she was about to indulge in. I remember thinking 'No… way!' I did not expect that this chick would be that experienced at this. Anyway, I break her off a piece and sat back to watch while I smoked my seasoned spliff, which was still burning. I wanted to see what happened with her once she smoked. I watched her take her first hit and inhaled a huge cloud of smoke. She looked over and smiled. I leaned forward and started kissing her even before the last of her smoke had exited her mouth and nostrils. She kissed me back and started feeling me up. I was already turned on from a mixture of her smoking a pipe, the memories of sex on crack and the anticipation of what was to come!

I gave her space to take another hit from the pipe but I stuck my hand down her top and played with her nipples while she inhaled and exhaled the fumes. I could see this got her. As soon as she finished exhaling, she started stripping off her clothes. So I did the same too. In no time we were naked. As soon as she started feeling me up I knew what I wanted. I wanted to get a blow job while hitting the pipe. So I stopped her and reached for some coke.

"Babes this is the first time I'm piping since 1990. But you know what, might as well."

I broke off a good sized piece and placed it on the pipe. "Blow me please babes when I'm on it?" Half question, half request.

She immediately got down on her knees and took my dick in her hands and then as I started to take a blast from the pipe, she put it in her mouth and started blowing me.

'Oh... fuck!' was going through my head. It was sheer bliss. I pulled on the pipe for as long as my lungs would go, prolonging the ecstasy as she kept blowing. When I came off the pipe to exhale and feel the rush of the crack going through my brain mixed with the sexual pleasures, I looked at the pipe and looked down at her and I knew I would want to do this again. I took another hit from the remnants of that piece of rock and the whole time she was glued to my cock. When I was high enough, I found myself lighting another couple of cigarettes to burn and breaking off another piece of rock - we were going to party. I sat her down on the sofa with her legs spread real wide and told her to take a hit. As she fixed the pipe for a hit I finger-fucked her while sucking on her breast but giving her the space to take a hit. As she did this I kept up the finger-fucking and kept her nipple in my mouth, all the time tickling her nipple ends. When she withdrew from the pipe to exhale, her legs were trembling from the work I was doing mixed with the high from the hit. Her legs spread even further as she soaked in the pleasures of the effects of the hit mixed with the sexual high. When she was done I could tell she was ready to be taken. I took the pipe back and prepared a hit for myself. She had already taken my cock in her mouth and was going from my cock to my balls, all the time sucking for the nation. I hurried to take the hit. I placed a much bigger piece on the pipe this time. One that should have me inhaling for a long time while being sucked off. "Oh... my... God!" What can I say? I think everyone should experience this just once in their lives. The pleasure was out of this fucking world. I hadn't had a pipe for nearly four and a half years, sex and the pipe for even longer. I put the pipe down and we started kissing. I placed her back on the sofa, spread her legs out wide and proceeded to stick my boy Freddie in her now wet pussy. She let out a soft moan as she took me in. We fucked and fucked and fucked until we both came. The climax was thunderous for me. It was like I had just been released from prison. She couldn't stop coming. So I took advantage of this and kept poking away. Every poke made her moan and twitch as she just kept coming. When we stopped, I got up, went to the bathroom, washed myself off, came back out and headed straight for the pipe. She was still lying on the sofa with her legs spread out and her eyes shut but with a slight smile on her face. I placed another rock on the pipe and started to pull on it. One look over at her sexy breasts and her spread-eagled legs as I exhaled was enough to get my erection back up.

I prepared a hit for her and called her over to take the pipe. It was now close to two in the morning. Although I knew Sandra would be suspicious the later I took to get home, I was having way too much fun to want to stop. Once she took another hit, I sent her to the bathroom and I then moved all our paraphernalia into her bedroom. I wanted to be comfortable this time. Round two started in her bed as soon as she came in. I was sucking on the pipe inhaling when she came in so she went straight for my dick and did what she did best. I gave her a hit and as we were on the bed this time, I was able to really finger-fuck her from behind this time. She took her hit on her knees and resting on her elbows while I finger-fucked her from behind. As she took a second blast from the pipe in the same position, I placed my dick in her doggy style. She soon put the pipe down as we had another round. Again it was just share explosions when we came. She came first so it was even better for her as I took a very long while to explode. But explode I did!

After this session I just lay there with my eyes shut. I should have realized that I enjoyed this a little bit too much for comfort. I soon gathered myself together and remembered home. I didn't want to take another hit because I didn't want to go home too high in case Sandra was awake. So I smoke a plain weed spliff just to come down some. It was around 3.30 I think when I got home. I felt real bad. In the cold light of day, I knew I had just broken two rules. Smoking the pipe and cheating. All in the same night. But I quietly got undressed hoping I wasn't smelling of sex or of another woman. As I got in bed, she asked me where I'd been and I said with the guys just catching up.

I awoke the next day, unsurprisingly wanting more of the night before. I had a hard-on as soon as I remembered what I'd got up to. Again, not a good sign at all.

I spent that whole day wondering if I should or shouldn't call Monique to hook up again later. I didn't think it was a good idea to do this two nights on the trot, not because of the effects it would have on my fight to not get hooked on crack again but more because I wasn't sure if I'd get away with it with Sandra. Funny isn't it? I should have been more worried about the former than the latter really.

I hooked up with Monique again and again until it became 'Our thing'. I'd call her and all I needed to say was, "What you saying, come round tonight?" And she always replied, "Yeah, what time?" After telling her what time about I would come over, I followed it up by saying, "Don't have anything on when I get there and burn some cigarettes for ash." That was it.

At this point I still was not freebasing at home or anywhere else apart from my seasoned spliffs, which I had now started smoking at home. My drug business was still doing OK but gym was now starting to lose out. I battled with myself daily for months as I tried to juggle the realities of being out with my plans for taking up boxing. But I think deep inside I really had given up and admitted to myself that my life as it was at that time was not compatible with training and going through the mill until I was earning enough to feed my family and myself. I felt I had let Mr Akay down big time. The first time I went all week without going gym was back in January but it still played on my mind daily because it was so much a part of my life in jail for a long time. So by now in March I really could see that I wasn't going to be a boxer.

To anyone reading this who has been there, seen it and done it, I'm sure you know what was coming next. Yes, I began smoking the pipe again without Monique or sex! It was horrid the first time I had to tell Sandra that I was going to take a couple of hits on a pipe one night after the kids had gone bed.

"What, are you mad Anthony?" She looked at me disbelievingly. Little did she know that at this point I had been piping regularly now for about three weeks with Monique.

She went on. "Why do you wanna do this to us? You've been doing so well since you got out. I knew the minute you started smoking your fucking seasoned spliffs it would only be a matter of time before you wanna pipe again. I knew it."

"It's only a one-off babes, trust me," was all I could really say.

"Can't you see that it won't be just a one-time thing? Anyway you know what? Your mind's made up, I'm going to bed. Enjoy yourself yeah!" With that painful last comment she got up and went to bed. I sat there for a moment thinking, 'Shit, do I really want to do this?' I really had to think because I knew the minute I broke that thing that held me back from doing this at home, there would be no more boundaries keeping me in check to some degree. As hard as I thought about it, I still fucking went ahead and started to build a crack pipe. That first time at home again was my downfall. Well to be honest the first time I smoked with Monique was really the beginning of the end.

So it was now late March going on to April and although I wouldn't admit it at that time I was now a crackhead again. It didn't take long for this to start showing - in my financial state, my social life, home life and in my business. My finances were starting to suffer from getting high on my own supply and then taking money from the heroin business to replace what I'd smoked off from my crack supply, I was starting to argue with Sandra badly as she wasn't happy with my late nights and piping at home. I visited people and family members less and less because I didn't want to see anyone in case they knew, and as for my business, whereas before I was open all hours, now there were times when I was preoccupied smoking either on my own or with Monique that I couldn't go to supply what the client wanted. When you do this too often, people go elsewhere. So I was starting to fall apart but couldn't see it at this point. I carried on doing what I was doing. I also now had another chick I was smoking with just as I did with Monique. Her name was Lorraine. I'd been in Maidstone with her baby's dad. A guy called Greg from West London. I only knew who she was when I got a call from her one day telling me Greg had died. Myself and Greg had hooked up on the outside on my release as he came out before I did. We rolled a few times but mainly I sold him large-ish quantities of crack whenever he asked. I didn't even know he was sick. So I get a call this day and it was a stranger introducing herself as Greg's baby mum. She said they were planning his funeral and she was going through his phone book and contacts to see who wanted to come pay their last respects. I was shocked he'd died so quickly and extended my sincere sympathy. I asked where she was and promised to pass by to leave her and the kid something from me. But I passed on the funeral. So about a week later I went by her house in Finsbury Park. When I saw her she looked real thin and real sad. She was a mix of Indian and white. She was all alone with this little boy who must have been about a year and half or two.

She explained all about Greg's very brief illness and death and how Greg spoke very highly of me, which was why I was one of the first people she called. I spent some time with her just offering my sympathies and support. When I left I gave her some cash, maybe a hundred or so.

A few days later I get a call from her again asking if I would come to hers to sell coke to her friend. One of Greg's clients before he died. I said OK and went over. To my surprise the client was a black chick, sexy and cute. I sold her what she wanted and sat down to talk with Lorraine for a bit. This chick disappears into a room off the passage that I guessed was Lorraine's bedroom. We carried on talking in the living room. I pulled out my rolling papers to do a coke and weed spliff, piping was still something only a few people knew I did so I didn't go around piping just anywhere. As I'm rolling my joint, the girl in the room calls out to Lorraine, she then gets up and walks to the bedroom where she stayed for about two minutes or so. Her little boy was left with me in the living room. After a couple of minutes they both come out and both had that look I know very well.

"You lot smoke yeah?" I asked, not referring to any one of them in particular. I had only met the black chick that day and as for Lorraine, this was only the second time I was meeting her.

"Yeah sometimes," Lorraine answered. "I used to only smoke with Greg though but since he died I now only smoke with my friend Debbie."

"Ok," I said. Not ever thinking anything other than why would

Greg smoke this with his child's mother.

I said, "Listen you lot don't have to go in the room to smoke, it's cool by me."

"Nah it's just the baby innit, don't want this room to be full of smoke," Lorraine replied.

"Can I put something on the pipe and smoke?" I asked.

"Yeah go on man," Debbie answered.

I had just the one hit, I think, then I asked Debbie for her number and gave her mine. I had big plans for her in the back of my mind. This was one chick I wanted to see naked and smoke with, for sure. Lorraine was not my type so what happened next was totally unexpected.

One night a few days later, Lorraine called me, saying she wanted fifty pounds' worth of coke. It was real late and I think Sandra could make out it was a chick. She also sounded to me like she had already been smoking. So I said OK, to give me about half an hour or so.

"Who was that?" Sandra asked. This is how I knew she must have made out it was a female asking to buy. But I guess something about the call got her back up.

"Oh you know my pal who died, it's his baby mother."

"So she smokes?" she asked.

"I don't know babes. I don't know if it's for her or someone else," I lied.

"How long you gonna be?"

"Just gonna drop it off see how her and Greg's little boy are doing then come home."

As I said those words, I knew I was gonna take something extra for myself to smoke while I was there.

So I got to Lorraine's and I was let in. The living room was an open space with the kitchen so you could see the kitchen. I looked over to the kitchen and noticed a pipe and smoking tools all over the counter. She looked high as a kite too.

"What, you been smoking on your Jack Jones?" I asked with a smile on my face.

She just nodded and handed me fifty pounds. So I gave her the stuff and relaxed in the sofa.

"Where's little Greg?"

"Sleeping in the bedroom." She went over to the kitchen area and started fixing the pipe to have a smoke.

"Bring the stuff over here innit," I said. "I'm gonna have a blast too before I shoot off but you go first."

She brought the pipe over and I went over to get the rest of the stuff, ash tray, cigarettes, safety pin to keep the pipe holes clear as she took her blast. I sat down just in time for her second blast and as she was doing this I put my hand up her top into her bra and started caressing her nipples. To my surprise she didn't flinch. She had a pair of the smallest breasts I have ever put my hands on, even going back to my teenage years. As soon as she put the pipe down, I lifted her top up over her head and took off her bra. I whipped out my dick and pulled down my bottoms. I carried on feeling her up and slowly progressed to her panties and to her pussy. She was now playing with my dick. I picked up the pipe and set my rock on ready for a blast. Before I took the hit I asked if she would blow me while I smoked. She agreed by going down and getting in position so I went ahead and took my blast. We still both had our bottoms on, mine down by my ankles and hers at her thighs. So after my blast I put the pipe down and started taking off my jeans and shorts. She stood up too and did the same. Now we were totally starkers. I took the second hit from what I had on the pipe as she latched back on to my cock. I then set up a hit for her and passed the pipe. I spread her legs as wide as they would go and went about finger-fucking her while she took a long pull of the pipe. This girl was the wettest chick I had ever felt. It was like a tap was leaking up in there. She came off the pipe, grabbed my cock and positioned herself to sit on it facing me. We fucked long and hard as I chomped on her tiny breasts. She was a fucking screamer. We banged until she was nearly waking up the whole road and then she came and that was another type of scream. I reminded myself to put my hood on when I left the house. We smoked some more and then I had to leave because I knew Sandra was alert about this sale. All in all I was gone over two hours and that still needed explaining.

As I drove home, I wondered what it would be like to smoke with those two, Lorraine and Debbie. I got excited just thinking about it. Got home around 2.30 . in the morning having left at about midnight. I got the usual look I get when she knew or could tell from my face that I'd been smoking again. She had a drink of water and went to bed again. I stayed up in the front room watching TV and coming down from my high before I got in bed.

I smoked a few times more with Lorraine and we were now sex partners. It was bad really because Greg wasn't even dead a month when we started. But I was always drawn back to Monique. We seemed to go that extra mile of dirty sex, which every man loves. I'd send her to go get a carrot, cucumber or whatever from the fridge to fuck her with in-between sex and she would never argue. I did not go down on women as we frowned on that type of thing in my world at that time. So as I wasn't blowing her as she was blowing me, the next best thing was to use tools on her while she piped.

My dream or fantasy to have Debbie and Lorraine at the same time smoking and fucking came true a few weeks later. I was called by Debbie to bring some stuff round to Lorraine's for her. It was in the early evening in early May or end of April so I wasn't really expecting anything to happen on this day as it was still bright outside. I got to Lorraine's and sat down. I wasn't sure if Debbie knew I had been fucking Lorraine since I last saw her. I asked about little Greg as I always did and was told by Lorraine that he was at his grandmother's house for the weekend. Debbie took her shit and paid me and went ahead and started putting a pipe together. When she had her back turned to us doing what she was doing in the open kitchen I signalled to Lorraine to ask if Debbie knew about her and I. She shook her head and put her finger to her lips meaning 'keep it quiet'. I nodded to indicate that I understood. I think Debbie still was not comfortable smoking in my presence, so when she had her shit sorted she went into the bedroom again. After about thirty seconds this time, I signalled to Lorraine to give me a minute and I then went into the bedroom. I walked in just as Debbie was blowing out her smoke from what I guessed was her first hit on the pipe. I placed a little bit more on it for her and told her to smoke it and I was gonna go after her. When she regained her breath she put the pipe to her mouth again and began inhaling. As she did this I started to feel her breast over her top pressing my body against hers from behind. As she starts exhaling I'm in her panties and feeling her pussy with one hand down her pants from behind and the other hand still outside her top but on her breast caressing. She didn't say a word, just handed me the pipe for my turn. As I took the pipe from her, I took her hand and placed it on my dick on the outside of my jeans and told her to feel me while I took my turn.

I nearly choked on my pull because Lorraine walks in just as I'm pulling on the pipe and Debbie's rubbing my now very erect cock. You know what; she didn't say a thing about it.

"Can I get some then you lot or ain't I allowed?" Lorraine said.

"Here," I said, my mouth still full of smoke as I attempted to speak, then handed her a piece.

I went out to the living room knowing I had Debbie; it was just a matter of time. I didn't want to let on that Lorraine and I were already 'fucking buddies' as that may push her back. For some odd reason the pipe stayed in the bedroom and we took turns going in there to smoke. I caught up again with Debbie in the bedroom as she fixed the pipe and this time I had undone her zips and had my hand up her pussy even before she started taking a blast again with her standing in front of me and pressed up against me tightly.

This time I place my other hand inside her top feeling her bare breasts and nipples.

"Should we all get naked and just party Debs?" I asked.

"Hmm hmm, not here," she said.

"Why not?" I whispered. She pointed in the direction of the living room, meaning Lorraine.

"She's cool, trust me. She will come in too!"

Debbie looked at me and said, "How do you know that?"

"Just trust me, I know what I'm saying."

"Nah not here man," she insisted.

I let her go when I heard Lorraine coming. I sat on the bed and watched as Lorraine fixed up the pipe to have a turn. Debbie left and went to the bathroom. It gave me the opportunity to pleasure Lorraine as she smoked. I hadn't done that to her the whole time. She had on a skirt, a really short one too. So it was easy access all the way. The thing with Lorraine I noticed is either she was super sensitive or she had a gene gone wrong in her system. The minute you got to her vagina, she was super wet, super turned on and just putty in your hands. By the time Debbie came back in the room, all the pretence was gone out the window. I had her sat on the bed next to me, panties off, legs spread out wide with one over my thigh so I could get in deep and she was winding and softly moaning with pleasure. Debbie went straight for the pipe held in Lorraine's hand and let us get on with it. When I went to take Lorraine's top off there was no resistance. In seconds I'd got her naked and I was taking my own clothes off.

"Go make another pipe, we need two," I said to Lorraine. So she walked off naked to the kitchen. In the meantime I turned my attention to Debbie. I whispered close to her ears, "You see what I mean now innit?"

"You lot've been banging from time innit?" And just shook her head.

I took the pipe from her hands and set it down on the bedside unit. I got hold of her top and pulled it up over her head. Turned her around and undone her bra. Next I undid her zip and started pulling her jeans down.

"Wait, wait let me do it," she said. Just then Lorraine came back in and yes, this is what any man dreams of, with or without drugs in the mix. The next time I was to have two chicks there wasn't a speck of crack in the place. But I will get to that later in the book.

For now I was lucky enough to have these two partying with me and I was going to party hard. Now we had two pipes between us. We were all sat on the bed and while they fixed their pipes, I enjoyed the company of two pairs of breasts and two vaginas! When they were nearly ready to smoke I asked them to get up turn with their backs facing each other, but close enough so each of my hands can go around their fronts and down to their vaginas to finger them at the same time while they smoked. I think they loved it because Debbie's leg went up on the bed giving me more room and soon after Lorraine did the same. I kept this up while they had their turn, going from breasts to vagina and kissing them too. We partied hard for a few hours, we had music, we had soft and strong drinks, we had weed and we had lots of coke. I must have missed out on about £600 to £1000 in the time we were partying. Sandra had called a few times too but I was too high to even want to speak with her. When I thought I'd done enough damage to my supply for one day I cut off one last piece big enough for a couple of hits each and began wrapping up to leave. I got there at around 6 p.m. that evening and it was now nearing midnight. Anyone who's ever had a smoking party will tell you how quick time flies. Before you know it, you have been at it for five, six, eight hours! I was so high I knew I needed to just smoke weed and drink brandy for another couple of hours to sort of take the edge off the coke high before I could go home or take any business. This is the problem with coke, you spend lots of money doing it and then lose money making time, if you work for yourself or get fired if you work. Either way no one can sustain it forever, as Whitney Houston's story shows you. Everything goes in the end and sometimes your freedom goes with them too!

When I got home I tried to sneak in to go sleep in the front room. I hadn't even got my trainers off before I heard her footsteps coming over.

"Yep, I knew it. You've been smoking innit? That's why you weren't answering your phone isn't it? How much of your food have you smoked today? You keep smoking your food and we'll see what you'll have left. You're gonna smoke yourself to death because you won't stop till you ain't got no drugs and no money to buy any. And then you're gonna go back to doing all that mad shit for money."

She went on. "I told you the first fucking night you wanted to smoke here. I knew it wouldn't stop. Fuck me Anthony can't you see where this is going?" Then, "You know what? Smoke yourself to death and next time you're in jail because you had to go back on road, don't think we're gonna follow you around again. You ain't even been out a year yet. Listen, do what you want." She calmly walked back to the bedroom and slammed the door.

She was right because within a couple of weeks from that night I was buying coke to indulge in my habit. I only had heroin for sale and barely at that but my coke was totally gone and I had at that point decided I was coming out of that business. Access was too easy. So I found myself buying smoking quantities rather than selling ones. I became a client of people I barely knew because I was too embarrassed to go to my friends. I mostly chose Jamaicans as I didn't roll in their circles. It was now about the third week in May '95, I'd been out just about six months and I was hitting the pipe nearly like before I went away but not yet there. I was a more social user now and more likely to party than I was to hide away in the room and smoke for days. No, I still had some control but that was being chipped away quickly.

One night in late-ish May, Sandra must have been out all day with the kids somewhere. I started off saying let me call for some to just have a couple of spliffs. I ended up piping some and this decision was to change my whole day, my whole life and the lives of my family members ever since. Why? Well as I said I started off with buying a sixteenth of an ounce for around fifty pounds. This was in the daytime around midday or there about. Once I piped a piece, I had to get more so I drove this time to save time, spent double that because I wanted a good smoke. When that was done I went again and this time I bought double again so now I'm down £350. I convinced myself I would pipe some and then seeing as Sandra was coming home soon I would wind down by smoking seasoned spliffs. I did that but all that does if you don't win the battle is you end up using up so much gear because you need three, four times more for a spliff than you need for a hit, that when it's all done you're gutted you wasted so much in spliffs and you want more to pipe because you haven't got the coming down effect you needed to sit your ass down and chill. So, I went on another Journey this time at about 8 p.m. As I was walking out the door I bumped into Sandra and the kids coming home. It was starting to drizzle. We spoke for a bit with me struggling to keep up the pretence of being normal. But I knew she could tell. I said hi to the kids and I walked to the car park while they walked towards the flat.

I always smoked in our third bedroom, which wasn't occupied as the boys still shared a room. I always put the stuff away there in that room too, on the top shelf of the bedroom wardrobe way out of sight even for Sandra to see, as tall as she was. Of course she could feel for it and reach it but I was meticulous about not leaving my shit around.

I purchased another £200 worth. It was now about 9 p.m. and I was down £550, money I needed badly as I was in a bad way financially. It was also starting to pour down a lot harder and windy as hell by the time I was driving home from buying the stuff. I parked up and ran home through the rain but getting soaked anyway. I felt so shit and angry with myself that I'd allowed myself to be taken on this day and spending so much. But… I went ahead anyway. I locked myself in the room, smoked, came out, tried to socialise with my family, went back in, smoked some more, came back out and so on. They went to bed, I was still up. It was now thundering as well as pouring buckets, not to mention the wind and noise from it.

The last thing anyone would do at this point is want to be out at 1 a.m. in that weather. Not if you're hooked, mate! I carried on smoking, understanding and knowing this had to be it. I got undressed when my last piece was done at about 2.30 a.m. I lay on the sofa trying to watch the TV and keep my mind off that evil voice saying 'Go on you know you want more!' The noise from the rain, wind and thunder was horrendous I remember. I lay there for close to an hour contemplating and fighting but still the buzz and the craving would not go away because I'd had so much. I then found myself starting to get dressed up again. Put my coat on. I knew there was only one person I could go to on a night like this. No one would come out to meet you at half past three in the morning in this weather. So I had to do the work running to my car, driving, then running to my guy's house and repeating the process again. I called ahead to make sure he was awake. He answered. I left.

The run to the car was pointless. I was soaked as soon as I left the safety of the block entrance. Got in my car. Fully wet. Drove to my guy's place. The drive was terrible, could barely see in front of you. When I got there, I parked up and ran to the entrance of his block. I pressed on his buzzer twice in an urgent manner because I was being battered by the wind and rain. Although there was a sort of lip you could stand under at the door, the rain was too strong and wind too powerful that it offered no protection at all.

I pressed again and again. I'm standing there in the pouring rain absolutely hating myself. As I'm about to turn around and walk away, he answers. A part of me was glad he did so I hadn't put myself through this for nothing. I went in and he let me in, I wouldn't go past the entrance of his flat because I was soaking wet and dripping. I cursed about him leaving me outside for so long and he apologised saying he fell asleep. I couldn't blame him, it was going on 4 a.m. He asked what I was doing out in this weather and I had to just blow it off as I was embarrassed enough as it were. No point running to the car this time, so I just walked to punish myself even more. Drove home and took my clothes off. The whole time I'm doing this it seems it's all in slow motion. I am not in any type of hurry to smoke. The feeling I had going through me right now was one of depression, disbelief and utter disgust in myself. The three D's! When I finally took the first hit, it was such an anti-climax that it wasn't worth it.

I sat down, looked at the pipe, looked at the rock sitting there and a light came on in my head.

I thought, 'You know what, you are going to throw that rock in the toilet, you will sleep for a day or so. And when you wake up you will never again smoke that poison.'

I got up like I was in a trance and walked to the toilet. I lifted the lid and threw the £100 rock I had just put myself through hell to buy in the bowl and flushed. I went, still in a trance-like mode, back to the sofa and just closed my eyes listening to the noise from the weather outside.

I awoke the next day to the kids' noise. I looked at the time and it was 8 a.m. I had only been asleep about three hours. I said hello and got up to go into the bedroom. I needed to sleep. I slept all day and deep into the evening.

When I woke up that night at around 9 p.m., I looked at myself in the mirror and said, "You can't smoke that shit ever again."

That, ladies and gentlemen was the last day I not only smoked crack cocaine but powder cocaine too, or any form of the drug.

It was May 1995. I will never forget that day for as long as I live! It has now been nineteen years.

CHAPTER FIFTEEN

I remember that first day, first three days, first week and first month clearly in my head. I have spoken about this process to lots of people in and out of our circles. People who were or are still hooked, people who knew people who were hooked, people who never touched it or did once a week, a month or a year therefore do understand and also people who turned their noses up at those who used. The one thing that I tell them is this, from my experience, rehab can work, yes, being locked up in prison or something similar can work yes, moving away from that environment and people in it can work, yes but the main factor that runs right through all those solutions is you! You can do it without rehab, prison, moving, counselling, hypnotism (I've heard people do this) or any other type of magical cure you may think you need. I spent four years in prison and that didn't cure me. But hating myself for being out in the rain when every normal person was home did it. And did it for good, I might add. How often do you hear of people who relapse from whatever treatment they went through for weeks or months and are back on whatever it is they were addicted to?

I believe that when that light comes on in your head, you do not need any of those methods of quitting to successfully stop whatever habit you have. Without that light coming on, you will either die from your addiction as many have or you will take your addiction to your grave. All those people who tell you they stopped drinking twenty years ago, or stopped smoking cigarettes ten years ago, all had that light come on in their heads. But even those who used all of those methods and kept off whatever addiction they had, the light also came on in their heads why they were able to stay on the path. What I'm saying is I believe you can do it with or without all that help as long as it's from within. Without that light coming on, that willingness, that desire from within, no amount of help given to the person makes a difference. If it does, it's always temporary.

I began seeing a difference in my whole being immediately. I smiled more, I stopped and chatted a lot more to neighbours who said hello. I had more time to play with the kids and spent time with Sandra, my mum and family in general. I immediately also started to see money building up again. I had come within a few pounds of disaster. I was down to an ounce and a half of supply and no spare cash. Once I woke up on the second day, I was able to think a lot clearer. Not because I was always in a daze or something because it wasn't like that. It is something I find difficult to explain. It was like a fog had been lifted off my mind, which had been there since the 1980s. Like a fog was there even when I got out but wasn't getting high on crack, but that fog was now gone. A certain type of peace of mind, of spirit and soul that I hadn't had in my adult life up until then. It was a feeling, not anything you could see or touch, just a feeling, a vibe within my being. It felt good. Even with the hustling for example, I wasn't so hungry about it all. I took my time building back up with no particular pressure. That wasn't how I did things before. I hadn't lost my drive, not at all - I was just seeing things with a different pair of eyes.

I started saving cash pretty much the first week after I quit that poison. By the end of the first week, I had doubled what I had in stock and savings. There was a feeling within me that I'd found a new buzz. Money! Now even though I always had that money buzz, there were other things that I chased. Every fifty pounds I put into the savings box gave me a buzz like I just took a hit from the coke pipe. It wasn't like that before. So just like you want another hit from the pipe, I looked forward in anticipation to the next £50 or £100 I was able to put aside.

By July of that year, '95, I had enough put aside to decorate and refurbish our home. This was something we hadn't done since Sandra moved in when I was still locked up back in '92. We searched for someone who could do the stuff that we couldn't do ourselves and set about doing the stuff we could, like painting and putting on ceiling tiles. I had the Piece de Resistance planned for the living room: a bar!

I designed this myself by drawing what I wanted and then got the handyman we hired to build it to specification. It was really cool. Having a built in bar in my home was a dream come true. Later in life it was having a pool table and a swimming pool in my home that was the thing, I also did get this when we moved to Spain in 2004.

So the house was done up, new beds, larger TVs and that spare room I used to smoke in was now kitted out so the boys had a bedroom each. I do believe in the same month I purchased a pretty red Ford Fiesta XR2i. This was the upgrade from the XR2 that I purchased when I first got out. That was still a pretty good car and in good condition. Now we had two cars in the family. It wasn't the first time we had multiple cars but it was the first time both cars were of a very good standard. The XR2i was about four years old, which is pretty new for people my age while the XR2 was about seven years old but a good seven as opposed to an abused one.

When the house was done it gave me even more reasons to want to stay home and just chill out. My wasteful spending had gone down by ninety-five percent or more and money was building up in a way that I only experienced when I was in jail and selling drugs because I wasn't outside spunking it off. Sandra and I were also much happier. By the time I suggested we refurbish the house and her seeing it happen in reality, she was starting to get sold on the idea that I may just have been serious about changing my life. All this within two or three months since that day in May.

Summer 1995 rolled on and autumn came and went. Things were so much better, and I was a totally different person. Don't get me wrong, I didn't break away from my people or crew. I was still rolling daily with the guys. Guys who were still smoking crack hard, we were raving hard still as UK Garage was now fully in the swing. There were still Jungle raves but that scene was fast being replaced by Garage and being left for the teenagers and teeny boppers. During those early days and weeks after I stopped using, I spent many hours with my crew while they were actually smoking and did not flinch or get tempted at all. I would basically sit down and smoke my weed if we were somewhere you could do that while my guys smoked their stuff. Again this is what I meant when I said it has to come from within. People sometimes feel they have to move from influences to be able to beat the addiction or habit, but from the very first day I quit, I was so sure that I'd had enough, that I did not restrict myself to being around just people who did not indulge. I was still going out every weekend after a couple of weeks of quitting, the smell as you walked in a rave then was still the smell of coke spliffs, people around me still skinned up and smoked but, it wasn't a problem from day one.

I started selling weed too at this time. Weed was steady and stable once you built up the clientele. I welcomed my second Christmas in 1995 with huge hope for the future. I hadn't touched cocaine at this point for seven months. The longest I'd gone without touching it on the outside. I was pleased with myself.

New Year was a blast. Always was and always will be after spending so long away and missing so many of them. Although I haven't been to prison now or seen a police cell now for twelve years, come New Year I still appreciate it with a different twang, that vibe that only people who have missed it multiple times can appreciate. And in the wee back of your mind you remember those sitting where you sat for those many years, and what was going through their minds at that point as the clock struck twelve.

1996 started really well. I had now been out a year. We were steady financially and the kids were getting older by the day. Koy was now five years old, Romaine was going on eight. I was twenty-seven years old. I pretty much sailed smoothly through the year with no hiccups.

I was still always being harassed by the local police as often as they could. I remember near enough stripping naked one day on Bruce Grove when the same police officers stopped me for the third time in two days. The first two times, they called for a van so I could be strip-searched in the back looking for drugs. That was in the morning and then late afternoon of the same day. Then comes the next day and I'm driving along on Bruce Grove, I just opened a pack of cigarettes and threw the plastic and foil wrappers out the window, when I looked up it's the same two officers again flashing me to stop.

I was so angry now that I pulled over jumped out my car and asked them what they wanted this time.

"We just saw you throw a silver wrap out of the window," one officer said.

"Ok so now you want to search me…" I finished off their sentence the way I expected them to. "No need to call the van I will strip right here and right now for you officers!"

With that I started taking off my jacket, then my top, threw them in the car, then next I pulled my jeans down and by the time my jeans got to my knees, the one officer says, "We don't have to do this here pull up your jeans."

"No mate, because all I threw out was the plastic and silver wrapping of my pack of Bensons and Hedges cigarette. You know that, it went flying. If there was stuff in it one of you idiots would have gone back to fetch it. All you wanna do is to have a reason to search me so let's cut out the bullshit and search me now. I ain't waiting on no van to come to get searched."

I was prepared to strip off there and then and they saw it. Eventually they relented and drove off with me giving them a mouthful.

But even with the police attention life was pretty good at this point. I knew that the biggest risk to a street guy's freedom is the active stuff you do, like street crimes, burglaries, thefts, shoplifting, armed robberies, home robberies and things like selling drugs on the streets. If you cut away all those things I just mentioned, you reduce your chances of getting locked up by maybe eighty percent! I wasn't doing any of these at that time. I was focusing mainly on just selling my drugs to customers I had and some of them I'd had now for over a year. Yes many of these guys will sell you out to cops in a heartbeat if they're caught doing what they do for money, but the less they know about you the further down your chances of getting caught go. So for example, a dealer who's too lazy or maybe too complacent and chooses to have his clients come to his drug house or even his home to buy is more likely to get caught than I am because I go to my clients and no one ever comes to my house for that. When the junkie gets caught stealing and is at risk of losing his or her freedom even for a few hours, the thought of withdrawal pains while in custody is enough to tell the police something in return for freedom and getting a fix. So if you sell from a base then that information can be passed on. If on the other hand you meet people who call you at different points then all they have to give is your number and nickname. And most of my junkies knew me as Boxer. The weed I mostly sold to people by delivering to their homes but very few would come to me. Weed was a different business altogether. Your clients tended to be mates as well or mates of mates, people you knew, while class A was really clients, full stop. So I was sure that as long as I had a hiding place for my stock whilst in transit to supply, I was half OK.

There were many times I was stopped carrying stuff but got away with it as I had the best hiding place of all. My body!

1996 passed fairly stable and quiet. That May, I drank and celebrated my first full year of being off the pipe. I didn't completely cut off from the chicks Monique, Lorraine and Debbie. I didn't see Lorraine or Debbie much anymore because I wasn't selling that stuff any longer but I kept in touch with Monique. We still screwed each other's brains out any time we got together. But the sex smoking I didn't indulge in anymore, obviously. Remember in the previous chapter when I was telling the story of me and the two girls? Remember I told you it was the first but not the last time? Well now I was deep into this new me, I had met quite a few chicks that were not from our clique, so to speak. When you have more time to notice things, chat and be more social you do sort of pick up on people from all walks of life. In the summer of '96, I was cruising down West Green Road when I pulled up to chat up a Greek or Turkish looking chick. This was a type of chick I'd never banged before. Done the black, white, mixed of all sorts and even a white and Chinese mix chick, but I hadn't done any Indian, Turkish or Greek. So I pulled up and we got talking. We swapped numbers and she gave me her address, which was on the same road, literally behind where we were standing at that time. I could spit from where I was and it would hit her window. She said her name was Maria and her parents were Turkish.

The first time I visited her, I met her young niece. Maria was around twenty-five then, I was twenty-seven and her niece was about nineteen or eighteen, not sure now but late teens anyway. We smoked weed and chilled and watched movies. Maria was cute and was very streetwise so she wasn't your everyday Turkish chick. We banged I think by my second visit to her flat. We became banging buddies and I really actually liked her. She had a swagger about her that black girls have with an ass that matched most too.

When my birthday of '96 was approaching, Maria asked me what I would like for my big day.

I had noticed a sexual vibe with her niece for some time now. She loved play fighting, sitting on me and all those little girl ways of sending sexual messages your way. She even slept in the bed with us once when I stayed over late at Maria's. Maria instigated a sneaky bang from behind but I was sure as quiet as we tried to be, her niece heard us.

So when she asked what I wanted for my birthday I cheekily and jokingly said two girls in a bed, thinking she would laugh it off. She asked what I meant.

"I mean like two in a bed?" and, "You know what I mean."

"Yeah, so where you gonna get that, I can't give you that. What else you want, come on be serious."

"I'm serious girl, it would be the best birthday ever and I will remember it for life," I said, still with a cheeky smile on my face. It's funny I said that because eighteen years later I'm talking about it even though I haven't seen or heard anything about her for maybe seventeen of those last eighteen years.

"Ok so how you gonna get that then?" she asked me with her hands on her hips in a feisty way.

"You and Larissa ain't it."

"*What?* You're mad. You've proper lost it mate!" Then. "Me and my niece? Are you crazy?"

"Why, ain't impossible!" I replied, all the time smiling. Because to be honest it was more a wind-up than any real attempt at suggesting.

"No way Jose, put that out your mind!"

"Well you asked what I wanted didn't you, so I'm just telling you what I want, innit?" came my cheeky reply. Still winding her up of course.

"Listen when you know what you reeaaally want then let me know. It's two weeks away so you got time!" Then turned around and walked off in playful annoyance.

After that conversation I definitely didn't expect my wish to be granted I can tell you.

But… a few days later, I was at Maria's again and this time her and her niece brought the conversation up all by themselves.

"So Anthony I hear you're asking my aunty to have us two in one bed for your birthday?" Larissa said out of nowhere.

I nearly choked on the weed spliff I was pulling on at the time. What? She had told her niece about our joke conversation? What the fuck! I composed myself after coughing for a second, which made them both laugh.

"No babes, I never said it like that. She asked me what I wanted for my birthday so I said two chicks at the same time. Then she asked how I was gonna get that and as a joke I said you two. That was it babes, I swear."

"Hmm hmm. That ain't what I heard!" she said this in a sing song way.

"Why are you lot bringing it up anyway, what you guys been talking about it yeah?" I came back at them.

Then they get all defensive and evasive. "Nah man, I told her about your cheeky suggestion, that's all it was. So don't think we was here debating it right," Maria says.

"It's cool you know, we can debate it now still if you want," I said.

"Debate what, there's nothing to debate," Maria said.

So I looked over at Larissa and said, "What do you think of my birthday wish Larissa?"

"I think you're mad. So hold on let's say Maria does that for you…"

"What us three?" I interrupted.

"As I was saying," she continued. "Let's say Maria does that for you will it be cool for you to do it back for her on her next birthday and let her have two of you in bed? Like you and your friend or something?"

"I'll think about it if she does mine first!" I said.

"Yeah right, I'd like to see that happen," Maria commented.

We went back and forth like that for a while, but I remember coming away from the conversation thinking, they might actually do this. They weren't overly disgusted at the thought; it was all still very light hearted. Me personally I have never been in a room with another naked man banging one, two, three or any number of chicks. It's not something I ever want to do. I've been in a house where we are in different rooms in the house and had our own chicks for the night with us and even once where we swapped. But never in the same room, never mind the same bed.

My birthday weekend came. It was a Monday that year, so I started celebrating from the Friday. I promised Sandra we'd go out the Saturday and go do something special on the Sunday, like go cinema and then Monday my actual birthday we'll do something with the kids.

In return I told her I was going out with the guys on the Friday before my birthday. The 'guys' was actually Maria and her niece. We went to this wine bar in Shoreditch to listen to some Soulful House music, which was another genre that was starting to come in on the circuit. I popped an ecstasy pill and those two had a half each. It was a great night. Peaceful, soulful, lots of singing and dancing because the tunes were like that.

We went back to her place at around 3 a.m. when the club closed and got there at around 3.30 a.m.

"How long you staying Anthony?" Maria asked as we kicked off our shoes and sat back in the living room.

"I'm good you know so let's do whatever, it's my night with you babes."

We made a couple of spliffs turned on the music and just chatted, the three of us. We were still flying from the E's so the vibe was really nice. After a while Maria asked if I wanted to go to the bedroom so Larissa could go on to the sofa as she was staying the night. So I said OK, picked up my bits and pieces, said good night to Larissa and walked to the bedroom leaving them both out there but expecting Maria in the room in a few seconds.

She came into the room and started to get undressed. She stripped off everything and got in bed. I was on top of the bed but when I saw that I quickly did the same and jumped in next to her. As soon as our bodies made contact it was on. We'd had such a great time out that it was nice to finish it off this way.

So we're rolling and kissing and fingering and she's blowing me and all that. As I'd taken a pill earlier that evening, I knew she was in for a great sex session. Anyone who's ever had sex on an E will tell you. You can go all night and start again.

"This special one is for you birthday boy," Maria said as she pushed me back on the bed and took my dick in her mouth.

The blow job was so nice that I had my eyes closed with a smile on my face and just enjoying the moment.

Then I hear something that makes me open my eyes! What the fuck?

Larissa walked in the room absolutely naked and smiling. Is this real or am I buzzing? I was thinking. She just walked briskly to the bed before I could even ask or say anything, lay down on the bed, right up on me but half her body still on the bed and took her right breast in her hand and stuck her nipple up to my mouth, making me have to react on instinct and open my mouth to let it in!

You know what guys, there are sometimes when you just don't talk! Sometimes when no matter how bad your instinct tells you to speak, you just keep your mouth shut.

I was getting a blow job from Maria, who didn't stop the whole time, I had Larissa's tits in my mouth and now my hands roaming up and down her body into every crevice and orifice. Why spoil it by talking? I went ahead, glad I was still buzzing on ecstasy, they were gonna get it on all cylinders tanight! Larrissa's body was really nice. Whereas Maria was of average height for a woman, about five-seven, Larissa was more five-five. She was small for what I would normally go for but she was very OK. I didn't think this was going to happen at all.

I'll leave you to use your imagination. This isn't *Fifty Shades of Grey*! It isn't a sex book. It's a story about our lives and how we live it.

What I will say though is as much as I wanted to bang Larissa first before she changed her mind or get jealous watching me do Maria, I had to do Maria first. Out of respect, she was my chick after all. But while we banged I kept Larissa busy. Every time we changed position, I put her in a position too, to allow me to keep them both happy. So when I was done with Maria, I washed and went to Larissa. We partied all night and fell asleep in the bed all three of us. My phone woke me up that morning. You can guess who it was. It was a shame to just get up and leave so I cuddled up with them for a good while to savour the moment.

Around this time the war that now exists between Tottenham and Hackney began. A lot of guys who got into it in the 2000s and are in it now do not even know what the beef was about. A lot of people have died since, all you have to do is go to Google and look them all up. It really started between Tottenham and Hackney when coolie Kenny Rowe (RIP) got shot in the stomach the first time. He was shot over some Young Offender Institution argument that spilled over to the streets. Clifford Angol aka Suttie (RIP), my old best friend in Maidstone, shot him in the stomach in a rave in West London. It wasn't Suttie's argument really because I don't think those two actually knew each other to even have beef. The beef was with who Suttie was with. But Suttie, I hear, was the one who pulled a gun out and fired. Kenny was from Clapton, therefore Hackney and was a good friend of mine. We were all friends going back to the 1980s when we were all early teens and late teens. Kenny ended up with what we call a Shit Bag but is really called a Colostomy Bag. This was about the middle of '96. The next year, in 1997, just about the start of summer Kenny was sitting in his car with his chick and got finished off this time. It was obvious who the police thought did it. He was really the first casualty in the Tottenham versus Hackney war that exists today. About a week later, Suttie, my old friend was sat in his car. He had just been released from questioning over the death of Kenny. A car pulled up and shot him six times. He's dead. Now even though he was West London, he rolled with us as well in North London. That started the tit-for-tat murders that have only now slowed down, eighteen years later.

1996 also saw us start growing from just street hustlers and or thieves, to serious gangsters. We were also starting to become 'international' so to speak. What I mean is that we were starting to hook up crews from all over London, crews from Birmingham, Manchester, Leeds and Luton in particular, but also places like Nottingham, Northampton and Southampton. I noticed at this time too that a lot more of us had guns. Not a majority like now, but it was becoming more and more common. We were still a very small minority. I say we because by the end of '96 I'd bought a small .22 revolver. My first gun since the one I got arrested with back in '90. These days it's a shock when a wannabe bad boy does not have one, even as early as eighteen years of age. So life became a lot more serious as '96 drew to a close and '97 came in. What we didn't expect was that the Post Code Wars of London had just kicked off. I don't know about Manchester and Birmingham and all those other places if they had these wars before '96 but I pretty much think they also started in those places round about '96 give or take a year. By 1997, I was going into my third year of freedom. I had had a couple of scrapes with the law but no charges. I was keeping my no-smoking-coke promise with ease. I truly was over it and feeling good. A lot of my old crew still smoked daily and lived that life that now to me looked so, so crummy a life. By that May it would be two years since that night. 1997 also brought what looked like it would be a change in the political landscape that had blighted us for eighteen years. It was the Tory party. The nasty Conservative Party. They had been in power with Maggie Thatcher since 1979. And then when she stepped down due to back-stabbing within her ranks in 1989, John fucking Major took over. A puppet PM if there ever was an example of one. He then won an election in 1992. The next five years and the scandals they got into helped annihilate them for the following thirteen years after they lost in '97. And even when Labour messed up so badly in the 2010 elections, the public still did not trust them enough to give them back the reins again on their own. We ended up with the first coalition government in my living memory. Tony Blair was the star. He was the Tory Slayer in my eyes. Tories are racist, anti- working class, greedy, cold and heartless. Then multiply all that by a factor of twenty, that's what you feel from them if you're black or ethnic or a foreigner.

I remember watching telly all night to see constituency after constituency fall to Labour. Tory MP after Tory MP lost their seats. Familiar big names were now no longer holders of a House of Commons seat. The whole country woke up to huge optimism. I know I did. It was great to see the back of that sleazy lot. Many of them were in prison too for cash for questions and all sorts of other sleazy cases.

Mid '97 was bittersweet but we carried on nonetheless. So did the tit-for-tat shootings that were now starting to take hold on the streets. There were now more and more people getting shot.

My personal life was OK-ish. I started to feel like I needed something in my life. Some sort of release besides raving and girls. I took on a young soldier called chubby to help me with selling drugs and meeting the clients. This gave me more free time to be around the new networks we were now building. Unintentionally I might add. Sandra and I were not getting on as well, mostly down to me and my escapades. I'd met another chick by now called Chika. She had the largest tits I ever saw, but more importantly she was born on my birthday. Or rather, we were born on the same day. I was now twenty-eight, she was twenty-two. She was the first person I'd ever met who was born on 14 October. Male or female. I knew of people but never met one. We got on great. She worked in my local pub, a black owned pub. We spent a lot of summer '97 in that pub it became our spot and Chika was my chick. Sandra and I were growing further and further apart. I wasn't feeling her anywhere near how I used to. I stayed out a lot at this time because the vibes just weren't there. Around the autumn of that year we found a place called Rio's. It was an adult, twenty-four hour sauna, gym, steam room and general wellness place in Kentish Town in North West London. Sandra and I would drop the boys off at her dad's on a Friday and we'd go there from about 11 p.m. till 4 or 5 a.m. It was one of those places where you can go nude if you wanted. Lots of dirty old men of all races would go nude. There was fucking in the two large Jacuzzis, fucking in the chill out rooms upstairs, disguised fucking in the steam room and anywhere else people screwed. I definitely banged discreetly in the Jacuzzi and in the private chill out rooms. Many times. We started going every Friday. A habit I kept until at least early 2000. With three different relationships.

This didn't save my relationship however. When 1998 came round, I had given Sandra back the four years we lost with me being away. I changed my car and bought a four-year-old Mazda 626 - the ones that look like a Lexus. It was a pretty metallic black one. By now I wasn't always going to Rio's with Sandra. But I always went on Friday nights. There, I met another Maria. A mixed race chick. Very pretty girl with the sexiest tits you ever saw. She worked behind the bar at Rio's topless. All the female staff who worked there had to work topless. It was like tits on show! What with all the other topless female visitors, some nude, others just topless.

Maria knew I had a girl as I went there with Sandra, I noticed she was always being rushed, harassed by men, chatted up, bought drinks and all sorts. She was their best looking member of staff by a mile. Young and old went after her. I was cool with her but kept my distance and gave her space. I probably was the only one not seeking her audience or company. One Friday night, early Saturday morning, I asked her to come to Aquarium later that night, Saturday night. She said she had to work that night but will let me know. I think I got a call at about 7 p.m. from her asking what time the rave started and finished. She said she might get off work for 1 a.m. and go home to change and be ready for 2. She gave me her address and hung up. We met up later that night and went out. That night I really got to know the real Maria. She was a nice girl and quite humble, which doesn't come across when she's at work. We had fun and then went back to mine. I now had a place in Finsbury Park. It was a two-bedroom flat but I was renting one out to a girl called TJ, a friend. I left the larger room kitted out for whenever I wanted space from Sandra. We spent all day Sunday together late into the early hours of Monday. From then on we were tight. She was also cool about me bringing other chicks there and I didn't ask her who she did or didn't date, we just hooked up whenever and kept it cool at the health spa. I watched or overheard sometimes when guys were trying to chat her up and I'd smile to myself because the guy didn't know we were seeing each other.

By May of '98, Sandra and I split up. She tried to patch things but there was no use in my opinion. I knew I could and would be a great dad whether I was with their mum or not. I moved out to my place and that was the end of about eight or nine years of life together as a family unit.

I kept on going to Rio's but a lot of times on my own and then going home with Maria when she signed off at 5am. It was now getting out a bit that we were seeing each other. A lot of the staff members knew and a tiny few of the guests and regulars. I saw Stephen Lawrence's parents there a few times when they were together and saw his dad there a lot more times after she stopped coming.

This became the routine for a while as well as making money but all in all aside from the war now brewing and at full pace, life passed without too much fuss. Tony Blair was looking like a great guy and the most popular PM either in history or in a really long time but for sure the most popular Labour leader in their history. There was a feel good factor at this time in the country. The records being made in

Garage music at this time is what is still played today and referred to as back to '95. They were soulful tunes and really carried a distinct vibe about them, this is even more noticeable now when you go to one of the Back To '95 raves. So the mood was good. Round about June of '98 I met the person I would be with for the next six years. Her name was Marcia. She was with her cousin and I was with my good friend Andre. We swapped numbers that first day and agreed to arrange a hook up. I called her that same week, a few days later and invited her and her cousin to Rio's.

They turned up, I was there with Andre so we sort of double dated although Andre wasn't interested in her cousin. While Marcia was tall and stunning, her cousin wasn't much. While Marcia had a figure and legs to die for her cousin was on the tubby side. But we rolled as a foursome. Maria did not look pleased. But I never had her down as someone I could settle into a stable relationship with yet I could see that potential in Marcia from the first time I saw her. That night at Rio's we talked and talked, she was a very interesting person. I think the most interesting girl I'd ever met at that point. Interesting in a way that I like listening to her, she brought a side out in me that I didn't know existed. I think I was hooked by the time we went home, me to mine and Marcia to hers. I couldn't wait to see her again. Monday I arranged to pick her up for lunch from work. We went and had a pub lunch. Something I hadn't done in fucking years. I didn't want the lunch to finish, we really clicked. By the following weekend we were fully dating. It was still summer and a great one too that year. Marcia and I went to the Notting Hill carnival that year, my first time since about '89 or something. Nine, maybe ten years. This chick was making me do stuff I liked but hadn't done for ages. We're like two months in and I had no intention of looking elsewhere. I was content with just the one girl for the first time.

When my birthday came round she surprised me with a weekend trip to Paris and a two-hour flying lesson voucher, already paid for. I was shocked. No woman had ever done that for me at that time. Chicks I was around regularly wouldn't think of buying me flying lessons to fly planes! I had told Marcia as well as most girls who I really got close to that my childhood ambition was to be a pilot. It was and still is my biggest regret that I didn't have the support from my folks to take up the career. Anyway during one of our deep conversations weeks before I talked about this and my passion for flying. Little did I know she would book me my first ever flying lesson. I booked the flying lesson for the day before our flight to Paris, which was booked for the day before my birthday. We drove to Chertsey Airfield in Surrey. The two hours consisted of one hour instrument lesson on the ground, in a classroom and one hour flying time in the air. When I took to the air with my instructor handling the controls and with the head phones for communicating with the tower so I could hear the tower and could talk to them, it was bloody magical. I was mesmerized. I, Anthony, was in the cockpit of a twin engine Cessna. Then he let me take the control once we got to flight altitude. Man, it felt at that moment like I had opened a whole new door in my life and I was loving it. I promised myself that I would now keep this up. You need forty hours of flying time to get your Private Pilot's License or PPL. I promised myself I would try my very best to achieve my PPL. We went on our weekend away in Paris and had a blast. It was my first time in Paris at that time and it was a nice treat. I hadn't travelled again since we travelled in '95 when we went Amsterdam and Belgium. I felt a bit bad not having the kids with me. But Marcia had a son too who was twelve years old at this time and he also wasn't with us, so it wasn't too bad. On our return I immediately set about booking more flying lessons and even started to look at how much a Cessna small aircraft costs. I found out that for forty grand you could get a nice old-ish one. One maybe about ten to twelve years old. But still had ten more years and more of life left.

When I told my brothers that I finally flew, they were well chuffed for me. For the first time my family wanted to know who I was seeing. They wanted to know who this chick was that I had been going on about. When we came back from Paris, I think Sandra also realized then too that I definitely had moved on. She tried one last ditch effort to get back together but it was too late for me.

I had also stopped seeing Maria and about four other chicks I had around me as soon as I got serious with Marcia. Monique included.

1998 saw Grays Inn Road rave take off big time. It was a new type of rave on the scene and one that I became king in. It started at 4 a.m on Sunday morning and finished at 4 p.m. in the evening of that day. There had been similar raves with those hours years before, around the early nineties in the Jungle and Acid rave days, one was called Turnmills. But Grays Inn Road was an instant hit. I had been going there with Maria in early summer when I first got to know about it. Now I was going with Marcia. It was easier to bring Marcia into my crew than it was Maria, so even though I'd gone raving alone with Maria, Marcia and I were going with my people. I got to know the woman who promoted the event, Fulvia. She was a sharp lady and knew what she was doing. We later hooked up to put events on as business partners, but that was to come later.

The wars on the streets had also intensified by the end of '98. Because of the killing of Suttie, West London was now fully involved in the war. Suttie had a lot of friends. At this point the older Tottenham guys my age, we were now nearly thirties or just over thirty, were not as involved in the day to day warring that was going on. Over in Hackney they were fully involved, over in West London they were too, but in Tottenham the few older guys who were fully involved needed soldiers and so they set about bringing the youngers into it. And into it they went happily. The main reason the Tottenham olders weren't in it like that was because many of us were too connected to the Hackney lot for years and years. I couldn't just start shooting at guys I'd raved with, done crime with, whose sisters I'd dated and so on. We ran into each other at local petrol stations, at raves and at mates' houses. Only a very few in Tottenham my age took it up. But by the end of '98 there were quite a few young guys gun slinging in the name of the war who didn't even know the characters or the stories involved.

This trend, started in Tottenham because of lack of interest by the older gangsters to get involved, carried on to the other areas slowly, where the gun men were getting younger and younger. Older guys my age, having seen how many serious young guns were coming out of Tottenham and eager to impress and make a name on the streets, started the same thing in their Manors. This new trend of trigger happy young guns, who weren't even thinking about jail or a life sentence, were quick to squeeze the trigger no matter where they were from. This infusion of the young crews escalated this whole mess. This escalation caused me a lot of problems later when I was promoting my own Garage raves.

Towards the end of '98, round about November, I made an approach to Fulvia, the lady who promoted the Grays Inn rave, to work with her on putting on a Sunday night event after hers. I figured I could harness her crowd and give them something to go to on a Sunday night. She had at least 600 to 700 people in the club every week, if not more, but when it was finished you were left wanting more. If I could promote this new event at hers for weeks before we opened, have her DJs, who were now my friends, promote the event on the microphone every week and their respective radio shows, then I would have a chance at making it a success.

Business was always something I knew I was good at. I just hadn't flexed that part of my brain up to that point, unless you call dealing drugs a business, which in a way it is but you know what I mean.

Gathering people to have a good time, to the sort of music you personally like, while all the time making money, this seemed like a good deal. There was something about the way I was now carrying myself that made me know I was ready to kind of leave the streets behind and look forward. I had now stopped wearing trainers. I used to live in them, now I wore shoes and pumps. Grown-up style. I think I also had more manners thanks to Marcia. All in all I was ready for the next chapter of my life to begin.

I went to Fulvia's house as we'd arranged to iron out my proposal to her. She agreed to my proposal so we set about putting things in motion. Marcia's cousin Buzby had just been deported back from the States after serving prison time there.

Now you see with Marcia, I was the first criminal she ever dated. Her last date was six years before we met, so she wasn't one of those chicks who was always in a relationship. I clocked this about her early on so I tried my best to hide my criminal activities from her as best I could. She knew I was gangster but did not really fully know until her cousin Buzby came back to the UK. The funny thing was, I didn't even know him before he left the UK about ten or so years previously, but when he came back and shortly after being introduced to him, we soon both knew exactly who each other were. One day he called me to the side away from the rest of the family and said, "Hear what Ant (her family called me Ant because she did), you're out of control! Been hearing about you."

"What do you mean Buzby, out of control?" I asked, not sure where he was going with this or even what he meant.

"I hear you lot from North got the streets on fire and ain't taking no prisoners. I hear it's all you and your man dem. I hear you're well in the mix. But it's cool cos you know how we roll. Just treat my little cousin good yeah and take care of her," he finished off saying. I thought he was cool. He was the only other gangster in Marcia's family besides the baby fathers of some of her cousins and her sister. I knew one of those very, very well. Nasty was his name. Nasty was Marcia's cousin Tania's son's dad but I knew him way before all of that. He was a good friend. But within the family itself Buzby was the oldest and he was the baddest. What he said in their family went.

Back to Fulvia and the raves, the problem we had was where to host the event. This was resolved when Buzby and big Froggy went into partnership to buy a wine bar right on the corner of Dalston Lane and Stoke Newington high street. I approached Buzby and offered to be a third partner in the business. I offered six thousand pounds to buy in. All three of us sat down to iron out what was what, Froggy, Buzby and I. It was much better to buy in than rent from them. It made more business sense. I would get a share of drinks sold seven days a week.

I proposed we each have a night where we put on an event and the rest of the week we serve food upstairs and run it as a normal bar. They agreed to this with the two of them having first pick for their individual nights. Buzby chose Saturday nights, Froggy Friday and I was left with Sunday, which was fine by me as this was the night I wanted.

Fulvia and I had flyers printed and a few posters for lamp posts and stuff and started promoting the rave at hers. We kicked off on launch night in December of '98. Luechie and Frankie came down. It was the first time my family had seen the bar that I was a part owner of. Funny enough Luechie knew Buzby. They went way back. He was a little older than Leuchie. I was now thirty, Leuchie was thirty-four and Buzby was about thirty-nine or forty then. The night passed off well. It was one of my proudest moments, to see something that I dreamt up coming to life. To see people turn up to my event and have a great time was great to see.

From the very beginning we had problems with the partnership of the bar. My night was an instant success. Buzby and Froggy both did not understand the Garage music scene. They were still stuck on the reggae music circuit. The nights they tried to start up were going nowhere fast. My crowd spent heavily at the bar because that was how we all rolled, they paid ten pounds at the door no problems, while their people argued about paying five pounds on the door and only bought bottles beer and the likes. The arrangement we had was that we kept our proceeds from the door to ourselves on our individual night but shared all proceeds from the bar but keep back enough to re-stock the bar obviously.

Mine and Fulvia's Sunday night was giving us a cool two and a half to three thousand pounds to split between us and pay doormen and stuff and my share from the bar added another thousand and more as the weeks went by.

Buzby and Froggy being much older friends than I was with either of them must have got together behind my back. They called me down to the bar one mid-week just before Christmas of '98. I wasn't at the bar all the time but I had a chick I knew working with their bar girl to make sure I wasn't being robbed. So I came to speak with them.

They wanted to re-write our unwritten agreement on how the bar was run and proceeds split. I listened even though I knew where they were going. Anyway, now they want all the nights and all the drinks to be shared equally. So we throw all in and we take all out equally regardless of whose event it was.

You see this now, when they left me Sunday nights they didn't think my night will work as well as theirs being Friday and Saturday. But I'd had Lennox Lewis turn up to my wine bar and queue's outside every Sunday night. My event created a traffic jam on Monday morning as revelers left at 6 a.m. meeting those going work.

Anyway, I told them to give me some time to think it over. I didn't want to rush into any decision regardless what answer I gave. It was complicated on my end because I had Fulvia to think about too. What they were proposing would mean the door takings on our night would now be split four ways. She wasn't going to benefit from the other side of the deal as she wouldn't be getting anything from their nights.

In the end I refused the offer. This created a bad vibe in the partnership that lasted for months into '99 until I asked for my investment back and moved to Trends. But that was another story entirely. All in all I had my first taste of owning my own bar or club and even restaurant, all of which I have owned since those days. Lately, I've owned a Thai Food restaurant in Barcelona! Yes you heard right Barcelona Spain. Keep reading.

So we saw 1999 in with a bigger bang than normal. I felt the future looked orange as they say. It had been five years since my release. I was doing OK financially, I was in a new relationship, the kids had met her and we were now starting to become a family unit. 1999 was promising to be a good year.

I was now a bar owner and a promoter and I seemed to be putting my past behind me and moving into a new era.

CHAPTER SIXTEEN

My year started with a bang. This was the year all conspiracy theorists had been waiting for. "Space 1999!" Remember that? It was finally upon us. The dreaded year 2000 AD was now just a year away! There were stories of all stored data being wiped out or disrupted at the least when the new millennium started. Stories about humanity as we know it coming to an end. Stories about the old Ethiopian time or the Chinese and their old calendar or biblical predictions all coming back to haunt us and even kill us all. The internet, which I was now starting to bite my teeth into, was awash with one conspiracy theory after another. Frankly, I don't know how we didn't just all capitulate and just commit suicide before it all ended. But thank God we didn't isn't it?

Spare a thought for those fuckers who did commit suicide thinking it'd all be over in a year or those who wasted money buying huge amounts of provisions ready for the worst. Me, I really just got on with it. When it happens it happens was my policy! But those who listened to Rasta men high on high grade weed preach what would happen to us all and then came and wanted to tell me all about it, I had no time for. I had better things going on in my life.

Remember chapter twelve? Well what you read in chapter twelve was to take you to the future. As the book started off in the Introduction with my being in lock-up again for the first time in eight years, chapter twelve was to bring you forward in time so the reader can catch back up to that present time. From this chapter on, time catches up. This chapter serves the purpose of bringing the past to meet with the future/present.

From here on in the past and present will meet and blend to trace the path that lead to my last and hopefully final time in prison, events in the background that lead to the events in chapter twelve, which I didn't go into in depth in that chapter.

So the bad blood at the wine bar was deteriorating fast. My nights were getting bigger and bigger. We were sometimes unable to let people in. There was no room on the wine bar floor. The capacity was 150 but we squeezed 200 and more in every week. Buzby's night on Saturday was struggling to get thirty or forty while Froggies didn't even really get off the mark at all. By January or February '99 Friday night became just a normal bar night. There were no door takings. So you can imagine how ghetto people are, they were fuming because I rejected their attempt at being smart, like I was a fool.

This bad blood flowed into their family with Marcia also getting drawn into it. Those who weren't asking but just listening to their big brother or big cousin Buzby thought I was greedy until they spoke to Marcia or myself then they really understood. What Buzby was telling his family was that my night became a success and I was not sharing with them, that instead I was sharing the spoils with some old Turkish woman. That woman was Fulvia, without whose help it would have taken me a lot longer to get the rave going, if at all.

The war on the streets was also intensifying fast. Soldiers were being knocked off left, right and centre. Guys were getting shot and survived, guys were shot and died and many more mothers were sitting at home with a son they had no clue just murdered someone that night, that week or that month even. We were watching a community of killers grow larger and larger, slowly but surely.

My relationship with Marcia was fast approaching its first year and I still hadn't felt the need to cheat once! They say a woman can change a man and that's true, but the man has to be ready for change. It wouldn't matter what a woman did to try changing her man, if his mind wasn't receptive to it, it would be a waste of time. I think I was ready for change when I met Marcia. So it made it easier for us both. She would always tell me to say thank you in restaurants when they took our order, when they served the drinks and when they served our food. I dressed more like a mature business man than a street guy but that was down to me. So I was changing a lot during this time, changes that stayed till this day. I went to a few more flying lessons but someone should have told me that it wasn't easy learning to fly over the skies of the UK.

Our weather was so shit that I drove to the airfield about seven times since my first flight in October '98 and was only able to fly two or three times due to bad weather. With every session being an hour I could see it was going to be a long process to clock up forty hours. I'd still only done four hours I think by March '99.

Life settled into a routine of doing my thing in the week days, going to Rio's with Marcia on Friday nights, going rave at Grays Inn on Sunday mornings and then doing my own rave on Sunday night. In between this I made a lot of time for the boys, my mum when I could and raising more money. The situation at the bar was getting so bad, I asked to be bought out by around May or so of that year.

This was also the year as I wrote in chapter twelve, that I set up Many Many Promotions. My first of many companies. As I said in twelve I was now building up a crew of doormen who would later become debt collectors for the company. At this time I also got into selling Vests and bullets as the street wars I talked about in the previous chapters took a greater hold on anyone remotely connected to gangsterism.

The older we got the more serious we were. The only thing I stayed out of was the war between East and North. It was ridiculous to me. I knew all the main players on the Hackney side. We all knew each other. Only a few years ago we would have fought on the same side against west, south or out-of-towners. So while they went at it I kept building and made my position known that I was not going to be caught up in it. The younger players I didn't know but the originals all knew who I was and knew where I stood. This stand is the reason why as I explained in twelve, all crews were able to come to my events and put down whatever beef they had.

By May or June '99, Buzby and Froggy finally bought me out by returning my six thousand. They were idiots really because although the door was mine, the bar made on one Sunday night what it made in a month without my rave. But it was what I wanted as the tension was only gonna come to blows or worse. About this time too, I believed I'd learned enough and built up enough of my own contacts to go it alone, away from Fulvia. For example, we used her door staff to start with, we used her regular Grays Inn Road DJs as our music providers, she did the box office obviously because she knew I was street so was weary, so even before we set up, to put her at ease we put that into the agreement. But by summer of '99, I knew those DJs would work for me and me alone, some of her bouncers were mates anyway from Grays Inn but were now truly friends from working on the same side for six or so months at that time. So I had all the tools I needed to go it alone. I had one more thing that she didn't leave me, and that was Pirate Radio Station connections. Through the success of the wine bar, I was building my own contacts in the nightclub industry. At this time I felt I'd found my calling. Something I could do that was as profitable, if not more profitable than crime. Just before I walked away from the wine bar, on one of my Sunday nights, a big Jamaican guy walked over to the entrance of the bar and just hung about. He offered help when it got crowded at the entrance and just generally looked like a big lost puppy. By the end of that night I asked him if he wanted a job. His name? Bigsy. That's how I met him. He was the only doorman that I personally recruited while I worked with Fulvia. It proved to be one of my best decisions. He paid off straight away with keeping an eye on Fulvia and her lot. He stayed loyal to the very end did Bigsy. He was shot at when I was shot. In the end he became my head doorman, my body guard, my right hand and watched my back for the next three years. I loved that guy. You know the old saying about the world being small, it turned out that he was the son of Marcia's sister Sam's boyfriends ex-partner. He was only twenty-three years old but looked thirty-five, bless him. I later recruited more and more doormen until I had about six guys. As I said in chapter twelve, I firstly had them doing freelance to make more money until I had a plan with Many Many Promotions LTD. As you know I took Many promotions into different sectors. I advertised in the Yellow Pages as a debt collection outfit, door staff agency and the rest.

I got into negotiations with the owner of Trends Nightclub, Danny about starting my Sunday nights there before I walked away from the wine bar. Trends I heard, was covertly owned by the Kray Twins. They were still alive at this point. Well maybe one of them anyway. Negotiations went well and I went ahead and struck out on my own in the rave business.

Fulvia told me something right at the very beginning that stayed with me the whole time I was in the rave business.

"Anthony listen," she said. "For as long as we work together, please do not get involved in selling drugs at the venues we host. It will be the worst thing you could do. The authorities will put it all down to you promoting events just for the purpose of having an outlet to sell your drugs. And then you'll have the full weight of their wrath. If you get caught as a raver selling or you sell to a police informant in a rave you might get three or four years. But if it is your event then it's more like seven and nine years. Plus you lose everything you own. So please listen to me and either do one or the other, don't do both."

This was sound advice when I really thought about it. It made sense. It was advice that I truly abided by. I sold my business phone that I'd had now for five years. Whoever had that phone was guaranteed to make money. I sold it for eight grand.

Having the rave also hooked me back up with a lot of my old skool friends I hadn't seen for years. With those guys came pavement work. Pavement work means armed robberies, security van jobs and the likes. I got involved in what I chose to get into and the rest I declined.

About this time I had another crew I carried these jobs out with. This I did to supplement my income. Seeing as I wasn't dealing anymore it was a case of making anything I could make as long as it was safe. I will not go down the list of the more incriminating stuff, but yes we had ink soaked notes on numerous occasions. We learned to clean them and test them at tube station ticket machines to make sure they were good to go. We took down big dealers regularly and every time I got drugs on a move, I made the guys give me cash for my cut. Many times I sat there while they smoked crack in spliffs or in pipes but when I was done I just walked off to go get on with my business. I was now fully cured of that shit. It was now four years since I had that crap go into my body.

'99 saw a roll call of missing guys. Guys shot dead in the wars that had now spread to lots of other manors. Wars that weren't linked to the Tottenham versus Hackney beef. Brixton guys were at war amongst each other depending on which part you were from. There was war between the Hackney guys themselves as Hackney sort of split into two sides. But both sides still had Tottenham as their enemies. It was becoming complicated to keep up with. Then there was your random shooting that had nothing to do with wars. Shootings that probably wouldn't have taken place if the atmosphere wasn't filled with shootings. Let me explain.

When you know more and more people who have used a firearm on someone and you're hearing more and more about people getting shot, and people doing it getting away with it, it becomes an environment that makes you want to shoot someone too, have your name talked about too, want to be feared and respected too. You want to also say, yes, I've done that too.

In this atmosphere everyone wanted to be a gunslinger. So it wasn't just the wars but guys were now more armed than ever before in the street history of the UK plus they were much more ready to pull it out and use instantly. No arguments! Fisticuffs were by now a distant memory. I think the only guys still using fists then were the Scottish.

It was in this atmosphere that as I said in chapter twelve, I started the bullet proof vests and bullets trade. Well someone had to capitalise. At least I was selling them something that may one day have saved them.

Marcia was now starting to know who I really was by the people who had lots of respect for me. I didn't have to say anything to her. She could see for herself slowly. One summers day in '99 we were out shopping for her down Fonthill Road in Finsbury Park. We came out of a shop and started strolling down to another shop when I heard someone shout out, "Yo Killer! Killer!" I ignored this call hoping it wasn't for me.

"Oi killer!" the person behind us shouted out again, "Killer!" and again but this time you could tell the voice was getting closer. Instinct told me to turn around, so I turned around to see this fool, a very good friend of mine Cashew smiling and walking over. God Damn it! Hasn't he got more class than to shout 'killer' on a busy shopping street like that? So I say hello very reluctantly as everyone was now watching to see who 'killer' was. Marcia walked on looking at a shop's window. I told her long ago that if I didn't introduce her to someone then that person wasn't someone she needed to know. So when I told her to give me a minute to say hi to this guy she knew I was pissed. When we walked off I was still so upset. I had told Cashew never to call me that ever again. No one ever really called me that. I don't know what he heard or why he called me that.

We were now fast approaching the dreaded Millennium. Trends had taken off and was a hit by the latter part of '99. I was now getting crowds of 500 and 600 plus every week. It was a smooth operation. I managed to buy my first ever brand new car! A Ford Focus. First owner. Felt great. I also bought Marcia a car after I'd taught her to drive over a few months. She could drive before but not really. So I made her drive us anywhere we wanted to go for months until she was capable. Bought her a second hand Renault Megane. I was getting so big in the game that I had well known DJs contacting me and begging for a set on my night. My posters were everywhere. It was great to drive from North to South and see my rave being advertised on lamp posts. I had companies putting my flyers out for me, putting posts up all over London and DJs promoting my raves on the radio stations.

Along with this success came temptation from females. More and more females wanted to know who the promoter was and wanted to be friends with the promoter. I fought hard to bat them off and keep my new found faithfulness.

I also at this point found myself drifting further and further away from my old crew, Toddler, Briggie, G Money, Nose, Nicky, and all the original guys I grew up with and ran the streets with for so long.

Many of them were still smoking crack. Some sadly had even taken up heroin due to doing time. Many of my friends who I grew up with, who used to turn our noses up at junkies together, were slowly going into using heroin. As they did new sentences in the latter 1990s came out, some had gotten hooked on the inside.

It is a shame really that government policy after government policy, no matter how well meaning they may be, are sometimes not well thought out. Did you know that the biggest reason for the rise of black heroin addicts was the policy brought into prisons to urine test inmates randomly to see what was contained in their urine samples? And the consequences of being found to have cannabis or any other drug in your urine were severe enough to make people find another way. Let me explain. Until my recent incarceration in 2002, I didn't even know these facts myself as there wasn't this so-called piss testing the last time I was locked up in 1994. But basically, the drug that stays in your system the longest was cannabis. Heroin, cocaine and most amphetamines leave your system after the fourth day, therefore if you use those, unless you're unlucky enough to get randomly picked for a piss test between day one and day four the evidence will not show up. Whereas with cannabis the evidence stays in your system for twenty-eight days at the least. What then happens is if you had a good job in prison, you lose it, if you had normal visits, or open visits as it's known, where you can touch, kiss and hold your family, you were placed on closed visits where your visits are conducted behind a heavy piece of glass. Even though you may not have been the person who brought the drug in, you could just have had a few puffs on a spliff. If you had parole coming up, you lose it, if you were going home in three months, two weeks could be added to your time for failing your piss test. In that additional two weeks, you could get piss tested again and if you failed again, an extra month is added again. And so it went. To get round these sanctions and consequences, people switched to using drugs that only stayed in you for a very short time. Slowly the black prison population followed suit. I must say that not all white guys use heroin inside and not all black and ethnic guys got caught up either, but anyone will tell you back in the day, heroin was the drug of choice for the white guys in prison and cannabis was it for blacks. Today the policy of piss testing turned even more white guys to the drug and converted previously crack and weed smoking black guys into heroin addicts. The thing is governments never learn. Look at the Prohibition story of the 20s in the States. That is the classic example that even banning and mismanaging the humble alcohol can cause the type of lawlessness that blighted the US for most of the 20s. The money the mafia and gangsters made in that time was only matched by the ruthlessness they carried out. Why we didn't learn from that, I will never know.

So a lot of my old friends who were still actively going to prison all these years I'd been out, sadly had got caught up in the heroin drug wave that was now in our hood. Some like Briggy had got so bad that he was now a tramp, literally! Every time I drove past him or saw him while walking to or from my car, he would ask me for money and I would give him whatever I had or felt to give him. For others jail became a revolving door. They were hardly on the outside, so were missing for years. Others just went from bad to worse. My hood was disintegrating. The up and coming gunslingers were the ones running the hood now by the late nineties. They were the ones at the raves and the last remaining of us old skool lot. So as I pushed forward with my life, I was slowly losing touch with my old crew. I know Toddler only stopped smoking crack in the mid 2000s, for example, but he was one of those who didn't take the heroin up. But to me smoking crack by the year 2000 was so yesterday, so stupid, that to me it was like 'Are you fucking kidding me? You still on that stuff?' Those who were like me, I moved onwards and upwards with. I built up new friendships and re-established old ones with guys from other manors who were on the raving circuit that I knew from past sentences in jail who were now big time at it or that I knew somehow from just being about. So this became the new me. There were still lots of us though don't get me wrong from Tottenham who were still up there and representing.

Leuchie was also doing well for himself. He'd had his first daughter in '96, Divonne, quickly followed by his son Dillon Junior or DJ for short. He was in a stable relationship with a lovely lady, Simone, who was the mother of his children. They were doing OK. I knew Leuchie dabbled every so often in the hard stuff and I envied him because he never got all fucked up on cocaine like the rest of us. He always just seemed to be able to smoke a raw coke spliff or a seasoned spliff without getting caught up in it. I couldn't do that. He would come out to my events every so often and I would smell he was smoking a seasoned spliff, but by Monday he was his normal every week day self again. So they were pretty much doing fine.

Kevin my brother, was now the one who looked up to me, was always at my events, helping out any way he could and banging chick after chick on account of the rave being his big brothers. By '99 my sister Cass had also had her first child, also a daughter. She was a year old in '99. She was named Taja. Frankie also had two kids at this point, two boys called Andrew and Bradley. His son was named after our brother Andrew. My mum, although she now had six grandchildren, never seemed quite the same person since her son had died over five years previously. To the rest of the world she seemed back to normal, but to the family we knew something wasn't quite right.

It wasn't long before my mum got ill. She suffered from high blood pressure, insomnia and a host of other ailments that she kept getting medicated for. She wasn't in any imminent danger or anything like that. These were ailments that a lot of people carried for years and years until they died of one or some other cause. So it was just a case of her not feeling well all the time but having medication to keep them all in check.

So came the year 2000. Oh my God, was I glad that I was out to see this historical moment. Billions of people had lived and died since the last time there was a welcoming of a new millennium.

When you really think about it, there will not be another on until the year 3000. A thousand years away. Wow! This was how I personally felt. To top it off, I never forget all the New Years I have missed in my life, so being able to be free to see this, not just alive but free too was huge for me.

We went to London Bridge to see the huge fireworks display London had put on. This was something I'd never done before. I never went and still do not go to places like Trafalgar Square and the likes for Hogmanay. But this year we did. I now had cousins who were now much older, so myself, Marcia, her son, my cousins all went to the Bridge to watch the display. We had lots of bottles of champagne that we used to spray over all who were within spraying distance of us. Including police men who to their credit took all in good spirit.

Tony Blair's government had built what became known as the Millennium Dome to commemorate the new century. It was beautiful.

The year 2000 promised new beginnings and hope for the future. And so it started. We went out later that night and partied, for once at someone else's event so we really raved till the morning came. I was just over the moon, I remember.

So I carried on my now semi-criminal life. Half retired from active service. Dabbling in things I deemed as safe-ish to avoid any trouble with the law. I picked and chose carefully what I got involved in. Life on the outside was too sweet to get locked away like a lab rat. I had a nice chick and I didn't want to even imagine what would happen to my relationship if I got locked up. As much as I was sure Marcia would stick by me, I didn't want to put it to the test.

As I mentioned in chapter twelve, it was around this time that I made the link to access bullets, guns and vests. I chose to deal only with bullets and vests. It was good business. The streets were getting very violent. Raves were becoming hazardous if you weren't careful or didn't roll right. My policy at this time was to never go out without my gun. I had changed my weapon by now to a street favourite, the Glock seventeen. It wasn't my only gun mind you, but I'd stopped carrying my six-shooter as most of these young guns carried a Glock that held seventeen rounds.

Raves and my events were the first places I decided to make sure I was always armed. It was an arms race like any other after all. Just like Super Powers and countries at war, you do not bring a knife to a gun fight. And you make sure that at least your weapon matches the other side's. The threat of equal destruction has kept Europe at peace for seventy years. The longest Europe has ever been at peace. And so can that principle save your life.

The proof came in about February or March of 2000. One Sunday night at my event in Trends. I had been trying since the turn of the year to implement a stricter and more upmarket dress code for my rave. We started banning trainers and the likes. My adverts now running regularly on many Pirate Stations were telling the raver about our new dress code. We made sure to be lenient to start off with as it is hard to just change how people came out, if they'd been coming to you a certain way. Some people took to it immediately, some others it took a minute to comply, although some already always came out dressed up and wearing acceptable footwear from the start even before the new dress code. So for weeks and weeks we would warn the same faces, tell them they would be stopped from coming in if they turned up again like that.

There were times when my door men after having warned the same crew many times would refuse them entry, the guys would then ask for me to be called, I would come outside, listen to their excuses and promises not to do it again and I would then override my doormen and let them through with a stern warning. So this shit went on like this for weeks. As I said I understood they were not used to the new standards I was trying to achieve and knew it was going to take time to bring all to my way of thinking and those who didn't want to change could find somewhere else to go for their Sunday nights.

So it was that one Sunday night, I was called outside urgently by Warren, one of my doormen. We didn't have radios then, we only brought those later on. So Warren runs to myself and Bigsy and tells me to come outside quickly because one other doorman and a raver both had each other at gunpoint. I thought, 'What the fuck now?'

We all three ran towards the exit. When I get outside, there was the doorman concerned with his weapon drawn and still in his hand, fully upset and with a lot of commotion around him. I told him to put the gun away as ravers were all around us and more were still coming and then asked what had happened. He explained that it was the same crew of about three young guns who were always being told to stop coming in trainers or they'd be refused entry. They were a very hot headed and troublesome crew, who obviously didn't like to be told what to do, even when it's your place. These guys had been refused the week before but I let them through on the understanding that that was their absolutely last chance. But this night, the very next week, they fucking came back again in the same way and wanted to force entry, showing my place no respect and showing me no respect too as we'd had an agreement the week before, that it was their last of many past chances.

My doorman says that when they turn up again all dressed in trainers and Jeans, he looked them dead in their faces and said, "Guys for sure none of you ain't coming in tonight. Not even the boss can save you tonight!"

With that, the hottest one of these hotheads pulls a gun and started raising it as if to fire, my doorman pulls his out and raises his too. They end up in a stalemate posture with each pointing his weapon at the others face. Now this is a bad situation and bad for business. We were now starting to look like a decent rave and were now attracting the normal nine to five raver and not just the hardcore people and gangsters. This wasn't the image I wanted this new crowd to see. The rave was better off with people from all walks of life not just hustlers, gunslingers, crooks and the hardcore lot.

I asked where they'd gone and I was pointed to the left. I walked off in search of them with Bigsy close behind. Turned left and walked down scanning all the time to see if I could see them. I'd walked about fifty seconds when I could see someone getting into the back of a grey two-door Peugeot, with someone else holding the front seat forward for the back passenger to get in. We walked up on the car just as the front passenger was putting the front seat back down having let the back seat passenger in.

266

Just as he was about to get in himself, I said, "Yow, which one of you pointed a gun at my doorman?"

"Why? What you gonna do Troubles? I don't give a fuck about you, your doorman them or your rave!" As he was saying this he started to reach for his gun, I could tell.

So I grabbed his hand that was pulling out the gun, wrestled it out of his hand, scuffling all the time. I got possession of his gun, still scuffling with him and in one motion threw his weapon as far as I could into a block of flats across the road. Then I pushed him into the open front door and onto the seat, pulled my weapon and shot him.

I hit him in the side of his stomach, I could tell. He let out a scream and shouted, "Aghhh, you just shot me man!"

I pushed him firmly into the car and told him never to come back to my place. "When you back out your gun, then you're trying to kill me. Take yourself to hospital."

I quickly walked back to the club before police got there. I went in and hid the gun in our hiding place inside the club and then went back outside to await whatever was coming. These little fuckers. I was fuming. This wasn't how I expected my night to go. Now look what they'd made me do. I was thirty-one and this kid must have been around twenty-one or twenty-two. Gave them chance after chance as they were good spenders at the bar for their age but to pull a gun on my doorman who was simply just doing his job and then to pull one on me too and maybe was going to shoot me? That was too far. And I was ready to deal with whatever became of this shit.

The whole night I was very much on edge. His mates had seen the whole thing and no one knows how these young thugs would react to stuff. They could roll up and shoot up the club, ride up on bikes and shoot it up or just wait to see me and shoot. They also had so many friends, these young kids that are willing to pick up arms so the revenge may even come from someone completely unexpected. But so be it. I'll deal with it however it came.

What happened next was so unexpected that it completely threw me off.

About the middle of that week, while still weary of every phone call, every knock on the door and every car or bike that pulls up at the traffic lights beside me, I get a phone call from a voice I didn't recognise. That wasn't unusual as my number was on every flyer, poster or radio station ad promoting my events and businesses. So it wasn't hard to reach my phone.

"Is that Troubles?" the voice asked.

"Yeah who's this?"

"Old school Troubles from Tottenham?" he repeated, like he wanted to be sure.

"Yeah, who's this though?"

"It's Sharkey."

"Which Sharkey? Big man Sharkey?"

"Yeah Bruv," he replied.

But just to be sure, "Sharkey from Holly Street?"

"Yeah bruv."

"Oh my days, how you doing, fam? Long time." This was an old friend of mine, much older, I think he was older than me by a good ten or twelve years but I knew him for being on the roads and also from jail. We'd served time in jail back in the day and had met up on the raving circuit lots of times. Good guy but a gangster too. He must have been about forty, forty-one.

"What's happening, Sharkey fam?" I asked.

What he said next came as a complete shock. "That was my son you shot Sunday night Troubles."

"What? Who?" I said, my brain scrambling for what to say. "That yoot was your son Sharkey?"

"Yeah Bruv."

This was followed by a very, very long pause on both sides. What could I say? I just digested this terrible information.

"Sharkey, your boy pulled a gun on my doorman, so the doorman then pulled his gun on him. They stood there toe to toe outside my rave. I get called outside. Time I get outside they'd walked off to their ride. So I went to look for them ain't it, just to tell them never to come back. I get to the ride and your boy pulls a strap on me. We start tussling and I get the strap off him and shoot him. Simple.

"Sharkey, it ain't the first time he's come to my rave to cause problems. We told him and his people for weeks about the new dress code, but they won't listen. Just the week before they got stopped at the door, they called for me to speech me, so I let them in but said it was the last time they were gonna get a by from me," I carried on explaining.

Then he broke his silence. "So you shot him bruv, you couldn't just buss him up, man?"

"Bruv, listen to me. *He pulled his strap out to blaze me!*" I shouted. Then went on, "Sharkey, you've known me a long time. You know I ain't rash but I ain't no fool either. Man's been out here a fucking long time. Your boy pulled his strap on me. Most man would've done him there and then. I blazed him in the side on purpose, not his head, not his chest and not his stomach. Do you understand? How is he?"

"He's still in Hommerton. Listen I wanna meet wid you," he said.

"Yeah, that's cool bruv, but listen and tell me now, is it beef?" I asked. "Cos if it is fam then let's go to war then. Just like your son wanna tell me he don't give a fuck about me, my rave or my doormen, I'll tell you right now, if it's beef, I don't give a fuck. I'll blaze who I have to blaze!" That was letting him know that friend or no friend, if I have to, I will smoke him too.

"Look Troubles, we know each other a long time. I just need to think about all this and talk to everybody there. I'm not saying I ain't listening to you or don't know my sons going down certain roads that ain't gonna be good for him, I know this. But he's my son."

"I hear you but bro, he tried to blaze me. At work, fam! At my place of business, after pulling on my people." I went on. "I can meet whenever you want, fam. But make sure you come in peace, fam. We're the bigger boys in all of this madness the yoots are going on with."

In all this I did not apologise at all. I didn't think I needed to. Whoever that person was that pulled his gun on me and I ended up shooting was always going to be somebody's son. Just because it turned out to be Sharkey's son made no difference. It was self-defence and self-preservation.

It turned out the boy, not mentioning any names for a reason, was treated in hospital for about ten days and was discharged. He was still in hospital when I met with his dad Sharkey. We met in McDonald's on Stoke Newington high street the very same week, a couple of days after the phone call. I was with Bigsy and he was alone. Leuchie and my brothers, Bigsy and the rest of the doormen had by now heard that the boy I shot was the son of an old friend of mine. Leuchie assured me that I'd done the right thing smoking the guy. He said he knew I didn't do it for rep whereas that kid would have shot me purely to boost his rep. And we both knew that even Sharkey himself would have done the same thing if he was armed.

The greetings when we arrived were laboured. We sat down. As he was alone, I sent Bigsy to go get us all milkshakes so we didn't stand out, sitting there and not eating or drinking anything.

"Is he gonna be OK bruv?" I asked, it was the closest I could get to apologising.

"I think so. His mum's there all day every day. I just came from there to come meet you."

"When's he coming out?"

"Don't know man, don't know." Then, "These fucking yoots them today. They wanna roll big but ain't got the marbles yet to roll big. When we were coming up we came up step by step. You got one step locked, then you go to a next step. But them yoot wanna fly up four steps at a time when they don't even get step two and three before that."

"Sharkey, trust me, fam, I'm watching it every day. They're carrying big strap and don't care to pull on anybody. It's crazy. All me and my guys were doing is working, fam. I never set out to shoot no one's child," I said. Then I asked what was really on my mind, "So how's this all gonna end now Sharks? Did he talk to Feds? Is it beef with you and me or him and his crew and me and mine. How's this gonna go?"

"He's chatting to no Feds. They've been there every day trying to chat to him but he ain't budging. I'm gonna talk to him and tell him you man are bigger man for him. He fucked with the wrong people this time and he has to let it go. But I know his brethren them are hotheads so I don't really know to be honest Troubles."

"Well fam, man's geared up for the worst right about now, so whatever is whatever ain't it," I replied.

"Don't go after my son again, fam. Let it die right here and now with him. I'll pull him out of any shit his man dem wanna do but I don't have nothing to do with his people. Just leave him out cos he ain't gonna be in nothing with you. You hear me?"

"Sharkey, I had nothing against your son. And I got nothing with his people. I'm only gonna go after who I think is going after me. Standard."

With that and a bit more talking, we said our goodbyes and departed. Ironically, as I told you in chapter twelve, I myself was shot later that year in September, outside the same fucking venue.

But these are the situations that led to me finding myself back in jail that February day two years later. Because without a shadow of a doubt, the police knew exactly who shot who. Trust me. The spontaneous shootings are the easiest to solve. When you plan it and protect your identity, you stand more of a chance. So I knew they knew.

And this event probably led to the later surveillance on my club, which was still in effect when I later became the victim myself.

I do take my hat off to the kid, though, for not grassing me up and holding his bullet like a true soldier. Thankfully for all concerned, the whole thing was quashed and no one got hurt further.

Life went back to normal. Home was a bit tense with Marcia having heard of the shooting but I was able to speech my way out of it. By that summer we'd been together two years and guess what? I was still faithful. This was unbelievable for me. It wasn't as perfect as before though by this time. Arguments about being out, about females at raves were starting to creep into our conversations. It wasn't all rosy as it was but it was still a really healthy relationship and I still wanted more of it.

We started a credit card printing operation at around this time as well. Thanks to my cousin Nigel and my old friend from back in the day Nyrone (RIP). My cousin approached me about cloning cards on to blank cards and using them to buy stuff to sell later. When I turned up for the meet with my cousin, it turns out the mastermind behind it all was Nyrone. Nyrone was one of the older lot like myself who had the potential to get involved in the wars going on but chose to stay out of it. So I embarked on a new money making scheme. I had been in credit cards back in the day of book and cards, where we used cheques to buy stuff, but I wasn't really a fraudster. It wasn't my game. I was always more a pavement sort of guy. But at this point these ways of making money were just as profitable as anything you could do on the pavement, maybe not the forty, fifty or seventy grand hits in one go, but they were a lot safer. One year, two years if you got caught whereas pavement work was seven, eight and eleven years if you fucked up. The less pavement work I did the less chance that I get a huge bird on my back. So with these cards we would place grabbers in a shop where we had girls we knew and even sometimes guys too. Grabbers were a device that allowed you to quickly copy the electronic details from an unsuspecting customer's card, when he or she went to pay at the till.

This came in handy big time as I purchased a lot of my champagne and spirits for the club on these cards and sold them at the rave. We paid Nyrone obviously, and kept the rest as profit. I travelled in the summer up and down England from Harlow to Norwich to Buckinghamshire to Reading in Berkshire. Filling up my boot with booty. We also bought stuff like the Play Stations when they came out, TVs, Camcorders and such stuff to sell on.

I was making money from all angles.

We were still sticking up the occasional drug dealer, the occasional security van, the occasional Jewellers and even on a couple of occasions a Book Makers. As the year 2000 progressed, life was good and I expected it to only get better. I sure didn't expect to get shot two weeks before my birthday.

We were now deep into the preparations of the opening night of the new club with Richie and Ken. The building and refurbishing works were going smoothly. It was going to be a West End type club and ambience but in Stratford. It was set to be my best home to date. And a permanent one too. A place I could sit back and just count the money coming in weekly. A move that I expected would one day lead me to owning my own place outright with no partners. That was the vision, that was the plan.

But I must have been getting a lot of attention from the police without me knowing it. They weren't bothering me as much anymore. I'm sure they knew that I wasn't dealing drugs anymore but

I'm sure they also knew that I was now an older, wiser, and a much more dangerous criminal not to be taken lightly. 2001 was fast approaching; I was less than a year and a half away from my arrest in February 2002. But I didn't know it yet.

As I told in chapter twelve, on the night of 30 September 2000 I was shot by an idiot that I'd saved from getting killed by my guys. People I knew. But that was the difference between thinking like and being a businessman and being a raver, an ordinary person out with his pals. And it nearly cost me my life. Because if I wasn't at my premises and didn't have my business cap on, I would more than likely have jumped on that guy just like Happy and the rest of the guys and given him a beating too. I more than likely would not have attempted to even stop the guy from being shot if I had seen the attempt at shooting him. But on that night, I took the side of a stranger against my guys and he repaid me by coming back to shoot me.

So roll on EQ's and the opening night. That was a success and I now felt at home. Then came the killing of my friend Philly at my Christmas Eve event. That really nearly put paid to the club, just three months in. I couldn't believe what was happening. The dream to have this new club as a base for many years into the future was slowly slipping away. I agreed with Richie and Ken to move my event in good time elsewhere because my DJs were now being vetted. It was unheard of. I'd never known any promoter to have to submit his DJ line-up to his local police station for approval. Never. But as it turned out although I believe it started with me, it didn't stop with me. It became a policy, which the police all over London began to adopt with those clubs or promoters whose events they deemed most likely to breed trouble.

Now in 2001, I started a whole new, rebranded event called Strawberry Sundays at the Aquarium club in Old Street. As I mentioned in the earlier chapter, it was the only club I know with an indoor swimming pool.

I brought in a partner this time, an old friend of mine from Plaistow way called Blanks. Blanks was much younger than I was, maybe by about three or four years, but was an established guy in his own rights. He washed our inked monies up for us whenever we needed to feed inked money back into circulation. We would, for example, give him ten grand and he would give us back eight grand of totally clean money. For a guy his age I had a lot of time for him. Hence I knew I could work with him, hassle free.

We kicked the events off in the summer of 2001. It wasn't an instant success, but it was getting there week by week.

The shootings carried on and even went up greatly at this point. I remember these were nervous times. Remember I was by now always rolling with my Glock and sometimes my revolver, depending on where I was going. My revolver I rolled with if I was going about my day to day affairs and my Glock when it was a mission or a rave or place I perceived may be dangerous to my health. Having been shot the year before, I took no chances. It was that bad sometimes that I'd go into a place for a meeting or a club and I would not feel totally comfortable with my gun being in my waist band so I'd bring my newspaper out of the car with me and fold the paper over in half with my gun in the middle of the fold. This meant I didn't have to pull the weapon out but could just take it out the paper or even pop you through the paper. I'd hate to think what my life would have been like, how paranoid I would have been living my life if I was still on crack at this point. But thank God I was as clear headed as anybody.

I wasn't making as much money anymore from the raves firstly because I didn't have the same numbers as before coming through my doors, secondly we were paying quite a lot for aquarium and thirdly I was sharing what we were making two ways. So my pavement work stepped up.

I remember going on one mission set up by this white wannabe-Jamaican chick. It was the most nervy move I'd ever been on. It started by me calling this Jamaican guy she said she knew and ordering half a kilo of crack cocaine. The move was lined up for that night at the girls' house in East Ham. I took my trusted regular driver for these moves Sly and my trusted soldier Nasty who would go in with me. And as extra back up but to stay in the car I had another trusted soldier with me called Yankee.

We went to the house knocked and were let in by an old black lady. I couldn't believe it. I didn't expect that there would be someone else in the home. I thought it would be her home, a flat or something. We go upstairs only to find that this mouthy and boasty bitch lived in a bedsit. She was fucking thirty-eight or something. She was renting from an old lady. But we pressed on anyhow.

The plan was for Nasty to act as my crack customer and me the dealer. As I didn't smoke, he was to taste the merchandise by doing a bit on a pipe he brought with him. The signal was when he said; yes this is good stuff.

On that signal we would move. But when we turn up there are two guys. One bigger than the other. So I made a sign to signal that the bigger one was mine, so he was to go for the smaller guy. I'd made up a money parcel filled with £500 of real money and newspapers cut to the size of money so they looked like bundles of money all the way.

We're in a bedsit remember, a room not big enough to swing a cat. On Nasty's signal, I jumped on the bigger guy, pulling my gun out in the process and had him in a head lock before he knew what hit him. Nasty went to do the same but I don't know what went wrong because they started tussling and scuffling for the gun. I watched the goings on warily and very worried. If that guy was to get Nasty's gun, it was anyone's guess who came out of this mess alive. The furniture in the room scattered everywhere. The girl started screaming, she didn't know we were here not to pay but to rob the goods. She runs right out of the house screaming her head off.

The fight with Nasty and the guy carries on for minutes, the whole time I'm nearly strangling the guy the way I was holding his neck so tight. I could not afford for him to also start tussling. I'm watching the whole thing closely and waiting for Nasty to get back control. He didn't. I made a decision in a split second to shoot this guy as soon as I had the opportunity. It was either we finished this shit quickly and get the fuck out or we'd get caught or get shot. As soon as I saw my opportunity, I shot the guy in the back. He goes down, Nasty gets back control of his gun and we grab the coke, our money and ran out. We run past the old lady at the bottom of the stairs asking us what happened. We got no masks on so we didn't hang about to talk. We run straight for the car and get the fuck out of East London. Phew! That really was a close call.

Un-fucking-believable. For a minute I wasn't sure who was gonna get out of that fucking bedsit. I took my cut and left the guys to their smoking.

2001 was littered with situations like this. It was a funny kind of year. At home wasn't too great either. I cheated on Marcia for the first time after three years of being faithful. It was with a chick at my rave called Natalie. Really pretty girl. She worked hard at it cos she'd been hanging around me for nearly a year before I even gave her the time of day. With this came two more affairs as things got even worse at home.

I really couldn't put my finger on why the relationship was going south. I was being the best guy I'd ever been in my life and I knew I was a far better man now than I ever was when I was in my relationship with Sandra.

One of these two other long-ish affairs that I had during this period was with a girl ten years my junior, who I ended up moving to Spain with in 2004 and marrying and having my last child with.

But then it was just an affair that was keeping me happy because I wasn't happy at home. She was twenty-two and I was thirty-two. I'd met her years before in '95 or '96 when I'd stopped smoking and was selling weed. She was one of the people I visited to drop off weed to at their homes. She was the little sister of a girlfriend of mine called Antoinette, her name? Jeanette.

I had bought a Mercedes 500 SL. A red one. Convertible. It was pretty.

I was driving down the road one day when I saw a taxi trying to overtake me on a one lane road. I had my roof off as it was a sunny day. I looked at the driver with an evil look as if to say; what the fuck are you doing? Just then he gets a bit worried with my look and points to the back of his car. When I look, I notice it was Jeanette in the cab. So I motioned for him to pull over so I could talk to her. He did and the rest is history. She had told the driver to catch up with me. I hadn't seen her since my weed days. Then she was a kid, that day when I saw her, with me not being happy at home, I saw a different girl.

We started linking straight away. I spent the first night at hers the next day. We dated from about the summer of 2001 up until the night before my arrest. She would come with me to the countryside while I picked up my drinks on my credit cards and whatever other bits and pieces I was doing. She was a single mum at the time so I also helped her out financially. We had fun that summer, Jeanette and I. That summer she turned twenty-three and in the October I turned thirty-three. Of the three girls I was now seeing behind Marcia's back, I soon dropped two of them and just rolled with Jeanette.

As Christmas 2001 fast approached, I kept losing friends and associates and life kept getting harder.

Then came the day that changed the world forever: 11 September 2001, or 9/11 as the Americans christened it. I remember I had booked a holiday to Spain with Marcia to try re-kindling things between us. It wasn't like we fought all day every day; it was just that the magic had faded quite a bit. We were supposed to travel on 15 September. That day on 9/11, I was very ill. Ill from a bad flu, I remember. I was in bed wrapped up at around 1 or 2 p.m. watching normal daytime TV. It was interrupted to show first one plane crashing into one of the towers. I think I switched over to Sky News at this point and actually caught the moment when the second plane hit the second tower. Wow! I couldn't believe what I was seeing. I stayed on the news channel until I saw as the first and then the second tower collapsed. Saw bodies trying to escape the flames and just jumping from those crazy heights. As I watched, I knew this was a huge, huge situation. But I never would have guessed how that day has now totally and completely changed all our lives forever.

Within Months Blair was at Congress in the US pledging to stand behind the US in all war efforts. A war that's still raging today thirteen years later.

Christmas 2001 was a very shaky one for the whole world. America and the UK were ranking up their forces for war, there was rhetoric coming from the Taliban, Nations were either falling in line with the US or they were standing to the side. Many of my friends and associates could not see that this was something that would affect us all, for many they thought it had nothing to do with them. How wrong they were. The first strike I felt was the bullet and vest business I was connected to. It stopped soon after 9/11. The importers were too scared to ship these in light of what just happened and the heightened security at all borders, land, sea or air.

New Year came and I was less than six weeks away from being banged up again but did not see it coming.

It was under these situations and atmosphere that I was driving to pick up my kids from school on 7 February 2002 when I was arrested.

I didn't know if Marcia would wait as things were bad, I didn't know what the future held when I found myself in custody nearly killed, by the way, by the twitching cop on that day on the A406.

All I knew was that a run of eight long years out of prison was over!

CHAPTER SEVENTEEN

Ok so I'm back in custody. In the same fucking police station. Stoke Newington. Again just like the last time in '90, I felt like I was a big catch. Ok no newspapers and paparazzi outside but the police knew they had got someone important off the streets.

Once my gun dropped out of my waist band and onto the ground in the police car park, I knew there was no getting out of it. I remember as soon as I hit the cells, I started planning a possible escape route. Not escaping from custody but a good defence or possible mitigation to damage limit my predicament.

I remember I was filled with uncertainty about my future with Marcia. You see, she had never visited anybody in jail. She wasn't familiar with that sort of thing. And as our relationship was and had been on shaky grounds for some time, I really wasn't sure if for the first time I was going to go through this alone with just my family. Whatever the situation, I knew I was in a better place mentally than the last time.

The flat Marcia and I shared was searched. They found nothing really other than one unused and one used bullet casing and a balaclava. I knew better than to keep anything else at the flat. That balaclava was to feature quite a bit in their questions later.

For some reason I always seem to get nicked on a Friday or Saturday. Either way I seem to always spend the weekend in police custody before going to court on a Monday and then Jail. Most people will tell you, once you're nicked and you know you're not getting bail for sure, it's all about getting to the prison you're going to. At least you get to see people and socialize to some extent, unlike police cells, which basically are twenty-four hours of bang up.

My interview was crazy. I was accused of everything. I was

accused of being a contract killer, a drug dealer, even though I hadn't sold drugs now for about three years or so, a gangland leader, an armed robber and anything else they thought up to accuse me of. They harped on the balaclava and said this was evidence that I was a contract killer.

My lawyer was there and as always I made my standard no comment statement. It came as no surprise that I was charged. I was charged with seven offences under the Firearms Act. I forgot to mention that I had dumdum bullets in the gun as well. A dumdum bullet is a very lethal bullet. It expands on impact and causes much more damage to the target. I was charged with possessing these as a completely different charge.

I got my first call to Marcia on the Friday night after they searched her place. I was sure she wasn't going to be pleased with officers turning her home over. We'd been together nearly four years at this time and engaged for two years and not once had the police been to our home. This could only make matters worse between us. But as I spoke to her I gauged her response and answers to get a feel of what was going through her head. It wasn't as bad as I thought it would be. She promised to bring me some food and fresh clothing the next day, Saturday. Next call I made was to Koy's home. Just needed to make sure they got home OK that day. With that I settled in to a night in the cells for the first time in many years.

On Monday, I was arraigned in court and surprise, surprise, I was remanded in custody.

My Journey this time started off in Wormwood Scrubs prison in West London. It was my first time there. They had a whole wing devoted to lifers. I was allocated to a cell on the lifers wing, funny enough.

The UK had brought in the US style Three Strikes Law. I'd heard about this when on the outside. It was scary then but was now my reality. I scrambled to catch up with this law, not knowing if it affected me or not. Being on the lifers wing was a great help in working out whether or not I would be caught up in this law or not. As far as I heard on the outside, it was three strikes but then when I got to jail, I was hearing two strikes and it didn't have to be the same crime. So your first strike could be an armed robbery while your second strike could be a stabbing or a shooting.

I always seem to get locked up when the police and authorities have got fed up of a whole section of society. Just like back in '90, this was another period when so, so many of my friends and associates were away. Some had got caught up in the shootings and were now on remand or already convicted of murder or attempted murder if their victim survived, some were doing life on the three strike law but didn't kill anybody so were serving as low a tariff as four years and five, lots and lots like me had been caught with firearms. The more the firearm explosion that I talked about through the late 90s went on the more people were getting caught carrying them. I had never seen so many people in on firearm charges at one time. Being on the outside for so long and not associating with the hardcore street criminals who went in and out of jail had left me a little out of touch with the prison politics, I discovered. So I started to quickly catch up with what I needed to know to survive.

My first few days in custody were about seeing what relationship or relationships I had on the outside. Marcia was being the woman I hoped she'd be and visited me in the Scrubs within a few days of arriving there. Jeanette was also standing behind me a hundred percent.

She also came up in the first week I was in jail. I had an older friend who was like my driver some of the time if I didn't feel to drive. I was really good friends with about three of his kids, some older than I was. His name was Cliff. Cliff was happy to drive Jeanette up to see me anytime she wanted to come up. Marcia drove so she made her way up herself. I was now settling into life in jail again.

Prison had changed a lot since I was last inside. We now all had electric sockets in the cells, we had prison provided TVs, even the old London jails had been updated to have toilets in them, I couldn't believe my eyes. You could have Play Stations and the likes, although I wasn't a video game addict. But all in all, regime was the same, food was as shit as I remembered it and it still smelt the same.

One thing I did notice though, was that the screws had got a lot younger! The last time I was inside, I was a young gun and majority of the screws were my dad's age and uncle type age group. Now I was older than quite a lot of them and some were my age or at least age group. Only a few were now old enough to be my dad. I thought this was bad. I really now understood how those old timers felt when

I was doing my last sentence when they were older than most officers. I was still just thirty-three years old but already I felt like an old man. Jail was filled with young guns who talked loud, weren't cultured, wanted to discuss their cases as loud as possible so everyone could hear they were in for murder or attempted murder or huge quantities of drugs or what major type of firearm they got caught with. While some of us were just plain pissed off that we allowed ourselves to get caught.

I went about preparing my case to at least try to fight it. And so one day I'm watching ITV's *London Evening News* and a detailed report was featured on the news about guns in clubs and shootings at night clubs. I watched it with interest and a light bulb came on in my head. The next day, I called my solicitors and asked them to get a hold of that report. You see, as much as I was bang to rights, I still had to look for a way out that would allow me to plead Not Guilty on some basis such as self-defence or even if I did plead guilty, I needed to have a backup to that plea in the way of mitigation.

The bottom line of the report was that guns and knives were flooding venues and parties like never before. Shootings were a regular occurrence at events and then the reporter had input from club owners, bouncers and Scotland Yard. An array of guns of all types and knives were placed on a table for the camera to show you, the viewer. The way I sought to use this was to say well, this was why I was armed on 7 February. I have been involved in that sector for nearly four years, I was shot in 2000 by a reveller that I saved from being attacked and so I'm still traumatized and paranoid and always worried for my safety. This would be the basis of my defence if I were to choose to plead not guilty or it would be my explanation for carrying a weapon if I chose to go guilty.

So I set my lawyers to work on acquiring the tape of this ITV report and preparing for a trial but also preparing for a guilty plea.

Life settled down inside. I saw that some things hadn't changed. Heroin was now the drug of choice for many more due to the piss test I talked about earlier. This was now my first time of being in the new system. I had enough friends in Scrubs who got their weed in so for the first few weeks, I just studied my new surroundings and decided what I wanted to do with myself while in here. People around me were older now anyway. They would not bring hard drugs into prisons now, not like eight years ago. Cameras in the visiting rooms were also one of the new additions to prisons that didn't exist when I was last inside. While outside I watched many a TV show, showing people passing drugs and getting arrested and convicted. It took a hard head these days to still chance it. I knew I would be prepared to chance it, but I wasn't sure who I now had around me on the outside that would. Marcia was a definite no-no and so was Jeanette. So as the weeks passed, I decided the best way forward was to find a staff member I could corrupt. Someone I could pay to bring me stuff straight to my hands on the inside, bypassing the cameras and sniffer dogs on the visits. It didn't take me long to find someone. It was all about having money.

One of my associates whom I knew vaguely on the outside, but we knew all the same people, told me one day that the girl who brought our canteen purchases was from around the corner from him. He was from Shepherds Bush, not far from the prison. The girls was maybe three or four years older than I was, a black chick. She wasn't an officer, she was an admin member of staff. She had keys to travel wing to wing within the jail, but did not have cell keys. She was also friends with my guy's woman on the outside and visited his home every once in a while. So I set about targeting this chick. I got friendly with her and kept telling her quietly every opportunity I got that if she ever wanted anything sorted on the outside to let me know. It was hard to talk to her type inside because you didn't come across them daily like the officers. You only saw them when they brought your purchases over and even then they always had an officer escort. So you seized your moment when an officer moved off to the next cells along the landing and left her to sort you out before she also moved along to the next cell. So these were the moments I seized. This went on for a few weeks, I could even tell she started looking forward to our two or three minutes together before she moved on. Every time I would offer her help outside she would say, "No I'm OK really, but thanks. If I do I'll find a way to let you know." I would ask her for her mobile phone number and she would decline giving it to me. What she didn't know was that I already had it from my pal Abs. He'd given it to me weeks before but I didn't let on that I had it. I wanted her to give it to me herself. I got impatient finally, and decided to shock her.

So one evening when I knew she'd finished at the prison for the day, I called her from the pay phones. I won't mention her name just in case she is still employed by Her Majesty!

"Hello?" she said when she answers her phone.

"It's me, your friend from B wing," I said.

I think it took her a minute to process that it was me calling because she paused for what seemed a long time then, "How did you get my number?"

I laughed and said, "Told you we're big out there didn't I? How was your day? Didn't see you this week."

"I'm alright, just doing my shopping. No seriously how did you get my number Spencer?" she asked not knowing what to make of my call.

"I'll tell you when I see you yeah, but listen I need a favour. They gave me a big bottle of Fanta instead of a Coca Cola, I've put the form in the wing office and I'm supposed to get it tomorrow. Can you get me a bottle of brandy and put it all in the Coca Cola and then top it back up with coke and close it back so it looks like it's all coke. Tell me how much it cost you and I'll give you three times whatever you paid. Please yeah, cos it's my birthday tomorrow." I lied about my birthday of course.

She was quiet for a minute then, "Is that why you're calling me? Do you know you're one crazy guy. How you gonna give me back the money?"

"I'm gonna get it dropped off to Michelle and then you can pick it up from her when you're ready."

"Ah now I know how you got my number. I'm gonna kill him when I see him."

"Don't kill him he did it true it's my birthday ain't it?" Then, "So is that cool yeah, please?"

"I can't promise, I'll see how it goes," she said.

"Ok that's good enough. I told you I'm gonna look after you ain't it, do this for me and trust me you're safe."

"Ok Spencer, I'll see you soon yeah, let me finish my shopping. And anyway are them phones safe to be calling me like this? Listen I'll see you when I see you yeah."

"Don't worry we'll talk. See you tomorrow?" I sort of asked to still seal the deal further. We hung up and I went and sat back to see what she would do.

The next day, she appeared at my door with an officer carrying a 1.5 litre bottle of coke and a piece of paper that is sent back from the canteen when you fill one of them in to say there had been an error in your order. She smiled and handed me both the Coca Cola and the form I'd filled in. I thanked her and she left. I opened the bottle and as soon as I did that, I could tell the bottle had been tampered with. I could tell it had already been opened. That was a good sign. I opened it and smelt, yes. It was brandy alright. I had her.

That was how it started. I didn't really need a drink. Far from it. But I couldn't just jump to class A drugs or even class B. I needed to get her comfortable. It was a test, one that had just worked. I did enjoy the brandy all the same and shared some out to close friends. I told Abs to make sure this was kept strictly between us. She was mine and I wanted to keep it that way.

You see I was now a big boy, I needed to come differently to how I operated eight years before. I had the money to do this and the brains, contacts and muscle to put it all together. That same day I sent Mr B, the old boy who sometimes drove me around, to go over to Marcia to collect £50, take £10 for his petrol and drive over to Abs' girl's house to drop £40 off for the girl. I figured she probably spent £15, so I gave her about three times what she spent.

Next time I called less than a week later, I promised her £100 to please bring me a mobile phone. I told her someone would drop it off to Michelle's house along with the hundred.

"How the fuck do I get that in then? What you trying to do to me?" she said all hysterical.

"Don't worry! Listen, canteen's in two days' time. I'm gonna order a box of cornflakes right, now what you do is bring the phone and charger in your work bag just like it's your second phone, no one's gonna say nothing. When you do my order, open the box of cornflakes at the bottom end of the box, take out the plastic bag inside with the actual cornflakes in and open that too. Then put the phone and charger inside that, glue it back and make sure the glued end is upright in the box and the untouched end is at the other end.

Then glue back the bottom of the cornflakes and bring me that when you wrap my order. So you're gonna need glue and that's it."

"Oh my God Spencer!"

"Anthony!"

"What?"

"Just call me Anthony, you ain't got to keep calling me Spencer. Listen it's a hundred for you honey. Michelle will have it there tonight so you can go get it tonight or you can get it tomorrow when you finish work. Are we cool?"

"So what if they ask why I've got two phones, what am I gonna say to them? We do get searched sometimes you know."

"Tell them it's your back up phone as your main one plays up sometimes." I continued. "Trust me girl, you're OK. Nothings gonna happen."

"My God, you lot are something else."

"Listen if you wanna go pick up the hundred in about an hour my brethren would have dropped it. Have a drink on me. I'll see you in couple days."

"Ok then. But if I get caught I will never forgive you and Abs and Michelle too."

"You're cool. Nothing ain't gonna happen. It'll be alright. Thanks again yeah."

This was a plan I put together in my head. I needed a phone in here. I needed to reach my people when I wanted to, at any time at night. I wasn't going to be able to use it a lot in the daytime as officers were out and about, but bang up time in the afternoons from 12 p.m. to 2 p.m. and after 8 p.m. when the screws left until morning, I was good to go. I knew I could get her to do it. What I didn't realize was that I would make it a business before I was shipped out of the Scrubs.

So roll on canteen day, I already knew that the chick had picked up the phone from Abs when he called his missus the next day after our conversation. So I looked forward to canteen. When my canteen order arrived I played it cool and signed for it. They shut my door and left. First thing I do is shake the cornflakes box. Yes, I felt it in there. Yes, I thought to myself. I can't wait to call Marcia and Jeanette that night. I knocked on Abs' wall to signal that the phone came. It was one of those really small Nokia flip phones, specifically chosen because it was light and small. Doing this was made possible because we now had sockets in our cells. At this point I knew I had her fully. My next step was to arrange my heroin to come in and not even tell her at first, but maybe later the more she got comfortable. Now I had a phone I could arrange things easily. It was a pay as you go phone or Top Up as it was called then. So the plan was to get Marcia and my brothers to top it up whenever I needed a top up. Marcia knew all about it as she was linking my old boy pal to give him the phone and money, so when I called her that night she answered in her usual 'not impressed' manner.

"So you got it then?" she said.

"Yeah babes, now we can chat all night if you want and you can call me too after eight o'clock not just me calling you all the time. Good innit?" I said. That was about as excited as she got. She didn't really understand how big a deal it was.

After we spoke, I called Koy at night on his mobile. Koy and his brother Romaine had had mobiles since Koy was about seven years old and Romaine ten. Phones that I bought and topped up for them the whole time. It was so I didn't have to go through Sandra to speak with them if I didn't want to. Koy was now eleven years old, Romaine was fourteen that February. They thought I'd got out when they saw I was calling them from a mobile phone number. But I told them that I would now be able to call them every night to say good night.

Next I called Jeanette. Now she's the one that was shocked.

"Oh my God! what's happening babes, they let you out?" she said all excited. "Did you get bail? Where are you?"

"Yep, open the door I'm coming up," I said in reply, teasing her and trying to draw out the surprise as much as possible.

"Is it, are you downstairs?"

"Nah, not really babes! I'm in Scrubs still," I said, deciding to call off the teasing. But it took her a second to really get what I was saying so I spelled it out for her. "I got a phone in innit. You know how we roll."

"Ah man. I really thought you got out you know! But that's wicked though. How did you get that then?"

"The same chick I told you got me the brandy last week."

"Ah that's heavy babes. You call the kids yet?"

"Yeah just spoke to them. What you up to?"

We spoke late into the night and then I called Marcia back. This was my nightly pattern for a few weeks. About six weeks into my time on remand, Jeanette suddenly decided that she wasn't happy about being the third wheel, as she called it. To be fair when I got with her, I wasn't sure if Marcia and I were going to survive. And that was how it was up until when I got arrested. So I knew Jeannette was waiting and watching to see how things would pan out with Marcia and I. But the reality was that Marcia and I were stronger since my arrest than we'd been for maybe six months leading up to my arrest. It dawned on Jeanette when she wanted Mr B to bring her up to see me on Tuesday, and I refused as Marcia had the day off from work that day and wanted to come up. She wasn't pleased about that especially as that was her usual day to come up. I think it dawned on her that Marcia was there to stay. I had to respect her wishes to be honest and respected her for it. I was engaged to be married to Marcia, I'd been with her nearly four years and we had a lot of history together. Jeanette and I didn't have all that. So I let her go. We stayed in touch over the telephone for a while after and even through my sentence but just seeing how each other were doing. It's funny but I ended up getting married to her in September 2005 in Scotland. But if you'd told me back then in 2002 that I'd one day be married to her, I would have told you to fuck off. We had a beautiful little boy in 2010, born in Marbella where we lived for ten years. We called him Marquez Anton.

So on with my current situation. It was now less complicated with Jeanette gone out of the picture. I was committed to the Crown Court in April. I plead Not Guilty. I was still half intent on fighting the case but half eyeing up a guilty plea too. Anyway I set about preparing for a fight. The guilty plea was only in my head, I didn't let on to my lawyers that I had half a mind set on that so they could keep working on a good defence.

It was different for me this time in jail. I felt like one of the godfathers. The young thugs like Aggro and them kids from East making a name for themselves were drawn to me. I was the one who calmed them down. I'd seen it all, been there, done it and had the scars to show for it. When I told them to cool it a lot of them listened. When majority did, the rest followed.

I also had fewer arguments with the officers than I used to in my younger days. I felt like the wise old man!

As May 2002 approached, the news I was getting from home wasn't good. When I called Leuchie it was the same message. When I spoke to my sister Carol, Frankie, Kevin, I was being told that our mum wasn't sleeping and she was losing weight. I knew about insomnia obviously, but I don't think I really saw it as a medical condition that can cause you problems. I'd never come across anybody who really, seriously could not sleep night after night and day after day to the extent it was taking a toll on them. So I suppose it didn't dawn on me. I hadn't seen my mum since just after New Year of that year, so about five months. She wasn't coming to see me as she did back in the day either, I was a big boy now.

But as worried as I should have been I didn't really get it, I have to say, looking back now. I got the occasional visit from Leuchie and his missus and kids and also from Frankie and Kevin from time to time. Marcia also brought Koy and Romaine up to see me when they could come. They were much older now, understood where I was and didn't understand why I would want to be there. So as you can imagine, I didn't want them coming up too often.

In May I started bringing in my drugs through my canteen chick. I had a box of large kitchen matches stuffed with brown and weed, then wrapped tight in cling film. This was dropped off to Michelle's house for my chick to pick up and put in the cereal box as usual. I then ordered the cereal as part of my canteen order and Bobs your uncle, I had it in my cell. With this method I was able to get ounces of the stuff in as well as large quantities of weed. It was great. All of the guys who got stuff in still got theirs in the old way of going out on visits and plugging or swallowing the drugs. I was over all of that. Summer was now here and it was my first summer away from my family in years and it hurt.

My trial was fast approaching; I'd been inside now about four months by June of that year. My arrangement with the canteen chick was paying off big time. My heroin business was back in full swing, but this time hassle free. Scrubs was a huge, huge jail and as long as you kept it cool, business could go on as usual. There were too many wise guys there and too many illegal activities going on. I had now turned the mobile phone thing into a business. I was now charging £500 to get you a phone. It still cost me a hundred mind you. The deal was, you provided the phone and I got it in for you. So I would have Bigsy, Mr B, a chick that was loyal to me called Natalie or about two or three others I could call on now I had a phone, to go meet your people, collect the phone and the money, drop it off to Mr B, if he wasn't the one who picked it up. Whoever I used for the pick-up got £50, I would then give Mr B £50 if he wasn't the one who did the pick-up, he would drive to West London to Michelle's house, drop off the phone and a hundred for the chick and Bob's your uncle the phone will come to me on canteen day and you get your phone. It was that simple. When Mr B did the pick up from the prisoner's people, I made £350. If I used someone else, I made £300. This money would be dropped off to Marcia by Mr B for me and banked. Mr B was the only one sent to meet with Marcia. So it all had to go through him. I also looked after Abs on the inside. I always gave him a few grams of Heroin for him to sell as well. This helped both him on the inside and his girl Michelle on the outside. If I got fourteen grams in, I'd give him three grams. This was equivalent to about £150 to £200 in prison currency and hard cash. He also never went without his weed or ash as having brown always meant you could swap that for class B anytime. So this little connection was feeding lots of people and making me money.

All this was new to Marcia, she never actually thought you could make money while inside. But then again, she'd never really been around anybody like me. To be honest neither had Jeanette. She knew bad boys and had visited her ex lots of times in prison before we rolled, but even she was shocked one day a few months after we cooled it off, when she came to see me with Mr B. Now usually the drug trafficking between prison and the outside goes one way. That's from the outside in, correct? Well I turned that on its head this one day. I knew she was coming with Mr B on a visit, I'd prepared a small parcel of weed for them both to share but only mentioned it to Mr B. I got it to the chick inside a Mars Bar packet that I'd then glued back. I handed it to her about two days before they came up. I then called the chick that same night and told her that I had Mr B whom she knew very well at this point and a friend of mine coming. I told her to call Mr B and arrange a spot where they could meet after my visit and hand them the weed in the Mars Bar packet. She even thought I was crazy. No one and I mean no one sends drugs out in that direction. But Jeanette was a single mum, working, but not well off and Mr B was a pensioner who was a big time gangster and earner in his time, but I used to look out for them both in different ways when I was out so I just thought I'd do something for them.

After the visit, Jeanette said they drove a couple of roads away from the prison and parked up, Mr B walked off and then came back to the car and said, "Here, Anthony sent this for you from in there!" She said she wasn't sure what he meant until he explained that the chick had called him the night before and told him that I had something for them and to meet her at such and such a place. She said she couldn't believe it.

When I called her that night, she was still amazed that I was locked up and was giving her weed to go home with. She also did say it came in handy and thanked me for it big time. That's how we rolled. She was just as shocked as Sandra all those years ago when I handed her the new £50 notes from the inside even before she'd seen it on the outside.

As my trial date approached I kept a close eye on the sentences that were being dished out for firearm offences. It ranged from three years to six. It worried me. I wasn't ready to do another six year stretch. No way. That was a sentence that went on forever. Three to four was OK but anything over that was a nightmare. Since I was last in, they had brought in new guidelines about how much time you did. If you got four years and under you did exactly half and anything over years was as it was back then, you did two thirds before release. So it was all about getting no more than four years. I could do two years inside as hard as that would be, but that was half the time I'd done eight years previously.

The more I looked at it the more I was sure that if I plead guilty I may just get away with four years or under. When my trial date was set, I got one last visit from my defence team. At this point I informed them for the first time that I was thinking of pleading guilty. My Barrister let out a sigh of relief and said this was what they had discussed on the way up to see me. They said that really was the best option for me and then use all the material we had as mitigating evidence. The fact I'd been shot a year and a half ago doing an honest day's work, the fact that I was worried for my safety, the fact that I was at the fore front of this wave of gun crime and all that.

I asked them what they thought of my idea to write a pleading letter to the judge so he got my perspective of things as I wouldn't get to speak because there wasn't a trial. My Barrister thought that was a brilliant idea. So as soon as I banged up that night I set to work writing a grovelling letter to be sealed and only read by the judge. Basically I told him all the bullshit under the sun. About my mum being ill, about losing my brother the last time I was locked up, about having been behaving myself since my last sentence, about being shot by a reveller whose life I'd just saved about carrying the gun because I was scared shitless but never intended to use it. And on and on. When I was done, I'd written about three or four A4 pages by hand and sealed it ready for court the next week.

I hoped that guilty plea and the story behind my case and my personal letter would all add to some leniency for me. Against me was my previous firearm offence and whatever intelligence led them to watch me over a week. They don't just watch you for a week and commit numerous officers if you're just an innocent guy. So I knew the judge would have this information available to him.

So the first day in court arrives and I'm brought upstairs to start picking the jury. But I'm sure the prosecution has been informed that I was changing my plea to guilty, so we all await the entrance of the judge. I'd already handed my letter for the judge to my Barrister, which when I asked him as we sat in court if he'd passed it on, he'd nodded yes.

Judge comes in and then after all formalities, confirming my name, date of birth and all seven charges read out, it was finally time to throw myself at the courts mercy. I was asked how I was pleading to the charges: Guilty!

That was it. I was now a convict and at the mercy of the judge. Well at least it wasn't Judge Hickman from years ago. I knew I was due some time off for pleading guilty and as long as he wasn't completely heartless maybe even a bit more off for my heartfelt sob story letter. We adjourned for him to take his sweet time to think how long he wanted to keep my ass in jail for.

When we reconvened in court, he started the usual. You have been convicted of a very serious offence. This type of offence is taken very seriously by the courts. This is an offence that must be punishable by a custodial sentence. The courts must be seen to deal with such offences so as to set an example to others who wish to travel our streets with such weapons. Mothafucker it is my streets too you know, I was thinking. Then he went on to say he had taken into account my guilty plea, taken into account my letter, which he had taken the time to read. He also took into account that I had been out of trouble for a relatively long period of time. But he has decided to sentence me to two years in custody on the possession of a loaded firearm in a public place, fifteen months in custody for the dumdum bullets to be served consecutively. Ok, I'm thinking, that's thirty-nine months, go on.

On the other charges he sentences me to fifteen months too. But before I freaked out, thank God, I hear him say all to be served concurrently to the previous two sentences.

Phew!

Ok, as I'm doing my maths mentally, I figure I've come in under four years. That means I will be entitled to do half of the thirty-nine months. That's nineteen and a half months. Basically a year and a half. Hmm, not bad. I was OK with that. It was August, so I'd already done six of the nineteen. I would be out in just over a year. Well all in all, it was a result. I was sure my letter had helped, I was also sure that all that material I'd gathered also contributed to my not so bad sentence.

I went back to jail happy in a way because I knew it could have been a lot worse. I would be out the next September. September 2003. A lot better than the last time, I can tell you.

Back in prison, I was now again a convicted prisoner. Visits were now back to three a month, if I remember right or maybe even twice a month. I now needed to send a VO anyhow. I planned on staying in Scrubs for as long as possible so I could be in London. But now I was convicted, time was ticking to me being moved. I had thirteen months left to serve and every month I served in London close to home was a month less I'd serve away from London. Not to mention my link in there, getting all my stuff through the canteen chick.

It wasn't long though before I was told I would be going to the Mount Prison in Hemel Hempstead in Hertfordshire. That was a result really. Hertfordshire is as close as you can get to being in a London jail even though you're outside London. I'd been to the Mount before to visit my cousin when he was serving time there. It was a ghetto jail I'd heard. But on the plus side, I also heard it was another one of those jails where you can cook your own food. There were now a couple of them, but not many.

I was probably allocated to the Mount within a month of my conviction, so sometime in September. But still I hoped I might stall it for as long as possible. So life carried on in Scrubs.

The war in Afghanistan was raging at full tilt. This was all that was making the news all day and every day. The Americans and the Brits were winning and were promising us, the public, that it would soon be all over. About this time, the US and that rat Bush the second decided that he needed to also invade Iraq and change the regime of Saddam Hussein. This plan - to all who followed news and history like myself for years - was an unnecessary war. And it was a battle from the start for the UK and US to sell the war to the world. The French, Germans, Russians and the other powers advised strongly against this move. It was a move seen by many as a personal vendetta by Bush against Saddam to finish off what his father, the first Bush, had started in defence of Kuwait a decade before. Dick Cheney, the horrible human being that was the vice-president, and Donald Rumsfeld, the defence secretary who was just as nasty as Cheney, would have none of it. It was a shame to see them use General Colin Powell as an errand boy to sell this bogus war to the world.

Their cover was that Iraq posed a threat to us all in the West and had WMDs - Weapons of Mass Destruction. This became the byword of the time. Wow, what the West would do to get their aims achieved is amazing. And you do have to take your hat off to them, because there are no history books out there where you will find the West ever fighting a war without being on the right side. We were always the good guys and someone else was always the bad guy. Every war we ever fight is a justifiable war, a noble war, a war to save the world or the people from doom. When it comes to propaganda, no one does it as good as the West.

The Iraq war was nothing more than a quest for oil and access to it. George Bush declared he had an open cheque to demolish and rebuild Iraq. Dick Cheney and his oil company cronies like Halliburton and British companies alike went in for the kill rubbing their hands together and licking their lips. Money was made by all concerned and is still being made by all concerned. But poor bastards on the ground in Iraq all the time were being killed. US and UK troops who will obey orders no matter what, were being killed and are still being killed. All for what. Well as we speak, Iraq is now far worse off than before we went in. It really is a shame. Recently I watched an interview by Pharrell Williams, the US black singer. And he said something that has stayed with me. He was asked the typical question by a stuck up journalist who was there to praise and clip his wing at the same time, as they do. He was praised for his hit after hit and then in the same breath he was asked about his stance on women's rights because his music videos demean women. After putting the journalist in his place and shutting him down intellectually, he said, "We have never seen the world run by seventy-five percent women and twenty-five percent men. Have you ever wondered what sort of world this would be if we had more women rulers of the world than men?"

I thought about this for a while and still do. Imagine if the EU rulers were ninety percent women and at the same time Hilary Clinton got into the White House, Brazil as they currently do have a woman in charge just like Argentina too. Then Russia, Isreal, South Africa, Australia, Canada, China and New Zealand all happened to have female rulers at the same time.

I beg the reader to just try and think what the world might look and operate like. The status quo will never change until we are all destroyed and have to start again. And to be honest, sometimes when I daydream, I long for something like an Ice Age or a Meteor to just strike us all. Erase all we know, erase borders, erase the rule books and just start all over with the way the majority think and go about things, not the way the status quo have created it.

So anyway on with my own personal politics and battles.

At about September still of 2002, I was given a job on the servery serving food. Wow, this was a great job. It really was the best job on any wing in a jail. Had access to food, was out all day, if I didn't have a mobile it would have meant access to the phones as much as I wanted up until lock up at 8 p.m. It meant being freer at the weekends too. Weekend was hell in London nicks. It was lock up at around 4.30 p.m. until the next day. But with the servery job I was out until 7 p.m. at least. It also gave me more access to the canteen chick as we were more or less 'staff'. I use the term 'staff' for myself loosely, but what I mean is I was now able to even help with canteen distribution sometimes, or I was out with screws and canteen staff when everyone else was banged up. Nothing sexual went on with her, we were just really cool and I had made her lots of money. She was making at least £600 to £700 extra on her wages a month from me.

On the home front, my mum's illness was getting more and more serious. Sometime in early October, just before my birthday I called home. This call was my first real insight that things were really bad. I called and had a few words with my dad. I asked how my mum was doing and all that, he said she was bearing up but was very weak. He said she was always tired because she didn't sleep much. She was still being bogged down with her insomnia condition.

I then asked to speak with her. I clearly heard my dad say to her, "Here Veronica, it's your son Anthony."

"Hello?" came her very, very weak voice. She sounded so weak I just couldn't believe it.

"Hello Frank?" She had just called me by my brother's name, thinking it was Frankie, even though my dad had just told her it was me on the phone.

"Mum it's me Anthony, It's not Frankie, mum. How are you?"

"Oh my Tony! I'm not sleeping, I can't sleep. I have pain everywhere. I don't know what to do anymore. I'm tired." Her speech felt like she was using every bit of energy she had in her to talk.

"Mum, it's OK. You're stronger than you think believe me you are. You will get thought this. I'm out in twelve months and I promise you when I come home, I will come and look after you a lot more than I have done for a while. Ok? That's a promise."

"Get some rest OK and I'll call at least twice a week from now on so you don't forget who I am." I sort of laughed at my joke to cheer her up .

"How can I forget you Tony?"

"Ok mum, stay strong yeah. I'll call again in a couple of days."

My dad came back on the phone and I had to ask him.

"Dad is she going be OK? She sounds so, so weak man."

"We pray every day that she gets stronger but it's the sleep that's making her not remember things and making her weak."

I came off that phone and was really worried for my family. Life without my mum was unimaginable. But just about five weeks after that phone call, my mother was gone!

But I wasn't to know this yet. I kept my word to keep call her. And did every two or three days. She never called me Frank again, but she always seemed to struggle to speak and struggle to really remember that it was me calling.

A few days after that call I had my birthday. I turned thirty-four. And then a few days after that, I got the message I didn't want to get. I was being shipped out to the Mount in the next batch. Oh well, that was it for my servery job, my contact in the prison and my short travel visits. But as I said it wasn't too bad, it was only about thirty minutes from Tottenham as we´re in the right part of London for a shorter journey. I also looked forward to being in a jail where you could cook, especially considering Christmas was around the corner.

I arrived in the Mount I think the third week of October. And oh my God, it was like a reunion. So many faces from the past and from the roads. I was welcomed like the old school head that I was. I immediately felt at home. I was among so many familiar faces that it was like being in my raves. There were so many guys there from my last sentence eight years before. Guys who had never stopped going prison. Then there were guys from more recent, on the rave scene. Real gangsters. Even one of my DJs, Top Notch, was there too. I had managed to get my phone there with me too. With all the searches and stuff.

I simply stored my phone in the same way as I got it in. I always made sure I had a box of cornflakes at all times. I kept the phone and charger in the plastic bag containing the cornflakes, shuffled it around a bit so the phone and charger go deep into the bag. Turned the opened side of the bag upright because the top of the box always stayed untampered with, then glued the bottom of the box back together. To any eyes it just looked like an unopened box of cereal.

This saved my phone many times, especially in the Mount. I was hooked up with a Jamaican guy who was one of the best cooks I'd ever met. Trust me, this guy could fucking cook. He was serving time for drug trafficking and was gonna be deported when he finished his sentence. He had no money and no one in England. I took him under my wings and told him I would do our weekly shop and he would cook. He agreed wholeheartedly and thanked me.

Listen this guy made me feel like I was at my mum's house every day. He changed the menu daily so we weren't always eating the same things. And sometimes we'd collect what the prison was serving for the day and re-cook it gourmet style. That way we didn't always use provisions I'd bought.

One day after about a month of being there, I was called to the office over the Tannoy system they had in there. I didn't even think anything of it. I was still new, so every so often they would call me to tell me about this or that, education, work, gym, chaplain, Imam, you know, just general stuff as a new arrival.

So I walked into the office to see two senior officers waiting for me. I still didn't clock what at first until I saw the look on both their faces at the same time. No! I've seen this look before. In Maidstone Prison!

I just looked at them and asked what was wrong.

"There's been some bad news at home Spence. You need to call your brother, Dillon is it?"

"Yes, Dillon Gov. Why, what's wrong?"

"He's just called the prison and was put through to the wing office. I'm afraid it isn't good mate. Call home. Do you have call cards? If not you can use the phone in this office."

"Thanks, it's OK. I got cards, I'll go call now. Thanks."

I left the office and walked as fast as I could. I wasn't sure who to call first. They couldn't call me and I couldn't use my mobile because here in the Mount we were out a lot more. So my phone was always put away until at least way after 9 p.m. We banged up at 8.30 or 9 p.m., I think.

I decided to call Leuchie first seeing as he called in.

"Hey Bruv, they said you called in man. What's happened?"

"Troubles man, I can't believe we're here again," he said first off. Then he took a long and loud breath, and said, "Mummy's gone bruv."

"What? What do you mean gone?"

"She passed this morning. Dad called an ambulance for her this morning. He said she had a stroke in the hospital after they got there but her body was too weak to deal with it. She passed a couple hours ago bruv. She's gone, Troubs."

It was like déjà vu. I'd been here before. In 1994. I went limp. My legs felt weak. The phone room was spinning and spinning. I tried to talk but couldn't. Why was this happening to me again!

"Ant," he called.

"I'm here. I'm here. I can't believe this bruv. I know she was weak but…"

"I know. I saw her Wednesday and she looked thin bad. She still couldn't sleep, fam. She's been in bed now for like a month. She was weak bad."

"So did she have the stroke at home?"

"No in hospital. Dad said she was struggling to breath so he called an ambulance. Then she had the stroke after they got there."

"How's Carol and Mikey them? Where's everybody?"

"Dads still at the hospital, Cass has gone there as well and me, Frankie and the boys are here at mum's."

"So what's gonna happen now, Leuch?"

"Tell you the truth, I don't really know Ant. We're just here waiting for the old man to get back." Then he asked what I hadn't even thought of yet. "Do you think they'll let you out for the funeral?"

"Boy I don't know you know. I just got here as well. I've only been here a month innit. I'm gonna ask, but I don't know Leuch. I just don't know."

"When you out again?" he asked.

"Ten months."

"Well they should let you out man."

"I'm gonna definitely try speech them, trust me. Listen I'm gonna call back after lunch, hopefully when dad's back. And tonight when I turn on the phone I'll call you lot. I need to go sit by myself for a bit."

"Ok. Nothing you can do right now. Don't let it twist you up too much yeah."

It was the morning of Saturday 16 November 2002. And I was now motherless. We knew she was sick and in a bad way. But when it came it was still a real shock to my system. I walked off to my cell to cry for my mother. I got there and lay down on my bed and cuddled to my pillow. I curled up in a ball like a child. I just stared at the walls waiting for the tears to come, but they wouldn't.

Just like the last time, I just could not find the tears to cry for my mum.

What the fuck was wrong with me. Why couldn't I cry? I was willing the tears to come but they just wouldn't. I stayed in my cell all afternoon, so much so, that I had guys after guys coming to look for me. I could hear them coming down the landing asking people if they'd seen me, until they got to my cell and looked in. As soon as they saw me lying on my bed, they knew something was up. When I told them they were shocked and offered words of sympathy. Some left me alone and some stayed in my cell with me for a bit. But they knew I just wanted to be alone at that moment, so eventually they all left.

Later that day I called my dad. He didn't seem in a bad way. Maybe he knew it was coming and therefore was more prepared than the rest of us.

He said something that I will never and have never forgotten. He said our mum had never gotten over Andrew's death eight years previously. He said she has been dying slowly ever since my brother died.

I suppose some people are like that. They just never get over the death of a child or a spouse. It may take a month or a year or even ten, but they just never mend their broken heart.

Me, I also think she gave up about a year before she died.

Sometimes people survive trauma by fighting and fighting while someone else gives up and lets go. I think my mum got tired of being sick and not being able to sleep. She gave up on life.

I told the officers that I was going to apply for a compassionate leave first thing Monday morning and that I needed to attend my mother's funeral.

Next day, Sunday morning, I went church for the service. I went straight up to the Vicar and told him of my mum's passing. I gave him my mum's name and mine. I asked him to please mention my mum in his service and to pray for her.

I sit down to the service with everybody else and the service starts. I'm going through the motions. The service gets to the point where we pray for this or that. The Vicar mentions my mum by her name, mentions me and her children and grandchildren and asks the whole church to stand up and pray for her and my family. And that's when it happened. Finally.

The flood gates opened and I was finally able to cry. I cried and cried and cried. I cried the tears I wasn't able to shed for my brother. I cried for my mum and I cried for myself. I finally cried.

When the service was over, the Vicar took me to one side just as I was walking out and offered his condolences. He said if there was anything he and the church could do, to make sure I let him know. I said thanks and left.

The next day, I applied to see the wing governor. I was told he'd be over that afternoon.

At around 3 p.m., I was called to the wing office again over the Tannoy speakers. When I get there, there's a queue of around four or five guys waiting in line to see him as well. So I join the queue.

About ten minutes later a black guy comes along, one of these muscle bound guys who'd been pushing weights in jail, some young fool that thinks muscle's everything.

I watch him try to intimidate one guy after another to push in, totally ignoring me like I wasn't there. Like if he pushed in front of some other guy, he wasn't pushing in front of me. So I told him to fucking join the queue.

He turns round and asked what I was going to do about it. That was it. He had just fucked with the wrong guy on the wrong day. I'd just lost my mother and this fool was taking the piss.

I kicked off. I beat him up and down the landing where we were all standing. Smashed him against the wall, the doors, and then I beat him some more. I tried to push him through the bullet proof like windows of the phone room, which must have really hurt because they were as thick as the bank teller windows. The officers must have heard the commotion and came out, but the Mount is a place you can have a really good fight as it was pretty open and lots of landings off the main landings. I got to him good and proper.

He must have thought because I didn't have as many muscles as he did that he could take me on. I pretty much fucked him up silly.

Then the officers pulled me away into the association room. They asked my side of the story and I told them I'd been waiting to see the governor when this idiot came along and tried to push in. I explained to them that I'd just lost my mum two days before and wasn't in the mood for foolish guys.

You know what, even the officers understood. They took him away and locked him in his cell, leaving me back in the queue where I'd started, to carry on with what I was doing. Normally, you are both done for a fight, but this time they just let it go.

The idiot came to me the next day, with his face looking like ten men had beaten him up and apologised profusely. He said he'd now heard from the grape vine that I'd just lost my mum and he was very sorry for my loss. I just told him to be very careful next time he tries pushing his weight around because he just never knew who he was messing with. He took my hand and shook it and asked to quash the whole thing. I suppose he was worried that I was going to come back with more.

The Mount was full of knives. And I mean fucking proper knives. They found a small gun when I was there. You don't believe me? Hell, even I couldn't believe it. Remember when I said I got away with my phone in that prison, well it was down to a gun being found and the whole damn place was locked off for about four days and spun upside down.

Having the fight wasn't good for me though because the governor was in the office we were fight outside of.

So anyway, I put my case to the governor and waited for his reply. He said to send in supporting documents that my mum had passed. Why would anybody lie about something like that.

I ask my family to send me all the stuff I needed. We still didn't have a funeral date at that time so I couldn't actually ask for a specific date. I just wanted them to approve it first pending a date.

I was surprised when in early December, with the date now confirmed for 18 December, they refused my application. I was shocked. Eight years previously, I had been let out with two whole years remaining of my sentence. This time I had a much shorter sentence and nine months remaining and had a serious family bereavement but was turned down. I reapplied, this time asking to be handcuffed to officers. This is what is known as an escorted leave. So you are released only for the funeral and you are cuffed to one officer the whole time, but with another one in attendance.

Again I was turned down. This really traumatised me. Was I really going to miss saying a final farewell to my mum? I turned to the Vicar who had said to ask if there was anything he could do. I put my case and pleaded with him to back me up to be allowed at least to go out escorted. He said he was powerless to do anything. He said he didn't influence the prison's decisions.

He went further and offered me what's known as a church visit. This is when your visitor or visitors are brought right into the belly of the prison as opposed to the visit room, which is normally at the front of prisons. They are brought through to the church and you are then brought to the church for a one to one visit with no screws around. The Vicar then leaves you and your people alone for long periods in the privacy of his office within the church. You're served tea and biscuits and all that. I'd had one of them with Sandra years and years ago just after Koy was born.

I accepted and a date was set for Marcia to come visit. Under normal circumstances, inmates ask for these visits to get sex in prison. I did, that first time. But this was different. I couldn't disrespect my mum by doing that. It was the best I was being offered for my bereavement.

I scratched my head for what I could do to say farewell to my mother. I came up with two things. I was now in a computer literacy course, an NVQ course, so I decided to write out a speech or letter to be read out at the funeral. Then I also made use of my mobile by asking that at the wake, when my mum's body was in the church, that I'd call my sister's phone and be allowed to say a few private words to my mum, by her putting the phone to my mum's ear so I could have a few minutes with her to say whatever came to my head to say. This was all I could do.

One of the things I said to her was that I was done with crime. I promised her that I would do all I could to give it all up, put down the gun and go a hundred percent straight. I told her that I couldn't risk being in a prison again and losing another family member. I also apologised for missing her funeral and not being there for her and Andrew in their hour of need.

That was my send off for my mum. I promised myself that when I got out I would get a real job for the first time in my life. I didn't know how I was going to do it being used to fast money for so many years, but I was going to try if it killed me.

The funeral went off without me, her favourite son. I was devastated.

Life in the Mount carried on. But I was never too far from thinking about my mum's passing. I kept going to church and kept praying that I find the strength to quit the streets. Christmas 2002 came and went and it was now 2003.

I pulled myself back to reality. In the Mount getting drugs in was a whole lot different to anywhere else I knew. We had drugs thrown over the fence and collected on the inside by joeys. Joeys were junkies or just hangers on.

This was cool as far as I was concerned. I had lots of money and lots of people on the outside who were prepared to come and throw the stuff I wanted over the walls. Mount was unique in the sense that there were public paths, busy ones, running down the outside of the prison walls. So your people could drive down or walk down right next to the walls and chuck stuff over. Now with mobile phones in there and lots of it, we were able to co-ordinate the throwing and the picking up of stuff to a tee.

As soon as stuff got thrown over, you got your joey to run over and pick it up. There were times though that the officers patrolled those walls and I saw once when a parcel actually hit an officer in the head. That was funny. Remember the people on the outside were throwing the stuff blind, so it was down to us on the inside to make sure the coast was clear before we gave the go ahead on the phone to throw.

This was how real knives got in and not prison made knives. This was also how the .22 pistol got in. How times had changed. Even I was in shock for a while when I heard there was gun in that prison.

I was also shocked to my core when we were told that the whole prison would be locked down for a cell to cell spin of the entire jail. And they did too. We were on timed meals where one landing at a time went for food. The kitchen was shut so we couldn't cook. They found lots of phones, knives and drugs. I got to keep mine through my tried and tested hiding method, which I always kept to myself. The screws actually picked up the cereal box and checked it to see if it was open. He shook it too and then just replaced it. The trick was to have a few different boxes. Weetabix, cornflakes, Frosties, and also have some you're eating from and some still unopened. So my phone survived the blitz and I was able to stay in touch with my people.

As 2003 rolled on I got tagged as a dealer and one day was moved to Blunderston prison in far away Suffolk. I was gutted to say the least. I went there in March 2003, with only six months left to serve. The rest of my sentence pretty much flew by. Having done four whole years previously, six months was nothing. And so it was that on a sunny September day in 2003 the gates opened to let me out once again. This time it was the first time I was seeing the streets since that day in February when I was on my way to see my kids.

I got some days back just at the end of the sentence. Marcia was expecting me on the date I'd been given when I was first sentenced and so was I expecting to go home on that day. I then recalled that I'd done three days in police station custody before going to court on the Monday. So I applied for my police station days back and got them. That meant that my release date was brought forward by three days.

I kept it quiet from Marcia but told my little brother Kevin to come pick me up from Liverpool street station where the Suffolk train went to. I also told him to call her and tell her that he was coming round to see her, so she would be there.

He picked me up from the station and we then drove to Hackney where we lived. He buzzed the flat and she answered. She buzzed him in and we then walked up the two flights of stairs up to our landing. I got him to knock the door, while I hid to the side, out of view.

She opened the door and just as she's greeting him I pop my head round and said hi, all calm as fuck. I'm sure I do not need to tell you what a pleasant surprise that must have been for her. Although I was coming home anyway on the Monday, the fact I'd got back three days meant I came home the Wednesday before. Because people aren't released on a weekend, I really got five days back.

It was great to be free again.

My main problem now was to keep my promise to my mum, lock off the streets, put down the guns and get a real job for the first time in my life.

And guess what, I did too.

CHAPTER EIGHTEEN

So the first thing I do after having a bath and something to eat is go to see my family at my dad's house. Cass my sister, Kevin who'd picked me up earlier that day came back for me, so he was there too. Mikey my youngest brother, who was now twenty-three years old was still living at home. He was the only one still at home. He was the one I felt sorry for the most with the loss of our mum. He was the one we all had to take care of as he still somewhat needed guidance. My son Koy is now the same age today as my little brother was when our mother died and I still assist him regularly, financially and otherwise.

Leuchie and Frankie weren't there at that time. The first thing my dad did was say a prayer with us all joining in. We prayed as a family and remembered my mum. My dad called on my mum above to watch over us all and protect us along with my late brother Andrew.

I was brought up to speed with the family stuff and how the family will move forward from my mum's passing nearly a year before. As I still hadn't visited her grave and it was getting late, we all agreed to go to the cemetery the next day. Dillon and Frankie were also going to come along as well as our partners. My sister was now married and we all had fiancés or long term partners. Even little Mikey had his girl Vanessa.

So the next day we go to the cemetery. It was a real difficult event for me. I just stared at the grave for a while and couldn't say anything. I was looking at my mum final resting place but did not see how she ended up in there, who put her in there or how she was put in there. I found it a bit hard to accept she was in this piece of ground. Maybe I needed to see her go in to accept she was the one really in the ground.

Of course I knew it was her resting place, but my brain seemed to doubt it for some silly reason I still can't explain. We tended her grave and placed all the flowers and stuff we'd brought with us. I spoke to her in private and again apologised for not being there in her final moments. I reiterated my promise made to her in her coffin and asked her to guide me and give me the strength to move forward with my plans for my life. We left the cemetery after about an hour. It was a beautiful warm September day, I remember. Like my mum brought the sun out because this day was the first day we were all by her side since she passed away. Everybody else had been there when she was laid to rest with the exception of myself.

Going to the cemetery that next day was like a cleansing for me. It was like I had been forgiven. I felt a lot lighter as soon as we left. I felt like I was now ready for the future.

I went home and worked out a plan to move forward.

First thing first, I needed to get myself a place. I needed to get on the social security. I needed to sell all remnants of my past life, like the guns and vest I still had. Then I needed to get a job.

It wasn't the case that I didn't want to live with Marcia anymore or anything like that, but I'd always had my own back up place since the eighties except for a few years when I was with Sandra and we had our place. I'd been forced to give up my place when I was away so I just needed to get another place. Social security or the dole was something I never did bother with either for all those years I was out making money, but now I figured it would help me until I got a job regardless of how little the money was and it was also much easier to get a flat when on social security.

I then set about selling a couple of weapons I still had. For this I called on my old right hand man Bigsy. I hadn't seen him in nearly two years. I'd spoken to him inside and he was one of those who helped hook up the pick-ups and drop offs I organised from inside. But he didn't visit because that was how I wanted it. It was good seeing him again and he expressed his sympathies at my mum's passing. He immediately went to work for trying to sell the weapons and vest.

Next I looked about booking a holiday for myself and Marcia to go on before that Christmas of 2003.

Then I started to look around for what type of work I could get. I wasn't sure what I was going to be good at. All I knew was that I had brains, I could sell sand to an Arab and I was tough. Hard labour work was a no-no. I wasn't good at DIY or building work or any of that sort of stuff. I wanted a suit and tie job. That much I knew. Marcia helped me with where to search for these things as I didn't know really how best to maximise my job seeking efforts and get the best results as quickly as possible. But as usual, I am a fast learner and soon was on my way seeking out the jobs I thought I could get easily and would pay me a decent living salary rather than a wage, if you know what I mean. I kept coming across sales jobs and I soon figured maybe that was my direction. Sales jobs had commission payments as well as a monthly income. I liked the sound of that. It meant I had a reasonably good monthly income and I could top this up by selling my heart out. The more I looked at them the more I saw that really there was no ceiling to what a salesman could earn.

So I went about applying for mostly sales jobs. I went for a few interviews by the beginning of October. One was a complete scam that I figured out in less than two weeks after training for the first week. They had people apply to become managers of 'soon to be opened' branches of their company. They trained you for a week talking about selling methods. Then sent you out the next week to sell fake perfume, which they claimed was legal as they had manufactured it themselves. Whoever sold the most got closer and closer to being a real manager of a branch when it opened. You weren't paid, mind you, and even the sales you made you got such silly money that I worked out half way through the second week, my first selling week, that this was mend to use us as outlets to sell their fake perfumes. I tried to tell people, tried to challenge the guy in charge and told him I knew what this was. Wise guy to wise guy, I had to pat him on the back. For him, the person behind it, it was a great scam. They had endless supply of applicants, week after week so had endless bodies pushing out their products. But by the end of that second week, I had sold so much stuff for them and earned so little that I quit and kept the remaining supply I had in my possession. I figured they owed me. It was probably about £500 worth of perfumes and aftershaves. I used most of these and gave a lot away.

So my search for work carried on. My birthday came in the

October and it wasn't my usual hype birthday, my mum's first year memorial was coming up in a month.

I booked our holiday at this time for 16 December to go to Malta for a week. That was one mission down.

Then Bigsy came through for me with a buyer for my guns and ammo as well as my vest. All in all it added four grand to my pocket and that was another door of my past life closed shut.

After my mum died and after my promise to her, I felt like I was going to need a daily reminder to remind me of the promise I'd made to her in her coffin. I wasn't sure how to go about this until I got to Blundeston prison from the Mount. It came in the form of two tattoos.

There was a really good tattoo artist in Blundeston who was always on call with so much people getting them done.

I'd decided I was going to have two done, one on each arm. On my left arm I had a photo of my mum smiling with flowers around it, saying, 'Rest In Peace 2002'. On my right is a picture of two boxing gloves with wings on them as if to depict them flying off, with a caption saying 'Hanging Up', then the gloves and then below the gloves was the year 2003.

What this meant was I was hanging up the life, the guns, the streets and all that came with it and the year was 2003. I didn't want to have pictures of guns so I decided on gloves. I knew what it meant and so did those around me. They are tattoos you do not see even with short sleeve shirts on. But for me every night when I get undressed and every morning when I go to take a shower, they are reminders of what I wanted to be from then on. Just a normal everyday guy.

I also had to change my circle of friends. This wasn't like smoking crack where I knew I had beat the habit and was OK to be around people who smoked. This was different. To change my life over completely, I couldn't associate with my old crew and associates. Really just a handful of people could be around me and those had to be people thinking on my wave length. People who like me, were changing too. And there were a few. But not many.

So in November sometime I went to Croydon for a mass interview. I'd never been to one of these before. It was in a conference hall with about a hundred of us applicants, and maybe ten or so interviewers. It was for AIG, the largest insurance company in the world at the time. The position was for insurance sales people, and it looked like they were hiring in huge numbers.

I went along and filled out all the stuff I was required to fill out and sat and waited for my turn. I hadn't worn a suit for many a year but I had to admit that I looked crisp in one.

We weren't going to find out the results of our applications for a couple of weeks, so I carried on my search. It was about the third week into November when I got a call from AIG that I had been successful and was starting work on 1 December. Great.

It wasn't paying a huge amount, about was twelve thousand a year, but the commissions were seven percent on business written. What was even better was that we only had to go into the office on Wednesdays in my branch in East London to hand in all written business of the week up to that day, have our weekly team meetings and catch up with managers and so on. The rest of the week we could come in and make phone calls to prospective clients to book appointments for presentations and sales or we can make the calls from home or our mobiles and sell, sell and sell.

I called them and told them that I had booked a holiday for a week slap bang in the middle of that month and was it possible to still go without jeopardizing my position. The call came back and gave me the all clear.

So it was that on 1 December 2003, I started my very first paid job, at the ripe old age of thirty-five years old. I had fulfilled one part of my promise to my mother and my son. I now just had to make it work for me financially.

I shouldn't have worried. We had a whole weeks training in the insurance products that we were to sell. This wasn't difficult for me as I had a good understanding of financial markets and products. I took to it like something I'd done before. We had a test at the end of that week just to make sure we got it all, which included a mock presentation to a client. The test was also to weed out those who were going to be shit at it. I passed with flying colours. My presentation was deemed the best not just by the woman instructing us but also by my colleagues. I made very good friends in that group that I went through training with. They kind of looked up to me, many of them.

So I started work proper in the second week of December. I hit the ground running, I'm sure you guessed.

Every Wednesday, we had to attend our team meeting, hand in our numbers in sales and the hard copy of the contracts signed by the clients. Well what happens also is that during these meetings whoever sold the most contracts in money value was asked to address the room and tell everybody what they did right and how they did it so as to give the team a kind of heads up on sales techniques. My group did the first whole week and turned up for the meeting the next week Wednesday even though we came by the office to book appointments and pick up forms and all of that. But my group's first meeting with the rest of the team was the Wednesday of the following week. When we had all our numbers totalled, I had done the most business in the whole team of sales people in Romford. My group was made of about fifteen guys and girls, but Romford branch had about one hundred or more sales people. This is not a lie. I had the best figures, beating people who had been employed over a year and more. It was my first full week. No one else in my group came close.

I was asked to speak to the team of people gathered there and tell them how I'd achieved such numbers. This was something I'd never done before, not in a setting such as that. I'd had team talks with my doormen and club staff and maybe this was what got me through this first time. It has since become second nature to me since as I went on to run businesses in Spain. My motivating talks to my staff were legendary amongst people in my industry.

But this first time I stood up, walked to the front of the huge room and started talking. I was proud of my talk. I handled it very well, I have to say. I told them how I did it even though I myself didn't even know how I beat all these guys who were well versed in the products we were selling.

They must have bought it all because I got a fantastic round of applause when I was done. Unbelievable really, because three months before I was doing time in Blundeston. Of course I hadn't declared this on my form when I applied for the job, if I'd done so I wouldn't be standing there speaking to a room full of people about how I went into people's homes to carry out a presentation and sell our insurance products to them. And those of you readers who think I should have done, are naive. The world as it was set up before I ever existed does not give people like me a chance. Yes we did bad, but the mechanism to turn your life around is very thin on the ground the way things are. Declaring that to them at that time would have made me fail in my quest for change. Whereas the result of me telling that lie is that since my release in 2003 I have not even had a traffic ticket never mind seen a police cell. It has now been eleven years since I was released. Now can anyone out there argue with this point? I rest my case.

This is the last chapter of this book. In this chapter I will be dealing with how I think the world has got it all wrong in my humble opinion. How governments are still getting it wrong as we speak. How our emphasis is still too overly weighed on labelling, punishing and finger pointing. But I will get to that in the second half of this chapter first I need to finish the story for the reader.

So my first week was a raving success. I didn't know I would be good at sales. I just knew that most of my associates and the ones before me, when they quit the streets always headed for manual work. Brick layer, painter and decorator, plumber, drivers mate and so on. I knew a few who went to work as post men, work for councils and lately some have taken to traffic warden jobs. I knew I didn't want one of those types of jobs. I wanted more out of life. I chose sales because of the limitless earning capacity it offered in the way of commissions on top of your salary. But as it turned out my first week was showing me that I might just have found my calling in the real world.

So on 16 December, Marcia and I packed our bags and went off to Malta. I left very much looking forward to coming back and looking forward to the future.

The holiday was a blast. We stayed on the main island. We also visited Gozo, which was Malta's second island. It was good to get away from cold England and just be somewhere else albeit for a week.

We flew back on the twenty-third feeling great about the year ahead. It was two days before Christmas, which meant we only had one shopping day to buy all our meat and food for the festivities and all our presents and all the other stuff we all buy over maybe a week. We only had one day to do all of this. There is a reason I'm talking about this, because what happens the next day changed my life completely.

So we get up very early on 24 December and start out to buy Christmas presents for our families and friends. We're everywhere literally. Then we get all of our food shopping done including our Turkey and New Year's meat. We carried out the mission at hand in military precision as we couldn't forget anything. No one likes doing any kind of shopping between Christmas and New Year with the exception of buying clothes during the sales. And even then, not really. We get to Wood Green at around 4 p.m., we are pressed for time at this point. As we're walking up to a shop I hear someone call out to me, I turn around and bump into an old friend I hadn't set eyes on for fourteen years, since my Tottenham college days. His name: Tony.

"Oh my God Tony, is that you?" I shouted as we gave each other a man hug.

"Yes Anthony man, long time!" he replied.

"Boy how long's it been. Have we even seen each other since college?" I asked as we tried to work this puzzle out.

We eventually worked it out and agreed that it was about fourteen years since we last set eyes on each other.

"So where've you been all this time?" I asked.

"After I left Tottenham Tech, I went university. And then I moved to Atlanta Georgia to work in Finance. I was there until 2000 and then when my boss moved to Spain in 2000, he offered me a position in his new company in Spain, so I moved to Spain with him. Been in Spain now since 2000. I'm just over to see my family and spend Christmas here," he explained.

"Wow, Spain yeah. So you've been there three years now. That's crazy. You know we just came back from Malta yesterday and it's been a crazy rush to get all our stuff done today. It's been a mad day. Babes come meet my good friend from back in the day." I called over to Marcia who was looking impatient as time was ticking away and we still had loads to do.

She came over all the same and I introduced them. She sort of looked at her watch to say we didn't have much time, not in an impolite way.

"Listen give me a number for you in Spain, I might come out there one day to see you. You never know."

"When are you going back bruv? Maybe we can hook up before you go back."

"Soon after New Year's."

I'm sure we both would have liked to have caught up some more but we were pressed for time and so we swapped phone numbers and said our goodbyes and left. Tony was a really good guy who thought I was a crazy kid when we were kids. He was one of the good guys in college who hung out with us in the day time but while we went out causing mayhem at night he was home tucked up in bed. That meeting lasted about five minutes. But it was the chance meeting that influenced my life for the next or last ten years. I will get back to that later.

So Christmas was a great one. Remember I had missed the one the year before, so it was great for me to be back spending it with my kids and family and friends. The office had broken up on the twenty-second while I was still in Malta, so I was off work now until 3 January 2004, I think.

Bless them I received my first legal working man's salary sometime around the twenty-seventh or twenty-eighth. I thought to myself, 'Welcome to the real world son.' It was only £830 or there about as I got a grand a month. It was nothing in terms of the amount, but it was very pleasing to me. My commissions had not been added on as we got paid our commissions a month behind. So you got December's commission in January and January's in February and so on. I knew I was due about £250 more, and that was just for about nine days' worth of work because we didn't start selling until after training, which was about the start of the second week in December and then I had to leave on the sixteenth. So all in all, I was content with my progress.

When January started, I booked another short trip for Valentine's the following month. This time just a weekender from the Friday morning till the Sunday night for Marcia and I to go away. That year I also planned a trip to Disney Land Paris for myself and Koy in the summer. But in the meantime, I focused on work.

I hit January with the same enthusiasm as I did in December. I kid you not, but for the next month, I was the top seller no less than three times out of four. I became used to making those speeches to the gatherings on Wednesdays. People came around me. People in the company I barely knew their faces, knew exactly who I was. Guys and girls.

On the home front things were slowly but surely turning sour once again. This time I was able to identify a flaw to Marcia's character that was killing the relationship. Maybe if I was a different kind of guy, I would have said OK no problem, it is what it is.

But I'm not that guy to just sit back and dislike you but put up with it. Too many chicks out there for that.

The thing was that the whole time we were together she went on sometimes about my criminal stuff, letting me know she wasn't in support of it. How she wasn't one of those girls who help their men count money when they get home from doing shit out on the streets. She wanted a guy who was responsible and didn't go to jail. You know, the usual stuff that my mum would have been glad to hear.

But when I would give her two grand for Christmas, she never complained. When we went shopping to buy designer clothes, she was happy to wear them. But still, I paid attention with one ear. When my mother died, she was the first person I told of my plans to find a job. When I came out, she helped push me in the right direction in my search for work.

But as time went on, I saw that she started saying things that made me wonder if she really was happy with what I was now bringing to the household. Gone were the thousands, gone were the two thousands, the jewellery, the champagne and the taking her shopping. I figured in jail that if I was going to be able to live on a worker's wage then I had to think like a worker, talk like a worker, sleep like a worker even fuck like a fucking worker! I couldn't be working and then roll like an earner or gangster. I figured this out while still in prison, so that was how I went about my daily life.

So my contribution to the house was far less than what it had been the whole time we'd been together. Her basic pay was more than mine at the time and even by the end of February when my January commission got paid I just about was catching up with her sixteen grand a year salary. I passed it within three months mind you, but in those first months I was earning less than she was. I would give her £400 a month and still we'd do shopping together and all that. I still had to pay my way to go visit clients at home anywhere in London. I still had my sons to look after and myself to clothe. Round about the end of January I started thinking to myself, all that talk about go straight, come off the pavement, do the right thing, was all bullshit because as soon as I did, you're showing a side that tells me you loved it the other way.

Now as trivial as that is to you, the way this manifests in a relationship is recipe for big problems. I loved my new path and no one was going to move me from it. I could see progress while others longed for the past. We started arguing a lot more again and I just turned off the girl. I threw myself into work and making comms.

The weekend away I'd booked for us both, I decided to go on my own. I don't think she thought I would go at all as we weren't talking at all at home. At this point my decision in going to get my own place started to look like a very smart move. The more we deteriorated the more all the reasons I started cheating on her after three years of being faithful started to come back.

She also seemed to be jealous of my son Koy especially, and not Romaine, my step-son. When my kids would come over I would make sure I cooked for us all to lighten the load for her even though I also cooked in the week when they weren't there. But this was a complaint. When we would argue it would be, 'You only cook when your kids are here.' In my books a lot of women would see that as something good, the fact that I didn't make her cook for them all the time while I sat down and watched TV.

There was an incident that also came back to me at this time, which happened before I went to prison.

The kids were over as usual at the weekend as well as Marcia's two nephews. They had all grown up together now at this point, her son, my sons and her nephews. They were all in her son's room, I thought, when I heard Koy let out a blood-curdling scream. I ran out to the passage to see Koy's fingers stuck in the hinges of her son's bedroom door. He was screaming his head off the poor kid because someone on the other side was pushing the door shut and trying to shut it with my son's fingers still caught in the door. I pushed the door open with all my weight to free Koy's fingers and it took force because even though her son was only fourteen at the time he weighed about sixteen stone. What pissed me off the most was that as I berated all of them in the room and consoled my son, she walked calmly over and consoled those I'd just told off. Completely ignoring the severe pain they had to have caused Koy's little nine-year-old fingers.

So the more I turned off her, the more I remembered why we nearly broke up just before I was locked up. So I headed off on my Amsterdam trip alone. I had relatives there as well so I stayed at theirs, which was always the plan. I wasn't there alone. I had a blast.

When I returned about the middle of February, I received two fantastic phone calls within a day of each other. The first was from the council telling me I had a place to view the following week. And the very next day I get a call from someone I didn't know.

"Hi, is this Anthony?"

"Yeah who is this?"

"You might not remember me, but I used to work for AIG. I left just as you started. My name is Eric."

"OK. Hi Eric, what can I do for you?" I asked.

"Yeah I left a couple of months ago to go work for another company called Royal London Insurance. They are the oldest insurance company in the UK. You started in December right? I left at the end of February."

"Right, sorry I don't think I know who you are but maybe if I saw you I'd remember the face. OK so what can I do for?" I asked again.

"Well my friends over at AIG have been telling me about you. I still have many friends there and I stay in touch with them. They say you are the man right now and no one can beat you this month."

"Ok well thanks."

"I was talking to my manager and telling him how good you are as a new guy to the company. Not many people do that."

"Right." I still wasn't sure what he wanted.

"My manager wants to offer you a position as an insurance consultant in his team here at Royal."

"Really? Why, what's good about Royal?" I asked still not sure.

"Listen mate, first you will get six thousand more in basic, then you will get a company car or if you already have one then you can opt to take the cash, that's another six grand. They will give you this every three years, then your commission is nine percent."

Wow, I thought to myself. Before I could even reply he said, "You are being head hunted my friend. You are like a good striker and our club wants you."

This was just crazy. I was being head hunted? Just two months into my first ever job? When people work all their lives and no one even notices them! I made a quick mental calculation and worked out that my salary would go up to £1500 a month, then there was this car allowance, which he said if I already had a car, would go straight to my pocket. I did still have my Mercedes SL500, so that was an additional six grand. And then there was the two percent raise in comms with them.

So I said, "That sounds good Eric. So what do I do now? I am interested and I would like to know more before I decide. As you know I just joined AIG and last month, January, was really my first full month because I went away in December and then you had Christmas and all that."

"That's fine. Give me your email address, my boss will get Admin to email you all the forms and get your details and all that. I have your number, which I will give to my boss and I am sure he will call you in a day or two." He went on. "Listen another thing is, they give you a company laptop computer, which is loaded with their clients and people who want to be clients around a few miles radius of your postcode. These are the people you will sell to. So it isn't like AIG where you have to generate your own clients. I used to go out of London in the morning to sell to one person and then rush back to South East London to another and then to West London to another because that was where they were. With Royal they have millions of clients already in every post code so your lap top will feed you people closest to you. It's much better."

He was right, my clients up to that point were mainly coming from people in my mum's church, my sister's church and people I knew. And with AIG when you sold to a client, you asked them for five names of people they could refer you to. That way you had a constant feed of potential clients. But they could be anywhere in London or the outskirts. This system sounded like my ideal system. I was sold on this even before we finally came off the phone.

"Ok Eric, thanks for the call, you have made my day. I will wait for the email from your people and do what I need to do. Thanks again and tell your boss I said thank you for the job offer."

When I came off the phone I wanted to share this amazing news with everybody. So I called my brothers, my dad and my son too. He had just turned twelve and he did understand and was happy for me.

Meanwhile the following week I went and viewed the flat they had for me. It was more than ideal and I accepted at once. It was a house split in half, then one half was further split in two. So there was A, B and C. The beauty of it was that B was half the house. The back half - and therefore it had the garden too. It was a one bedroom split level, so I had the kitchen and living room downstairs and upstairs the bedroom and bathroom. At the front of the property on the ground floor was flat A and upstairs was C. So A and C both had one level flats while mine had two levels and the garden.

I really began to feel like my mum was watching over me and making things happen really quickly for me to reward me for keeping my promise to her.

I set a date to move out of Marcia's and into mine for 4 March 2004. About ten days from the viewing. That was how quickly I wanted to move into my place and away from any kind of distractions.

When the forms from Royal London arrived, my heart sunk. It was like I was applying to join the police and taking an exam all in one. They wanted to know dates and times and where and what I did my whole life since leaving school. It was daunting, so much so, I almost gave up before I even started. But I tried my luck. I filled them out. I replaced times spent in prison with being self-employed, I mentioned my company Many Many Promotions but stretched the time I had it to cover some missing periods like my last sentence. And then I included my current position with AIG. You would think that seeing as they came to me, the process would be less tedious. Nope.

When I was finished, I sent it all back and waited. A few days later I got a queries reply. Saying things like, what did you do from this period to this period, and please be more specific about this or that. 'Shit!' I thought. 'This isn't going to work.' But I carried on and tried to answer the questions. Again I sent the answers back and again I waited. A day or so later, more queries.

Finally after the third or fourth back and forth, I finally got the letter I was waiting for. A letter of acceptance to the position of an insurance consultant and a contract. Oh my God, I did it. I got in. I really felt my mum up above had a hand in this.

I had already spoken to the guy that would be my manager a few days after the call with Eric. This day he called me again and welcomed me to his team and said he knew I would do well. He asked when I was handing in my notice to AIG, and I told him I would do that immediately. I was starting work on 1 March with Royal London. Exactly three months since I'd joined AIG and since I started my first ever job.

Beginning of March was a time of change. I changed jobs and on the fourth, I moved out of Marcia's place and into mine after decorating the place to a decent standard and kitting it out with the necessary stuff. I was looking forward to having just myself and my kids spend time at my place with no mums, no girlfriends or fiancés, just us rolling and doing what we wanted.

The new job was too good. We worked from home booking appointments and going to see people to sell them insurance products. We only met for group training or meetings because everything with Royal was done on line. It really was as they had said.

As I settled into my new job and my new place, I started a casual relationship with a chick I knew from around my new place, a chick called Donna. She was the first true Jamaican girl I had ever dated. But she wasn't Jamaican like those loud mouth and uncultured ones that put me off Jamaican chicks. She rolled more British than Jamaican, which was why I even entertained dealing with her. It was ideal for me as we banged and texted and talked and not much else. We didn't go cinema or dinner or anything like that. She never met my kids even though I met her six-year-old a couple of times at the hair dressing salon she worked at.

As March turned into April and April into May, I was again smashing work to pieces. My figures were always high but did not realise how high in comparison to the other sales people until a few weeks later.

But one day, I was walking up to the shop on my road, which was a busy road and a through road to access many areas in Hackney, when I saw a familiar figure walking up towards me. I knew that walk, it was Jeanette.

I hadn't called or heard from her since a few months before my release from jail and definitely had not contacted her since my release.

"Hey you, what you doing on my road?" I asked her smiling when we got close enough to speak and hug.

"Do you live on this road now yeah?"

"Yeah got a flat just up there, number seventy-nine. Moved here in March. What are you doing here?"

"You know I'm a social worker now, one of my girls just got a place in the unit over there, so I was just checking on her and now I'm going back to the office." She pointed to the building her client was now living in.

"Ok that's good. How's your little man, how's he getting on?"

"He's fine babes he's getting big now, what about Koy, how's he and Marcia?"

"Koy's cool thanks. Me and Marcia, we're done. I moved out in March man. Moving on and doing good. You know I'm working now ain't it?"

"Is it? Ah well done babes, what work you doing?"

"Insurance Consultant babes. We sell insurance products and stuff."

"OK. Sounds good. So which number are you again? Next time I'm down here I can pop in and see your place?"

"79B babes. Press the buzzer for B. I'm home in the mornings cos I work from home. Here, let me take your number and give you mine."

We swapped numbers that April day and stayed in touch regularly. I wasn't looking for a girlfriend to be honest but it was good to see her again after all this time and she looked good.

Royal London had sales numbers results announced quarterly to award prizes to the top three sales people in, listen to this, the whole of the South East region. Yes, not just the branch but the South East of England. From London to Essex to Surrey and beyond. If I remember rightly, somewhere in the region of 300 or 400 sales people. The event was held in June with all the top bosses in that region, the regional managers, then managers and then us sales people. I'd seen these types of events on TV but I never thought I would one day actually be a part of it all.

The prizes for the three top guys in the region was a stay over at the Holiday Inn hotel where this whole thing was being held, a free health and massage treatment and a hamper of goodies in the hotel room when they got there.

I knew I was always hitting and going over my weekly targets and had never been below my target but I did not really think my team was in the running at all. There were many guys struggling to meet targets in my team. Guys who called me up weekly and asked if I had hit the target because they were struggling.

So we had this event and it was really great because you got to meet guys from outside London and from other parts of London. The boastful ones, the big mouths and the saleswomen. Anyway, we got to the bit where they announced winners. They started with which part of the region took the award for the most sales, like London or Kent or Essex and so on. London won that. Then which particular office brought in the most sales in total and I think an office in Essex won that. Then the one most of the loud mouths were waiting for came. Which three sales people did the most business. They started with third, then second and then first was...

I heard my name get called! What! Me? I quickly composed myself and walked up to get my prize. It was an envelope with a voucher for the health treatment and a hotel room key.

I was asked to make a speech, which I made and thanked them. I was still in shock if I'm honest. I really, really did not expect it. My manager came over to me and congratulated me. He told me he had a hint that it was someone in his team and it could only have been me.

Wow! After having drinks with everybody and a meal that the company paid for, I went upstairs with one girl from Essex who came third and a guy from a South East London team who came second to see our rooms.

When I walked into my room, it had my name on the television: Congratulations Anthony Spencer.

I called my son, called my brothers and sister and told them the news. Next I called Jeanette and told her. Last I called my dad. Maybe now he would really be proud of me. If he was, he didn't show it the way I thought he might have done.

My dad was never really proud of me until he came to visit me in Spain and stayed in my house with a swimming pool and basketball/tennis court many years later.

I had my massage and treatment and stayed the night in my room with a nice Essex girl next to me. You see, most of the people always stayed over. But while the rest paid for their rooms, us winners had our rooms paid for. There was a club that all those who stayed over went to for the night. It was full of us Royal staff, from managers to sales people and one or two regional managers. I scored with a crisp looking babe from the Basildon team and of course I was the star so all I had to do was ask and she came. It was great being a part of a working company. Belonging to something. I was loving this life.

My earning was now in the region of three thousand a month after tax with my comms. Working wasn't bad after all. I was still seeing Jeanette quite a bit. She would stop at mine and I would pass by hers too. We were just really good friends now. I still wasn't looking at her as a potential new steady girlfriend. She even slept in my bed a couple of times and we top and tailed it all night.

I was too into having just myself and the kids alone that I wasn't in a rush to change anything. The kids knew who she was but they also knew that we were just good friends who had dated in the past.

In July I took Koy with me to Disneyland Paris for five days. It was a dream come true for both of us. I was a kid again. But I have to tell you, the Space Mountain put me off roller coasters for life. I was sick the whole day after just one ride. Koy went back on numerous times. I havent been on a roller coaster again since that day.

We came back as I had appointments for work, but we were soon off again to Holland to stay with my cousins whom I'd stayed with, in the February of that year. This time we were gone for a week. This was part of my annual leave.

In September came very good but shocking news from my bosses. I was promoted to a manager's position. This was too much to believe.

When I went to work after running my own business for so long and being the boss, I accepted the fact that I may never be a boss again in my life. I accepted that fact to be able to go to work. Not just that, I also was at peace with the fact that I was going to start from the bottom of the pile. The new guy. The nobody, in a way. If I hadn't had been at peace with this simple fact, there was no way I would have settled into working life the way I did.

Now here I was, nine months after first starting work and I was being pushed up to management. I was now on the managers starting salary of thirty-five thousand a year, had fourteen people to manage and got seven percent of the total written by my team. I was required to motivate and train my guys and also to still do business myself. I was now surely on my way back up where I belonged.

They say if you are cut out to lead, no matter where you find yourself that quality will always shine through and things end up correcting themselves. I was a leader again and my guys looked up to me.

I had another week to take off towards completing my annual leave. We had four weeks off a year and I had only taken two of those.

So still in September I started thinking of going to Spain. Somewhere warmer. I asked Jeanette if she would like to come Spain with me as friends. Hmm, OK maybe a bit of fun would take place while there but really I wasn't looking for a partner. I just really didn't feel like to go out to Spain alone. She agreed. I told her I would pay for the flights and hotel but she had to bring her own money as we would share expenses. This was a new concept to me as I always picked up bills in the past. But like I said earlier, I needed to start thinking like a working man, roll like a working man and definitely spend like a working man.

So before I bought flights, remember Tony - my friend that I'd run into on Christmas Eve while shopping with Marcia? I placed a call to him. It was the second time I'd called him since that meeting. I called him in June to say hello and told him I may take up his offer to come over. I was addicted to travelling by now. It was something I'd promised myself when I was banged up that last time, that I would start travelling at least three times a year, even if sometimes it was just for weekends away. So I called him and asked him to source a good hotel for us to stay in for the five days I was planning on going for. One day of shopping with her before the flight and one day of rest after the holiday, made up the seven days I was taking off work.

But just before I booked our exact dates, a deal I was putting together to sell insurance covers in bulk to two estate agents to cover all the properties they had on their books, which was going to net me about ten grand in comms, came through. It was a huge deal and one I came up with in my head. I had put in a lot of ground work knocking on random estate agents until I found two who were happy to listen. I met with them with my regional manager before this call came through a couple of weeks before. When the call came through, they asked to see my boss and I again to negotiate further. This was what made me put the trip on hold.

The deal came through in October. I earned about twelve thousand from the package! With about half that amount every year when they came up for renewal. This success pushed me to try a lot more estate agents. I called all my team guys together and trained them in what I did and how I had pitched it. Then I sent them out there to look for more of these. This type of deal was not taught to me, we were not trained for it. But seeing as we sold building, contents, and all the types of cover that a property needed, it kind of made sense to me and that was what led me to try this new avenue out.

My birthday that year was great. I went raving for the first time since I got out, over a year ago. Believe it or not. Remember, I was now rolling just like a fucking worker. I didn´t know how to rave light. So I stayed away from raving.

I went out with Jeanette and an ex of mine that I dated when I was still with Sandra, a girl called Remi that I'd run into a few months before. We went to a 'Back To 95' rave. It was a great night. Still did the champagne.

November came and I got back on the holiday tip. I was still owed two weeks, which I had to take before March, four months away. So I got back in touch with Tony again and restarted plans to come to see him in Marbella. This time we set dates for leaving on 3 December and returning on the eighth.

Something had happened though between the last time we tried to go in September and this time when we had booked the fights in late November, between Jeanette and myself. We had been spending double the time together we had spent before this period. Way too much time for two people who had dated in the past. We sort of were getting closer. And then whereas I didn't see her before as my wifey, all of a sudden I was warming to her. I was seeing her in a different light. But, we still weren't sexing. We still kept it the way it had been since I bumped into her again back in April or May. I was still seeing Donna the hairdresser and was just about to start seeing a neighbour of mine, Sharon. I think it was the threat of Sharon, who was a wifey type thing, that made Jeanette start the transition from just friends to maybe more.

So we headed off to Stanstead airport to fly off to Marbella. I remember that morning like it was yesterday. The cold was terrible and the fog came down as low as our heads and as thick as anything you'd ever seen. It was a very good day to leave the UK. Our flight, along with many others, was delayed by hours. We boarded the plane but couldn't take off. We were due to arrive in Spain at just gone 11 a.m. Spanish time, 10 a.m. UK time. By 10 a.m., we were still on the plane and on the tarmac at Stanstead. I placed a call to Tony to let him know about an hour before as he was picking us up.

When we eventually took off, we were shocked at how bright the skies were above the clouds and fog. It was an amazingly sunny day and yet ten thousand feet below was like one of those horror movies.

We had got so bored waiting that we had started kissing each other's faces off.

We kissed all the way to Marbella.

When we got there and came out of the airport, it was so warm I was burning up under my jumper and shirt. In December. I had taken off my thick sheepskin flying jacket, which was what I had on top of my jumper back in London.

Tony came back and met us, bless him. He drove us to our hotel and helped us check in even though they spoke English. He then told us he'd come back to take us out later. So we settled in to start our holiday.

It was a brilliant time away with Jeanette, which marked the start of our relationship once more. We were now officially dating but this time she was not the third wheel!

We had a blast and got to meet a lot of British guys living and working out there.

Tony's life was very impressive. He owned a hospitality business that catered for high end clients who wanted to entertain guests who came to Marbella for business. Footballers who wanted to be entertained and all that kind of stuff. He hired them out yachts, he had a helicopter on standby, he had a formula three racing car for those who wanted to race round tracks. I was well impressed.

We talked late into the Sunday night we were invited to his and his girlfriend's beautiful seaside apartment for dinner. He told me how easy it was to make it over here if you could sell. He knew I was doing very well for myself in sales. The figures he was quoting were unreal.

The next day he called me and said he wanted to introduce me to someone he had a lot of respect and time for.

We were leaving on the Wednesday back to the UK and it was now Monday. Tony called back that night and said this guy called Nelson, who owned a large real estate company who was his good friend would be free for us to meet on the Wednesday morning. Our flight was that night so we would have all day to enjoy the last views, lunch and then meet with this guy Nelson.

I still wasn't sure what I expected from the meeting to be honest but I was keen to just see what this was all about.

That Wednesday we checked out of our hotel room and stored our luggage in the hotel storage space to collect later on our way to the airport. We strolled around town, did a bit of last day shopping, window shopped and had lunch. Tony met us at the restaurant and took us uptown to this plush part of town. When we arrived, we walked into the richest looking office I had ever seen in my life. The guy who seemed to be in charge greeted Tony with a hug and said hello to us too. He beckoned us through and said Nelson was expecting us. He took us through into a huge private office with a well-tanned, well-muscled fifty-something year old white guy sitting behind the most impressive desk I had ever seen outside of the movies. That desk alone must have cost upwards of ten grand. He stood up and shook our hands and again gave my friend a hug. They went off chatting about Nelson's last time at the tracks driving the formula three racing car. They chatted away for about ten minutes all excited, and then Nelson remembered us.

He said to me, "I hear you're a good salesman Anthony, I can always do with really good salesmen around me."

"Yeah well, I just won an award the other day for smashing the whole of the South East of England. I beat about four hundred hundred sales people," I said.

"Impressive," he said in his New York twang. "Well, have you ever sold property?"

"No, never. But I don't care what you sell, give it to me and I will out sell anyone," I replied. This was fast turning into a job interview that I didn't ask for. But I found myself selling myself like any good salesman would do.

"I like that, I like that. When do you go back to the UK?"

"Tonight."

"So let me say this. If you want, I have a job for you with me. You will be trained and given all the tools to be successful. You will be given a corporate apartment until you don't need it anymore. Hell, I have guys here still in my apartments even after two years. But the really good guys move on and get their own place. I believe you will be one of those guys." He went on. "If you're good at this you could earn yourself anywhere around ten to twenty thousand a month."

I looked at Jeanette and she knew I was sold. All I could say was, "Ten to twenty grand?"

"Yep and even more. Tony, tell him."

"Yes Ant man, he's right. That's why I brought you to meet him," Tony assured me.

Tony was a very honest and good hearted friend. I have told him this many times since. If it was anybody else sitting there with us on 8 December 2004 in that office, I would never have trusted everything I was told. Too wise and too shrewd. But as it was Tony, all of a sudden I started to see me living in Spain.

We basically ended the meeting with me saying I was going to put things in place and return. He told me he had a guy who went to Thailand every December after making lorry loads of money, spend the next six months there doing nothing and then came back in June and worked again until it was December again. He said this guy was leaving on the twentieth and I was welcome to have his desk.

The twentieth, I thought. That was twelve days away! Wow, it was going so fast I really needed to think about it carefully. I looked over again at Jeanette and she had tears in her eyes. I asked what was wrong in front of everybody.

"I can't believe it, you just got offered a job in Spain," she said, crying tears of joy.

Well that was good, at least she was happy about it, I thought.

We thanked him and promised to be in touch and left.

As we walked back to Tony's car, I still wasn't so sure. I didn't come to Spain to look for work. I was in a very good job, I had just got promoted three months before, I had just earned my biggest commission with the estate agent deals, I had a team that needed me and looked up to me, I was with a company that valued my talents and then there was my kids and my home.

Jeanette held on to me tightly as we walked to the car a bit quiet.

"You're thinking about it ain't it bruv?" he asked me.

"Boy, I can't believe I have the opportunity to live abroad and earn good money too."

"Listen Ant, you don't have to take it up. I think you will smash it. You have what it takes and if you do well it will definitely change your life. I've known you a long time and you were a soldier from the first time I set eyes on you. But think it over and get back to him even if you don't take it up. He's a good guy and you know what, you sell land and property to Americans in Nevada and Florida and the Americans love an English accent," Tony said to me.

"Babes, you know what I'm thinking? I'm thinking, if I can smash it in London doing what I'm doing right now, then I definitely can smash it here. And If I smash it here we're laughing." This was what was going through my mind, so I thought I'd share it with my new girl.

We thanked Tony and promised to call him too once I knew what I was going to do. He dropped us off at the airport and we went to wait for our flight.

It was all we discussed the whole time waiting for the flight, on the flight and all the way to my house where we spent the night. Her little boy was at her mum's so we chilled the night and talked some more about it.

Jeanette was all for it. I think I was too but it was a little different for me. I had to leave my kids here, well Koy really, while she would bring her son with her. My job commitments were greater than hers, although she also managed a care home for teenagers. I managed a team of sales people, a job that had been trusted to me and a team that believed in me.

By the morning as we bathed and got dressed to face the world, I was seventy percent sure I was going to take up the job.

I needed to make a list of things to do, and I set about it.

Top of my list was to make it right with Koy. Second was to try my best to rent my flat out. It was my safety net if things went wrong.

Third, make it right at work. I needed to have my job open to me if, again it went wrong.

Fourth, find a safe place for my car or plan to sell it.

Fifth, make it right with my guys and see if I could place them in other teams, for now.

Sixth, bring my bills up to date, even the ones not due yet.

Seventh, talk to my family.

I went about these as soon as I made the list. I now had eleven days if I wanted to start on the twentieth. I did not have to, I could have said January, or March or whatever but I wanted to meet that date.

Koy was happy for me. He was excited about the prospect of visiting his dad who lives in Spain. I promised to come and get him for his first half term break after Christmas.

My flat was sorted thanks to Donna my Jamaican chick. I told her I was now in a relationship and was moving to Spain as I got offered a very good job. I only really asked her and a few other people including Jeanette to ask around if anybody they knew, wanted to rent a flat. I was surprise when she said she'd take it. Well that was perfect. It was someone I knew, she was a clean living girl and worked hard. I was ecstatic.

Next was my job. I asked for a meeting with my regional manager and explained. I pleaded with him to keep my position open for me for at least three months. I asked him to move my guys to whomever they wanted to work under and not to force them to a team they didn't want to be in. He said he was OK with that but this had to be cleared by his boss. So as I waited for their response, I convened a meeting with my team at the office.

When I told them, one of the girls cried. They genuinely did not want me to leave. It got worse. They totally as one asked that they stay together and did not want to work for anyone else. They asked me to ask my immediate boss to take charge of the team for the three months and that if I didn't return in three months then they will move to other teams. Wow. I wasn't sure this was possible as regional managers manage managers and not teams. But I promised them I would try.

I was well liked within the company and a good guy so I used all my push and speech and yes, I got the deal for them. I suppose to my bosses it also meant that there was a high possibility that I would return.

So after getting all these sorted, I started to see myself working in Marbella. In sunny Spain, wearing shirts in December and January instead of sheep skin coats and rain.

My brothers Kevin and Mikey took it the worse. I actually had an argument with Kevin. A bad one, which stopped us speaking for months until he apologised when things were showing signs of being the best move I'd ever made in my life about six months in. My dad, he just gave his blessing. I think he just thought, 'Look at this boy now, just as he settles and is doing well, he decides to leave and go to Spain.'

As the day came closer, Jeanette was also sorting her stuff out. We agreed to leave her place empty as a fall-back on place if things went wrong, so we didn't rent it out. She ran to all the necessary school authority offices to get her son's school papers together, medical papers and all that. She packed in work too and at the right time all our affairs had been put in order.

And so it was that on 20 December 2004, we left the British Isles for good and moved to Spain in pursuit of a new life and new dreams. I had only put down the madness just over a year ago. Started work for the first time just over a year ago. Was just released from prison just over a year ago. But here I was, going on a journey that had I not made the decision to quit the streets, would never have happened.

And it was a journey that made all our dreams come true. For my son, my now wife Jeanette, my step-son, her mum, dad and many, many more people around us.

I have no regrets!

AFTERWORD

This is a book I have been writing for seventeen years. I started this book in 1997 because of an idea I had going round in my head. I hand wrote the first eleven chapters and had them finished in about two weeks. Then for the next seventeen years the written work stayed unfinished. It followed me everywhere I went in that period. I had asked a few people to read the work in the first year or so after writing it and everyone who read all or some of it gave me the same feedback. Finish it, they said.

Nobody read it again for fifteen years and it gathered dust. Until last year in 2013 when my German secretary asked to read it after I told her I had started a book that I needed to finish. She read it and just like everybody who had read it before her, she said I had to try to finish the book. To help me on my way, she promised to type out my handwritten work and save on a pen drive for me so that when I was ready to finish it, it would be easier to complete. This she did in-between her work schedule and I am forever grateful to her for this.

This one act and seeing all the work on a computer screen was my inspiration, a year later, to complete the book, That fact along with the tools available to an unknown writer today that were not available before at the time the first chapters were written. In particular, Self Publishing and the many routes available to independently publish your work.

This story is a work of fiction. It is fiction tinged with a few dashes of my own personal experiences.

But it is not my story. It is the story of around one billion people across the world, give or take a few hundred million either side. It is a story that people in London, Leeds, Manchester, Glasgow and Edinburgh's inner cities will relate to. The people in the Townships of South Africa, the Favelas of Brazil, the ghettos of the US, the ghettos of Russia, Israel, Nigeria, Colombia, Jamaica, Haiti, India and Pakistan.

This is their story. It is all of their stories. Those who made it and got out, those who did not and died trying, those who raised children in those circumstances and are still doing so and those who are still stuck in the battles described in this book.

Either way, the system that I kept referring to in the book, which was created maybe a thousand years ago in Europe by the Aristocracy to keep people not from their side of the fence in boxes with labels, has evolved over the said period to become what we see today. Unfortunately, even when a nation has taken control of its own destiny from colonial rulers, this system has not been tweaked or changed. They have simply carried it on because those decision makers all of a sudden now find themselves on that nice side of the fence and love it.

And let's face it, we all do. No matter where we came from, when we make it in life we become to a large part, just like those people a thousand years before and lock ourselves into our communities and those like us. We moan at people who struggle sometimes and forget how hard it was to break into the society, that community or that group of people on the ski slope or the First Class section of an airplane. I have done all of the above. But I also remember starting work and struggling.

But this is not my story. For example, I achieved a high enough standard of education in reality, whereas in the book it depicts someone who only attained a level of O levels or GCSE as it is known in the UK. But that fact is a disease that keeps those billion people exactly where they are today because until we, as a world community, really make honest tracks to make sure that every single person born on planet earth from now on reaches a high standard of education, people will always have this story to tell.

How is it that Europe throws enough food away yearly, to feed the whole of hungry Africa for three years non-stop? Why is it that Europe can build tunnels under seas and build sky scrapers that withstand all that nature can throw at it, transport all types of things over seas and oceans, even things like bridges from one place to another, oil, goods and anything else they want, but we cannot coordinate a joint effort to collect all of our unused food and ship to those starving people of the world in a timely fashion so that the food gets to them before it goes rotten?

How is it that when disasters strike in third world countries, we in the west donate hundreds of millions and send so called charitable NGOs over to 'help', but yet one year later these people are living in tents with no sanitation or amenities and dying of hunger. More people then end up dying from the diseases and hunger long after than died from the original disaster. Is it because that is how they are seen? Meanwhile those 'helping' on the ground are living in the best hotels those countries can give them.

But yet when it happens in our countries, for some reason I just... can't... work... out why I don't see tents anywhere. I see churches, community halls, town buildings all hosting the unfortunate victims. And guess what, within a few years we are on the mend. I use the term we, because if you are in Japan, US, UK, Canada, Australia, New Zealand any EU country and a few others, then we are all included as one. The sad fact is that the amount usually donated by the unsuspecting public, when exchanged into these country's currencies is enough a lot of the time to rebuild these places to a higher standard that they started with. But it isn't done. Why?

And it isn't just the poor countries, this is an illness in our own backyards. Any reader that really thinks the US, UK, France, Germany or any G8 country cannot get rid of homelessness is foolish to say the least. Yes, you are.

Every one of the G8 country earns enough money, has enough know-how and enough land to not have people sleep on their streets. But they don't do much about it. Yes there are people who would prefer to live out in the open and sleep rough, but you will find that those people have other issues such as mental illness, which again we can solve. But do very little about.

Why is it that if a homeless man walks into a restaurant and picks up a plate of leftover food a client has just left and attempts to empty it into his own plate to take out with him, he is stopped and or the police will be called but the same plate of food will be thrown in the bin to be sent to landfill sites for disposal?

I know why these things are as they are. It is simply because this was the road map set up for us all a long time ago. At a time that is totally unrecognizable to the time we live in now. It was a way set up by kings and queens of the richest, most powerful, most armed and equipped and most greedy nations of the world along with their ruling elite at a time when it was easy to brainwash and groom the masses. It was done so well and now for so long that this is how it is. And we all accept. When the masses started to gain their voices, the Magna Carta was born to placate them. Democracy was born. The idea that 'you too can become one of us' was born.

And so it remains. And so we all, without exception, strive to get on that promised side of the fence.

Whole countries, not just families and individuals. It is good to strive for better do not get me wrong. But it is the way we go about it and the reasons we go about it. And the ignorance that besets us on that journey. Meanwhile all those who planned it all from the very beginning are looking down on us all from their seats in Hell and are amazed at just how covertly evil and heartless we have all become and how skilful we are in our pursuit of what they set down for us back in 700 AD.

I wrote this book to tell a story and to enlighten some quarters about the struggles of billions across the world. It is also meant to give inspiration to all those in prison, on drugs, broke, homeless and down on their luck. These types of books are popular among that section of society. This is meant to tell them that it is possible to change. It is possible to turn things around. To tell them not to keep making it easy for the world to forget them. The more you stay in the labelled box you are in, the easier it is to keep you there and you will find that policy after policy will not favour you. You will be used as political football so someone else's family can get up another notch in society. To reach that promised side of the fence.

The story you have read in this book relates to a combination of myself and maybe fifty of my friends and associates and has been wrapped up as one person's story, with a lot of fictional tales and scenes. But, this is your story too if you have grown up in any of those places I mentioned at the top of this Afterword.

The common man needs to understand that there is very little help for them out there. No part of the world is there a set up or plan to help you become like them. It just does not exist. Those who have done it have had to do it on their own. If it is too late for you, then please do what you must to give your next generation as much a chance as possible. You need to understand that the more your descendants do nothing about it, the further behind your bloodline falls. So if you think you have it bad now, look down from Heaven or Hell, wherever you end up, in about a hundred years from now and see the hardship your descendants will be in. Then look again in two hundred years' time! Because I can tell you now, no one can change how it is. And if they could, they are on the side of the fence where they do not need to and do not have the desire to. So things will be this way, always.

I also wrote this book in very basic everyday language, English, which is used by most of the population. It is written in a way that the upper levels of society if they choose to read this, will get it but more so that those who reside at the bottom end will definitely relate to it fully.

Those at the top end of society, were they to come across this book, will more than likely revert to type and put down the drug dealing, the robbing of people, the shootings and all that stuff they blast regularly on TV, in the Houses of Parliament and on programs like Question Time. But let me ask you, the everyday person, not them, what is the difference between someone who sells heroin to a user and BP, the British oil company that goes to a third world country and carries out its oil operations in a way it could never do in any developed country? In a way that kills a thousand babies a year and pollutes the water so badly that skins peel off them and they are constantly ill in a place where the health care service to help them does not exist?

What is the difference between someone who robs a whole family's possessions and the staff at Barclays who set plans to crush a family's livelihood even though their business was a viable one, and when it is done, those responsible are paid handsomely by the bank, everybody celebrates and the bank sells off the assets at a profit. Because I really do not see one.

The powers-that-be see one though. To me all involved are doing terrible things to people they can do it to. For money.

If you did not use heroin, the dealer will not use you to make money, full stop. And if those poor countries were not corrupt and allowed BP to do what they were doing, then BP would not. But just like our rulers lock you up for dealing those drugs, when it comes to BP, why do they not say to all companies within their control, "The standards we expect you to keep here in the UK must be uniform anywhere you operate." You know why? If they did that BP would make less money and therefore pay less to the Exchequer. The fact it will save whole communities is put to one side. It costs more money to operate correctly than it does to operate carelessly.

This double standard is how we live. And we have accepted it. That is why I tell you, the ordinary man, that there is no help out there for you. You need to do what you must do to get your family out of these areas and into better places and better schools. To give them a chance at a better life. Hong Kong was built on the Opium Trade by the British. Many finance houses were built on either slave trade or some other illicit trade going back years. Many wealthy families today had ancestors who were rogues and thieves. Go to Essex and ask yourself how many of these wealthy Essex families had ancestors who were dealers and armed robbers and general roughnecks. Fast forward forty or fifty years and the smart ones who sent their kids to good schools have changed the history of their families for good.

My advice to all those in prison today, the best thing you can do for yourself is to make sure that for every illicit penny you earn, you dedicate half to pulling the next generation out of the mess. Failure to do this will bare huge consequences for your future descendants.

It is too late for many. But unlike the government that has no plans to make it better for you and yours, you my friend can start today. The inner city dwellers need to stop allowing their kids to have kids at a young age. You had your kids young and struggled and yet while still struggling, while still not fully baked yourselves, you allow your sixteen-year-old or seventeen-year-old to bring another victim into the world. I think it is so ridiculous it is sad. I remember when grandparents were old and wise. Today our new generation of grandparents in the inner cities are early to mid-thirties! And you know what, the inner city dwellers do not seem to see that this sickness only exists in their neighbourhoods. Over in Chelsea, when kids get pregnant, and yes they do in Chelsea, they know exactly what to do. Either abortion or adoption. Only the poor seem to not get this fact. And it hurts me to watch. Watch a woman on benefits have six kids and then before the youngest one is in school her teenage daughter has a child too! This is recipe for poverty, chaos and imprisonment of generations to come in the same social lock up. Do not look down from above a hundred years from now and see things that cause you sleepless nights even in death.

Finally, I have a second part to this novel. I haven't started work on it as yet, I want to see how this is received first. That second part will be about our story once we left the UK.

Leaving the UK made us realise that Britain is especially good, better than any developed country, at classifying people and whole communities and whipping up whichever sentiments the powers-that-be wish to whip up. The British press is one of the cruellest in the world. And it is run by none other than the same people who run our country. If they wish to demonise green coloured people tomorrow, it's done. If they choose single mums it is a done deal. If they tomorrow believe Romanians are the enemy, or asylum seekers or benefits claimers, you are doomed if you belong to that group.

As I write this book it is Europe that's the enemy. There was a time when it was the Irish, then blacks as a whole, Rastafarians, then black young men, then single mums, then Somalians, then asylum seekers, Muslims, then Romanians and now Muslims and Europe.

We have a sickness in this country that is deep within the DNA of the UK. Phobia of the highest order.

We lived in a real European country that embraced the rules from out of Europe. What Brits do not realise is that many of the rules the Brits fight against are actually rules meant to better the life of the ordinary man. But the way the press spin it, the stupid nation buys it wholeheartedly. The press belong to the same people who want the status quo in the UK to remain the same. But try telling that to the man on the street and you will be wasting your time.

The second part to this book will cover all of this and how the kid done well. And how sometimes we must not be scared to leave our shores to find a better life.

I thank you for listening and giving humble me your valuable time.

THE END

RIPs

Here I wish to remember some fallen soldiers over the past twenty or so years. Some of the names below did not pass away down to violence. They are just people I would like to remember and immortalise in this book. I hope they all rest in peace wherever they are.

RIP MUM

RIP ANDREW

RIP SCOTTY (Park Lane, Tottenham)

RIP RODNEY ADAMS

RIP SUTTIE

RIP KENNY ROWE

RIP LOURDES (Farm)

RIP TITCH (Wayne)

RIP TENOR TITCH (Junction)

RIP NOOKIE

RIP LAVERNE

RIP POPCORN

RIP PATCHEYE

RIP COREY WRIGHT

RIP MARK DUGGAN

RIP ROGER SYLVESTER

RIP GRANTIE

RIP BUCKHEAD

RIP YELOW BABY

RIP ANTHONY MORRISON

RIP STREKKER

RIP JAMIE (Ex-Soldier)

And to all those other fallen soldiers that I haven't remembered to mention, rest in peace. You are not forgotten.

Printed in Great Britain
by Amazon.co.uk, Ltd.,
Marston Gate.